THE
YEAR'S BEST
SCIENCE FICTION
AND FANTASY
FOR TEENS

THE YEAR'S BEST SCIENCE FICTION AND FANTASY FOR TEENS

First Annual Collection

EDITED BY

Jane Yolen and Patrick Nielsen Hayden

TOR

A Tom Doherty Associates Book   *New York*

THE YEAR'S BEST SCIENCE FICTION AND FANTASY FOR TEENS: FIRST ANNUAL COLLECTION

Copyright © 2005 by Jane Yolen and Patrick Nielsen Hayden

A Tor Book
Published by Tom Doherty Associates, LLC
175 Fifth Avenue
New York, NY 10010

www.tor.com

Tor® is a registered trademark of Tom Doherty Associates, LLC.

ISBN 0-765-31383-9 (hc)
EAN 978-0765-31383-6 (hc)
ISBN 0-765-31384-7 (tpbk)
EAN 978-0765-31384-3 (tpbk)

Printed in the United States of America

0 9 8 7 6 5 4 3 2

For SFWA's presidents, past and future.
It's a dirty job, but someone has to do it.
—J.Y.

For Terry Carr.
—P.N.H.

CONTENTS

PREFACE

Welcome to the best young adult science fiction and fantasy stories published in the year 2004. They will make you laugh, cry, whoop for joy, and gasp in astonishment, and will tickle your seventh sense—that sense of wonder.

Back in the Cretaceous Period, when I was a young reader, there was no such thing as Young Adult fiction. YA literature was something invented in the mid-1960s by librarians who looked at reading scores and feared children were not reading after they became teens.

Of course we were reading. We were hopping from children's books right into adult books, without training wheels. Especially those of us who read fantasy and science fiction.

So the book you hold in your hand now is chock-full of SF and fantasy stories Appropriate for Young Adults published last year—2004. However, the majority of them have been gleaned from adult magazines, Web sites, collections, and anthologies. Why? Because there is very little being published in the field specifically for Young Adults. So we have taken it upon ourselves to seek out the gems for you. They range from the powerful science fiction dog story "Sergeant Chip," which—like all great war stories—speaks to what is happening today even as it posits a future war, to the dark fairy tale of "A Piece of Flesh," which sets faerie and paranoia side by side. They range from the epic fantasy of "Blood Wolf," with its touches of science fiction, to the historical fantasy of "The Wings of Meister Wilhelm," and the urban fantasy of "CATNYP."

Each story has an introduction that speaks to you about the science fiction or fantasy tropes used in the piece. But it also gives you the titles of other, similar kinds of stories or novels that you might want to look for, books and stories not written in 2004 but along the same lines.

And we also have an honor roll of stories that almost—but not quite—made it into the book, because we loved those stories, too.

Finally, there is an extra bonus, a golden oldie, published exactly one hundred years ago, in 1904. In this case it is a ghost story by Rudyard Kipling. Recognize the name? Of course you do. He wrote *The Jungle Book,* a powerful set of dark, interlinked stories in which the lost Indian child Mowgli is brought up by wolves. Kipling wrote *The Jungle Book* long before Disney Inc. got its hands on the story and turned it into a singing/dancing cartoon romp. When you read the Kipling ghost story in this volume, you will begin to understand that fantasy, horror, and science fiction have a long and noble tradition in literature. Stories written a hundred years ago are just as alive and viable as stories written today. And to truly get what the writers today are doing, you'll need to have some knowledge of the past because— trust me, writer to reader—we writers count on you to have read the old good stuff, too.

—Jane Yolen

ACKNOWLEDGMENTS

For all manner of help and support on this project, the editors would like to thank Jack Dann, Ellen Datlow, Jim Frenkel, David Hartwell, Sharyn November, Sheila Williams, our editors Jonathan Schmidt and Susan Chang, our publishers Kathleen Doherty and Tom Doherty, art director Irene Gallo for her usual outstanding jacket design, and, of course, our spouses, David Stemple and Teresa Nielsen Hayden.

For starting me down this road, I'd like to thank Richard J. Hurley, editor of *Beyond Belief,* a paperback anthology of science fiction stories for young readers published by Scholastic Book Services in 1966.

—Patrick Nielsen Hayden

The Faery Handbag

KELLY LINK

❖

We all start out believing two things: that our families are normal, and that the stories they tell us (think Santa Claus, think Tooth Fairy) are true. Growing up, we find that some of that was true, and some of it was false—and, maybe that some was true in ways we didn't appreciate at the time. Thus Kelly Link's story, about the joys and sorrows of having the coolest grandmother in the world.

If you like this story, try the short stories of Francesca Lia Block, the magical novels of Joan Aiken, and Susanna Clarke's Jonathan Strange and Mr. Norrell.

I used to go to thrift stores with my friends. We'd take the train into Boston, and go to The Garment District, which is this huge vintage clothing warehouse. Everything is arranged by color, and somehow that makes all of the clothes beautiful. It's kind of like if you went through the wardrobe in the Narnia books, only instead of finding Aslan and the White Witch and horrible Eustace, you found this magic clothing world—instead of talking animals, there were feather boas and wedding dresses and bowling shoes, and paisley shirts and Doc Martens and everything hung up on racks so that first you have black dresses, all together, like the world's largest indoor funeral, and then blue dresses—all the blues you can imagine—and then red dresses and so on. Pink-reds and orangey reds and purple-reds and exit-light reds and candy reds. Sometimes I would close my eyes and Natasha and Natalie and Jake would drag me over to a rack, and rub a dress against my hand. "Guess what color this is."

We had this theory that you could learn how to tell, just by feeling, what color something was. For example, if you're sitting on a lawn, you can tell what color green the grass is, with your eyes closed, depending on how silky-rubbery it feels. With clothing, stretchy velvet stuff always feels red when your eyes are closed, even if it's not red. Natasha was always best at guessing colors, but Natasha is also best at cheating at games and not getting caught.

One time we were looking through kids' T-shirts and we found a Muppets T-shirt that had belonged to Natalie in third grade. We knew it belonged to her, because it still had her name inside, where her mother had written it in permanent marker when Natalie went to summer camp. Jake bought it back for her, because he was the only one who had money that weekend. He was the only one who had a job.

Maybe you're wondering what a guy like Jake is doing in The Garment District with a bunch of girls. The thing about Jake is that he always has a good time, no matter what he's doing. He likes everything, and he likes everyone, but he likes me best of all. Wherever he is now, I bet he's having a great time and wondering when I'm going to show up. I'm always running late. But he knows that.

We had this theory that things have life cycles, the way that people do. The life cycle of wedding dresses and feather boas and T-shirts and shoes and handbags involves the Garment District. If clothes are good, or even if they're bad in an interesting way, the Garment District is where they go when they die. You can tell that they're dead, because of the way that they smell. When you buy them, and wash them, and start wearing them again, and they start to smell like you, that's when they reincarnate. But the point is, if you're looking for a particular thing, you just have to keep looking for it. You have to look hard.

Down in the basement at The Garment District they sell clothing and beat-up suitcases and teacups by the pound. You can get eight pounds worth of prom dresses—a slinky black dress, a poufy lavender dress, a swirly pink dress, a silvery, starry lamé dress so fine you could pass it through a key ring—for eight dollars. I go there every week, hunting for Grandmother Zofia's faery handbag.

❖

The faery handbag: It's huge and black and kind of hairy. Even when your eyes are closed, it feels black. As black as black ever gets, like if you touch it, your hand might get stuck in it, like tar or black quicksand or when you stretch out your hand at night, to turn on a light, but all you feel is darkness.

Fairies live inside it. I know what that sounds like, but it's true.

❖

Grandmother Zofia said it was a family heirloom. She said that it was over two hundred years old. She said that when she died, I had to look after it. Be its guardian. She said that it would be my responsibility.

I said that it didn't look that old, and that they didn't have handbags two hundred years ago, but that just made her cross. She said, "So then tell me, Genevieve, darling, where do you think old ladies used to put their reading glasses and their heart medicine and their knitting needles?"

❖

I know that no one is going to believe any of this. That's okay. If I thought you would, then I couldn't tell you. Promise me that you won't believe a word. That's what Zofia used to say to me when she told me stories. At the funeral, my mother said, half-laughing and half-crying, that her mother was the world's best liar. I think she thought maybe Zofia wasn't really dead. But I went up to Zofia's coffin, and I looked her right in the eyes. They were closed. The funeral parlor had made her up with blue eyeshadow, and blue eyeliner. She looked like she was going to be a news anchor on Fox television, instead of dead. It was creepy and it made me even sadder than I already was. But I didn't let that distract me.

"Okay, Zofia," I whispered. "I know you're dead, but this is important. You know exactly how important this is. Where's the handbag? What did you do with it? How do I find it? What am I supposed to do now?"

Of course she didn't say a word. She just lay there, this little smile on her face, as if she thought the whole thing—death, blue eye-shadow, Jake, the handbag, faeries, Scrabble, Baldeziwurlekistan, all of it—was a joke. She always did have a weird sense of humor. That's why she and Jake got along so well.

❖

I grew up in a house next door to the house where my mother lived when she was a little girl. Her mother, Zofia Swink, my grandmother, baby-sat me while my mother and father were at work.

Zofia never looked like a grandmother. She had long black hair which she wore in little, braided, spiky towers and plaits. She had large blue eyes. She was taller than my father. She looked like a spy or balle-rina or a lady pirate or a rock star. She acted like one, too. For example, she never drove anywhere. She rode a bike. It drove my mother crazy. "Why can't you act your age?" she'd say, and Zofia would just laugh.

Zofia and I played Scrabble all the time. Zofia always won, even though her English wasn't all that great, because we'd decided that she was allowed to use Baldeziwurleki vocabulary. Baldeziwurlekistan is where Zofia was born, over two hundred years ago. That's what Zofia said. (My grandmother claimed to be over two hundred years old. Or maybe even older. Sometimes she claimed that she'd even met Genghis Khan. He was much shorter than her. I probably don't have time to tell that story.) Baldeziwurlekistan is also an incredibly valu-able word in Scrabble points, even though it doesn't exactly fit on the board. Zofia put it down the first time we played. I was feeling pretty good because I'd gotten forty-one points for "zippery" on my turn.

Zofia kept rearranging her letters on her tray. Then she looked over at me, as if daring me to stop her, and put down "eziwurlekistan," after "bald." She used "delicious," "zippery," "wishes," "kismet," and "nee-dle," and made "to" into "toe." "Baldeziwurlekistan" went all the way across the board and then trailed off down the right-hand side.

I started laughing.

"I used up all my letters," Zofia said. She licked her pencil and started adding up points.

"That's not a word," I said. "Baldeziwurlekistan is not a word. Besides, you can't do that. You can't put an eighteen-letter word on a board that's fifteen squares across."

"Why not? It's a country," Zofia said. "It's where I was born, little darling."

"Challenge," I said. I went and got the dictionary and looked it up. "There's no such place."

"Of course there isn't nowadays," Zofia said. "It wasn't a very big place, even when it was a place. But you've heard of Samarkand, and Uzbekistan and the Silk Road and Genghis Khan. Haven't I told you about meeting Genghis Khan?"

I looked up Samarkand. "Okay," I said. "Samarkand is a real place. A real word. But Baldeziwurlekistan isn't."

"They call it something else now," Zofia said. "But I think it's important to remember where we come from. I think it's only fair that I get to use Baldeziwurleki words. Your English is so much better than me. Promise me something, mouthful of dumpling, a small, small thing. You'll remember its real name. Baldeziwurlekistan. Now when I add it up, I get three hundred and sixty-eight points. Could that be right?"

❖

If you called the faery handbag by its right name, it would be something like "orzipanikanikcz," which means the "bag of skin where the world lives," only Zofia never spelled that word the same way twice. She said you had to spell it a little differently each time. You never wanted to spell it exactly the right way, because that would be dangerous.

I called it the faery handbag because I put "faery" down on the Scrabble board once. Zofia said that you spelled it with an "i," not an "e." She looked it up in the dictionary, and lost a turn.

❖

Zofia said that in Baldeziwurlekistan they used a board and tiles for divination, prognostication, and sometimes even just for fun. She said it was a little like playing Scrabble. That's probably why she turned out to be so good at Scrabble. The Baldeziwurlekistanians used their tiles and board to communicate with the people who lived under the hill. The people who lived under the hill knew the future. The Baldeziwurlekistanians gave them fermented milk and honey, and the young women of the village used to go and lie out on the hill and sleep under the stars. Apparently the people under the hill were pretty cute. The important thing was that you never went down into the hill and spent the night there, no matter how cute the guy from under the hill was. If you did, even if you only spent a single night under the hill, when you came out again a hundred years might have passed. "Remember that," Zofia said to me. "It doesn't matter how cute a guy is. If he wants you to come back to his place, it isn't a good idea. It's okay to fool around, but don't spend the night."

Every once in a while, a woman from under the hill would marry a man from the village, even though it never ended well. The problem was that the women under the hill were terrible cooks. They couldn't get used to the way time worked in the village, which meant that supper always got burnt, or else it wasn't cooked long enough. But they couldn't stand to be criticized. It hurt their feelings. If their village husband complained, or even if he looked like he wanted to complain, that was it. The woman from under the hill went back to her home, and even if her husband went and begged and pleaded and apologized, it might be three years or thirty years or a few generations before she came back out.

Even the best, happiest marriages between the Baldeziwurlekistanians and the people under the hill fell apart when the children got old enough to complain about dinner. But everyone in the village had some hill blood in them.

"It's in you," Zofia said, and kissed me on the nose. "Passed down from my grandmother and her mother. It's why we're so beautiful."

When Zofia was nineteen, the shaman-priestess in her village threw the tiles and discovered that something bad was going to happen. A raiding party was coming. There was no point in fighting them. They would burn down everyone's houses and take the young men and women for slaves. And it was even worse than that. There was going to be an earthquake as well, which was bad news because usually, when raiders showed up, the village went down under the hill for a night and when they came out again the raiders would have been gone for months or decades or even a hundred years. But this earthquake was going to split the hill right open.

The people under the hill were in trouble. Their home would be destroyed, and they would be doomed to roam the face of the earth, weeping and lamenting their fate until the sun blew out and the sky cracked and the seas boiled and the people dried up and turned to dust and blew away. So the shaman-priestess went and divined some more, and the people under the hill told her to kill a black dog and skin it and use the skin to make a purse big enough to hold a chicken, an egg, and a cooking pot. So she did, and then the people under the hill made the inside of the purse big enough to hold all of the village and all of the people under the hill and mountains and forests and seas and rivers and lakes and orchards and a sky and stars and spirits and fabulous monsters and sirens and dragons and dryads and mermaids and beasties and all the little gods that the Baldeziwurlekistanians and the people under the hill worshipped.

"Your purse is made out of dog skin?" I said. "That's disgusting!"

"Little dear pet," Zofia said, looking wistful, "dog is delicious. To Baldeziwurlekistanians, dog is a delicacy."

Before the raiding party arrived, the village packed up all of their belongings and moved into the handbag. The clasp was made out of bone. If you opened it one way, then it was just a purse big enough to hold a chicken and an egg and a clay cooking pot, or else a pair of reading glasses and a library book and a pillbox. If you opened the clasp another way, then you found yourself in a little boat floating at the mouth of a river. On either side of you was forest, where the Baldeziwurlekistanian villagers and the people under the hill made their new settlement.

If you opened the handbag the wrong way, though, you found yourself in a dark land that smelled like blood. That's where the guardian of the purse (the dog whose skin had been sewn into a purse) lived. The guardian had no skin. Its howl made blood come out of your ears and nose. It tore apart anyone who turned the clasp in the opposite direction and opened the purse in the wrong way.

"Here is the wrong way to open the handbag," Zofia said. She twisted the clasp, showing me how she did it. She opened the mouth of the purse, but not very wide and held it up to me. "Go ahead, darling, and listen for a second."

I put my head near the handbag, but not too near. I didn't hear anything. "I don't hear anything," I said.

"The poor dog is probably asleep," Zofia said. "Even nightmares have to sleep now and then."

❖

After he got expelled, everybody at school called Jake Houdini instead of Jake. Everybody except for me. I'll explain why, but you have to be patient. It's hard work telling everything in the right order.

Jake is smarter and also taller than most of our teachers. Not quite as tall as me. We've known each other since third grade. Jake has always been in love with me. He says he was in love with me even before third grade, even before we ever met. It took me a while to fall in love with Jake.

In third grade, Jake knew everything already, except how to make friends. He used to follow me around all day long. It made me so mad that I kicked him in the knee. When that didn't work, I threw his backpack out of the window of the school bus. That didn't work either, but the next year Jake took some tests and the school decided that he could skip fourth and fifth grade. Even I felt sorry for Jake then. Sixth grade didn't work out. When the sixth graders wouldn't stop flushing his head down the toilet, he went out and caught a skunk and set it loose in the boy's locker room.

The school was going to suspend him for the rest of the year, but instead Jake took two years off while his mother homeschooled him. He learned Latin and Hebrew and Greek, how to write sestinas, how to make sushi, how to play bridge, and even how to knit. He learned fencing and ballroom dancing. He worked in a soup kitchen and made a Super-8 movie about Civil War reenactors who play extreme croquet in full costume instead of firing off cannons. He started learning how to play guitar. He even wrote a novel. I've never read it—he says it was awful.

When he came back two years later, because his mother had cancer for the first time, the school put him back with our year, in seventh grade. He was still way too smart, but he was finally smart enough to figure out how to fit in. Plus he was good at soccer and he was really cute. Did I mention that he played guitar? Every girl in school had a crush on Jake, but he used to come home after school with me and play Scrabble with Zofia and ask her about Baldeziwurlekistan.

❖

Jake's mom was named Cynthia. She collected ceramic frogs and knock-knock jokes. When we were in ninth grade, she had cancer again. When she died, Jake smashed all of her frogs. That was the first funeral I ever went to. A few months later, Jake's father asked Jake's fencing teacher out on a date. They got married right after the school expelled Jake for his AP project on Houdini. That was the first wedding I ever went to. Jake and I stole a bottle of wine and drank it, and I threw up in the swimming pool at the country club. Jake threw up all over my shoes.

❖

So, anyway, the village and the people under the hill lived happily ever after for a few weeks in the handbag, which they had tied around a rock in a dry well which the people under the hill had determined would survive the earthquake. But some of the Baldeziwurlekistanians wanted to come out again and see what was going on in the world. Zofia was one of them. It had been summer when they went into the bag, but when they came out again, and climbed out of the well, snow was falling and their village was ruins and crumbly old rubble. They walked through the snow, Zofia carrying the handbag, until they came to another village, one that they'd never seen before. Everyone in that village was packing up their belongings and leaving, which gave Zofia and her friends a bad feeling. It seemed to be just the same as when they went into the handbag.

They followed the refugees, who seemed to know where they were going, and finally everyone came to a city. Zofia had never seen such a place. There were trains and electric lights and movie theaters, and there were people shooting each other. Bombs were falling. A war going on. Most of the villagers decided to climb right back inside the handbag, but Zofia volunteered to stay in the world and look after the handbag. She had fallen in love with movies and silk stockings and with a young man, a Russian deserter.

Zofia and the Russian deserter married and had many adventures and finally came to America, where my mother was born. Now and then Zofia would consult the tiles and talk to the people who lived in the handbag and they would tell her how best to avoid trouble and how she and her husband could make some money. Every now and then one of the Baldeziwurlekistanians, or one of the people from under the hill came out of the handbag and wanted to go grocery shopping, or to a movie or an amusement park to ride on roller coasters, or to the library.

The more advice Zofia gave her husband, the more money they made. Her husband became curious about Zofia's handbag, because he could see that there was something odd about it, but Zofia told him to mind his own business. He began to spy on Zofia, and saw that strange men and women were coming in and out of the house. He became convinced that either Zofia was a spy for the Communists, or maybe that she was having affairs. They fought and he drank more and more, and finally he threw away her divination tiles. "Russians make bad husbands," Zofia told me. Finally, one night while Zofia was sleeping, her husband opened the bone clasp and climbed inside the handbag.

"I thought he'd left me," Zofia said. "For almost twenty years I thought he'd left me and your mother and taken off for California. Not that I minded. I was tired of being married and cooking dinners and cleaning house for someone else. It's better to cook what I want to eat, and clean up when I decide to clean up. It was harder on your mother, not having a father. That was the part that I minded most.

"Then it turned out that he hadn't run away after all. He'd spent one night in the handbag and then come out again twenty years later, exactly as handsome as I remembered, and enough time had passed that I had forgiven him all the quarrels. We made up and it was all very romantic and then when we had another fight the next morning, he went and kissed your mother—who had slept right through his visit—on the cheek, and then he climbed right back inside the handbag. I didn't see him again for another twenty years. The last time he showed up, we went to see *Star Wars* and he liked it so much that he went back inside the handbag to tell everyone else about it. In a couple of years they'll all show up and want to see it on video and all of the sequels too."

"Tell them not to bother with the prequels," I said.

❖

The thing about Zofia and libraries is that she's always losing library books. She says that she hasn't lost them, and in fact that they aren't even overdue, really. It's just that even one week inside the faery handbag is a lot longer in library-world time. So what is she supposed to do about it? The librarians all hate Zofia. She's banned from using any of the branches in our area. When I was eight, she got me to go to the library for her and check out a bunch of biographies and science books and some Georgette Heyer romance novels. My mother was livid when she found out, but it was too late. Zofia had already misplaced most of them.

❖

It's really hard to write about somebody as if they're really dead. I still think Zofia must be sitting in her living room, in her house, watching some old horror movie, dropping popcorn into her handbag. She's waiting for me to come over and play Scrabble.

❖

Nobody is ever going to return those library books now.

❖

My mother used to come home from work and roll her eyes. "Have you been telling them your fairy stories?" she'd say. "Genevieve, your grandmother is a horrible liar."

Zofia would fold up the Scrabble board and shrug at me and Jake. "I'm a wonderful liar," she'd say. "I'm the best liar in the world. Promise me you won't believe a single word."

But she wouldn't tell the story of the faery handbag to Jake. Only the old Baldeziwurlekistanian folktales and fairytales about the people under the hill. She told him about how she and her husband made it all the way across Europe, hiding in haystacks and in barns, and how once, when her husband went off to find food, a farmer found her hiding in his chicken coop and tried to rape her. But she opened up the faery handbag in the way she showed me, and the dog came out and ate the farmer and all his chickens too.

She was teaching Jake and me how to curse in Baldeziwurleki. I also know how to say I love you, but I'm not going to ever say it to anyone again, except to Jake, when I find him.

When I was eight, I believed everything Zofia told me. By the time I was thirteen, I didn't believe a single word. When I was fifteen, I saw a man come out of her house and get on Zofia's three-speed bicycle and ride down the street. His clothes looked funny. He was a lot younger than my mother and father, and even though I'd never seen him before, he was familiar. I followed him on my bike, all the way to the grocery store. I waited just past the checkout lanes while he bought peanut butter, Jack Daniel's, half a dozen instant cameras, at least sixty packs of Reese's Peanut Butter Cups, three bags of Hershey's Kisses, a handful of Milky Way bars and other stuff from the rack of checkout candy. While the checkout clerk was helping him bag up all of that chocolate, he looked up and saw me. "Genevieve?" he said. "That's your name, right?"

I turned and ran out of the store. He grabbed up the bags and ran after me. I don't even think he got his change back. I was still running away, and then one of the straps on my flip-flops popped out of the sole, the way they do, and that made me really angry so I just stopped. I turned around.

"Who are you?" I said.

But I already knew. He looked like he could have been my mom's younger brother. He was really cute. I could see why Zofia had fallen in love with him.

His name was Rustan. Zofia told my parents that he was an expert in Baldeziwurlekistanian folklore who would be staying with her for a few days. She brought him over for dinner. Jake was there too, and I could tell that Jake knew something was up. Everybody except my dad knew something was going on.

"You mean Baldeziwurlekistan is a real place?" my mother asked Rustan. "My mother is telling the truth?"

I could see that Rustan was having a hard time with that one. He obviously wanted to say that his wife was a horrible liar, but then where would he be? Then he couldn't be the person that he was supposed to be.

There were probably a lot of things that he wanted to say. What he said was, "This is really good pizza."

Rustan took a lot of pictures at dinner. The next day I went with him to get the pictures developed. He'd brought back some film with him, with pictures he'd taken inside the faery handbag, but those didn't come out well. Maybe the film was too old. We got doubles of the pictures from dinner so that I could have some too. There's a great picture of Jake, sitting outside on the porch. He's laughing, and he has his hand up to his mouth, like he's going to catch the laugh. I have that picture up on my computer, and also up on my wall over my bed.

I bought a Cadbury Creme Egg for Rustan. Then we shook hands and he kissed me once on each cheek. "Give one of those kisses to your mother," he said, and I thought about how the next time I saw him, I might be Zofia's age, and he would only be a few days older. The next time I saw him, Zofia would be dead. Jake and I might have kids. That was too weird.

❖

I know Rustan tried to get Zofia to go with him, to live in the handbag, but she wouldn't.

"It makes me dizzy in there," she used to tell me. "And they don't have movie theaters. And I have to look after your mother and you. Maybe when you're old enough to look after the handbag, I'll poke my head inside, just long enough for a little visit."

❖

I didn't fall in love with Jake because he was smart. I'm pretty smart myself. I know that smart doesn't mean nice, or even mean that you have a lot of common sense. Look at all the trouble smart people get themselves into.

I didn't fall in love with Jake because he could make maki rolls and had a black belt in fencing, or whatever it is that you get if you're good in fencing. I didn't fall in love with Jake because he plays guitar. He's a better soccer player than he is a guitar player.

Those were the reasons why I went out on a date with Jake. That, and because he asked me. He asked if I wanted to go see a movie, and I asked if I could bring my grandmother and Natalie and Natasha. He said sure and so all five of us sat and watched *Bring It On* and every once in a while Zofia dropped a couple of Milk Duds or some popcorn into her purse. I don't know if she was feeding the dog, or if she'd opened the purse the right way and was throwing food at her husband.

I fell in love with Jake because he told stupid knock-knock jokes to Natalie, and told Natasha that he liked her jeans. I fell in love with Jake when he took me and Zofia home. He walked her up to her front door and then he walked me up to mine. I fell in love with Jake when he didn't try to kiss me. The thing is, I was nervous about the whole kissing thing. Most guys think that they're better at it than they really are. Not that I think I'm a real genius at kissing either, but I don't think kissing should be a competitive sport. It isn't tennis.

Natalie and Natasha and I used to practice kissing with each other. Not that we like each other that way, but just for practice. We got pretty good at it. We could see why kissing was supposed to be fun.

But Jake didn't try to kiss me. Instead he just gave me this really big hug. He put his face in my hair and he sighed. We stood there like that, and then finally I said, "What are you doing?"

"I just wanted to smell your hair," he said.

"Oh," I said. That made me feel weird, but in a good way. I put my nose up to his hair, which is brown and curly, and I smelled it. We stood there and smelled each other's hair, and I felt so good. I felt so happy.

Jake said into my hair, "Do you know that actor John Cusack?"

I said, "Yeah. One of Zofia's favorite movies is *Better Off Dead*. We watch it all the time."

"So he likes to go up to women and smell their armpits."

"Gross!" I said. "That's such a lie! What are you doing now? That tickles."

"I'm smelling your ear," Jake said.

❖

Jake's hair smelled like iced tea with honey in it, after all the ice has melted.

❖

Kissing Jake is like kissing Natalie or Natasha, except that it isn't just for fun. It feels like something there isn't a word for in Scrabble.

❖

The deal with Houdini is that Jake got interested in him during Advanced Placement American History. He and I were both put in tenth-grade history. We were doing biography projects. I was studying Joseph McCarthy. My grandmother had all sorts of stories about McCarthy. She hated him for what he did to Hollywood.

Jake didn't turn in his project—instead he told everyone in our AP class except for Mr. Streep (we call him Meryl) to meet him at the gym on Saturday. When we showed up, Jake reenacted one of Houdini's escapes with a laundry bag, handcuffs, a gym locker, bicycle chains, and the school's swimming pool. It took him three and a half minutes to get free, and this guy named Roger took a bunch of photos and then put the photos online. One of the photos ended up in the *Boston Globe,* and Jake got expelled. The really ironic thing was that while his mom was in the hospital, Jake had applied to MIT. He did it for his mom. He thought that way she'd have to stay alive. She was so excited about MIT. A couple of days after he'd been expelled, right after the wedding, while his dad and the fencing instructor were in Bermuda, he got an acceptance letter in the mail and a phone call from this guy in the admissions office who explained why they had to withdraw the acceptance.

❖

My mother wanted to know why I let Jake wrap himself up in bicycle chains and then watched while Peter and Michael pushed him into the deep end of the school pool. I said that Jake had a backup plan. Ten more seconds and we were all going to jump into the pool and open the locker and get him out of there. I was crying when I said that. Even before he got in the locker, I knew how stupid Jake was being. Afterward, he promised me that he'd never do anything like that again.

That was when I told him about Zofia's husband, Rustan, and about Zofia's handbag. How stupid am I?

❖

So I guess you can figure out what happened next. The problem is that Jake believed me about the handbag. We spent a lot of time over at Zofia's, playing Scrabble. Zofia never let the faery handbag out of her sight. She even took it with her when she went to the bathroom. I think she even slept with it under her pillow.

I didn't tell her that I'd said anything to Jake. I wouldn't ever have told anybody else about it. Not Natasha. Not even Natalie, who is the most responsible person in all of the world. Now, of course, if the handbag turns up and Jake still hasn't come back, I'll have to tell Natalie. Somebody has to keep an eye on the stupid thing while I go find Jake.

What worries me is that maybe one of the Baldeziwurlekistanians or one of the people under the hill or maybe even Rustan popped out of the handbag to run an errand and got worried when Zofia wasn't there. Maybe they'll come looking for her and bring it back. Maybe they know I'm supposed to look after it now. Or maybe they took it and hid it somewhere. Maybe someone turned it in at the lost-and-found at the library and that stupid librarian called the FBI. Maybe scientists at the Pentagon are examining the handbag right now. Testing it. If Jake comes out, they'll think he's a spy or a superweapon or an alien or something. They're not going to just let him go.

❖

Everyone thinks Jake ran away, except for my mother, who is convinced that he was trying out another Houdini escape and is probably lying at the bottom of a lake somewhere. She hasn't said that to me, but I can see her thinking it. She keeps making cookies for me.

❖

What happened is that Jake said, "Can I see that for just a second?"

He said it so casually that I think he caught Zofia off guard. She was reaching into the purse for her wallet. We were standing in the lobby of the movie theater on a Monday morning. Jake was behind the snack counter. He'd gotten a job there. He was wearing this stupid red paper hat and some kind of apron-bib thing. He was supposed to ask us if we wanted to supersize our drinks.

He reached over the counter and took Zofia's handbag right out of her hand. He closed it and then he opened it again. I think he opened it the right way. I don't think he ended up in the dark place. He said to me and Zofia, "I'll be right back." And then he wasn't there anymore. It was just me and Zofia and the handbag, lying there on the counter where he'd dropped it.

If I'd been fast enough, I think I could have followed him. But Zofia had been guardian of the faery handbag for a lot longer. She snatched the bag back and glared at me. "He's a very bad boy," she said. She was absolutely furious. "You're better off without him, Genevieve, I think."

"Give me the handbag," I said. "I have to go get him."

"It isn't a toy, Genevieve," she said. "It isn't a game. This isn't Scrabble. He comes back when he comes back. If he comes back."

"Give me the handbag," I said. "Or I'll take it from you."

She held the handbag up high over her head, so that I couldn't reach it. I hate people who are taller than me. "What are you going to do now," Zofia said. "Are you going to knock me down? Are you going to steal the handbag? Are you going to go away and leave me here to explain to your parents where you've gone? Are you going to say goodbye to your friends? When you come out again, they will have gone to college. They'll have jobs and babies and houses and they won't even recognize you. Your mother will be an old woman and I will be dead."

"I don't care," I said. I sat down on the sticky red carpet in the lobby and started to cry. Someone wearing a little metal name tag came over and asked if we were okay. His name was Missy. Or maybe he was wearing someone else's tag.

"We're fine," Zofia said. "My granddaughter has the flu."

She took my hand and pulled me up. She put her arm around me and we walked out of the theater. We never even got to see the stupid movie. We never even got to see another movie together. I don't ever want to go see another movie. The problem is, I don't want to see unhappy endings. And I don't know if I believe in the happy ones.

"I have a plan," Zofia said. "I will go find Jake. You will stay here and look after the handbag."

"You won't come back either," I said. I cried even harder. "Or if you do, I'll be like a hundred years old and Jake will still be sixteen."

"Everything will be okay," Zofia said. I wish I could tell you how beautiful she looked right then. It didn't matter if she was lying or if she actually knew that everything was going to be okay. The important thing was how she looked when she said it. She said, with absolute certainty, or maybe with all the skill of a very skillful liar, "My plan will work. First we go to the library, though. One of the people under the hill just brought back an Agatha Christie mystery, and I need to return it."

"We're going to the library?" I said. "Why don't we just go home and play Scrabble for a while." You probably think I was just being sarcastic here, and I was being sarcastic. But Zofia gave me a sharp look. She knew that if I was being sarcastic that my brain was working again. She knew that I knew she was stalling for time. She knew that I was coming up with my own plan, which was a lot like Zofia's plan, except that I was the one who went into the handbag. *How* was the part I was working on.

"We could do that," she said. "Remember, when you don't know what to do, it never hurts to play Scrabble. It's like reading the I Ching or tea leaves."

"Can we please just hurry?" I said.

Zofia just looked at me. "Genevieve, we have plenty of time. If you're going to look after the handbag, you have to remember that. You have to be patient. Can you be patient?"

"I can try," I told her. I'm trying, Zofia. I'm trying really hard. But it isn't fair. Jake is off having adventures and talking to talking animals, and who knows, learning how to fly and some beautiful three-thousand-year-old girl from under the hill is teaching him how to speak fluent Baldeziwurleki. I bet she lives in a house that runs around on chicken legs, and she tells Jake that she'd love to hear him play something on the guitar. Maybe you'll kiss her, Jake, because she's put a spell on you. But whatever you do, don't go up into her house. Don't fall asleep in her bed. Come back soon, Jake, and bring the handbag with you.

❖

I hate those movies, those books, where some guy gets to go off and have adventures and meanwhile the girl has to stay home and wait. I'm a feminist. I subscribe to Bust magazine, and I watch Buffy re-runs. I don't believe in that kind of shit.

❖

We hadn't been in the library for five minutes before Zofia picked up a biography of Carl Sagan and dropped it in her purse. She was defi-nitely stalling for time. She was trying to come up with a plan that would counteract the plan that she knew I was planning. I wondered what she thought I was planning. It was probably much better than anything I'd come up with.

"Don't do that!" I said.

"Don't worry," Zofia said. "Nobody was watching."

"I don't care if nobody saw! What if Jake's sitting there in the boat, or what if he was coming back and you just dropped it on his head!"

"It doesn't work that way," Zofia said. Then she said, "It would serve him right, anyway."

That was when the librarian came up to us. She had a name tag on as well. I was so sick of people and their stupid name tags. I'm not even going to tell you what her name was. "I saw that," the librarian said.

"Saw what?" Zofia said. She smiled down at the librarian, like she was Queen of the Library, and the librarian was a petitioner.

The librarian stared hard at her. "I know you," she said, almost sounding awed, like she was a weekend bird-watcher who'd just seen bigfoot. "We have your picture on the office wall. You're Ms. Swink. You aren't allowed to check out books here."

"That's ridiculous," Zofia said. She was at least two feet taller than the librarian. I felt a bit sorry for the librarian. After all, Zofia had just stolen a seven-day book. She probably wouldn't return it for a hundred years. My mother has always made it clear that it's my job to protect other people from Zofia. I guess I was Zofia's guardian before I became the guardian of the handbag.

The librarian reached up and grabbed Zofia's handbag. She was small but she was strong. She jerked the handbag and Zofia stumbled and fell back against a work desk. I couldn't believe it. Everyone except for me was getting a look at Zofia's handbag. What kind of guardian was I going to be?

"Genevieve," Zofia said. She held my hand very tightly, and I looked at her. She looked wobbly and pale. She said, "I feel very bad about all of this. Tell your mother I said so."

Then she said one last thing, but I think it was in Baldeziwurleki.

The librarian said, "I saw you put a book in here. Right here." She opened the handbag and peered inside. Out of the handbag came a long, lonely, ferocious, utterly hopeless scream of rage. I don't ever want to hear that noise again. Everyone in the library looked up. The librarian made a choking noise and threw Zofia's handbag away from her. A little trickle of blood came out of her nose and a drop fell on the floor. What I thought at first was that it was just plain luck that the handbag was closed when it landed. Later on I was trying to figure out what Zofia said. My Baldeziwurleki isn't very good, but I think she was saying something like "Figures. Stupid librarian. I have to go take care of that damn dog." So maybe that's what happened. Maybe Zofia sent part of herself in there with the skinless dog. Maybe she fought it and won and closed the handbag. Maybe she made friends with it. I mean, she used to feed it popcorn at the movies. Maybe she's still in there.

What happened in the library was Zofia sighed a little and closed her eyes. I helped her sit down in a chair, but I don't think she was really there any more. I rode with her in the ambulance, when the ambulance finally showed up, and I swear I didn't even think about the handbag until my mother showed up. I didn't say a word. I just left her there in the hospital with Zofia, who was on a respirator, and I ran all the way back to the library. But it was closed. So I ran all the way back again, to the hospital, but you already know what happened, right? Zofia died. I hate writing that. My tall, funny, beautiful, book-stealing, Scrabble-playing, story-telling grandmother died.

But you never met her. You're probably wondering about the handbag. What happened to it. I put up signs all over town, like Zofia's handbag was some kind of lost dog, but nobody ever called.

❖

So that's the story so far. Not that I expect you to believe any of it. Last night Natalie and Natasha came over and we played Scrabble. They don't really like Scrabble, but they feel like it's their job to cheer me up. I won. After they went home, I flipped all the tiles upside down and then I started picking them up in groups of seven. I tried to ask a question, but it was hard to pick just one. The words I got weren't so great either, so I decided that they weren't English words. They were Baldeziwurleki words.

Once I decided that, everything became perfectly clear. First I put down "kirif" which means "happy news," and then I got a "b," an "o," an "l," an "e," an "f," another "i," an "s," and a "z." So then I could make "kirif" into "bolekirifisz," which could mean "the happy result of a combination of diligent effort and patience."

I would find the faery handbag. The tiles said so. I would work the clasp and go into the handbag and have my own adventures and would rescue Jake. Hardly any time would have gone by before we came back out of the handbag. Maybe I'd even make friends with that poor dog and get to say good-bye, for real, to Zofia. Rustan would show up again and be really sorry that he'd missed Zofia's funeral and this time he would be brave enough to tell my mother the whole story. He would tell her that he was her father. Not that she would believe him. Not that you should believe this story. Promise me that you won't believe a word.

Blood Wolf

S. M. STIRLING

❖

*Epic fantasy takes a hero on sweeping adventures across vast
landscapes. In S. M. Stirling's story, young Blood Wolf has left
his familiar backwoods home and come to a city as strange and
new to him as another world would be.*

*Often epic fantasy comes in trilogies or multivolumed chron-
icles in order to accommodate such sweep. Indeed, Stirling has
already written about the world of this story in several of his
Nantucket novels, beginning with* Island in the Sea of Time, *in
which the Massachusetts island of Nantucket, complete with its
few inhabitants and small store of modern technology, is hurled
back into the Bronze Age. In the struggles that ensue, the Nantucketers conquer much of the ancient world: It's against this
background that the story of Blood Wolf takes place.*

*If this kind of story appeals to you, you should try Ursula K.
Le Guin's* Earthsea *trilogy, Lloyd Alexander's* Chronicles of
Prydain, *Sean Stewart's* Nobody's Son, *or Patricia McKillip's*
Riddlemaster of Hed *trilogy.*

His name was *Kreuha Wolkwos*—Blood Wolf, in the tongue
of the Keruthini folk—and he was the greatest of all the
warriors of his people, although still unwedded and barely
old enough to raise a thick yellow down on his cheeks. Even before
that fuzz sprouted he had been called a man in the *korios,* the war-
band of the youths who spent the summer living like a wolf pack in
the woods off what they could hunt and steal. Now even house-
holders and the clan chiefs called him a man, for six heads of his

taking—the oldest weathered down to a skull, the newest still ripe—were spiked to the lintel above his father's house-door. This year he had come to his full height, a finger's-span below six feet, rangy and long-limbed; agile enough to run out on the yoke-pole of a chariot while the team galloped, fast enough on his own feet to chase down deer and cut their throats with his knife. At a full run he could throw his narrow-bladed javelins through a rolling hoop of rawhide half a hundred paces distant, and in a wrestling bout few men could keep their shoulders off the ground once Blood Wolf's hands closed on them. At the Sun Festival he had thrown the sacrificial bull by its horns and then danced the night through by the side of the Spring Queen.

Two horses and eight cattle were his by *soru-rechtos,* booty-right, taken in lawful raids, besides sheep, bronze, cloth, and a girl who would be valuable if she lived to womanhood. Many men hated him for his toploftiness, but none had dared face him for some time. Two of those heads on his father's lintel were fellow-tribesmen, slain within the sacred wands after due challenge. His name was often spoken around the hearthfires, and all knew that—if he lived to be a householder—the ruler of the tribe, the High *Reghix,* would make him successor to the broad lands of his father. Then he would surely become a great chief whose name lived forever.

Right now that pride was lost in a dull misery as he scrambled to the lee side of the boat and puked helplessly, bringing up only a spatter of thin, bitter bile into an ocean that heaved gray and white with foam beneath a cold October sky of racing gray cloud.

His stomach had been empty since the first few minutes of the day-long voyage from the mainland to Alba, the White Isle. One of the boatmen pushed him aside as he adjusted a rope, and he was too weak to return a blow for the insult. Only when the fifty-foot length ceased moving beneath him did he raise his head.

"Get your arse out of our boat, wild-man," the crewman said.

His accent was strange to the young man's ears, and the order and sometimes the endings of the words he used, but comprehensible—

many tribes distantly related to the Keruthinii folk had settled across the salt water in Alba, the White Isle. That didn't mean they were his friends; the opposite, if anything.

The seaman also scooped up the horsehide bundle that held Blood Wolf's goods and threw it on the planks of the dock. Two more grabbed the youth by the belt of his wolfskin kilt and half-carried, half-threw him out on worn oak-wood. That done, the crew ignored him as he crawled up the splintery surface toward his goods. Gradually the shaming weakness left him, and he could sit, then stand, spit some of the vile taste out of his mouth, begin to feel like a man once more. He had crossed the Channel to Alba; beyond Alba lay the Summer Isle, and beyond that the River Ocean, and the Island of Wizards, Nantucket.

First he looked to his weapons: round shield, spear, a light bronze-headed axe, and his precious steel knife, bought from Alban traders. Then he swung his pack onto his back and walked landward as he gazed around, trying hard not to gape at the magical city of Southaven. The shore tended north and south here, but little of it could be seen; great piers of timber framework filled with rock stretched out into the water. Beside them lay ships, more than he could count on fingers and toes both, many times more, their bowsprits looming over the broad cobbled harborside street thronged with folk and beasts and wagons. There were more folk here than in his whole tribe—six or seven tens of hundreds.

The ships' masts were taller than trees, their rigging and yards a spiky leafless forest, but that was nothing beside the ones out on the water with chimneys of *iron* sticking up from their middles and belching black smoke, and great wheels on either side churning up foam.

"True wizardry," he murmured to himself, grinning.

And in the tales, didn't the great warrior always come off well from his meeting with wizards? Either gaining their friendship and battle-luck, or overcoming and plundering them. He snuffed deeply—silt, fish, salt water, horse-manure, odd sulfur-tinged smoke, but less sweat and ordure stink than you'd expect—and looked along the street. At the thronging folk dressed more richly than great chiefs or tribal kings and more strangely than his eyes could take in; everything from home-like kilts and shifts to shameless string skirts on bare-breasted cloaked women, long embroidered robes, with the odd-looking trousers and jackets and boots that the majority favored, making a dun-colored mass. And at the nets of cargo swinging ashore, laden with sacks and bales and kegs of the Gods alone knew what unguessable wealth; at buildings of baked brick, some five times a man's height, with great clear windows of glass—and remembered the price the Keruthinii chieftains paid for a single tumbler or goblet of it. . . .

His belly rumbled. It had been more than a day since he'd eaten, and that had gone to the Channel fish. It was a cool brisk day with a strong wind under scudding cloud, enough to awaken any man's appetite.

"Stop, thief! Stop him!"

Kreuha's head whipped around. The cry had been in En-gil-its, the tongue of wizards and wizard traders; he'd learned a little of it. And the call was repeated in half a dozen other languages, two of them close to his own:

"Kreuk! Kreuk!" That was the ancient call to raise the hue-and-cry after one who stole by stealth.

A man came pushing through the crowd, vaulted a pile of barrels, leapt and scrambled over a four-wheeled wagon piled with bales of some dirty-white fibre; that gave him space to pick up speed, heading for the frayed edge of town south of the small-boat docks. He was holding a sword in his hand; Kreuha's eyes narrowed at the sight. The blade was like none he'd seen, slightly curved and as long as a man's leg, with a round gold-chased guard and a hilt made for two hands. Sunlight glittered on the bright metal, picking out a waving line in the steel a little back from the cutting edge.

Kreuha laid his pack and spears down and ran three bouncing strides to put himself in the man's way. The thief stopped, sweating and snarling; he was a few years older than the newcomer, shorter but broader, with a shock of dark-brown hair and beard. The arms below his sleeveless singlet were thick with muscle and lavishly tattooed. But there was something about the way he stood, the sweat and desperation that made him blink—

"Give me the sword," Kreuha said, crouching slightly and spreading his hands so the man couldn't dodge past him. "And I will return it to the owner."

And be richly rewarded, he thought. He'd heard of such weapons. The lords among the wizard-folk wore them. *This one is no warrior, only a thief.*

"If you try to strike me, I will kill you and take it," the Keruthinii tribesman continued calmly.

The man hesitated for an instant and then cut desperately, a sweeping two-handed roundhouse blow at waist level. It was clumsy, and Kreuha could see the prelude coming a full three heartbeats before the steel began to move, but it was hard enough to slice him to the spine if it landed—the more so as the blade looked knife-sharp. Kreuha leapt straight up as the sword moved, and it hissed like a serpent as it passed beneath the calloused soles of his feet. One long leg smashed out, and his heel slammed into the thief's breastbone with a sound like a maul hitting a baulk of seasoned oak and a crackling noise beneath that. The man was shocked to a halt, staggered backward with his face turning dark purple, coughed out a spray of bright arterial blood, and fell bonelessly limp.

Kreuha landed on his feet and one hand, then bounced erect. The sword spun away, landing on the cobbles and sparking as steel struck flint-rich stone. The tribesman winced at the slight to a fine weapon and bent to retrieve it, marveling at the living feel it had in his hands. He was considering whether he could take the head when a party of strangers came up, breathing hard from their run.

❖

"Oh, hell," Lucy Alston-Kurlelo said, looking down at the body of the dead thief. He was extremely dead, and stank. "I *knew* I shouldn't have hired him."

She turned to glare at the Southaven policeman. He spread his hands, including the one holding a revolver: "I offered you hands from the lockup willing to sign up rather than work off their sentences here. Ardaursson was a brawler and a drunk and a thief, and this looks like a clear case of self-defense. I didn't say anyone you bought out of lockup would be any good."

Lucy shrugged. That was true enough; there simply weren't enough deckhands to go around, with demand so high; more so as the *Pride* was going far foreign, a long high-risk voyage, not schlepping back and forth across the Pond between Alba and Nantucket. The thief had been a fisherman by trade, worth any dozen farmers or dockside sweepings . . . if he'd been honest.

"No charges?" she said.

"No charges. Plain enough case of taken-in-the-act; I'll file the report."

And you did *supply this piece of garbage yourself,* she thought to herself. Instead of arguing with the peace officer—officials in Southaven had gotten very assertive since the local Town Meeting was admitted to the Republic two years ago, and though young, the policeman came of a prominent local family—she looked at the kilted youngster who'd kicked in the luckless thief's chest.

Pretty, she thought. In a chisel-faced blond athletic way. And he was obviously fresh off the boat from the European mainland. No east-Alban tribesman would still be carrying bronze-headed spears, even in the backwoods of the north; hell, most of them were in trousers these days, some building themselves brick houses and sending their children to missionary schools.

Not from anywhere near the trade-outposts at the mouth of the Loire and Seine and Rhine, either, she thought.

At a guess—

"Khwid teuatha tuh'on?" she said: What tribe is yours? Of what people do you come? *"Bawatavii?"* she went on: *"Jowatani?"*

Those were the nearest coastal groups over the water, but he looked a little too raw for that. He'd been staring at her in wonder from the moment she showed up. Lucy was used to that; black people weren't common in Nantucket and extremely rare elsewhere. Her own birth-mother had been Alban, her father an American—a Coast Guardsman who later turned renegade and eventually ended up as a king on the upper Nile. One of her two adoptive mothers had been true coal-black, as opposed to Lucy's own light milk-chocolate, and there were still people in Alba who thought Marian Alston was some sort of spirit or demigoddess . . . though her deeds had more to do with that than her appearance.

"Keruthinii teuatha eghom h'esmi," he said, shaking his head and visibly gathering himself. "I am of the Keruthini folk." He drew himself up proudly: "Those who drove the Iraiina to Alba in my grandfather's time."

She grinned; that had happened just before the Event landed the late-twentieth-century island of Nantucket in 1250 B.C.E. It'd been a typical tribal scuffle between two small bands of scruffy bandits. Evidently it was a legendary battle-of-the-heroes thing with this boy's people, now that the tribal bards had had a generation to work it over.

Then his jaw dropped a trifle more as he noticed she was a woman; he might not have at all, save that her jacket was open on a well-filled sweater.

Still, he recovered fairly well. "This is yours?" he said, turning the *katana* and offering it hilt-first—and surprised her by saying it in gutturally accented but fairly good English. "You are from the Island of Wizards?"

Well, not just pretty, but fairly smart, she decided, carefully examining the edge—this was a pre-Event heirloom, carried back in time with the island of Nantucket to the Late Bronze Age—and then wiping it clean with a cloth before slipping it into the sheath whose lip rode over her left shoulder.

Not *just* an heirloom, though. The layer-forged metal had minute etchings along three-quarters of its length, where the salt and acids of blood had cut into the softer layers between the glass-hard edge steel. Only some of them were from her mother's time.

"It is and I am," she said. "Lucy Alston-Kurlelo, captain of the merchantman *Grey Lady's Pride* . . ." She saw his eyes open slightly at the family name; curse of having two famous mothers. "And I'm shipping out soon. Interested in a berth?"

For a moment the man's face—he looked to be in his late teens, considerably younger than she—grew keen. Then he looked wary.

"On . . . ship? Ocean?" He pointed out toward the salt water. At her nod he raised his hands in a warding gesture and swallowed.

Lucy laughed and flipped him a gold ten-dollar piece. He caught the small bright coin and nodded with regal politeness. She sighed as she turned and led her people back toward the ship.

"Well, let's go see what other gutter-scrapings, shepherdesses, and plowboys we can rustle up," she said to her companions—first mate and bosun and two senior deckhands; her younger brother Tim was supercargo and in charge back at the dock.

They nodded in unison. The Coast Guard kept the North Atlantic fairly free of pirates, and Tartessos did the same for the waters south of Capricorn and the western Mediterranean. You could take a chance and sail shorthanded on the crowded runs between here and home, and you needed to squeeze every cent until it shrieked to meet your costs even so.

Where the *Pride* was going, Islander craft were all too likely to meet locals who'd acquired steel and even gunpowder without developing any particular constraints on taking whatever they wanted whenever they could. You needed a crew big enough to work the guns and repel boarders; the extra risk and expense was what kept competition down and profits high on the Sumatra run and points east. It was also one reason she and her sister-cum-business-partner Heather never shipped together on these long voyages.

No sense in making *two* sets of children orphans with the same shower of poisoned blowgun darts.

❖

The strangers departed while Kreuha was marveling over the gold-piece; he had seen copper and silver coins from Alba and the Isle of Wizards, Nantucket, but this was the first one of gold he'd ever held. He held it up to the fading light of afternoon; there was an eagle clutching a bundle of arrows and a peace-wreath on one side, and strange letters and numbers on the other.

One of the strangers had remained, a young brown-haired man in blue tunic and trousers, with a wooden club and one of the fearsome-wonderful fire-weapons at his belt—the awesome type called *revolver,* which let the bearer hold the deaths of six men in his hand. He pulled a metal whistle free and blew three sharp blasts on it.

"Ual kelb soma krweps," he said, to Kreuha in something close to the warrior's own language: "To summon help with the body."

Blood Wolf nodded, although he didn't offer to help himself—dead bodies were unclean, and he didn't know how he'd get a purification ceremony done so far from home. The man went on:

"I am . . . you would say, a retainer of my chief. A warrior charged with keeping order and guarding against ill-doers among the people. In English, a *policeman.*"

Kreuha's brows rose. *That* was a duty he didn't envy; you'd be the target of endless ill-will if you had to offend people as part of your duty. He'd never walked away from a fight, but now that he'd come to man's estate he didn't go looking for them, not *all* the time. His lips moved, as he repeated the word softly several times, to add to his store of En-gil-its terms.

"It's also my duty to advise strangers," the armsman went on. "No slight to your honor, stranger, but it's forbidden here to fight unless you are attacked." He looked at Kreuha's spears. "How were you planning on finding your bread in this land?"

Kreuha drew himself up. "I am Kreuha Wolkwos, the Blood Wolf," he said. "Son of Echwo-Pothis, Horse Master; son of a chief who was son of a chief, and I am foremost among the men of war of my people. I come to find some great lord of the wizard-folk who needs my arm and faith, so that I may win fortune and everlasting fame."

The armsman—*policeman*—made a wordless sound and covered his brow and eyes with a hand for a moment. Then he sighed. "You think that, do you?"

"How not?" Kreuha said, puzzled. "Already a lord . . . well, lady, mistress . . . from Nantucket itself wished me to follow in their fighting-tail. Surely I would quickly rise in any such band."

"Oh, Captain Lucy," the policeman said, nodding. "Well, you *were* lucky to get that offer, and you'd probably see some fighting on the *Pride*. Hard work too, but she's run on shares." At Kreuha's look, he went on: "You get a share of the gain at the end of the voyage."

Kreuha nodded—a lord always shared booty with his sworn men. But then he remembered the *voyage* here to Alba, and gulped again. "I cannot . . . not on the sea. A lord by land, yes."

It was more than the memory of his misery; it was the *helplessness*. How could the Blood Wolf be mighty if his belly made him weaker than a girl?

The policeman grinned, the more so at Kreuha's black look. "Nobody ever dies of seasickness," he said. "They just wish they would—until it passes, which may take a day or two."

He pointed out a building with a tall tower attached to it, a street or two back from the dockside. "That's the Town Meetinghouse. It's a hiring hall, too. If you can't find work, go there and mention my name: I'm Eric Iraiinisson. They can always find something for a strong back, enough for stew and a doss, at least." Sternly: "Remember also that here robbers are flogged and sent to the mines for many years, and robbers who slay or wound are hung up and their bodies left for the crows."

Kreuha nodded with stiff dignity; just then two more men and a woman dressed alike in the blue clothes came up. They had a horse with them, and tossed the corpse onto its back with brisk efficiency.

"I have gold," he pointed out. "Cannot gold be bartered here?"

Eric Iraiinisson nodded. "While it lasts," he said.

❖

Kreuha saw eyes upon him. This *tavern* was full of men who looked a little less alien than the smooth folk of the upper town; there he'd noticed stares and smiles at his dress and manner. Here there was a dense fog of sweat and woodsmoke from the hearth, and plain rushes on packed dirt below, and plain stools and benches. He had feasted well on beef roasted with some spice that bit the tongue, and beer that was good though strange. Now a man had offered to pay for his drink; he knew of coined money, but such was rare and precious in his tribe still, not something to be casually thrown about on an evening's bowsing. Still, the amber drink was *whiskey,* something that only the High Reghix had tasted at home . . .

"I will drink, if you will drink with me again afterward," he said. "Drink from my bounty. I have gold!"

Remember that whiskey *is more potent than beer,* he reminded himself. Still, it couldn't be *much* stronger than ice-mead, and his belly was full of bread and meat to sop it up.

"Arktorax thanks you," the man said, then grinned at him and tossed off the small shot-glass, breathed out satisfaction, then followed it with a long swallow of beer. Kreuha imitated the stylish snap of the wrist, throwing the amber liquid at the back of his throat.

"*Ai!*" he wheezed a moment later, when he'd stopped coughing. "What do you make this out of, dragon's blood?"

"Barley," Arktorax laughed; he fit his name of Lord Bear, being bear-tall and thick. "It's made from barley. But if it's too strong for you—"

Kreuha's fist thumped the table. "By He of the Long Spear, nothing's too strong for a Keruthinii of the Wolf clan! I've drunk the vats dry and danced all night, at our festivals."

He soothed his throat with a long draught of the beer. It made a pleasant coolness after the fire of the whiskey, but the flame had turned to a comfortable warmth by now.

"That's the problem with being a Keruthinii," he went on, signaling to the wench who served the tables. "You're so tough and hardy you can't get drunk."

His new friend laughed long and loud. "Are you boasting, or complaining?" he said, and tossed off his glass in turn.

Kreuha missed the considering look in his eye, and the glance he exchanged with the impassive figure behind the plank bar. Instead he laughed himself, until the tears ran from his eyes. The next whiskey went down far more smoothly than the first, and tasted good: there was a peaty, sweetish flavor to it he hadn't noticed the first time. That called for another beer, and when it came he stood, swaying a little.

"Drinks for all!" he said. A roar of approval went up, bringing a flush of happiness to his cheeks. Everlasting fame was the warrior's reward. "Let no man say Blood Wolf son of Horse Master son of Stone Fist is a niggard with sword-won gold!"

"Sword-won?" Arktorax said.

"Aye!" Kreuha shouted. "Gold won by winning a sword!" He was also accounted something of a poet, at home. "Listen and I will tell you of how I won it, bare-handed against a wizard blade—"

He was half-chanting it by the time he was finished, and men crowded around to slap him on the back and shout their admiration. *A fine lot, a fine lot,* he thought a trifle blurrily. His boon companion looked a little wary when he mentioned the black warrior-woman, but not everyone could be as stout in the face of the unknown as Blood Wolf. "—and so I came here, that men might know of my deeds," he said.

"So you're the one who killed Frank Athadaursson with one blow of his foot!" a woman said admiringly. "You must be a *real* man, beard or no . . ."

Hours later he lay with his head on his hands in the quiet of the near-deserted tavern, giggling occasionally. His stomach threatened to rebel, but even that thought was funny. . . . His eyes crossed as he watched his own reflection in the glass before him. It was that that saved him, an image of an arm raised behind him.

Reflex pushed him to one side, falling to the rushes of the floor as the small leather sack of lead shot cracked down on the beer-stained wood of the table rather than the back of his head. He lay gaping as the barkeeper turned and raised the cosh again, then lashed out with one foot. By purest luck that plowed into the fat man's groin, and he doubled over in uncontrollable response. Kreuha scrabbled away on his backside, as the woman and his friend Arktorax—the man he'd thought was his friend—came at him with ropes and a canvas hood.

His back hit the rough brickwork of the wall, and he scrabbled upright, lashing out left and right with his fists. Another man's fist thudded into the tough muscle of his belly, and he felt the night's drinking and the long-ago meal leave in a rush of sour bile. That saved him; Arktorax stepped back with an exclamation of disgust, and Kreuha turned and turned again along the wall, as if he were rolling down a slope. His hand found the latch and he fell forward with a splash into a muddy street under a thin cold rain that shook him back to the edge of consciousness. He rose, plastered with a thin layer of earth and horsedung churned to gray slime, and turned to meet the rush from the tavern, trying to scream out the war-howl of his clan.

Where is my axe? he thought. *Where—*

Shadowy figures rushed at him. He lashed out with a fist, head-butted an opponent who tried to grapple with him, then screamed with shocked pain at what that did to his drink-fuddled head. Blows landed on him in turn, many, more than he could begin to count and from all directions. He went down again, and feet slammed into body and head—feet encased in hard leather boots. Instinctively he curled himself into a ball and covered his head with his arms.

Blackness, shot through with the sound of a whistle.

❖

Kreutha came back to consciousness slowly. He recognized the symptoms—splitting headache, nausea, blurred vision—of a bad hangover combined with being thumped on the head. The place where he woke was utterly unfamiliar; there were strange shouts, metallic clangs, stenches. And bright light, light that hurt like spears in his eyes. Despite that he opened them—and saw a cage of iron bars not far away, with men inside gripping the metal with their hands. He bolted straight upright, letting the blanket fall away—

"Easy friend, easy!" said a voice in his own language.

Blood Wolf looked around, blinking and squinting and holding up a hand against the light of the bright mirror-backed coal-oil lamps. The voice came from Eric Iraiinisson, still dressed all in blue, jacket and trousers. A hand rested on his revolver, and Kreuha forced himself to wariness. Then he noticed that he was *outside* the cage, unbound, and that a corridor led to a door that swung open and closed as folk passed by. A woman dressed in blue like the man sat behind a table, writing on many papers before her; even then Kreuha shuddered a little at the casual display of magic. The Alban traders he'd met had carried revolvers, some of them . . . but the knowledge of writing on paper had proved to be a weapon nearly as strong and far harder to understand. He'd heard that the priests of the wizard-folk would teach it to those who took the water-oath to their God. It might almost be worth it.

"You're safe here," the man in blue said. In English, he continued: "I'm chief policeman of the dockside station . . . in your language . . . hard to say. I guard the peace in this area. I found you in the street."

I am *safe*, Blood Wolf thought; and with that the nausea came back, redoubled. It showed on his face.

"The bucket, use the bucket!"

It was a big wooden one, but already half full; he knelt in misery and then staggered erect when the last cupful of sour stomach-acid had come up; he was spending far too much time these days puking. That thought made him smile a little, a very little, as the policeman guided him back to the bench and handed him a blanket; Kreuha clutched it around his shoulders, and took the cup of hot steaming . . . something-or-other that he was handed. Sipping cautiously, he found it unlike any of the herbal teas wisewomen had given him for childhood complaints. It had cream in it, and a delicious sweetness without the musky flavor of honey, and under that a bitterness. Still, it warmed him and diminished the pain in his head and brought something like real wakefulness. The two tablets he swallowed with it seemed to help as well, for all that they were tiny, white, and tasteless; the effect was like willowbark tea, but stronger and quicker.

When he had climbed far enough out of wretchedness to talk, he looked up to find the man-at-arms also dealing with papers. Occasionally other armed men—and a few armed women—would come in, sometimes leading prisoners in the manacles known as *handcuffs;* many of the captives were drunk as well.

"Is it the custom here to make men drink and then fall upon them?" he asked the . . . *policeman, that is the word.*

Eric Iraiinison laughed. "No, it's the custom to arrest men who break the town's peace," he said. "This is a seaport, and a fast-growing one, with many folk who are strangers to each other and many rootless young men. When ships come in and crews are paid off, we get a lot of traffic here."

"I broke no peace!" Kreuha snapped. "I was set upon dishonorably, by stealth!"

Eric nodded. "And so you're not under arrest. The three assaulting you would be, if I could find them—and evidence against them."

"Ai!" Kreuha's head came up; he was owed vengeance for this indignity. "I can give you faces, and names. Arktorax son of—"

He told all he knew, then scowled as Eric shook his head.

"I know those three," the policeman said. "They're *criminals*—" he dropped the English word into the conversation, then paused to search for an equivalent "—evil-doers, breakers of taboo and custom. If you were to take them to court, they'd lie truth out of Creation. They're crimps, among other things. If you'd fallen asleep, you'd have woken up in the foc'sle of a sealer or a guano-boat, with a thumbprint on a contract and no way back until you'd worked a year for a pittance and daily swill."

Fury flushed more of the pain out of Kreuha's system. "They

sought to make a slave of me?" he cried, springing erect, his hand reaching for a missing axe. "I will take their heads! I will feed their living hearts to the Crow Goddess! I will kill, kill—"

Eric's hand went to his revolver; Kreuha considered that, and the blood-debt he owed the man, and sank back.

"Not quite a slave," the policeman said. "If I could get them on *that,* I'd be a happy man; the penalty's death. Or if I could prove crimping charges, that would be nearly as good—ten years' hard labor. But they're careful, the swine; they never pick on citizens and never do anything before witnesses. We don't keep track of every stranger who wanders in here—we can't."

"Is no man here *man* enough to take vengeance on them?" Kreuha said indignantly. "Or to call them doers-of-naught before the folk? I will challenge them to fight me between the wands—the men, of course, not the woman."

The policeman chuckled. "You remind me of my grandfather," he said. "Or me as I might have been, if Nantucket hadn't come out of time. . . . Fighting to the death is against our law here. It's treated like murder, killing-by-stealth. You could invite them to meet you outside our Township boundary." He pointed northward. "The Zarthani still allow death-duels. Arktorax and his friends won't do it, of course. They'll laugh at you, no more, and so would most other people."

Kreuha stared in horror. "Did the wizard-folk take all honor from you Iraiina when they overcame you and ground you beneath their heel, then? You were warriors in our grandsires' time, even if we prevailed in the end."

To his surprise, the policeman's chuckle turned into a full-throated laugh. "You *do* remind me of my grandfather's grumbles," he said, then held up a hand. "No offense. No, we fled here after you put defeat upon us, took in the Nantucketer renegade Walker, and he led us to war and yet more defeat, and then the Nantucketers did something far more . . . *drastic*"—that was in English—"more *powerful,* you might say, than grinding us down."

Kreuha shivered, imagining the vengeance of wizards. "What?"

"They lifted us up again, helped, taught us their faith and all their secret arts." He pulled a silver chain around his neck, showing a crucifix. "My father they took to Nantucket—he was young, our chief's nephew and heir—and the sons and daughters of many powerful men—and sent them to their . . . *schools,* places of learning. My father lived for years in the house of the Republic's chief like one of his own sons. When he saw all that they had, how could he be content to sit in a mud-floored barn and think himself grand because it was the biggest barn? And so he sent for teachers and missionaries, and . . . well. *My* sons could be Chief Executive Officers of the Republic, if they desire to go into politics."

The conversation had mostly been in something close to Kreuha's tongue, which Eric spoke easily enough. The young warrior noted that when the policeman spoke to his own subordinates—who must be his own tribesfolk, or mostly—he used English.

He shivered slightly, he who had never known fear before a mortal foe. *Mighty wizardy indeed, to make a whole tribe vanish as if it had never been.* Then he shook his head. That was an Iraiina problem, not his. Or perhaps not a problem for them either.

"I thank you for your courtesy to a stranger," he said formally and began to rise.

Eric reached over and pushed him firmly down again with a hand on one blanketed shoulder. "It's a cold wet night to go out with nothing but a kilt—and if you are truly grateful, you could help me deal with that God-damned crimp and his gang."

Kreuha's eyes went wide. "I thought you said—"

"I said you couldn't chop them up with a war-axe in fair fight," the other man replied. "But we in the Republic have a saying that there is more than one way to skin a cat."

Slowly, as Eric outlined his idea, Kreuha's smile matched that of the man across from him. If the wizards of Nantucket had taught the Iraiina all their arts, then they must be a crafty, cunning, forethoughtful crew.

I like it, he thought. Aloud: "Tell me more."

❖

"Arktorax!" Kreuha called jovially.

The little tavern was half empty on this afternoon; with the tide beginning to make in a few hours, crews would be back on their ships and fishing boats, and most ashore were at work. The big hearth on the inner wall had a low coal fire burning, and two big pots of stew simmering on iron hooks that swung out from the chimney wall. The tables were littered but mostly vacant, their few occupants looking to be oldsters or idlers, and a harlot or two.

Arktorax was sitting with a cluster about him, throwing dice from a leather cup; he rose, his expression a little wary, one eye puffed up and discolored. Long greasy blond hair swirled about his face as he turned to face Kreuha, carefully putting his back to the wall without seeming to hurry about it.

"Ah, I see you took some blows also," Kreuha said. "Shame and eternal shame to me that I was too drunk to ward you—or myself. Between the whiskey and the crack on my head, I don't even know how badly I did! But I did remember I left my gear with your friends here."

He seated himself, and Arktorax took the bench across the table, waving a hand. A wench—it was probably the same one who'd helped to befool him last night—brought a plate with a loaf of bread and lump of cheese, and two thick glass steins of foaming beer. The barkeeper called her over, and after a moment she returned with his spear, axe, dagger and bundle of goods. They might be wealth in the Keruthinii lands, but here they were only a pittance of scrap metal.

Kreuha made himself smile as he lifted the stein. In daylight, he could see what a shabby den this was—his mother would never have allowed rushes this fusty or garbage-strewn—but the crofters and gangrels here drank from glass mugs! And the beer was better than any his father brewed, as well. For a moment he saw himself as this Arktorax did, as a woods-running savage to be plucked and sold.

No, he thought. *Lord Bear here thinks he has fallen on a sheep in a pen. He will find it's a wolf—a Blood Wolf.*

"The police took you off," Arktorax said, relaxing a little and cutting a slab of the bread and cheese. "Officer Iraiinisson, that would be."

"Yes," Kreuha said, and scowled with rage. It was a genuine enough expression; the other man didn't need to know it was directed at *him*. He went on, his voice rough:

"And threw me in a cage full of vermin, and barked questions at me as if I were some thrall to be thrashed for not shoveling out the byre! By He of the Long Spear, by the Crow Goddess, I swear I will have my vengeance for last night's work!"

Arktorax nodded. "He's given to questions, is our officer Iraiinisson, and no mistake," he said genially. "You told him all, I suppose."

Kreuha grimaced. "I did not, not even what little I knew. I am not a spear-captive, to be kicked and cuffed. And he said he would not let me leave this place, so long as I did not tell him what he would know!"

"There've been complaints about him in the Town Meeting more than once. I complained, the last time he ran me in on suspicion— and had to let me go," Arktorax said. "He's had a feud with me for years, the son of a pig, but he and his kin have too many votes behind them."

"Why don't you kill him, if he's defamed your honor before the folk-moot?" Kreuha said. "I would give much to see his blood."

The big burly man looked at him blankly for a moment; they were speaking the same language, more or less, but it was as if Arktorax had just heard words without meaning to him. He smiled, shrugged, and switched to English:

"Was your mother a whore by choice, or did her father sell her?"

"I'm sorry," Kreuha said, with an effort at self-control greater than he'd needed to remain motionless on night ambushes. Eric had warned him they'd probably test him so. "I speak none of the wizard tongue."

Arktorax chuckled. "I asked if you would like me to assist in your vengeance," he said smoothly, with a genial grin.

"I would like that very much," Kreuha said. "Very much indeed."

The planning went swiftly. This time Kreuha turned down whiskey; that would not arouse suspicion, not after last night. He did grumble a little, as the urchin Arktorax hired sped off toward the police station and they left the tavern, the barkeeper and the woman in tow.

"Can you shield me from the blades of his kin?" he asked. It wasn't a question he would have made, or at least put that way, on his own.

"Just this way—" Arktorax said.

The building they entered was large and dim; empty as well, up to the high beams that held the ceiling. Mysterious piles of boxes and barrels hid much of the floor, stretching off into dimness.

"Yes, of course, my friend," he went on, clapping Kreuha on the shoulder. "You will vanish from this place as if you had never been."

The fat man chuckled, and spoke in English: "Just as we planned; Captain Tarketerol will be most grateful."

Kreuha smiled and nodded, the skin crawling between his shoulders. That was a Tartessian name; the wizard-folk of Nantucket kept no thralls, but the men of the far southern kingdom most assuredly *did*. Perhaps the villainy of these three was worse than Eric had thought . . . which was very good.

"And Officer Iraiinisson will be dead," Arktorax said. "We three can swear you were with us—and that's the truth, isn't it?"

He laughed, and then there was a long while of tense waiting, until a knock came at the door. The woman swarmed up a ladder to peer down at the doorway, and then turned to give a signal: the policeman was alone. That had been likely anyway, since there were only a score of the blue-clad armsmen in Southaven.

"Kreuha Wolkwos?" Eric Iraiinisson's sharp voice came through the boards.

"I am here," Kreuha said, taking stance in an open space not far from the portal.

The light was dim and gray, through small windows high up

around the roof, but there was enough for someone who'd hunted deer and men by moonlight.

"And the Blood Wolf is ready to speak as you wished," Kreuha went on.

The door opened, letting in a spray of light along with a mist of fine rain. Kreuha poised with his spear, and the policeman staggered back—

"Kill!" Arktorax shouted, pushing him with a heavy hand between the shoulders. "What are you waiting for?"

Kreuha dove forward, rolling around the spearshaft and flicking himself back erect, facing the man who'd pretended friendship. The Keruthinii grinned like his name-beast and bayed laughter that might have come from his clan totem indeed.

"I am waiting for you to put your head in the rope," he said—in English, thickly accented but fluent enough. "Arktomertos," he added, in a savage play on the man's name: *Dead* Bear.

The crimp roared anger, turned, snatched up a barrel and threw it. That took strength; it was heavy, and the policeman dodged, falling backward into the street. When the wood staves struck the thick timber uprights of the door they cracked open, and fine-ground flour exploded in all directions. The fat man who'd been Arktorax's henchman turned to flee; Kreuha's arm cocked back as he squinted through the dust, then punched forward with smooth, swift grace. The flame-shaped bronze head took the barkeeper between the shoulders and he fell forward with the spearshaft standing up like the mast of a ship sailing to the ice-realms where the spirits of oathbreakers dwelt.

That left Arktorax. The big man drew a broad-bladed steel knife from beneath the tail of his coat and lunged, holding it underarm and stabbing upward in a stroke that would have opened the younger man like a fish filleted for the grill. Kreuha bounded back with panther ease beyond the reach of the blow, his hand unslinging the bronze-headed axe slung over his back as, for the first time since he'd set foot on the boat that brought him to Alba, he felt at ease: here was something he understood.

Arktorax wailed as he stumbled forward, drawn by the impetus of the failed stroke. The keen edge of the bronze skittered off his knife and gashed his forearm. He dropped the knife and tried to catch it with his left hand; Kreuha struck backhanded, then again, and again, smiling.

He was holding up the head when Eric Iraiinisson came through the door—this time with his revolver drawn. He swore in English, then by the hooves of the Horse Goddess.

"I didn't mean you to kill them!" he said at last. "We were to capture them for trial—"

"You didn't mean to kill them," Kreuha grinned. "I did, Eric son of the Iraiina—and ask your grandfather why, some day."

The policeman shook his head. "This means trouble."

"Didn't you say your law allowed a man to fight in self-defense?" Kreuha said. *No. I can't keep the head,* he decided regretfully; he did spit in the staring eyes before tossing it aside, and appropriating the dead man's knife and the contents of his pockets.

"Yes . . . but there's only one witness, and I'm known to have accused him before," Eric said. "It could be trouble for me as well as you—he does have kin, and friends of a sort here."

Kreuha grinned. "Then let me not be here," he said. "I've been thinking of what you said earlier."

Eric looked at him, brows raising. "Now that's forethoughtful," he said. "Maybe you'll go far, young warrior. If you live."

❖

"All *right*," Timothy Alston-Kurlelo said.

Lucy and her younger brother both stood in the forward hold, watching a cargo-net sway down. It dangled from a dockside crane, which made the rate of descent something she needed to keep an eye on—if they'd been using one of the *Pride*'s spars as a derrick, she'd have trusted her deck-crew.

Two sailors had ropes on the net and were guiding it to the clear space at her feet; orderly stacks of other goods rose fore and aft, covered in tarpaulins and tightly lashed down. The early morning air was cold; the first week in November was usually chilly and raw here in southern Alba, and she could scent the faint mealy smell of snow.

"I'll be glad to get out of the harbor," she said, mentally running over the list herself.

Simple goods for the raw-native trade: spearheads and axe-blades, saws and hammers, kegs of nails, chisels, drills, printed cotton cloth, glassware and ornaments, cheap potato vodka. Wind-pumps and ore-breakers and stationary steam engines for the mining dredges Ellis & Stover had set up out east these last five years; treadle sewing machines and corn-shellers and cotton-gins, threshing engines and sugar-cane crushers for the Islander settlements in the Indian Ocean. . . . She took a deep satisfied sniff of the smells, metal and oil and the pinewood of boxes and barrels. Even the bilges were not too bad; the *Pride* had been hauled out for complete refitting in the Fogarty's Cove shipyards on Long Island not four months ago.

"Won't we all," her brother said; he was a slim, dark young man in his teens, chin blue-black with stubble despite his youth, holding his clipboard with a seriousness that made her smile.

"This is the last of the chocolate," Tim said as the net creaked to the decking.

Longshoremen sprang to unhitch it and begin stacking the cargo under the direction of the bosun and his mates; they knew the captain's fanatical insistence on neatness and having everything precisely in place. She grinned inwardly; that was another reason she and Heather didn't ship together if they could avoid it. She drove Heather crazy by being finicky, and Heather's blithe confidence that everything would come right in the end with a lick and a promise infuriated *her,* the more so since it seemed to work about as well as her methods instead of resulting in the immediate ruin it should. They'd been raised like twins—they were the same age almost to the day, as close as they could figure it—and loved each other dearly, as long as they didn't have to watch each other work too closely.

It's a very good thing Alston-Kurlelo Shipping and Trading has three merchantmen and a headquarters to run, now, she thought.

Lucy nodded to Tim, then sprang and planted a foot on the hook of the line that had held the cargo net and a hand on the cable. A man on deck whistled and waved, and the line jerked upward. She judged her distance easily as her head came above the hatch coaming, then jumped down to the deck, her mind on her return cargo. Tin, of course—alluvial tin washed from the streams was cheap enough to compete with the hard-rock mines here in Alba, with their high fixed costs. The West Alba Mining and Smelting Corporation had annoyed everyone during the long years it had a virtual monopoly.

Hmm. Can't expect more than a few hundred tons ready for loading. What else? There was always market for teak, but it was bulky in relation to its value. Would it be worth another thousand miles of easting to top up with cinnamon and cloves in the Celebes, then return via the Horn? If she did that, she could make a brief stopover on the coast of Peru; the locals there had silver in the ingot, and cocoa, and some excellent handicrafts. . . . *Best keep a careful eye on prices via radio.* That helped only so much, though. You still had to take months covering distance.

The deck was busy, too, with sailors making all secure for their departure on the evening tide. The mates and the senior hands were busy as well, showing newcomers how to coil a line, or shoving them into position to clap onto a rope and haul. There was an occasional foot to a backside as well; she frowned, but there wasn't much alternative until the raw hands learned enough to be useful. Until then everyone was doing their own work and half the trainees' as well, and there weren't as many even for simple pull-on-this as she'd have liked. Another group was being shown down the line of guns bowsed up against the bulwarks, sleek blue-black soda-bottle shapes, thirty-two-pounders bought surplus from the Coast Guard a year ago. She suppressed a wish for a Gatling; that would eat half the voyage's profits, and she had over a hundred employees, two children, and four nieces and nephews to support.

"All's well, Mr. Hands?" she called to the master-gunner.

He turned and touched a knuckle to his forehead. "As well as can be expected, ma'am. Arms drill as soon as we make open water? These handless cows—"

"A week or two after," she replied. "When they can be trusted to go aloft and reef."

She was *very* unlikely to meet a pirate before then, but sailing into a bad blow was entirely possible. And when she'd reached the Roaring Forties and started to run her easting down before the endless storms . . . then she wanted every jack and jill able to hand, reef, and steer.

"In the meantime, signal the tug we're ready," she said, as the crew began to batten down the hatchway. "Prepare to cast off!"

A noise on the docks drew her head up. A man was running down the quay, dodging carts and goods and passersby; a young man, with long fair hair and a mainlander's leather kilt. Her eyes widened slightly. *That's the woodsrunner, the Keruthinii,* she thought. And despite the recent rain, looking rather ghastly with flour-paste; doubtless there was a story behind that. He dashed for the gangway where crewmen were unfastening the lashings.

"Belay that!" she called, as they snatched up cargo-hooks or put their hands on their belt-knives. "Let him on board!"

She went over to meet him; her first mate fell in behind her, and a pair of the older hands with belaying pins from the rack around the mainmast, held casually but ready. He bounded up the plank with a stride that made him look as if his legs were rubber springs, then halted and cried her hail.

"What are you doing on my ship?" she asked quietly.

The young man—*Blood Wolf,* she dredged out of her mind; typical melodramatic charioteer-tribe name—was breathing deeply but easily, and he grinned with a cocky self-confidence.

"I came to see if you still wish my allegiance, chieftainness," he said. "For I wish to leave this *dunthaurikaz,* and see far lands."

Lucy snorted, hooking her hands in the brass-studded belt she wore over her long sea-sweater. "I'm not taking you on board if you've broken Southaven law," she said.

He offered her a piece of paper. She snorted again; it had the municipal stamp, and the Republic's eagle; she recognized Eric Iraiinisson's handwriting and signature, as well. Apparently the youngster wasn't wanted . . . exactly.

And I could use another hand. This one looks to be quick-thinking as well as strong.

"It's fifty cents a day and your keep," she said, and looked him over.

"Eight months to a year round-trip and a share of the take to depend on how you're rated when we make the chops of Nantucket Channel and pay off. And you do what you're told when you're told, or it's the rope's end or the brig. Understood?"

He grinned again. "Command and I obey," he said with a grandiloquent gesture, then went down on one knee and placed his hands between hers.

She knew the ceremony; this wasn't the first time she'd gone through it, either.

"Mr. Mate!" she called.

"Ma'am?"

"Sign this man on; rate him ordinary and see he's issued slops and a duffel." Louder: "Prepare to cast off!"

The crew bustled about; Lucy went up the treads to the quarterdeck, taking her place beside the wheel, with the helmsman and pilot. She looked southward, to where the gray water of Southaven Water waited, and the world beyond. Down on the deck, Blood Wolf was looking in the same direction, and she could hear his clear, delighted laughter.

Sleeping Dragons

LYNETTE ASPEY

❖

This is either a First Contact story (if you believe it to be science fiction) or a Hidden Prince story (if you think it's fantasy.) Either way, it's a gem.

Other stories you might try after this one include Nina Kiriki Hoffman's "The Laily Worm," or Roger Zelazny's magnificent novel Lord of Light.

When I was a little girl, I thought that all babies hatched from golden eggs. I don't mean that Ryan's egg was made of real gold. Rather, it was like a smooth rock the color of beach sand at sunset, and when Dad put it into my arms, my skin tingled. That it would hatch, after all the care I lavished on it, seemed perfectly natural to me, although Dad was surprised. He had brought it back for me from Vietnam as a gift, and it was *supposed* to be a dragon's egg.

The first sign we had that something might be happening was when fine veins appeared in that smooth, hard surface and it started to leak. Soon after, I was disappointed to find myself with an infant brother instead of a baby dragon, but Ryan was hard to resist. When he smiled, he looked just like a chubby Buddha, with soft black hair and honey-colored skin.

One day, Dad warned, someone might come to take him away, but until then, he was our secret. It was an easy one to keep, living as we did a long way from anywhere, even by Australian standards.

I was seven years old, and Ryan nearly two, when the old man came. I remember being cross because Ryan had plonked his fat bottom into the middle of my play, sitting on my paper and chewing my crayons.

The afternoon sun was too strong for the old curtains to keep out, but I enjoyed playing on the carpet amidst the patchwork sunlight. There was the hum of insects and the squawk of birds in the eucalyptus trees outside. From my father's study, I could hear the tap-tap-tip of his keyboard.

As usual, Yellow Dog lay stretched across the entrance to the hallway, from where he could keep an eye on us all.

"'Ainie," said Ryan, levering himself up the way toddlers do. "Knock. Knock."

I didn't bother looking up. "Who's there?" Usually it was Dog, or Dad, or Dino the dinosaur, but instead of playing, Ryan trotted out of the living room, into the kitchen. When he had nearly reached the door, Yellow Dog rose up on stiff legs to follow. I could see them from where I sat; the little boy with his hand on the back of the old dog, looking out. A moment later, Yellow Dog started barking.

Then came the scrunching sound of boots, and a shadow appeared at the door.

"Daddy?" I called, but he was already there, standing with one hand on the wall, the other on his heart. He paused for only a beat, before a few long strides took him across the kitchen. He scooped the baby up and hugged him close. Yellow Dog's hackles were bristling.

I got up and sidled closer. The shadow at the door resolved into a man-shape as I approached, the outline blurred by the dirty gray of the fly screen and the bright sunshine behind. I could see that the stranger was shorter than my father, but I had the peculiar impression that he was also much *bigger*. It was his shadow, I thought, noticing how it reached across the room. It fell over the dog and my father, and I was afraid to come any closer in case it touched me too.

The stranger was staring at Ryan. "Bắc Vương," he whispered. *King*.

"Chùa Bắc." *Honored Grandfather.* My father's voice was shaking. "Bắc cần gí?" *What do you want?*

"Your Vietnamese is still terrible, Jon Ashton," said the shadow man. At the sound of his voice, Yellow Dog's hackles settled, as if a hand had stroked them down.

Ryan burbled from his perch on Dad's hip. I think a cloud must have passed over the sun then, for the bright light suddenly faded and the stranger resolved into nothing more threatening than a sturdy old bloke with neat grey hair, bushy eyebrows, and eyes like shiny black pebbles in a nest of wrinkles. "We must talk," he said.

I remember thinking that Dad was acting very strangely. He turned and saw me standing in the corner, where the carpet became linoleum, the demarcation between our living room and the kitchen. He brought Ryan over to me and wrapped my arms around him.

"Don't come outside, Elaine," he said. Then, to the dog, he commanded, "Stay." Yellow Dog sat back on his haunches, ears pricked. Dad stroked the dog's wide, smooth head, slipped his hand under his muzzle and lifted his head up so that they looked eye to eye. "Guard," he said, and then he went outside, shutting the fly-screen door firmly behind him.

Yellow Dog padded over to the door and lay down beside it. The crafty animal knew me far too well. I gave a few good tugs on his collar anyway, just for good measure, before Ryan and I lay down across his tummy so that we could watch and listen through the screen door. I was delighted to see the baby's merciless little fingers grabbing a handful of thick fur.

Yellow Dog, aware of the price to pay for his obedience, gave a huff of discomfort, settled his muzzle onto his paws and waited for Dad to come back and relieve him from duty.

I could only hear snippets of their conversation. The two men were standing side by side; my tall, fair father and the stocky, dark stranger. Dad murmured something and passed his hands over his eyes, as he sometimes did when he was very tired or sad. He kicked at the ground with his boot, sending up little clouds of red dust.

A wide firebreak of bare earth surrounded our house, and, beyond that, nothing but bush; scrubby saplings and tall ghost gums, their skin of bark peeling away to reveal smooth, silver trunks. The afternoon breeze was heavy with the smell of eucalypt.

"He is too vulnerable here," I heard the old man say.

Dad muttered something, shoved his hands into his pockets.

The stranger laughed out loud. "Hide him? And if you could, what do you think he will become in that time?" He gestured toward the house. "You cannot protect them both."

From somewhere close by, a kurrajong warbled, and another joined in chorus. I breathed in the tangy bush smell. The *whumpf whumpf* of Yellow Dog's panting was loud in my ears.

Dad's voice was a low, angry hum.

The old man shook his head, and it appeared to me that dust motes danced around his shoulders. Dad's hands came out of his pockets and clenched into fists and his voice rose. "You think I'm going to give him up? Just like that?"

"It is a mistake to think of him as your son."

I glanced down at Ryan. He had stopped torturing Yellow Dog, his attention captured by the old man. I wondered if he knew they were talking about him.

"I have guarded his secret all my life, as my ancestors have done for thousands of years. His destiny is not with you."

"The egg came to me legitimately," said Dad, sounding desperate.

"And my daughter will pay the price of her betrayal. Oh yes. In the meantime, where is the proof that this child is yours, eh?"

Dad started to say something else, but the old man held up his hand. "I do not blame you for what happened and I do not threaten lightly. It is my duty. I *must* take him back."

Dad put his hands back in his pockets. I caught the words: "not now, so sudden, let me."

The old man was quiet for a while, then he nodded. He looked back at us and waved, as if he was the nicest person in the world, before walking off down the rough dirt road and quickly disappearing amidst the ghost gums.

❖

Dad hardly spoke for the rest of the evening, and I knew that look on his face well enough not to pester him. After he had put us to bed, I heard the creak of the veranda's old wooden floor at the back of the house and the slap of the screen door.

I got up and went to my window, but I couldn't see anything, so I padded out to the veranda, stepping carefully in the dark, knowing which floorboards would not complain. The night breeze was cool and pleasant. I pressed my nose against the fly screen, careful not to breathe in too deeply in case the dust made me sneeze.

He was standing in the yard, naked, head thrown back and long brown arms wrapped around his pale chest. I could see his shoulders and the muscles down his back all bunched and bulging. He was looking up at the stars, and he was crying.

I stepped backward, sorry for having spied on him, and my foot came down on the wrong floorboard. It betrayed me with a loud *creak*.

Dad turned toward me, although I don't think he could see me in the dark, and there was so much pain in his face that I was sure I had done something terrible.

"I'm sorry, Daddy."

"What are you doing out of bed?"

I said the first thing that came to mind. "You didn't tell us a story." Which was true enough.

"Go to bed, Elaine."

"But, Daddy," I whined.

"Now!"

I fled back to the bedroom and dived under my blankets, burrowing as deep as I could. I counted the long minutes before I heard the footsteps outside my door and breathed a sigh of relief.

The bed tilted down as he sat next to me. He gently pulled the covers from over my head, and tucked them around my shoulders.

Dad had put on his dressing gown. He toyed with the frayed edge of its belt while looking at the crib, where Ryan slept. "I do have a story," he said.

I snuggled up against his knee and he absently retucked the edge of my blanket. "A long time ago, there was a man called Kinh Duong, and he was the ruler of the Land of Red Demons. Kinh Duong fell in love with the daughter of the Dragon Lord of the Sea, and they had a son, whom they named Lac Long Quan. In time, Lac Long Quan grew up to become the Dragon Lord of Lac, and he ruled the land of the Red River delta. One day, Ti Lung, the Earth Dragon, warned him that there would be trouble with the people in the north unless he found a wife from those lands to keep the peace. After a long search, Lac Long Quan met a beautiful woman called Au Co."

"That's a funny name," I said.

"And you think 'Elaine' wouldn't sound strange to her?" he asked. "Do you want this story or not?" I nodded enthusiastically. "Okay, then. Au Co had already lived for a long time, and some even believed that she was immortal. Even so, she married Lac Long Quan and it seemed that they were happy, but then she did something strange."

At seven years old, I could imagine things very weird indeed, but Dad no longer seemed happy telling me this story. He looked down at his feet for a long time, absently picking at his dressing gown.

"Something strange?" I prompted.

Finally, he said, "The story goes that instead of babies, Au Co had a hundred eggs, from which were born a hundred sons."

My skin tingled with the memory of Ryan's egg.

"The Dragon Lord loved his wife," Dad continued after a pause, "but she didn't want to live in the lowlands, where he ruled. She craved the high places of the world. So, Au Co took fifty of her sons and went into the mountains, leaving Lac Long Quan and their other fifty sons in the delta lowlands."

"She had another egg, didn't she?" I interrupted again. "Or maybe the last one didn't hatch."

"I don't know, 'Lainie," he said softly.

The baby stirred in his sleep. Chubby fingers opening and closing like caterpillars.

"You won't give Ryan to that old man, will you, Daddy?"

"His name is Mr. Pham," he said, standing up.

"But—"

"Enough!" Then, in a gentler voice, "Go to sleep."

He closed the door firmly behind him when he left the room. I turned over on my side and saw that the moon was just rising. Some of its pale light filtered through the sparse trees outside, and caught the bars of Ryan's crib, making a shadow bridge across the space between us.

❖

The next day, we drove to Wallindah for supplies. Ryan sat in the middle of the front seat, strapped into his baby chair. He had a terry-toweling hat pulled down over his forehead to shade his eyes, one chubby fist gripping his beloved dinosaur. He was chuckling, happy to be going on a car ride. I was happy too, because I knew that he would fall asleep almost straight away, and it would be nice to have Dad all to myself.

I remembered to bring some cushions to sit on, so that I could see out the window, and so that the bouncing of Elsie, our ancient Land Rover, wouldn't make me bite my tongue.

Wallindah is a typical one-street town, with a hardware store, a bakery, and a general store that is also the post office. It has a gas station and a farm-equipment supplier and two pubs. A few cars and trucks were parked in the street, some with panting dogs lying underneath. There were only a few people moving around. It was the middle of the day, and sensible folk had retreated out of the heat into one or the other pub.

Dad parked in front of the general store and told me to stay in

Elsie with Ryan. He made sure both of us had our water bottles and left my window wound down. The sun was behind us, but it was hot, and I was sure that my bottom was melting into the pile of cushions.

Dad opened the back door and Yellow Dog jumped out, happy to stretch his legs and find something to pee on.

Ryan woke up as soon as we stopped. I could tell, from the way his eyes followed Dad into the store, that he was preparing to yell up a storm. I knew just how he felt. Since it was going to happen anyway, I couldn't be accused of having started anything. I snatched away Dino and threw it out the window.

Ryan's dark eyes narrowed vengefully, even as his face crumpled into an agony of distress, and his little legs started kicking in fury. I felt a rush of joy at having triggered such a reaction, but the anticipated yells never came. Distracted by something outside, Ryan suddenly forgot his tantrum.

"Caw, caw," he said.

I turned, and there, looking in at us through the dusty windscreen, was a huge crow. It tilted its head to one side, studying us from a bright, black eye. Its beak was half-open, probably from the heat, but it seemed to me that it was smiling at us, or laughing.

Ryan kicked again, bouncing his little body up and down against his restraints. "Caw. Caw."

I didn't like the bird. "Shoo!" I said, and lunged forward, wanting to scare it away. It hopped back a few paces, lifting its wings slightly, and then ruffled its feathers. It turned its head to one side and studied me, then hopped up to the windscreen and tapped its huge beak against the glass. Tap, tap, tip.

Elsie was old but well built, Dad said, and I knew that there was no reason to be afraid of a stupid bird when I sat behind solid, reassuring glass. I quickly wound up my window anyway.

Ryan leant forward in his chair, staring at the bird. He waved a chubby arm about as if he, too, wanted to shoo it away.

The crow watched him for a moment, and then bounced away on its skinny, leathery legs. Its claws click-clicked on the dirty metal of

Elsie's hood. It jumped onto the metal frame of the bullbar, at the front of the car, turned around, jumped into the air and flew straight for us. BANG! It hit the glass in a fury of exploding black feathers, beak, and claws.

I screamed and threw myself over Ryan, but he didn't even whimper. When I looked into his eyes, they were as black and round as those of the bird. I scrabbled for the door handle, suddenly desperate to get out of the car. Behind me, Ryan cooed, "Da, Da."

There was Dad, with Dino in his hand, staring at the bloody smear on our windscreen and the crumple of black feathers on the hood. He looked down at me from beneath the wide brim of his hat, and we connected in a moment of instant understanding.

Run away, I thought. We have to run away.

He put the shopping in the backseat, letting the dog jump in, before going around to the front. He lifted the bird by a broken wing and dropped it on the ground. He jumped into the car, and, without a word, handed Ryan his toy, checked our restraints, then gunned Elsie's engine and drove out of town as fast as the old car would go.

Ryan squawked in my ear, making his Dino noise, "Raar, raar." I steeled myself to look into his eyes, but I saw nothing there except baby innocence and stubborn insistence.

"Daddy, why did that bird want to get at Ryan?"

"It was probably sick in its head, honey."

I looked over at my beloved father. His face was hot and red, his hair dark and flat from having sweated beneath his hat. His Adam's apple bobbed up and down. He usually drove with one arm out the window, but both hands were clenched on the wheel.

"Where are we going?"

"Sydney."

I didn't need to ask why. I turned to stare out my window, letting the flow of familiar country pass by in a blur, knowing that he did not believe what he had said about the bird.

"Ryan killed it," I said.

He glanced at me, eyes squinting. "Don't be silly."

"He did!" Dad kept his eyes on the road, but he was frowning. "I think the old man sent it." I continued.

He shot me a quick look. "What?"

"The crow. It was watching us. It had his eyes."

This time he *really* looked at me. "A bird is just a bird," he said.

I stared back. "And babies don't really hatch from eggs?"

Between us, Ryan was pulling Dino's legs with his grubby little fingers. He looked up at me, from beneath the floppy brim of his hat. "Raar, raar," he said.

❖

Ryan soon fell asleep again, the dinosaur slipping by degrees from his curled fingers, his long lashes nested above the curve of his chubby cheek. A line of drool spooled from his soft lips, spiraling down to the car seat.

We stopped to fill up the tank and get some snacks. I was mad at Dad for taking us away from home, and took it out on him by pinching Ryan until he woke up, cranky.

Yellow Dog and I both needed to pee, so I let the dog out of the car and we both took off in search of a toilet. When I got back, Ryan was happily chewing on a biscuit and Dad had found a bucket of water and a sponge to wash the windscreen. I watched as the crow's blood mixed with the soapy water, trailing down the filthy glass, carving red channels like river deltas into the caked dirt, until it was all washed away.

That night, we stayed at a roadside motel. There was a "No Pets Allowed" sign, so we kept Yellow Dog hidden in the back of Elsie until we could sneak him into our room.

"You love Ryan, don't you?" I asked, as Dad herded me into bed. Ryan and I shared the double, but he was already asleep, lying flat out on his tummy.

Dad looked unhappy and tired. "Of course."

"I bet Mr. Pham doesn't."

Dad gave me an exasperated look. "'Lainie, I'm tired. Please don't try it on."

I knew I had to keep the whine out of my voice, I had to make him understand. "I'm not, Daddy. It's just that I don't care about Mr. Pham, or his ancestors. Ryan hatched for *us* and we love him. That must mean he was *meant* to be with us. Doesn't it?"

Dad stared at me for such a long time, I became upset, thinking that he was mad at me for listening to his conversation. Suddenly he got up and went into the bathroom. I heard him washing his face. He came back in and sat down.

"Ryan needs someone who understands his nature," he said. "Someone who can help him become what he is meant to be."

I was crying now. I wanted to stay serious and calm, instead I wailed, "But *you're* his daddy!"

Disturbed by our voices, the baby stirred and hiccupped, but he didn't wake.

"What are you going to do?" I whispered.

"What I have to," he admitted. "I will make sure that Mr. Pham has everything Ryan needs, and then we'll say good-bye and go home."

I felt my temper rise, the one that Dad said was just like his. "He's *my* baby dragon!"

It was only later that I realized what I had said.

Dad understood. He was a good listener. He looked away. "I love Ryan too," he said, "but I should never have taken the egg."

The burn of my temper was already fizzling out. I groped for something to say. "Did you steal it?"

He shook his head. "If someone tried to sell you a dragon's egg, would you believe them?"

I shrugged. *Why not?*

"I didn't, but I had promised to bring you back something beautiful, and although she told me the stories, she didn't believe them any more than I did."

"She?"

He gave me a small smile. "Mr. Pham's daughter. I liked her, and I wanted to help, so I bought the egg." This time it was his turn to shrug. "She used the money to leave her village, and I don't think Mr. Pham, or I, will ever see her again."

I didn't want to think about my dad liking *anyone's* daughter. "Do you know any more stories about Au Co?"

Dad rubbed his eyes. Sighed. "A short one, then sleep. Deal?"

I accepted with a serious nod. "Deal."

He gathered his thoughts for a second. "Do you remember those nights, when we counted stars, and I told you that around some of them are worlds?"

I nodded. Of course I remembered.

"Well, somewhere out there is a world called Kandoarin, and that is where Au Co came from."

"How?"

"I don't really know that part. The story goes that Au Co had a special power, something called *Kansaith,* which meant that she could travel long distances very quickly."

"Like flying?"

"No one knows. Au Co was the only person to ever come here from Kandoarin, and that was by accident. She used her power during one of Kandoarin's eclipses, but the forces that she harnessed were too great for her to control. Instead of traveling from one part of her world to another, she tore a hole in the fabric of space."

Yeah, right. "Are you making this up?"

"Okay, so I've modernized it a bit in the retelling," he admitted, grinning. "That's what happens to myths."

"It doesn't matter," I said. "I like the idea of Au Co falling through a hole in the sky."

Dad was in full storytelling mode now. "Maybe she did fall out of the sky, but before she could get here, she had to build some sort of bridge."

In my mind's eye, I saw the arc of the Milky Way. "Do you think it's still there?"

"Even if it is, I don't think it would be the sort of thing you or I would recognize. But Au Co only came to Earth because she couldn't go back to Kandoarin."

"Why not?"

Dad sighed, a little theatrically, I thought. "How am I going to finish if you keep interrupting me?"

I ran my finger across my mouth, zippering it shut.

"Better," he said. "So, Au Co realized that she had done something terrible. There are dangerous things living in the cold between the worlds. One of these things slipped through the hole that she had made and attacked Kandoarin.

"She was the only one who had the power to destroy it, or force it back through the rift, but she was too afraid, or too tired, to fight. This thing from space coiled itself around Kandoarin's heart and made the mountains tremble and cities fall."

I loved it when Dad waxed lyrical, but outrage forced me to break my vow of silence. "She ran away!"

Dad took an alarmed look at Ryan, and put his finger to his lips to shush me. "Maybe there was nothing she could do," he said quietly. "The tragedy had happened, and if she tried to go back, it would only kill her. Instead, she used her skill and power to survive. She found herself washed up on Earth, where she had to learn how to live amongst people very different from her own. That takes courage, doesn't it? She never tried to use *Kansaith* again. Maybe she was afraid of making the same mistake, or perhaps she had used up all her power, but Au Co spent the rest of her life thinking of what she had done, and wondering how she could make it right again."

"She didn't!" I whispered fiercely. "She got married and had eggs instead!"

"She was a long way from home," Dad said patiently, "and you watch too much television." He came over and gently pushed me down, pulling the blanket up to my chin. "Anyway, that's how the story goes. It was all a very long time ago. Since then, the Red River delta became the land of Van Lang, then the kingdom of Nam Viet became Vietnam." He finished tucking me in and stared down at Ryan. "All that time, Au Co's descendents guarded the last egg, until even they stopped believing in the stories."

I leant over and stroked Ryan's hair, until it occurred to me that it was the color of crow's feathers. I looked up at Dad, disturbed by the thought. "Is he going to breathe fire when he grows up?"

Dad got up and turned off the light. "We had a deal, remember?"

"But—"

"Sleep!"

Something woke me up later that night. Through bleary eyes, I saw Dad carrying the baby around on his shoulder, a half-empty bottle in one hand, singing nonsense tunes in a soft, exhausted voice.

❖

Dad was short-tempered with the both of us the next day. I thought that was unfair, since it was Ryan who had kept him up all night. It wasn't my fault that it was hot in the car, and boring. Even Yellow Dog demanded breaks more often than usual.

I watched the scenery change from countryside to dense forest. "What do you think Kandoarin is like?" I asked, wanting to fill the silence.

"Da," said Ryan. He leaned against his seat restraints, and started to wave his hand backward and forward beneath the sunlight streaming through Elsie's windscreen.

Dad took off his sunglasses, squinting at the road while he rubbed one eye and then the other. He scratched the stubble on his cheek.

We caught up with the traffic ahead; a red Toyota tailgating a long, wide truck, waiting for its moment to overtake.

"Maybe like here," Dad said after a long pause. He took a quick glance down at Ryan. "Probably different."

Ryan looked up at him, finger shadows danced across our laps. "Da, ook."

Dad's smile was the saddest thing I'd ever seen. The lines around his mouth had deepened. He brought his eyes back to the road and gave a jaw-cracking yawn. "I'm going to have to take a coffee break soon," he said.

"How different?" I demanded, feeling ignored.

Ahead of us, the driver of the red Toyota had still not succeeded in overtaking the truck. I could see him arguing with the woman next to him, even while he moved the car out into the opposite lane to check for oncoming traffic. He nipped back into his lane just in time.

"Bloody idiot," said Dad.

"Da, ook," said Ryan. "Uddy idiot."

I giggled.

"Oh, well," murmured Dad. "Just get on with it," he told the red Toyota.

Ryan turned to me. He pointed to the truck. " 'Ainie, ook!"

"It's just a stupid truck," I said. "Bloody idiot."

"Elaine," Dad warned.

Ryan was jumping up and down in his seat now. "Ook! Ook!"

Yellow Dog started whining. "Oh, for goodness sake," exclaimed Dad. "What *is* it?"

The red Toyota pulled out into the other lane and started overtaking the truck.

"Bang. Bang," Ryan said softly. He looked up at me, put his hands to his ears. "Bang, bang, 'Ainie."

There was a loud crack, followed immediately by a BOOM! A cloud of dust billowed as the truck swerved first one way, then the other. Its front tires hit the verge, kicking up a cloud of dirt and pebbles that spattered and clicked on Elsie's hood and windscreen.

"Shit," swore Dad, braking hard. Ryan and I were thrown against our seat belts, and I felt Yellow Dog hit the back of my chair with a heavy thump. Dog and I both yelped.

The road was suddenly strewn with long, thin shreds of rubber, writhing like big black snakes, and the front of the truck listed to the right. It swung across the road and caught the Toyota, dragging the small car underneath its high chassis. The truck's huge, double tires locked into a skid, jammed against the already crumpled Toyota.

There was another agonized screech of metal, and a horrible crunch, as the truck's load shifted, and, in slow motion, it twisted and started to go over.

Elsie shuddered and jounced, slowing but still carried forward by her momentum. Dad was shouting something but I didn't understand. I could only hold my breath as the distance between us, the mangled Toyota and the overturning truck, shrank.

Then we hit the oil. Elsie's brakes locked, we spun, and slid sideways even as the truck landed with a crash and a long arc of sparks flew out like firecrackers. The accident was still happening; smoke, dust and burnt rubber, my father's shouts, and Ryan's high-pitched wailing filled my world.

The wreckage ahead of us became a creature of motion and form. As we slid toward it, I saw a face emerge; not the face of a person, but of something dark, alive and angry. The cloud of dust and smoke opened at the center, became a mouth into which we were sliding. Smoke belched out of its jaws and the vague shape of the red Toyota was its tongue. The bright sunlight pierced the clouds, and became two hot, white eyes.

Beside me, Ryan was struggling against the pressure of his seat restraints. He was gasping, his hands pushing palm outward. His "go away" sign.

Go away! Go away!

I moaned. The mouth of the smoking monster closed in around us and I waited for the crunch, knowing that it was going to hurt. I felt a pressure push me *back* against my seat, the Land Rover stalled, and then there was nothing but dead quiet.

The darkness began to shred as light wove its way back into existence. Dad's breathing was a hoarse whisper. I think he was trying to speak. His hand touched my arm.

"I'm okay," I tried to say, but nothing came out except a croak.

The tattered smoke and dust cloud thinned and then blew away, revealing wreckage, but no monster, except the accident's carnage . . . and Elsie, safe—on the other side of it.

I looked across at Dad, slumped in his seat, his hands clenched to Elsie's steering wheel. Then he sat back and took a shuddering breath. He started the car and drove us off the road, on to the verge. "Stay here," he said.

He got out of the car, took a few steps, and vomited. Hands on knees, he breathed deeply and then managed an unsteady shamble back to the accident.

I unclipped my seat belt, turned around, and knelt over the back of my seat. Yellow Dog was still in the space between the seats. He looked up and whined, too shocked to move.

"'Ainie?" Ryan whispered. I looked at him and his eyes were huge and wet. "Raar, raar," he sniffled. He rubbed his nose, spreading snot across his cheeks. I pulled out the hankie Dad kept behind his car chair and wiped it away. He pawed at me, wanting to be released, so I unclipped his belt. He crawled onto my cushions and we clung to each other.

The police and ambulance came soon after, and Dad returned to us. He sat in his seat for a long while, staring out the window. "Those two people are dead," he said quietly, and then he turned to look at Ryan.

He leant over and picked him up, put him back into his seat and clipped him in. Ryan protested until Dad kissed him on the cheek, pressing his nose against the little boy's soft skin. "Thank you," he murmured.

A policeman appeared at Dad's window. He handed Dad a piece of paper. "Here's the station address, Mr. Ashton, if you recall anything else, let us know. You'll probably be asked to appear as a witness."

Dad took the paper. "Of course. Thanks." The policeman nodded, glanced curiously at Ryan and me, before turning on his heel.

"Did you tell them what happened, Daddy?"

"The truck's front tire blew out, the driver lost control and hit the Toyota," he said. "They know what happened."

"But, we were *behind* the truck, and then—" I faltered, my voice trailing away.

Dad started Elsie, looked over his shoulder, and pulled out onto the road. Something crunched as he mishandled a gear. "Yes," he said. "Aren't we lucky."

❖

That evening, we were lost in Sydney city. Dad pulled a tattered old street map out from the glove compartment, studying it during stops at traffic lights. He seemed to know where he wanted to go, but "they" had apparently changed the road system since he had last visited the Big Smoke. I drifted in and out of sleep, with my head against Ryan's chair and he with his head slumped to his chest in deep exhaustion.

I woke when Dad opened the door on my side and gently lifted me out. Monkeylike, I wrapped arms and legs around him, my head on his shoulder. Holding me with one arm, he unclipped Ryan from his seat, and, with a practiced scoop, put him up onto his other shoulder. He kicked the door shut.

Through half-closed eyes, I could see tugboats and rotting hulks moored alongside huge wooden pylons. There was the slap of water against slippery stone walls and the smell of spilt diesel. I heard the familiar *eek* of rats and the scuttle of things disturbed by our passing. Yellow Dog whined and pressed close to Dad.

The warmth of my father's body and the broad expanse of his shoulder lulled me back to sleep. I tucked my thumb into my mouth and remember nothing more until the morning.

❖

I woke up to sunlight slanting through a broken glass window, on a comfortable mattress, with a soft blanket tucked around me. Ryan was asleep next to me, curled up around his thumb and Dino, a rich smell wafting up from the gap between diaper and back. I crinkled my nose and looked around.

We were in a warehouse. Narrow shafts of light found their way through the mismatched corrugation of the roof and dirty glass windows high on the walls, spotlighting clouds of dust. Aromas came from everywhere; hanging baskets full of herbs and grasses, drying flowers hung from the rafters and from the rusting iron girders that crisscrossed the space above, a wok set upon a huge old-fashioned iron cooker in one corner.

Scattered around the warehouse floor was an expanse of garden ornaments and strange relics of all shapes and designs. Carved stone beasts with tusks and huge eyes crouched next to plaster flamingos. Fat, grinning Buddhas sat next to toga-draped Venuses. In the spaces between, there was a sense of pressure, like an oncoming thunderstorm. The air felt electric.

I saw Yellow Dog lying on a patch of carpet in the corner, near a stove and small sink. A door opened behind him and Dad came through, ducking his head beneath the door frame, with Mr. Pham close behind. The old man was dressed in loose, white cotton trousers and a long overcoat with wide sleeves. He looked comfortable and cool.

Yellow Dog's tail thumped on the carpet. Mr. Pham paused to pat him, but he ducked his head away. I could see his thick fur shivering, like it did when flies annoyed him. Mr. Pham stood, with his hand outstretched, until Yellow Dog whined and rolled onto his back.

I heard the old man chuckle, and didn't like it. Dad didn't seem to care. He stood listlessly to one side, stoop-shouldered, one hand leaning against the edge of the stove. He had changed his shirt for a clean T-shirt, but he still looked bedraggled, as if with one small push, he too might roll over.

I went to the mattress and knelt next to Ryan. He stirred, opened his sleepy, dark eyes. His thumb came out of his mouth with a sucking sound and he gave a little sigh of resignation. " 'Otty?"

I nodded and he rolled over onto his bottom and opened his arms to be picked up. There was a damp squishing against my hip, and I grimaced, trying not to take too deep a breath. Ryan's head was against my shoulder, his soft hair fluffy against my cheek.

"Ryan's needing a change," I said, taking him toward Dad, but Mr. Pham intercepted me with ease. With a firm hand, he herded me back to the mattress. He produced a diaper and a small towel from one voluminous sleeve, and pins, wipes, and powder from the other.

I stared at him in astonishment, wondering what else he might produce, but that seemed to be all for now. He put the towel down on the floor and gently pried Ryan from my grasp. With practiced hands, he quickly cleaned and changed him, while Ryan gazed up solemnly.

I saw Dad staring at us, with the same look on his face that I had seen when he had cried to the stars.

"Daughter, please take this to your father."

My name is *Elaine*, I wanted to say. I took the folded diaper but didn't move.

"Ryan used *Kansaith* yesterday," I said. It sounded like an accusation. I sensed the words hanging in the air, amidst the flowers and the baskets, heard faint whispers bounce from Buddhas and stone creatures, echoes that sounded like a breeze through dry grass.

I lowered my voice. "What is this place?"

The old man glanced around. "It is an edge," he said.

"That doesn't make sense."

Mr. Pham pursed his lips. "A shore, a threshold—a door." He lifted Ryan to his feet and spent a moment admiring his handiwork. "And here," he said with pride, "is the key." He studied the little boy for another moment, as if he were memorizing every crease, every fold of soft skin. Ryan squirmed, wriggling to get free.

"'Ainie," he pointed to the strange collection of *things* surrounding us. "Ook."

The old man smiled at this. "He knows. Oh, yes. He can *feel* it." He cocked his head sideways, looking at me in a way that reminded me of a bird considering its next meal. "Can *you* feel it, daughter? There is great power in the relationship of simple things to each other." He looked from me to Ryan, back again. "I had not considered that such power might also exist between children."

Relationship of simple things—was he calling me stupid? "What about the crow that attacked us," I demanded. "And yesterday—I saw a face; with big jaws and white eyes."

"What about it?" he asked. "Perhaps you have one of those over-active imaginations, eh?"

I know it was you, I wanted to say. *You're trying to scare us.* I shook my head firmly.

Mr. Pham was still kneeling, so we were eye to eye. I studied that broad face, as brown and lined as drought-cracked mud, with cheekbones so high they cast shadows. His long silver hair was drawn back from his face into a ponytail, and beneath grey eyebrows bristling with unruly hairs were eyes so black, I could not see the pupils. Strange eyes.

Ryan's eyes.

"I don't like you," I said.

The old man nodded. "Good. I don't like you, either."

Ryan had crawled onto the mattress to retrieve Dino. "When he grows up, I'm going to teach him to fly," I declared. "And he's going to breathe fire." *And eat nasty old men,* I finished silently. At that point, Dad came over, clearly intending to scold me. He went to take my arm, but Mr. Pham motioned him away and he stopped in his tracks, swaying like a drunk.

"Daughters need a firm hand," he told Dad. "They must be taught respect."

Mr. Pham rocked onto his toes, rising gracefully to his feet. He didn't look so old anymore. "Are you a sorceress? You will need to be, if you are to hide from that which hunts him."

"I'm not scared." *Of you.*

His bushy eyebrows drew together. "You should be."

Ryan decided to rejoin us, bouncing his way across the mattress on hands and knees. Gripping his toy with one fist, he put his other arm around my leg. "'Ainie-ay," he sang in his lispy voice.

I put my arm around his shoulders. "Ryan hatched for me."

"And you think that I am jealous?" He seemed to think about it for a moment. "Perhaps," he admitted, "if I permitted such feeling. But I do not. Nor grief. Such things must be put aside." He gestured at Dad; fingers moving in slanted light, shifting dust motes and shadows.

"We have to go now, 'Lainie," said Dad in a toneless voice.

I pulled Ryan closer and he hugged me back. He pointed Dino at the old man, "raar."

Mr. Pham's eyes narrowed. Suddenly he raised his arms and the light in the warehouse dimmed. A copper-colored gloom descended upon us. The sleeves of his white tunic slid back to his shoulders, revealing muscled, brown arms and a fine layering of tattoos, like glittering scales.

I quailed. "Daddy?"

"So, *you* would teach him?" thundered the old man. "And when Kandoarin's eclipse comes and its doom awakens, what then? Tell me, little girl, will the Youngest Son be ready?"

Between us, dust motes danced, as if the air was fluid, their movement captured in shafts of filtered light, whirlpools of motion, like froth stirred into coffee.

A low, deep sound pulsed above my head, the beating heart of some great beast crouching amidst the rafters and beams. The shadows deepened, melded into a darkness that pooled around our feet.

"Already the hunter is stirring. Without me, it will find him, and crush him, and all will fail." He lowered his arms and the throbbing sound dimmed, became the panicked beat of my own heart.

Mr. Pham held out his hand to Ryan. "Bắc Vương," he said. "Come to me."

"No!"

Startled, I saw my exhausted Dad draw himself up. Yellow Dog had come to heel. He crouched at Dad's feet, brown eyes focused on the old man, lips slightly raised over sharp canines.

Dad's voice was hoarse. "I don't care what you are," he said. "Don't threaten my children!" He rubbed a hand across his forehead. "I've had enough."

Mr. Pham nodded stiffly. "Yes. It is time for you to leave."

"Right," said Dad. "Ryan."

He immediately left me and waddled over, lifting his arms. Dad hauled him up, put him on a hip.

"Elaine."

I gleefully dropped the dirty diaper and rushed to take his hand.

"I nearly made a terrible mistake," Dad said. "I was afraid of things I half-believed. Now I *do* believe, and you know what? I don't care. I don't care what he is. I am a father. That is *my* duty. C'mon, Dog."

We turned our backs on the old man. The door was just *there,* we were headed toward it. I felt the brush of Yellow Dog's fur against my leg. I felt like skipping.

We walked fast, but I hadn't realized how *big* the warehouse was—our efforts to reach the door only seemed to push it away. Dad stumbled to a stop. "You bastard," he muttered.

"Daddy?"

"It's okay, honey. Everything will be okay." We turned around again, slowly.

I was half expecting a drum roll, or Mr. Pham to sprout fangs or wings, or perhaps the beasts of plaster and stone to come alive. As Dad said, I watch too much television.

Mr. Pham was just standing there. A strange, magnetic old man, with eyes that glittered in the weird light and a shadow that stretched across the warehouse, pooling around our feet like black ink.

"The Youngest Son knows what he must do," Mr. Pham said. He lifted a hand and motioned. *Come.* Ryan wriggled out of Dad's arms, as impossible to hold against his will as an eel. In a blink, he was out of our reach and toddling over to the old man. It happened so quickly. He took a few steps away from us, and suddenly he was enveloped in dust motes twisting into forms that swam in the air and shimmered like a mirage; multicolored scales, the curve of horns and claw, the glint of black eyes.

The old man threw back his head and laughed out loud. Then, with a conqueror's flourish, he went down on one knee. As he did so, his shadow shrank back, like a dark tide receding. He put out his hand for Ryan to take, and I knew that the moment he did, they would disappear, like Alice's rabbit.

Into that outstretched hand, Ryan gravely placed Dino the dinosaur. "Uddy idiot," he said cheerfully. Then he turned around to come back to us, leaving the old man stranded in confusion, holding a thoroughly gnawed and misused rubber toy. Mr. Pham looked straight at me, and I saw his fury, felt the heat of his intent across the space between us.

A wide, cheeky grin split Ryan's face as he put up his arms, ready for takeoff.

"Well, I'll be damned," said Dad, scooping him up.

Mr. Pham surged forward, only to be met halfway by a bristling, furious Yellow Dog, flashing canines full of promise. So we stood, my father and I, and the dog, in a little triangle, and we were as one.

"Simple things," I reminded the old man.

"Willful, disobedient child," he said to me. He looked at Dad and his face was suddenly very sad. "Your love will cost you dearly," he said. "I would have spared you the suffering." He locked eyes with Ryan, and then he opened his hand, letting Dino drop to the ground. It bounced once, and vanished.

Like a screen coming down between us, the gloom gathered around Mr. Pham, softening his form, blurring his features. He stepped back, into the shadows.

We turned and rushed for the door, and this time nothing conspired against us. We emerged into a tiny shop front, stacked full of rolled-up carpets and dusty furniture. A pair of floor-to-ceiling windows, half-covered in tattered posters stuck to the outside, faced out onto yet another bright, sunny day.

There was old Elsie, parked outside. We were going home. Nothing bad had happened. Dad had kept us together, and I sensed that I had changed. I felt grownup, a big sister, strong in ways I couldn't describe. One day, Au Co's youngest son will cross his bridge, but not yet. For now, he chooses to be with us, and that is a powerful magic.

I looked up and saw my little brother gazing down at me from over Dad's shoulder. "Knock. Knock," he said.

I grinned back at him. "Who's there?"

"Me!" He announced. Lifting his hands, he curled them into claws. *"Raar."*

Endings

GARTH NIX

❖

A story, and what a story means, are two different things. Sometimes a teller gives you both. When they do, you know the meaning they tell you, but nothing more. And sometimes a teller gives you just the story, so you have to find the meaning yourself; but you may find that a story holds more than one meaning, or a bigger meaning than any teller could ever catch in a nest of explanations. Trust the tale, and see where it goes.

*If you like this tale, you might like the wonderful fantasy tales of Lord Dunsany (*The Book of Wonder *is a good place to start), Sylvia Townsend Warner's* Kingdoms of Elfin, *Neil Gaiman's* Sandman *and* Books of Magic *series of graphic novels; or Garth Nix's own trilogy* Sabriel, Lirael, *and* Abhorsen.

I have two swords. One is named Sorrow, and the other Joy. These are not their real names. I do not think there is anyone alive who knows even the letters that are etched into the blue-black blades.

I know, but then I am not alive. Yet not dead. Something in between, hovering in the twilight, betwixt wakefulness and sleep, caught on the boundary, pinned to the board, unable to go back, unable to go forward.

I do rest, but it is not sleep, and I do not dream. I simply remember, the memories tumbling over one another, mixing and joining and mingling till I do not know when or where or how or why, and by nightfall it is unbearable and I rise from my troubled bed to howl at the moon or pace the corridors.

Or sit beneath the swords in the old cane chair, waiting for the chance of a visitor, the chance of change, the chance . . .

❖

I have two daughters. One is named Sorrow, and the other Joy.

These are not their real names. I do not think even they remember what they were called in the far-distant days of their youth. Neither they nor I can recall their mother's name, though sometimes in my daytime reveries I catch a glimpse of her face, the feel of her skin, the taste of her mouth, the swish of a sleeve as she leaves the room and my memory.

They are hungrier than I, my daughters, and still have the thirst for blood.

❖

This story has two endings. One is named Sorrow, and the other Joy.

This is the first ending:

A great hero comes to my house without caution, as the sun falls. He is in the prime of life, tall and strong and arrogant. He meets my daughters in the garden, where they stand in the shade of the great oak. Two steps away lies the last sunlight, and he is clever enough to make use of that, and strong. There is pretended amour on both sides, and fangs strike true. Yet the hero is swifter with his silvered knife, and the sun is too close.

Silver poisons and fire burns, and that is the finish of Sorrow and the end of Joy.

Weakened, the hero staggers on, intent on finishing the epic that will be written about him. He finds me in the cane chair, and above me Sorrow and Joy.

I give him the choice and tell him the names.

He chooses Sorrow, not realizing that this is what he chooses for himself, and the blades are aptly named.

I do not feel sorrow for him, or for my daughters, but only for myself.

I do drink his blood. It has been a long time . . . and he was a hero.

This is the second ending:

A young man not yet old enough to be a hero, great or small, comes to my garden with the dawn. He watches me through the window, and though I delay, at last I must shuffle out of the cane chair, toward my bed.

There are bones at my feet, and a skull, the flesh long gone. I do not know whose bones they are. There are many skulls and bones about this house.

The boy enters through the window, borne on a shaft of sunlight. I pause in the shadowed doorway to watch as he examines the swords. His lips move, puzzling out what is written there, or so I must suppose. Perhaps no alphabet or language is ever really lost, as long as some of it survives.

He will get no help from that ancient script, from that ancient life.

I call out the names I have given the swords, but he does not answer.

I do not see which weapon he chooses. Already memories rush at me, push at me, buffet and surround me. I do not know what has happened or will happen or might happen.

I am in my bed. The youth stands over me, the point of a sword pricking at my chest.

It is Joy, and I think chosen through wisdom, not by luck. Who would have thought it of a boy not yet old enough to shave?

The steel is cold. Final. Yet only dust bubbles from the wound.

Then comes the second blow, to the dry bones of the neck.

I have been waiting a long time for this ending.

Waiting for someone to choose for me.

To give me Joy, instead of Sorrow.

Dancer in the Dark

DAVID GERROLD

❖

If you want to settle yourself to always stay in the same place, and always believe the same things, despair will suit you better than joy, because despair always stays the same too. You can brace yourself against it. Joy and beauty will take you by surprise, and lead you away into places you'd never imagined because you didn't know things could be so good. Joy and beauty are sneaky that way.

David Gerrold has written a story about a boy growing up in a strange place. Just go along with it, and it'll explain itself in time.

If you like "Dancer in the Dark," try Edgar Pangborn's classic science fiction novel Davy; *Zenna Henderson's* The People: No Different Flesh; *and Orson Scott Card's tales of a post-apocalyptic America collected in* The Folk of the Fringe.

When Ma finally died, they said they didn't have a place for me and it wasn't safe in the city anymore, so they decided it would be best to send me somewhere west where I could live on a farm. They said I would like it. Hard work and sunshine. And I'd get over Ma's death in no time. You'll see. They said.

They put me on a train with a whole bunch of other tight-faced people and went away. The train sat in the station for half a day, all of us waiting scared, before it finally chugged out. It was cold and shivery in the car, and there wasn't much to eat. You could get a drink from the faucet, but the water tasted funny.

Out the window, there was a lot of smoke, and where there wasn't smoke, there was burnt-out buildings, some old, and some still smoldering. I never been on a train before, I thought they went faster than this, but no, this was all stop and go, mostly stopping and waiting. And when we did go, we went slow, like the driver was being careful to watch the tracks to make sure they was still there. Once we went real slow through a corridor of burning buildings.

I was stuck way in the back behind a family, sort of, with a couple of older sisters and a lot of young-uns, except they weren't a real family because they wasn't related. They was just traveling together, and the older sisters weren't sisters at all, they was just supposed to keep the littleuns together. The kids all stunk real bad, they didn't have any clean clothes, and they'd pissed and crapped themselves, more than once. And they cried a lot, trying to keep warm. So I just turned to the window and stared out at whatever there was to see, which wasn't very much because once we got away from the big towns, the dark was spread real thick in a lot of places.

Mostly the dark looked like black fuzziness floating in the air. I'd never been inside the dark, but I heard stories. Everybody heard stories. It's like being shoved inside a thick blanket, you can't see, you can't hear, you can't breathe, and you just stumble around blind. It has something to do with the dark making it hard for things to move, like light or air or blood through your veins. You lay down a couple miles of dark around something and nobody can get through, no matter how much tinfoil they're wearing on their head.

Somebody else said that the whole country was sectioned off now. Dark everywhere. The trains ran through special corridors with walls of dark on each side, just enough room for the tracks and nothing else. You could maybe jump off the train, it wasn't going very fast, but so what? You couldn't get through the walls of dark, you couldn't go anywhere except follow the tracks. So you might as well stay on the train.

Sometime in the middle of the second night, we got to our first stop and they took some of the people off. There was all kinds of dark here, all around everything, even above so we couldn't even look up and see the stars. We didn't know where we were. Even though everybody was real tired, they woke us all up while all these men in different uniforms came marching through. They looked like soldiers from five or six different armies. They pointed at people in their seats. You, you, not you, not you, yes, yes, no, no, and so on. Another man in a different kind of uniform, I think he was the train conductor, came running after them, shouting about how they couldn't just take only the workers, they had to take a balanced cross-section, otherwise it wasn't fair.

I was hoping they'd take me, I wanted off the train real bad, I didn't care where we were. I even asked one of the soldier-men to pick me, but he shook his head and said I was too skinny. I tried asking a couple of the others, but they ignored me, so I slumped back down and pulled my blanket up and tried to go back to sleep. There wasn't nothing else to do. I was hungry and cold and stinky and not feeling too good inside. But at least there was some empty seats now and if you had one next to you, you could stretch out.

We had two more stops the next day, one just before noon, and the other late in the afternoon. Each time, another bunch of soldiers came through and took off some more people. After the last stop, there was almost nobody left on the train so they made us all move to the last car. They didn't say why. But probably because it was easier to watch us all in one place.

When they woke us up again, it was still dark. Darkfield dark. I couldn't tell what time it was, somebody said it was 3:30 in the morning. They made us gather up all our things, I didn't have much to gather, and then they herded us off the train and into a fluorescent station. The light hurt my eyes and the room smelled real strong of that disinfectant they use everywhere now. There was a red line across the room and we weren't allowed to cross it. On the other side, there was a line of grumpy-looking people, farmers and townsfolk. I guess they didn't like getting out of bed at this hour either. They looked us up and down like we were something bad-smelling. I guess we were.

Every so often, I sort of got a whiff of myself. I felt dirty and itchy, and I wanted a bath or even a shower. My feet hurt and I was shivering in my blanket.

The guy who looked like the conductor read a statement to the folks on the other side of the line, something about what they was agreeing to and how they had to treat us, stuff like that. They all looked bored, like they'd heard it all before. Then he read another statement to us on this side of the line, about our rights and stuff and how we didn't have to go if we didn't want to, but we couldn't refuse either. Which didn't make any sense.

And then they started letting people pick us. A big farmer pointed at one of the skinny girls and asked her if she could cook and clean. She nodded, and he grunted and said, "Okay, come along," and she picked up her little suitcase and followed him. There was a sad-looking man and woman, they looked at the two littlest children and whispered together for a while, and then crossed the line and picked them up and left real quick, like they feared someone wouldn't let them take the babies.

It went like that for a while, until there weren't many of us left. There was this hard-looking woman standing across from me. She looked like she'd been baked in the Sun until all the juice had been burned out of her and all that was left was this dry crunchy thing. She was looking at me like she couldn't make up her mind if I was worth the trouble. Finally, she said, "Boy? Are you gonna work, or you just gonna eat?"

"I can work," I said.

She walked over to the conductor and they talked together for a bit. He shook his head a lot. I got the feeling that I wasn't the first kid she'd picked out. And maybe the other one didn't work out. But finally, whatever, she came back and pointed at me and said, "Get your things." And that was it. I followed her out through the big double doors to a dirty parking lot surrounded by dark. A couple of tall light poles showed a few cars and the building we'd come out of and not much more than that.

"You got a name?"

"Folks call me Em."

"Em?"

"Yeah."

"Short for Emmett?" she asked.

"Em for Michael."

"Michael, yes. That's better than Em. You can call me Miz."

"Yes, Miz."

She pointed toward a beat-up old flatbed truck. She tossed my duffel into the back. I started to climb up after it, but she opened the door for me and said, "Get in."

We drove west on a road that was lined with dark. There might have been stars above, I couldn't tell. We had headlights, but they was mostly useless. They picked out the line of the road and that was all. She didn't say much and I didn't feel like talking either. I was too cold. I bunched up part of my blanket like a pillow and tried to rest my head against the window. It was worse than the train. We must have driven two hours. By the time we got where we were going, there was a feeling of light behind us. Hard to tell though, with all the dark.

Then there was a hole in the dark and she turned right and then left and then right again, and then we came out onto a big gray slope leading up to an old gray house. Behind it there was a dirty barn that had once been red, real tired-looking and leaning to one side, like it wanted to lie down, like if you gave it a good hard push, the whole thing would collapse, except there were a bunch of boards jammed in at an angle, propping it up so it couldn't. The old woman pointed. "You'll sleep in there. There's straw for a bed, and some old horse blankets. You can wash in the horse trough. Don't bother the cows. I start milking at six. I want you up and mucking out the stalls every morning. As soon as the cows are turned out. There's a couple barrels of disinfectant. You keep those stalls clean, you hear? As clean as you want your own bed—or your dinner plate. It's almost six now, so wash yourself up, you stink like a pig. Then get started. After milking, I'll bring you a plate. Don't want you in the house, boy. Lord knows what you're carrying."

"Yes, ma'am."

She stopped the car in front of the house, yanked on the parking brake real hard, like she was angry. "You like eggs? You ever had fresh eggs? Don't look like it. You're thinner than a ghost. When was the last time you ate?"

"Day before yesterday. I think. On the train, they gave us some leather to chew on."

"Damn fools. That's no way to treat anyone. Even deepies."

"Deepies?"

"Displaced Persons. DP's."

"Oh." Remembered my manners. "Thank you for takin' me in. I'll work real hard for you, ma'am."

She grunted. "Damn right you will. No free meals out here. Well, don't just sit there. We got work to do."

After milking and mucking, we pulled down a couple of bales of hay from the loft and broke them open for the cows. There was only three cows and they looked kinda sickly, but I don't know much about cows, so they coulda been fine too. But they walked real slow and stupid, like some of the people I'd seen in the city, the sick ones that they'd herd away every so often. But maybe that's how cows are. One of them looked at me for a bit, but she didn't look dangerous or anything. I didn't think you could make friends with a cow, so I just kept on shoveling cowshit.

Then there was the chickens, there was too many to count, they kept moving around all the time, bobbing their ugly little heads and clucking like old ladies. Miz poured out some corn for them and they all came cackling up. They was funny to watch. Later, after they'd finished the corn, they wandered around the fenced-in part of the yard, scratching for bugs and worms.

The biggest part of my job was feeding the refiner. This was three or four big metal tanks in a row, all piped together like a connected series of garbage disposals. I had to dump all the garbage into it every day, and everything else that wasn't nailed down—old corn stalks, dirty straw, stinkweeds, whatever. I had to scrape up the chicken guano and dump it in, plus wheelbarrow loads of cow manure and pig shit. Miz had indoor plumbing, but we both had to use the outhouse, because it pumped right into the refiner too. The methane that came off the top was piped around to fuel the stove at the bottom. The refiner was a big stinky stew pot, simmering and bubbling, sometimes grinding and chewing. But I didn't mind working the refiner, except for the smell. It was the only time I was really warm.

At the far end, out came oil. Enough for the truck, enough for the water heater, enough to power the refiner for another few days. Sometimes there was even enough to sell the extra in town. What didn't get turned into oil came out as mulch. And a scattering of metal bits and rock. The metal bits we saved for town. I had to check the refiner when I got up, twice during the day, and again before hitting the straw. Miz said if we had two more pigs, we'd be fat. But we didn't have enough corn to feed any more pigs. We were already too close to the bone, she said.

Out back of the house, Miz had a garden for vegetables, mostly stuff like tomatoes and potatoes and cucumbers and things like that. Some pumpkins and watermelons too. She also had a big patch of corn. Not a whole field, but enough to feed us and the chickens and even some for the cows. Like everything else, though, the corn had a sickly look. "Hard to grow things when there isn't enough light for them. Not good for plants, not good for people either. Still, it's better'n dyin'." She sniffed. "One good thing about the dark, though. We don't get as many rabbits or foxes sneakin' in. They don't like the dark anymore than anyone else. But you still have to watch out for burrows, because sometimes they will dig under. Saturdays, we go to town and get whatever supplies they still got. Sometimes there's a movie, but don't be expectin' it. Sundays, we go to Meeting. When we get back from Meeting, you can have time by yourself. But you stay outta trouble. Stay away from the dark. Don't go darksniffin' like the last damnfool I had out here. And no, I ain't sayin' nothin' about that. And don't you go askin' no questions neither, if you're smart."

But I didn't have to ask no questions. There was plenty enough people willin' to tell me everythin' they knew. First time we went to town, while I was loadin' sacks of chemical fertilizer into the back of the truck. Town wasn't much, just a scattering of old buildings on one side of the old highway, like someone just dropped them there any which way. Surrounded by dark, of course. Only way in or out is through the corridors, that's three roads and the train tracks. So there's not a lot to see. Funny lookin' kid with a broken tooth comes up and says, "You Miz's new boy?"

"Guess so."

"You wanna be real careful. Not like Doey. She tell you what happened to him?"

"I know what I need to know," I said, pretending to ignore him.

"No, you don't. You're a city boy. You don't know shit."

"I know enough to keep my nose outa other folks' business." I hefted the last sack in.

"You just stay out in the barn, boy, you know what's good for you. Come winter, she's gonna want you to come in and warm her bed, you'll see. Keep yourself bad-smellin', that's what Doey did. Till he ran away—ran into the dark, he did."

Miz came out of the feed store then, saw the kid and her face got real fierce. He saw her the same time and skittered off like the rat he was. Miz came up to me and stared at me hard. "What'd that boy say?"

Already knew better than to lie. Miz wasn't easy even on the best of days. I just sorta shrugged. "He said you had another boy named Doey. He ran away."

"That all he said?"

"Yes, ma'am."

She sniffed like she didn't believe me, but she didn't push it. "Well, you stay away from that J.D. boy. He's bad news. That whole family is. Now get to work. Help me load all this."

Miz explained that the train had come through again, so today was a good day. Some of the stores had new things on the shelves, even some new magazines in the racks. Miz bought a couple, bought one for me too. "Readin' is good for you, as long as you don't do too much of it. Puts funny ideas into your head. You start daydreamin', you won't get your chores done."

She bought me some new jeans and a couple of work shirts, a pair of boots and some thick socks. For herself, she stocked up on spices; she was starting to run low, she even bought a bottle of vanilla. "Might try makin' a cake or something. When was the last time you had cake?"

"Had a birthday party once, when I was little. My ma bought a cake."

"Store-bought cake? Ain't the same. You get your chores done, I'll make you a cake so good you'll think you died and went to heaven."

Second time I heard about Doey was the next day at Meeting.

Meeting was a ways off, I couldn't tell how far, but we were driving for at least an hour, maybe more, down a long corridor of dark, all twisty, up and down, with a couple of sharp turnoffs into passages that felt even darker. When we got there, we weren't really anywhere, just a wide open space with an old school-looking building in the center of a hard-dirt clearing. The dark around was cut by seven different openings, but one of them was walled off with tall orange cones and Miz told me to stay well away from that one. I didn't ask why, she wouldn't have said anyway.

Inside, the room was gloomy, lit by kerosene lamps. No generator here. But it was warmer than outside and it was a chance to sit quiet-like and almost doze. It was kind of like church too, so you had to keep your eyes open. There were these old ladies up top all singin' real faraway and soft like they was a choir of angels or something. The music was real old-fashioned, but it wasn't too painful.

Then the mayor got up and talked about living the hard life and staying clean and trusting God and following the rules because the reason that things had gotten so bad was that so many people had stopped following the rules, and we'd all made a big mess of things, so now we had to do penance for a thousand years or more while we tried to put things back together the best we could, but the only way to do that was to stay away from the dark and follow the rules. He went on and on like that for a long time. Then there was some discussion of chores that had to be done in the coming days, including putting down some new dark lines just to the west. He asked for volunteers for a work crew.

After Meeting, some folks climbed back into their trucks and drove off right away. But most folks gathered for tea and little sandwiches and even a cake. It looked real pretty. And everybody stood around in their clean clothes and talked polite and pretended everything was going fine, which it wasn't, but nobody would say so, because nobody wanted to be accused of doing the devil's talk. But you could see it in their faces, all hard and narrow and pinched. The sandwiches and cake disappeared fast. Some of these folks was hungry. Miz stopped me, wouldn't let me go to the table. She whispered, "You let that food be, son. It's not for us. It's for them that hasn't any. We have food at home. Some of these folks, this is their only meal today." So I went outside and stood around by the cars with the other men, just stood and listened.

"Hey you, new boy!" One of the men turned around and pointed to me. A big man. Beard. Overalls. A broken eye.

"Yeah?" I answered the good eye.

"You coming out with us, tomorrow? Help lay some dark lines?"

I shrugged. "Dunno. Whatever Miz says."

"Miz'll say yes. If I ask her. Can I trust you to work? Not stand around?"

"I can work."

"You have to promise to stay away from the bright. And keep your glasses on. And don't take off your silver. That's how we lost the other one. Whatsisname. Doey. You heard about that?" He peered at me.

Didn't answer, just sorta shrugged again. Safest way. Better to have them think I'm stupid than wrong. You can get killed being wrong. That's a city lesson. But it might be true out here in the dark lands as well.

"He don't know shit," said someone else. "Just another dumb city boy."

"He can carry. I'll talk to Miz. We need the hands. Besides, if we lose him, nobody'll care. Not even Miz. She'll just hook another one off the train."

And that was how it was decided that I should work on the dark team one or two days a week. I think Miz was glad to not have me around so much. There wasn't enough work to keep me busy every day. Or maybe she was just glad not to have to feed me. Sometimes the food was a little thin, even at her place. There just wasn't enough light. Somebody said that made everybody sad all the time. Depressed, he said. And then someone else told him to shut up. That was the devil's talk. Next he'd be complaining about the dark lines and the lines were the only things keeping them out. And then somebody said, "Not in front of *him*," meaning me, and that was the end of that conversation.

A few days later, an old truck pulled up in front of the house and a couple of workmen I didn't know got out and paid their respects to Miz. She handed them a paper bag with a bit of lunch in it, nowhere near enough to feed one hungry man, let alone three, but it was all she could spare. I climbed into the back of the pickup and made myself comfortable among the tools and wires.

We drove for half an hour, through the town, up the old highway for a while, and then off to the right where the corridor ended in orange cones. The workmen got out then and we all put on heavy black goggles and breathing masks and shiny silver capes and heavy work gloves. Then we drove on. The driver steered the truck carefully around the cones and up the passage to where the dark lines simply stopped. Beyond the lines, the ground rolled away like a rumpled gray bedsheet. There were already two other trucks here and five other men. One of them had a map rolled out on the hood of his truck and he was drawing lines with a crayon.

When nobody was looking, I lifted my goggles just a bit and snuck a peek at the brightlands. Immediately, I wished I hadn't. It knocked me backward. It was like being slapped in the face with a red-hot splash. I stumbled into the side of the truck, I fumbled the glasses back into place. My eyes were watering, I held them shut tight and tried to wipe at them without being blinded again. I felt really stupid, then I heard the men laughing at me and I got angry. They could have warned me. But then, one of them, a big soft guy everybody called Tallow, came up and put a black cloth over my head. He reached under the hood, pushed my goggles back, and mopped my face with a damp rag. It smelled faintly of disinfectant. He said quietly, "Don't take it bad. You only done what everybody else here did their first time too. We was all watching you. You got it over with quick. Now that you've seen a little bit of what's out there, you know what we all got to be careful about. Your eyes will stop hurting in a bit."

"You looked too, your first time?"

"Yep. Worse than you. I wasn't much older than you neither. I went out with my cousins, they said it wasn't nothing to be afraid of, you just take off the gloomies and look, see? So I did. That was real stupid. I stepped in it as deep as anyone could. It was most of an hour before I could see again. You got off easy, boy." Then he leaned in close and whispered, "It was real pretty, wasn't it? After a while, you're gonna start thinking that you'd like to take another look. Don't you be tempted, you hear? Don't you even think about it."

"I won't," I said. "I really truly won't." And I meant it. My eyes were still hurting bad. But then, I asked, "What was all that? What did I see?"

"You never mind that. It wasn't nothing."

"It must have been something. It damn near knocked me down."

"Don't you get too curious, boy. It ain't safe. You just follow the rules."

"Just tell me what it was, that's all. So I'll know. And then I won't ever ask again. Promise."

Tallow sighed. "You can't ever talk about this to anyone, you hear? You're not supposed to know. Nobody is. They don't want folks going out to see it for themselves." He lowered his voice. "They call it colors. It's what happens when light gets too bright. Your brain can't handle it. It's called overload or something like that. It's a little piece of madness, is what it is. You don't want to get sucked into it. You won't never get back. You'll just wander out there into the brights and die of your own hallucinations. That's what happened to—never mind."

"Doey?"

"Yeah, that was his name. Damn fool was too smart for his own good. Don't you go getting too smart now, you hear? You just keep remembering how much your face hurt."

"I will."

"You do that. Now that you know, you keep your gloomies on, you hear? And that breathing mask too, so you can't smell anything either. The air is just as bad. And don't say nothing to no one. No matter what. If you know what's good for you."

Tallow felt around under the hood, pulled my goggles back down over my eyes, and then made me check to see that they were properly seated. And the breathing mask too. When we were both satisfied, he pulled off the hood. I blinked and looked around. Everything was safely gray again. As long as I didn't think about what was really out there, I was okay. As long as I didn't say what I'd seen, I was okay. I didn't even tell Tallow about the after-image still burning in my eyes. It looked like a naked boy. But he wasn't there when I put the gloomies back on, and I looked around everywhere. And I didn't tell him about the honey-smell either. Through the glasses, the bright-lands looked flat and hard and empty. But I didn't have a lot of time for looking. There was too much work to do.

Putting down darklines wasn't hard. Just tedious. Mostly, it was boring.

First, we pounded stakes. The stakes were heavy Y-shaped things anchored in an iron base. The base was pointed like a bee sting. It had to be pounded deep into the ground, three feet or more; then the long leg of the Y part was stuck all the way into it. Then, after all the stakes were in place, we strung the wire, hanging it from one stake to the next.

I didn't do any of the actual stringing, that was done by the others. They had the strength for it, I didn't. I held cable, feeding it out from a big roll so it didn't hang up while the crew manhandled it into position. They used pitchforks so they wouldn't have to touch the line themselves. It was a thick naked braid of wire. The outer threads were deliberately broken and frayed, so the line looked like it had silvery scraggly hair. The wire was supposed to be fuzzy, so the dark would be deeper and stiffer, so I had to wear thick gloves, because the frayed bits had sharp ends. Even with the work gloves, I still got a few pokes and jabs and had to pull a couple of wire splinters from the heel of my palm.

When it was lunch time, we all hiked up the corridor a ways, far enough so that none of the bright could get in, so we could finally take off our gloomies and air-masks. Even here, safe between the dark lines, it still felt too bright. Or maybe that was an after-effect. I didn't ask. There wasn't much to eat, and what there was, wasn't very good. Stale bread, dried up cheese, wilted lettuce. Everything felt tired. Still, it was better than hunger. There wasn't much talk among the work crew. Everybody seemed to have something personal to think about. I thought about the naked boy. Was he really there? No, probly not. How could anyone stand naked in the bright? We finished eating as quickly as we could and pulled our goggles and capes back on, then hiked back out into the bright.

When the line was all strung, it was a chest-high fence. Not enough to stop anybody or anything. Least, not until it was turned on. The end of the line split into three separate wires that were fed into a terminator box. They put a terminator box at each end of the line, then they threw first one switch, then the other.

I pointed a the line. "How's it work?"

He waggled his hand. "It's what's called a seduction current. Something like that. It's powered by ambient photons. That's a fancy way of saying it sucks the extra light out of the air. The more light it sucks, the thicker the dark it makes."

"But nothing's happening," I said. The cable hung limp between the stakes.

Tallow grunted. "It takes a while. In a month, there'll be another patch of land safe to grow on. It'll go to the Martins. They might be able to get some winter wheat in. Might be enough to make it to spring."

"Why does it take so long?"

"It has to be slow. Otherwise, it would only make dark during the daytime, and we need the dark at night too. It usually takes a month or so for a line to suck enough light to get up to full strength, but after that, it only gets darker and stronger. Some of the older lines around here have enough residual in them to go for a year or more. Enough time to replace them if they go down. We'll come back out next week and see if it caught. Sometimes the terminator boxes are bad." He stepped over and peered closely at the wire. So did I, but I couldn't see any difference.

"Can I ask you something?"

"What?" Tallow seemed annoyed, like he was getting tired of me.

"How does the line know how much light to suck? What you said about the older lines getting stronger—do they ever suck too much light? Could they make it too dark?"

"Eh?" Tallow squinted, suddenly angry. "Don't you go anywhere with that. We got enough talk already."

"I was just asking—"

"You was just asking too much. That's not safe, boy. Don't ask questions, just follow the rules, you hear?" He strode away from me, began loading his tools into his truck. The other men too. Like they couldn't be away from here fast enough. Pretty soon, we all piled into our separate pickups and headed back down the corridor. They dropped me back at Miz's place and that was that.

I worked on the line crews off and on all summer long, when I wasn't mucking out stalls for Miz. Tallow didn't talk to me much, probly afraid he'd already said too much. None of them ever talked to the city boy, so I mostly kept to myself. Every so often, I thought about the colors I'd seen. I wondered if there was a safe way to look at them, a safe way to be naked; but I didn't ask those questions. I didn't ask any questions at all anymore, and I didn't answer any either. I pounded stakes and unrolled wire. One day, I looked at myself in the mirror, I actually had muscles. But I was still hungry all the time. And cold. Miz managed to keep food on the table, but it wasn't a lot. Sometimes we had cornbread. Sometimes just mush. We had eggs too, but the hens weren't laying regular. A couple of times we even had chicken. That was pretty good. We didn't starve, but nobody was getting fat either.

One Sunday, while we were at Meeting, one of the cows wandered into the dark; either she didn't have enough sense to keep away or maybe she was daydreaming the way cows do and the dark just pulled her in. She wasn't in her stall and she wasn't in the field either. I finally found her, ass-end sticking out of the dark, and went running up the hill to the house. It took both me and Miz to drag the cow out, but she was never the same. She wobbled on her feet. She looked like she'd been smacked in the face with a shovel. That night, she fell down in her stall. She wouldn't get up, so the vet came out to look at her. He did some doctor stuff, then took Miz off for a talk.

I didn't hear what they said, but Miz looked angry and frustrated. Finally she nodded her head. The vet came back into the barn and put the cow down. Put a gun to her head and thump, just like a street-killing, execution style. It took all three of us to jack the cow up with a block and tackle. We hung her by the hind legs and cut some veins to drain the blood. The vet opened up her belly and the organs spilled out onto a canvas tarp. Some of it, Miz fed to the hogs, the heart and brains and tongue, she put into a big tub for pickling. I got the feeling she'd done this before, especially the way she stripped off the hide and stretched it out for tanning. We left the cow hanging so the meat could age two-three days, you can't eat it right away, it's too tough; hanging makes it more tender. Two days later, the vet came back early with a couple of helpers, and we all started hacking and sawing. We were a week smoking the meat. We pickled some of it too, in great big jars. We didn't eat much of it ourselves though. It didn't taste very good. Like it was old and stale. Even when you put gravy on it. Miz said that was the effect of the dark.

Finally, on Friday, we wrapped and boxed everything we could. On Saturday, Miz and me packed as much as we could fit into the truck and she drove into town, where she traded that cow for hard goods, spices, and even some jars of fruit from somewhere up north. Some people would eat it, she said. Just not us.

Miz didn't take me with that day, she wanted me to stay behind, in case anybody came wandering by. Word was that some bright-landers had wandered through town recently and nobody was sure if they'd moved on yet. I hadn't seen them, but I'd heard about them at Meeting. They all wore long black capes, just dark enough to keep them from going mad, except maybe they were a little mad from all that time in the bright. And maybe they'd come through looking to see if there was anything worth stealing. Maybe they were out there now, just waiting on the other side of the dark. But I didn't think it was the brightlanders Miz was fearing. I think it was our own neigh-bors. Some of them were real hungry, even eating tree bark. Miz had a big pot of stew simmering on the stove for Sunday's Meeting. Maybe some of them folks wouldn't wait. So I stayed behind, sitting on the front porch, watching the chickens scratching through the re-maining patches of grass.

Moments like this, I watched the dark. Sometimes, if you watched it close enough, you could see it move. It looked like it was flowing real slow, like a river of slow time. Sometimes it wasn't all dark, some-times it was dark gray; that was mostly at night. The dark leaked. It couldn't hold all the light it sucked and some of it seeped back out. Just enough to make everything look like moonlight.

But the closer you got to the dark, the worse you felt, like it wasn't just sucking light, but life as well. Everything close to the dark looked bad, all dusty-dull and shabby, turning gray and old in the gloom. I tried to stay away from it, especially now that I knew how it worked. But there was something about it, something I couldn't explain. I always felt like it was pulling me into it. Miz called it dark sniffing. I had to watch myself. I wondered if someday I'd get so lost in some dream that I'd wander right into it, not even realizing what I was doing. That's what happened to the cow.

That's when the colored boy appeared.

First I smelled flowers. Yellow and pink flowers. Bright red flowers. I stood up, looking around, wondering where the flowers were. Then I saw him.

He stepped out of the dark at the bottom of the hill and started up the path to the house like he lived here. I saw him instantly. He stood out like a flash of the brightlands. Where everything else was gray, he was all the different colors a person could be. He glowed like he was lit from within. He was gold all over. His hair flashed in shades of red and blond; his skin shimmered like sunset. He was shining and naked. I'd never seen anybody so beautiful. He could have come from the far side of the sky. Wherever he'd come from, I wanted to go there. I wanted to glow too.

He came all the way up to the porch. He put one foot on the bottom step, then stopped. I knew who he was. "You Doey?"

He nodded. He held out a hand to me, like inviting me to dance. I was real tempted to take it, he was so beautiful. But I didn't. After a moment, he lowered his hand.

"Was that you I saw in the bright?"

He smiled, a dazzle of happiness. I'd never seen anything like that. It just made me hurt with longing all the more. He was insane, of course. He had to be. How could he not?

"Do you talk?" I asked.

He laughed. A gentle chuckle of sound, like a shared secret. "Yes, I talk. I also sing. I dance. I laugh. Do you?"

Shrug. "I dunno. Never tried. Never had much reason to try."

He stepped up one step. He reached out with his hand. I took a step back. He drew his hand back, then took another step up, this time onto the porch. And this time, when he extended his hand, I didn't move away. With outstretched fingers, he touched my shirt, my chest. Through the faded cotton, I felt a hot rush of feeling I couldn't explain. His eyes met mine. His eyes were green and blue and violet. Not the sad shabby colors of the faded flowers around the edges of the old gray house, but the glistening sparkle of the deep edge of the rainbow. His eyes were bright. Everything about him was bright. The touch of his fingers—it felt like he was pumping energy into me. I felt *alivened*. Was this the magic of the bright? Was this how people went crazy? I didn't want the moment to end. I wanted to fall helplessly into it, dissolving into a bath of color, just like Doey.

I reached up with my own hand, took his mine, held it, felt the warmth, both strong and soft at the same time, released it, reached across and touched his chest as he'd touched me. Placed my palm flat against his hot and glowing body. There was nothing I needed to say, there was everything I wanted to say. There was perfect understanding and a thousand thousand questions. I'd never known a moment like this. Never felt a hot surge of feeling like this. I thought I was going to faint. Or fly apart in pieces.

"Yes," he said, finally.

"Yes?"

"Yes, you know how to sing and dance and laugh. You just haven't had a place to do it."

My mouth was dry as dust. "Will you—can you take me there?"

He smiled and leaned forward. Close enough to kiss. "When you learn to glow."

"How do I—?"

He touched my lips with a golden finger, silencing my question.

"Hush," he whispered. "Not yet. Not yet."

And then he whirled and spun, a twirl of light and color. He leapt and danced and flew, arms outstretched, all the way down the hill and back into the wall of darkness that surrounded the house. And then he was gone. Leaving only the fading scent of color. The afternoon was dull and gray again. I felt tears on my cheeks. Both joy and despair at the same time.

I almost ran after him, almost. Something held me back. All the words, all the warnings, all the gloom that wrapped the world. He was right. I wasn't ready to let go. Not yet. Not yet. Oh, that bastard boy of color. How did he do that? How could he flirt and fly? How did he live? Where had he gone?

Sank down into a chair, an old wooden chair that creaked in pain as it accepted my weight. A faded cushion, hard and flat as cardboard. What mad thing had just happened here? Damn that Doey! I hated him, I loved him, I envied him, I feared what he was, and I wanted to be him more than anything.

I was comfortable here. Working for Miz. Working on the lines. I was comfortable, wrapped in dark. I didn't have to care. I didn't have to think. I only had to follow the rules. I could do that. Okay, I wasn't happy, but I wasn't unhappy either. I was comfortable and after being hungry and tired and cold and uncomfortable for so long, comfortable was a good place to be. It was enough. I didn't need happy. Happy didn't exist anyway. Certainly not here. And then the glowing boy stepped out of the dark and looked in my eyes and touched my heart and left me gasping with desperation. Because now that I knew what happy was, now that I knew it did exist, how could I ever be comfortable again anywhere?

Now that I knew what happy felt like, I also knew I didn't have any. Instead, now I knew what lonely felt like.

Did he know how cruel his words were? "Not yet. Not yet."

I felt so torn up inside I didn't know what I felt. I put my head into my hands and started sobbing, I don't know why. Cried for Ma, cried for me. Cried for the whole stupid everything. Who made up this stupid world anyway? Why did we have to put down all these walls of darkness? What was on the other side that everybody was so afraid of they wouldn't even talk about it? And why did I feel so awful?

After a while, I felt all hollow and empty. So I got up and went to the barn. Stood around for a bit, then finally started mucking out stalls. Not because I wanted to, but it was something to do. And if I didn't do it, Miz would have words, lots of words. I hated all her words. I just never knew it until now.

When Miz got back, she sniffed the air and looked at me sharply. "What happened here?" she asked.

"Nothing," I said.

"Don't lie to me, Michael. Something happened here. I can see it in your face. You're all hot and flushed. Your cheeks are red." She put a hand on my forehead. "You're burning up. You have a fever."

"It's nothing," I said. Maybe too loud.

She grabbed me by the arm and dragged me to the horse trough. "Take off your shirt," she demanded. I did so and she pushed me down to my knees, pushed me head first into the sour brown water. She picked up a horse brush and began scrubbing my back with it. I couldn't scream and I couldn't breathe and I was trying to do both at the same time. She yanked me up, gasping. Before I could stop myself, I called her all those words she'd made me promise never to say again. She didn't even hesitate, she just whacked me across the head with the heavy wooden brush, knocking me backward.

"You're still an evil old bitch! And beating me to death ain't gonna change that."

"You think I'm stupid?" Miz shouted. She was loud. "You think I don't see what you're turning into? You want to go out there and get colored? You want to glow? You want to turn into some kind of fairy dancer? You want to die in delirium? Why do you think we put up all the darklines? Because we like the dark? You think we like being cold and hungry and miserable all the time? No, we do it because we don't have any choice. We have to protect ourselves. All of us. Even you—you stupid city boy."

I didn't say what I was thinking. She made me feel angry. But what if she was right? Everything was all confused. If the dark was so good, why did it feel so bad. And if the bright was so bad, why did it feel so good? I pulled myself bitterly back to my feet. Already, I was trying to figure out how I could get away from here. I could probly get a loaf of bread out of the kitchen, maybe some vegetables, put them in an old potato sack or something. But where could I go? And how could I get there? Walk the roads? Maybe, but to where? And if anybody else came down the road, they'd see me for sure. No place to hide in the corridors. Follow the train tracks? Maybe. But where did they go? Just to another place like this. I didn't know. I needed a map or something. But there had to be someplace somewhere better than this. I shook the water out of my hair, brushed it back with my hand. My arm and shoulder hurt where she'd slammed me against the trough. My back hurt from the scrubbing of the brush. And my head was throbbing like a nightmare. I hurt all over. And I stank of the foul water. And I was cold. Evening was coming on, and the dark was expanding.

Out in the barn, wrapped in a blanket, shivering against the night, listening to the wind scrabbling against the old wood, all the voices argued back and forth. Evil old bitch. I don't care what she thinks. This is sick. Everything is sick. These people are dying. I don't want to die with them. They're all sick and dirty and dead inside. I don't want to be like this. But there's no way out. It's a trap. All the darklines, all the rules, all the walls everywhere.

And just what's out there on the other side of the lines anyway? What's so horrible that you can't look at it direct, can't see it without being eye-poisoned? Doey wasn't wearing any gloomies. He was naked like one of those angels in the old books. He was as beautiful as a girl with long flowing red hair, but he was stallion-cut like a prize. He was both at once. I'd never seen anyone or anything like that. How did he live out there? How did he see without being blinded? What did he say? Learn to dance. No. Learn to glow. How do you glow? How do you learn? All those questions, and nobody to ask. Nobody to trust.

Next morning was Meeting. I wasn't going to go, but Miz didn't take no arguments. She just told me to clean myself up, put on a clean shirt, and not go around smelling like a pig. But once we were in the truck, she did say one thing. She said, "I didn't want to hurt you yesterday, Michael. What I did, I had to do. I had to break the spell. You were all glassy. I had to dunk you in the water and scrub your back hard and smack you to put you in all that pain to pull you back from wherever it was you were drifting off to. I've seen that look before, saw it on Doey. Didn't act fast enough with him. He danced away one night. Ain't going to lose you too. I see you starting to glow, I'm going to beat you—not because I want to hurt you, but because hurting you is the only way to pull you out. You understand that, don't you?"

"Yes'm. Whatever."

We pulled up at Meeting early, but we wasn't the first ones there. Bunch of folks all clustered by their trucks, talking. They looked over as we drove up, and a couple of them walked over to talk to Miz. She glanced at me, then moved off a ways so I couldn't hear what they were all saying. I pretended like I didn't care anyway and wandered down to where the older kids were scratching in the dirt with sticks. J.D. was there, the kid with the broken tooth, the kid from town who'd first told me about Doey. Nobody had names out here, only initials. He stopped what he was doing, tossed his stick aside, and said, "You hear?"

"Hear what?"

" 'Bout the Trasks?"

"What about them?"

"They went out."

"Out where?"

"You stupid, city boy? Out."

"Oh. Out."

"Doc drove over to see if they was all right, if they had enough food. He had a couple spare bags of beans and rice. He got there, they was all gone. The whole family. Ever single one. Even the baby. And one of their fields was starting to glow. Big hole in the darklines—all snapped, like somebody cut 'em. Doc didn't have no gloomies. He got out of there fast. Scared-like. That's what I heard, anyway. They're going to send out a hunting party, I bet. Go shoot some bright-eyes. They're going to need every gun in town. You know how to shoot, city boy?"

"I can shoot," I said.

"Then you'll get to go, for sure. They won't let me go. I already asked. They said I was too small. That's a damn lie. They just ain't forgiven my pa for losin' a gun last hunt. They say he stole it. But he din't. The brighties did. Turned it into something weird, I bet."

"How would you know?"

"I know lotsa stuff. More than you."

"Yeah? You think so?"

"I know so."

"Yeah? How do you know anything? You ever been out there?"

He shook his head. "Not gonna say what I know."

I wanted to tell him about the bright-eyed boy. I wanted to ask him if he'd ever seen the naked colors. But something told me that probly wasn't a good idea. So I just shrugged. Whatever. Drop it. Turned away, back to the others. More folks was arriving now. I hiked up the hill to where Tallow was standing, waited behind him for a bit until no one else was talking. He finally noticed me. "You want something?"

"You going hunting?"

"You got a gun?"

"Miz does, I think."

He scratched his neck thoughtfully. "Probly not a good idea. You being a city boy. And we're going out deep. Miz won't like that. But maybe you can hold the wire at the safe end. Might could use you that way. You just don't say nothing right now. You talkin' about it just makes a bad idea seem worse."

Then Miz came over with Doc. He looked at me, took my chin in his hand, turned my head side to side. Looked into my eyes. Put a hand on my forehead. Asked me to stand on one foot, put my arms out, and shut my eyes tight. Stuff like that. Turned to Miz. "He looks all right to me. You probly got to him in time. But if you want me to wrap him in darkline for a bit, suck some of the brightness out of him, bring him by one day, and we'll give him a bit of treatment."

"I'll do that, thanks," she said. "You be in tomorrow?"

"Better wait till the end of the week," he said. "It's going to be a busy few days. Let's get this Trask business taken care of first. I think this lad will be fine for the moment."

Eventually, we all got inside and got settled, but nobody was thinking about Meeting. Everybody was still whispering. It was like the room was full of bluebottle flies. The mayor said that he was sorry about the bad news, everybody had probly heard it anyway, but he had to officially confirm it. The darklines had broken by the Trask farm and it looked as if the Trasks had been enchanted. And yes, there would be a committee meeting to decide what to do next. Volunteers should make themselves known to the usual folks.

After that, there wasn't much else to say, because nobody was listening anyway, so we broke up early. Folks didn't eat much, they was mostly too upset. The whole family was gone, even the baby. Not even bodies left for a proper funeral. Lots of talk floated around. Somebody was going to have to get out there and take care of the livestock. Miz said she could take the cows and the chickens if nobody else needed them, but she didn't want no more pigs right now. They ate too much. A couple of the other folks spoke up, laying claim to tools or dishes or furniture. Blankets and quilts. Pots and pans. A little of this and some of that. Eventually, it was all sorted out, who was going to go out and pick stuff up. Tallow opened his truck and passed out gloomies to the folks who were going to need them.

Miz collected goggles and masks for us and some capes too, shiny on one side, black on the other. And gloves, just in case. We didn't even head home, just straight out through town and off around the hill to the Trask place. I don't know how Miz knew the way. All the corridors looked the same to me, just narrow twisty roads through the dark. But I tried to pay attention anyway, just in case. Miz kept talking, the whole trip. She was angry about everything. "Should never have let the Trasks settle so far out, way out on the borders with nothing between them and the bright. Damn fool stupid idea from the start. And now a whole family is lost. And the farm. And it's not like we have families or farms to spare. Lord knows what shape the poor animals are in. Put your goggles and mask on, boy. We're almost there. And you put that cape and gloves on before you get out of the car, you hear?"

She pulled up short of the farm and pulled on her own cape and goggles and gloves and breathing mask. She pushed the goggles up on her forehead and inched the truck forward, a little bit at a time. I pushed my gloomies up just enough to see under the frames. We came around the last curve and there was the brightness leaking in around the edges of the broken dark. We both pulled our goggles down at the same time. "I told you to keep those things on. You're susceptible. You can't take any more chances."

We pulled up in front of the barn. It was old and saggy. It leaned to one side and it looked like it was ready to collapse, even worse than Miz's barn. Miz looked off toward the bright before getting out of the truck. Half the darkline was down, the dark just faded off into filigree wisps. Beyond, the fields glowed harsh and stark in our gloomies. Without the goggles, they would have been impossible to look at.

Miz made a clucking sound of disapproval. I followed her into the barn. There were three cows tethered, all of them lowing uncomfortably. Miz told me to load up the sacks of feed, while she set about milking the cows. Afterward, I loaded the cans into the truck. Then she blindfolded the cows and led them out of the barn, tying their tethers to the back of the truck. Then she went and found a stack of empty crates and we began collecting the chickens. Some of them were clucking quietly in the barn, those we crated; but others were lying stunned on the ground outside. A few were wandering around dazed. Those she picked up and swiftly broke their necks.

"Can't they be saved?" I asked.

Miz shook her head. "Too dangerous. Too much bright in 'em. This is better. Safer." There were a few little chicks too, all safe in the incubator. She put these in a crate, dropped a canvas over it, and I loaded the crate into the back of the pickup. We walked around the barn then, looking to see what else we could find. The two pigs in the back were both gone. Miz shook her head at that. "Probly ran into the bright. Pigs are like that," she said.

Then we saw it. The fourth cow. It was staggering, all glassy-eyed and confused. It looked bright—not as bright as the brightland, but brighter than it should be. Miz said one of those words I'm not supposed to. She went to the truck and pulled out her shotgun from the back window.

"Don't you want to walk it into the barn?"

"What for?"

"That's a lot of meat—"

"Nobody's going to eat this beef. It's sick. You want to get sick too?"

"Can't you have Doc wrap it in darkline and drain the bright out of it?"

"You can't drain it. Draining takes the flavor out. And you can't let people eat meat that's been brightened either. That's even worse. No, this cow is gone." She lifted the shotgun, moved closer, then moved closer again, until the barrel was almost touching the cow's skull. I didn't want to see it, but I couldn't look away either. The rifle flashed. The cow dropped to the ground with a thud. She stepped closer and fired the second barrel. Just to be sure.

Miz checked the house then. She wouldn't let me go in, but she came out carrying a pillow case full of spices and other things from the kitchen. Even a small jar of honey, I found out later. That was a surprise. The Trasks weren't supposed to be doing that well.

Back in the truck, barely inching along the road, not moving faster than the three tethered cows could follow, Miz started talking again. She looked old. Older than the first day. And tired too. Like she'd been drained a few times. "This isn't right," she said. "Letting cows and pigs and chickens and corn go bad like that. And all those vegetables. Nobody should have been out this far, with only one line of dark between them and that—that brightmare. Now look what it's gone and done. A family gone, a cow gone. Two pigs running loose in the bright. All those chickens. All that food. What a waste. What a waste."

It took most of the day to bring the cows in. It was a long drive and we couldn't go very fast. But we were back before dusk settled in. I was glad of that. I didn't like being out in the dark. Not any kind of dark at all.

I slept badly. Tossed and turned in the straw all night. Finally, just before dawn, I got up and walked out of the barn. I tried to look up at the stars. Once in a while, you can still see them, some of them, but not tonight. Everything was black. Just dim shapes of black against blacker. I thought about lighting a lantern, but I didn't want to wake Miz, so I just stood barefoot and listened. Nothing much to hear. Just wind. A lonely cricket. Not a lot of insects anymore. I heard that one in town. That was the real reason everything was dying. The insects couldn't get through the darklines. No bees, no ants, no bugs, no spiders, nothing.

Not even a glimmer of bright from over the hill. Sometimes you can see it, mostly its reflection off the clouds. But not tonight.

Finally, I went back into the barn, back to my straw. Pulled my blanket around me and just sat with my arms wrapped around my knees, rocking softly. I used to do that when I was little. I don't remember much from when I was little, we moved around so much. But I remember I spent a lot of time sitting in the dark and rocking. Sometimes Mom would come and sit with me, wrapping her arms around me, and we'd sit as quiet as we could, not making any noises, so they wouldn't find us.

Thought about what I'd seen. Everything. All the bright leaking over into the fields. Miz didn't know, but while she was milking the cows, I'd lifted up the edge of my gloomies and snuck a quick peek—not at the bright directly, but at the fields it was just creeping into. That didn't hurt so much. I could see the colors, all the dazzling colors, everything at once—the rustling golden corn in the field, the crisp green stalks so clear it was like they cut the air, the rich dark soil like a warm bed, even the sky above glowed blue. I'd never even known such colors were possible. I wanted to see more. But then, I heard a noise behind me and just as quick-like I pushed the goggles back down over my eyes. I didn't want to get caught. Not by Miz. Because Miz wanted to take me to Doc. And wrap me in darkline. And drain the bright out of me. Like the beef. Drained beef. "You ever taste drained beef? You won't like it." Maybe that's what's wrong with these people. They've all been drained.

But what if Miz hadn't made a noise right then? Would I have kept looking until it was too late, until I was sucked away into the brightland too? I wondered what that might feel like—to dance naked in the stars. To whirl and dazzle and laugh. Madness, yes. But even madness looked better than this life. Miz wanted to wrap me in dark and make me just like everybody else. My stomach rumbled and I wondered what people ate in the brightlands. Magic corn? Enchanted beans? I didn't know. Nobody knew. Anybody who knew hadn't come back to tell. Maybe they was all dead, lying bright and starved? Maybe the bright pigs was eating them. Maybe this and maybe that and maybe some of the other. Nobody knew. Or if they did, they wasn't saying.

Finally, I just rolled over, curled up and tried to sleep. Thinking about stuff doesn't do any good. It doesn't work. It just makes my head hurt. Enough. Enough already. I wrapped myself tight in my blanket and eventually shivered myself to sleep.

For the next couple days, Miz didn't say anything more about getting me darklined, but I knew she was still set on the idea. She kept giving me these looks. But maybe she also felt bad about having to do it, because she made some honey-cornbread and cut me an extra thick slab with lots of butter. Or maybe she just felt I had to have my strength up so I could survive being drained. She didn't say. And I didn't ask. I was starting to think about running again. We still had the gloomies and the capes in the truck. Maybe if I could find my way to the Trask farm, I could go outside the darklines and cross the bright to some other place. Supposedly, the town council had some maps somewhere, but nobody was allowed to see them.

Tuesday evening, Tallow came driving up unexpectedly. He talked with Miz a bit, then told me to get into the truck. Tomorrow morning, we were going out to fix the darkline at the Trask farm. And maybe do a bit of hunting too. Miz sniffed unhappily. I could see she disapproved. She didn't trust any of this. She came right out and said it. "That boy's got too much bright in him. He ain't been drained. If you don't tie him down good, you know he'll just get sucked into the colors. I swear, you lose him and I'll skin you bad, Tallow, I will."

"Nah, you'll just get another one off the next train. Like you always do." Tallow grinned back.

Miz didn't think that was funny. She sniffed again in that funny way she had. "Oh, hell. Wait a minute." She went to her own truck and pulled the rifle down out of the back window, and the box of shells next to it. She cracked it open and popped the two shells out, dropping them into the box. She walked back over, and motioned me to open my door. She handed me the shotgun and the box of shells. "Don't you load this thing unless you need it. And you bring it back clean, y'hear? Tallow, you teach him how to use it. It's on your head now."

Tallow grunted and climbed into the truck. He pulled his door shut and put the engine into gear. We rolled down the hill and into the corridor of twisted dark. Tallow laughed. "Miz is good folks, but some folks say she's been drained one too many times."

I thought about that. It kind of made sense. "You ever been drained?" I asked.

"Most folks around here have. For their own good."

"Oh," I said.

"It doesn't really hurt. It just makes you queasy, a little. Like having the runs, sort of. After a couple days, the feeling goes away. And the bright can't get to you as easy."

"Did the bright ever get to you? I mean, before you were drained?"

Tallow's face tightened. "Y'know, boy. This ain't really anything you want to talk about. You don't want to go asking too many questions. Folks'll start talkin'."

"Just curious, that's all."

"Yep, that's all. That's what they all said. Just curious. You don't want to get too curious about the bright. You want to stay away from it. That's why we smacked you with it the first day on the lines—so's you'll know. You've seen all you need to see. Right?" When I didn't answer, he repeated himself. *"Right?"*

I shrugged. "Whatever."

Tallow stopped the truck with a screech. I jerked forward with the suddenness of the stop. He turned to me and grabbed my shoulder hard. "Listen up, city boy. You don't know what you're dealing with here. That ain't a question. It's the truth. You don't know shit. So when I tell you how it is, I'm not just running my mouth 'cause I like hearing my jaw flap. I'm telling you what you need to know so you don't get sucked away like all the others. We used to be three times as many people and ten times as much livestock and crops. Where do you think all those folks went? All those animals? They didn't listen and they didn't take care and now they're gone. You want to be gone too? Just keep asking questions. You ask too many questions, we'll open the dark and toss you out in the bright ourselves. This is for your own good, city boy. If you want to live, you better learn to listen."

"I thought you liked me," I said. I didn't know why I said that.

"This ain't about liking. Even if I didn't like you, I wouldn't want to see you turn into one of them damn fairy dancers."

"You've seen them?"

Tallow didn't answer. He let go of my shoulder and turned away and put the truck back into gear. I rubbed where he'd grabbed me so hard.

"You didn't answer my question."

"That's right. I didn't." Tallow didn't say anything else for the rest of the drive. That left me with lots of time to think about all the things he wasn't saying. I got the feeling he knew more than it was safe for anyone to know. And maybe he didn't want anyone else to know how much he knew. But it was only a feeling and he'd made it real clear that he wasn't going to answer any more questions of any kind. I felt bad about that. Because maybe if he'd said he'd seen a fairy dancer, I could tell him I'd seen one too. And maybe then we'd each have someone we could trust enough to talk about it. Except I didn't dare tell him, because he might tell someone else; and he couldn't risk saying anything to me either, because I was just another stupid city boy.

"We going out tonight?"

"Tomorrow. Early morning. But I don't have time to drive out and pick you up then, so you'll sleep behind the feed store tonight with some of the other boys. You keep your hands to yourself, you keep your mouth shut, and you don't ask any questions. I'll keep Miz's shotgun in my truck. No sense in having you shoot yourself in the foot, or anybody else either."

Behind the feedstore, it was just a big empty space under a sagging roof. A few bags of feed, here and there, just enough to make a rough bed. It wasn't much, but it was better than straw. Four or five others talking together, nothing important. I recognized two of them, but J.D. was the only one whose name I knew. They glanced at me, but didn't say anything. Just another city boy, using up space, eating up food. I grabbed a stretch of canvas to use as a blanket and made myself comfortable off in a corner, away from the others.

They had a kerosene lamp, but that was all. The light pretended to warmth, but the night was just as cold here as anywhere else.

After a while, J.D. wandered over, wrapped in a blanket. "Hey, city boy. Can I sleep by you?"

Shrugged. Not yes, not no. J.D. pushed a couple of feed bags into position and stretched out on top of them. "You know something you're not saying." It wasn't a question.

I didn't answer.

"If you tell me what you know, I'll tell you what I know."

I rolled over on my side, turned away from him. I trusted him less than anybody. J.D. like to talk, liked to pretend he knew stuff. Safest not to tell him anything.

"Aw, c'mon—"

"Fine. Okay. You go first."

"No, you," he insisted.

"Forget it then." I settled myself again.

Silence for a bit. Just enough time for me to figure out what was going on. They'd sent J.D. over to find out what I knew, if I'd ever seen anything.

A minute more and I figured out the rest of it. It didn't matter what I said. J.D. was going to make something up for me.

"Okay," he said. "I'll tell you. Folks keep seein' Doey. Miz's other boy. He's a fairy dancer now. We're goin' out to find him. Hunt him down like a blind pig. That's what my maw says—"

I sat up and looked at him. "J.D. Go away. Get away from me. You got devil-talk inside you and I don't want to hear it. Get away from me or I'll punch you." I said it loud enough for the others to hear. That was enough. J.D. gathered up his blanket and went scuttling back to the others.

He hadn't told me anything I didn't know already. It wasn't that hard to figure out. Even the rest of it, the part he hadn't said. Not just Doey, but the Trask family too, if they were still alive. Anyone and anything in the brightlands. Didn't need to be smart to figure that out. Just scared and angry and tightened up inside.

But something about this didn't feel right. Going out and shooting people. Even if they were all colored. No matter how little you felt inside. Just fix the darklines, that's all. Put up more lines if you have to. But going out into the bright. That didn't sound like a good idea. Not for this reason, not for any reason. Not unless you were planning to never come back. I just wish I knew more about what was out there. But if anybody around here knew, they weren't saying, and it sure wasn't safe to ask.

Next thing I knew, Tallow was kicking me awake. "Time to go, city boy. Move your ass." I rolled off the sack of feed onto the hard black dirt. It looked as dark in here as it was out there, but Tallow was waving a lantern, and that outlined everything in brown gloom. Two other men were kicking the rest of the boys awake. I didn't see J.D. anywhere.

I pulled myself to my feet, scratching and aching and hurting all over. My stomach hurt the worst. "Is there anything to eat?" Nobody answered.

I followed them all around the building to the front, where six or seven trucks had pulled up. Somebody had set up a table with a big plate of hard biscuits and even some hot coffee, seven or eight men just lining up. I fell in line behind them, then got pushed even further back when three more arrived. "Wait your turn, city boy. Let the men eat first." Pigs.

Bitter coffee and a couple of biscuits later, they formed up teams. I recognized most of the men from the darkline team, plus a few folks from Meeting. And a couple of the big stocky women too. Some of them had guns. This wasn't any darkline crew.

After a bit of discussion, people figuring out who was going to ride with who, that kind of stuff, Tallow pointed me toward one of the trucks, and I climbed into the back with two other boys. I said hello, but they ignored me. After a few last-minute instructions, the trucks all headed out toward the Trask place. The headlights of the ones following us made an ominous line snaking through the dark.

We couldn't drive very fast, it wasn't safe, so by the time we arrived, the sky was just starting to show an edge of gray—or maybe it was the glow off the distant brightness. I couldn't be sure, and I wasn't going to ask. We stopped down the hill from the Trask place and safely behind the bend in the road, so no one would accidentally get a glimpse of brightness before they got their goggles on.

We bumbled around in the gloom for a while, while the Sheriff and a couple of others organized everybody into teams. I was pushed over to stand with Tallow. He was carrying Miz's gun as well as his own, but he made no move to give it to me. I wasn't sure why I was even here, nobody was talking to me.

Finally, everything was sorted out and we all put on our shiny capes and our gloomies and our breathing masks and we started off. We trudged up the last of the road, around the bend of the corridor of dark, and finally up the hill to where the ground was starting to glow. And beyond that, we could see where the glare was leaking into the air from the brightlands. Kind of like the dazzle of light from an open refrigerator in a midnight kitchen.

Two of the men rolled a cart with three huge spools of darkwire on it. For some reason, everybody kept close to the cart. Even though the wire wasn't powered, folks still acted like they were safer staying close to it. Once we got to the top of the hill, I looked around for the dead cow, but where I thought it should be, I saw only a hump, covered with little white flowers. We all waited while the Sheriff and his deputies looked out across the brightland through special binoculars. They whispered to themselves for a bit, pointing and nodded and finally agreeing. After some more conferences, the guys with the cart installed one end of the wire to a convenient post; they hooked up a terminator box to it, there was another terminator connected to the end of the wire inside the big drum.

Then, when that was done, we all headed out into the bright, with the cart leading and the men unspooling the wire as they went. We didn't install any posts, we weren't putting up a darkline. This was only a safety line. All you had to do was follow it back. You could do it with your eyes closed, if you had to. I hoped I wouldn't have to.

Just the little bit of leakage around the edge of my goggles was painful.

Nobody told me where we were headed, so I just followed Tallow. At least, I thought it was Tallow. In the harsh glare, with all of us caped and goggled, everybody looked alike, all different shades of gray and white and whiter. To keep from stumbling, I spent most of the time watching the ground directly in front of me, following in the footsteps of the man I thought was Tallow. We hiked into the brightness where the ground turned white like salt—that's what it looked like through the gloomies; it must have been glittering gold without them.

We hiked through scorched fields, abandoned to the bright. An old dirt road cut straight through, but it was already starting to get overgrown. On either side, twisted trees groped in the glare. They looked like they were alive, their limbs slowly moving, waving, even reaching. We kept clear of them. And the bushes too—they looked like they were all burning. They were so bright, even the gloomies couldn't keep out all the color. They looked burnished with a hint of red and gold, like they were all wrapped in shivering flame. Everywhere else, I saw stalks of something that might have been corn once, but was something else now; they looked like torches.

None of this made much sense to me. How was anybody going to hunt anything in a place like this? Ten feet away, everything blurred out in yellow and white. It was like fog on fire. And nobody was saying much either. If they knew what they were doing, they weren't telling.

Finally, someone in front of me stopped and pointed. A couple of others stopped, so I did too. At first, I couldn't see what they were looking at, but finally I made it out, way out there, way beyond the place where the road just dazzled out, there was a tall old house, an outline of a house, a glimmering hint of a house. I guessed that was where we were heading, I tried to make it out clearer—but then somebody punched me in the back and growled, "Keep moving, bait." So I pushed on.

It was hot out here. Once, I tried looking off to the east, tried to see the Sun, the source of all this brightness, but the gloomies just went black. They overloaded and shut down. And I had to walk blind for a few moments until they reset themselves.

Eventually, we reached the house. It was in a field of grass so bright that the goggles showed it black, they didn't even try to resolve it. The house itself looked like it was made out of glass. The walls had gone glistening and transparent, and all we could see clearly was just the structural outlines, the edges and corners. It looked like it had been here forever, standing tall and stately, with porches and gables and even a widow's walk around the front and sides. And a tall cupola. It was almost a castle. Even Miz's house wasn't this big.

The two men with the cart cut the wire and tied one end of it to one of the porch posts. Once they did that everybody felt safer. A few folks started to go up onto the porch, but Sheriff stopped them, said the house was off-limits to everybody. Except the lure.

Then everybody busied themselves, separating into three teams. Each team had a cart and a roll of wire. Each team tied one end of their wire to the porch, connected a terminator, then headed out a bit and waited. One team was pointed straight out south, the other two east and west.

Tallow was on the western team, but when I went to follow, he grabbed me by the arm and walked me back to the house. "No, your job is to wait here and make sure nothing happens to the wires."

"By myself?"

"Nothing's going to happen. You're perfectly safe. You have four active darkwires terminating here."

"Then why do you need me to stay here? I thought I was going with you."

"I promised Miz."

"Then give me the gun."

"You won't need it."

"Then why'd she give it?"

"Stop asking so many questions. Go sit up on the porch. You'll be able to see farther."

"Can't see anything in this bright. Neither can you. And why'd he call me 'bait?' I'm the lure, aren't I?"

Tallow grabbed my shoulder. Hard. Just like last time. "Listen to me, city boy. If we take you out there, you'll get sucked away so fast you won't have time to scream for help. You stay here because I say you stay here. And if you want to argue about it, we can tie you down with darkline. And that won't be just an hour of draining, it could be a day or two or forever. You want that?"

I didn't answer. Not right away. "You say nothing will happen?"

"Nothing will happen."

"You sure?"

"Get up on the porch. Oh, wait—" He fumbled under his cape, passed me a sack. "Here's some more biscuits and a bottle of water. In case you get hungry."

"How long are you going to be out there?"

"As long as it takes." And then, he added, "Probly back by after-noon, certainly before nightfall. We don't want to spend the night out here, that's for sure; this place glows in the dark. You just stay awake and make sure those wires stay tied." He started to turn away, then turned back. "You'll be all right."

And then he was gone. All of them were gone. They hiked out into the bright and faded away in the distance like wavering shadows.

Tallow said I could go up on the porch, but I wasn't sure it was safe. The Sheriff hadn't let anybody else go up there. But maybe that was just because he didn't want anything disturbed. What the hell. I put one foot on the glassy first step. It held. Another foot on the next step. It held too. One more step and I was on the porch. It felt yellow everywhere. Dusty yellow. And it smelled of sweet sharp lemons. Even through the mask. And honey. And honeysuckle. And green melons. It was wonderfully delicious. Could the men out in the fields smell it too? What kept them from ripping off their masks and rolling around in the delicious air?

And the sounds—now that I wasn't surrounded by hulking men with their three-day sweaty stinks, the underfoot crunching of dirty boots, the lumbering hooves of upright beasts, the clatter of machinery and the stink of gun oil—now that all of that was gone, I could hear the tinkling music of translucent leaves, rustling in the delicate touch of the breeze. The wind sang like a distant chorus, very faint and far away. Silvery insects rattled and buzzed. And now, much nearer, something soft and small kept calling, *"Hoo-hooo, hoo-hoooo."* I wanted to go looking for it, whatever it was—bird or cricket or owl, I didn't know, but it sounded like the voice at the edge of the world, but so close by now that I wanted to find it, wanted to peer over the edge and see what was there on the other side. It felt like it was just around the corner.

This probly wasn't a good idea, thinking like this. I wondered if I would be safer inside the house? Maybe inside, I'd be out of the wind and away from all the flavors sweeping across the fields. Cinnamon and musk and jasmine. How did I even know all those different scents?

The doorknob glittered like diamond. I turned it and the door swung open. Inside, the house was silent, still, and empty. No furniture here, only an empty shell, a suggestion of a life once lived, exploded outward into solar dazzle and flare. The windows glowed with the creeping brightness of the world outside. The light felt muted here. I wondered if it would be safe to take off my clothes and dance in here.

I wandered from room to room, touching each wooden or metal or glass surface. The doors, the walls, the glass of the mirrors. Everything tingled. My fingers caressed. I didn't remember taking off my gloves. I wasn't even sure where I'd left them. This wasn't good. I shouldn't be doing this. All the voices in my head were screaming. Run away, now! Grab the wire and head back into the dark. Don't get sucked away. But all the songs were singing even louder. The music whirled and roared. Come dance aloft, be free. Be clear. I cowered shivering under my cape. Eyes clenched shut against the fiery noise.

The smells of sweet apricots and cream and gently scented candles. Overwhelmed, I held myself and counted, one and two and three and breathe and one and two and three and breathe—

No. No. I wouldn't give in. Not going to get sucked away. Never. Ever. Didn't come this far to be a golden bird fairy dancer. All the walls are here for a reason. The carefully constructed dark, the comfortable black essence of nothing at all.

Upstairs, the house is wide open. Tall windows with billowing white drapes, open to the balcony surrounding the house. Outside, the view went on forever. So bright below, so clear up here. Out to the horizon, the sparkling fields, the waves of rippling air, the colors sparkling and dancing. If I take off my cape, I can feel it like the comforting radiance of the refiner. I stand, arms outstretched to feel the heat, the delicious soul-filling heat. It soaks into my flesh, heals my bones, warms my spirit. I giggle at the wash of sensation. I can feel myself glowing.

In the cupola, I twirl alone. Naked and free. Finally warm, and finally here. The frozen winter of my past retreats before the blasting Sun. I thaw and come alive. Joyously alive. I laugh with silly pleasure. I am enchanted. The delight of heat.

Am I ready to see? Can I take off the goggles?

Here on the fenced roof of the cupola, the highest part of the house, I can see the world as far as the darklands, the carefully drawn boundaries of exclusion, every tiny little line etched into the face of the land like the wrinkles of time. The gloom of fear.

In the other direction, out toward the east, the south, the west, the land sparkles and shimmers. It dances with light and aliveness. Why would anyone try to hide from all this laughter?

I peeked under the glasses. It wasn't pain I felt, it was color, bright color, brightness overwhelming. It wasn't pain at all, just the sudden shock of coming alive after being dead so long. An awakening from the grave of gloom.

Lift the glasses slowly. Eyes ready to clench. At first, the dazzle startles. A splash of intensity. Hold my hand in front of my eyes—I can see through my fingers—I am translucent. Pink and gold and glistening. I have taken on the colors of the world. The crimson of my blood gives my skin a rosy blush. The blue of my veins resonates. I am a roseate glow of violet and vermilion. I lower my hand, and all the rest of the colors of the world flood in. All the smells and sensations. All the wonderful noises. All the heat and the light and the delicious flood of everything roiling together in a cascading symphony of being.

As I focus, I see . . . them. They've been there all along. Waiting for me. I just couldn't see them until now. Laugh and wave in radiant delight. They recognize me as one of them now. The dancing one is Doey. The others, also dancing, used to be the Trasks. I can hear the children singing.

And then, without passing through the intervening space, I am down among them, laughing with them. A moment of pause. Doey and I, face to face. Can I dance with you now? What a silly question. We're already dancing.

There are men with guns, hunting you. Hunting us. I wave toward the horizon. Doey laughs. He holds up the ends of the darkwires. The terminator boxes have been removed. The wires are dead—no, not dead, coming alive, infusing with clarity. Even metal can be bright.

Doey sparkles. Laugh with me and we'll dance the ends of these wires out to the distant south, out into the solar dazzle. Anyone who follows these lines will end up enchanted in the luminous day. The men will either dance or die. Whatever they choose. Doey twirls and passes out the tingling wires. I join him singing.

A Piece of Flesh

ADAM STEMPLE

❖

The world of Faerie is not necessarily full of sweet fluttery winged beauties or long-limbed, handsome, pale-faced elves. Look at the old fairy tales and you will find them packed with bloody-minded characters, amoral and nasty. Humans are simply there to be used, abused, or toyed with. Stemple is not afraid to go there in his story "A Piece of Flesh," which looks straight in the face of faerie horror.

If you like this story, you could try Dahlov Ipcar's novel about a new mother taken away into faerie, A Dark Horn Blowing, *or Terri Windling and Ellen Datlow's anthology* The Green Man.

I was not looking forward to another addition to our already large family. And I let my newly pregnant mother know it.

"What are we? Peasant farmers in the Middle Ages?" I asked. "Do we need a dozen children to work the fields?"

"A dozen?" my mother replied. "Vee, be reasonable. There are only four of you." She ticked them off on her fingers. "You, George, William, and little Charles. And baby here," she patted her stomach as she spoke. She wasn't showing. Yet. "Baby here makes five."

"Sure, five now. But when will it stop?" I had been perfectly happy as an only child. For the first six years of my life I had been a pampered princess. And then, as if rubber-stamped, my three younger brothers popped out, one after another, each almost exactly a year apart. They were loud, obnoxious, and dirty, and they soon had the run of the place. There was little I could do about it: I was older and smarter, but I was badly outnumbered.

And then, completely ruining my fourteenth birthday party, I got the news that there would soon be one more little monster to make my life even more miserable.

"And I suppose you'll want me to help you take care of the new baby?" I asked.

"Want you to help? Victoria Ann, I *expect* you to help is more like it."

I stomped off to my room in a snit and locked the door behind me. I moped the rest of the day away and let my birthday party dwindle and die without me. My parents could make whatever excuses they wanted to the guests. I didn't care. I was doomed to a life of diaper changing and babysitting until I was well out of college.

Maybe the baby won't be born, I thought. *Maybe there will be a terrible accident—a miscarriage or a car accident or something.*

That night, and for many after it, I lay awake thinking up scenarios where the pregnancy was averted or the baby disappeared. But try as I might I couldn't convince myself that Mom could ever recover from such a blow. She loved all of us so much.

I'll have to try something new then. Maybe if she knew she had other options . . .

On the first day of Mom's second trimester, I came home late from school.

"Where have you been, Vee?" asked my mother. She didn't sound angry, just tired.

"Jeanine is failing chemistry. I stayed after in lab helping her," I lied.

"Try to call next time."

"Mom, I'm fifteen minutes late! Relax!" I scampered upstairs before she could respond. I had work to do.

I slammed my bedroom door without going in. Instead, I tiptoed down the hall to my parents' bedroom. I reached under my shirt and pulled out the sheaf of adoption agency applications I had gathered after school when I was supposed to be studying with Jeanine. I stuck a few on Mom's nightstand and hid a few more in her dresser drawers. In case she missed those completely, I stuck one right on her pillow.

It wasn't subtle, but I was running out of time.

At breakfast the next morning, I waited for some comment on the gifts I had left her.

Nothing. It was a typical breakfast, light on conversation and heavy on good-natured brawling between my three brothers. When my parents spoke to me it was only to ask, "Pass the toast, please," or "More eggs, Vee?"

I went to school and spent the day wondering what had happened. *Had they found the pamphlets? Had they read them?* There was still no mention of adoption when I got home. The subject wasn't brought up at dinner or when I left for swimming at Allie's house or when I returned just before dark, wet and tired. I went to bed confused.

Everything became clear when I saw what had been left on my pillow: a four-color brochure for a very private, very strict boarding school hundreds of miles from New Dresden.

Message received.

The decision to have a child had been made, and I could either live with it or . . . actually, there was no "or." I wasn't going to boarding school, so I was just going to have to live with it. No more was said about either the adoption applications or the school brochure for the rest of the pregnancy.

❖

I woke in the pitch black one night and lay awake listening to the murmur of the television from downstairs. Mom was in her ninth month and shooting pain in her lower back woke her up every morning at three AM. She had taken to sitting in front of the tube for an hour or so with an ice pack tucked behind her before getting back into bed.

I thought about how helpless she had become and imagined how much help she would need with four children (and one young woman) to take care of. I began to think hard about children in general and my little brothers in particular. I listened to her shut off the

TV, plod up the stairs, and struggle into bed. Still, I stayed awake. Thinking.

When the sun finally shone in my window hours later, I had come to a conclusion: despite their faults (and there were many!), I did love each and every one of my little brothers.

I supposed I could love one more.

I snuck downstairs and made breakfast before my mother got up: eggs, toast, sausage, and a tomato. I put it all on a tray and brought it to her in bed.

"Mom," I announced as she came blearily awake, "I'll help you with the new baby."

"In exchange for what?" She sounded doubtful of my sincerity.

"Nothing." I said. She looked like she couldn't decide whether a snort of disbelief or a heartfelt thank you was in order. "No really, Mom. I thought about it for a long time last night. You're going to need someone to help around the house. The boys are too young and Dad is . . . well . . . Dad." She nodded and bit off the corner of her toast. "That leaves me. And I love you and Dad and all my brothers and I will love the new baby as well." I got the last part out in a rush because Mom was tearing up.

"C'mere, Vee!" she said and I hugged her over her breakfast tray, the lone tomato exploding into my shirt. We cried and then laughed at my ruined shirt and then cried some more.

❖

Two weeks later, my littlest brother was born. Mom and Dad let me hold him first. I cradled him in my arms and looked into his watery blue eyes. My eyes were blurry with tears as well. I was thinking about all the terrible scenarios I had devised for him, and now I saw his little Winston Churchill face on each of those babies in my mind. I couldn't believe I had ever had all those horrid thoughts and I swore to make it up to him.

I am your second mother, I mouthed silently to him. *I will love you and protect you all the days of your life.*

Mom and Dad named him Victor, after me, and we all hugged and cried on the hospital bed until they came and took little Victor away to the nursery.

One week after Victor was born I started fall semester. School was held a quarter mile from my home in a squat building that was big enough to house twice the number of students who used it. I guess New Dresden, Wisconsin, didn't get quite the population explosion it thought it was going to when the school was built.

Nestled in a river valley inhabited mostly by Norwegians and Swedes, the immigrants who settled New Dresden had managed to carve out an almost entirely German enclave that stands to this day. Roll call at school sounded like a list of beers—Schmidt? Here! Grolsch? Here!—and lederhosen and polkas figured heavily into the community-led summer activities. There were a few non-German families in town but for the most part they kept quiet about it.

Not mine though.

My family was English. Despite the fact that our last family member to actually stand on British soil did so in the nineteenth century, and probably in direct response to the overall German-ness of the town, my family was aggressively, overbearingly, painstakingly English. We drank tea and ate mince pies. We threw big parties for the Queen's birthday and Guy Fawkes Day. On a pole in the front lawn hung a gigantic Union Jack and smaller ones adorned the bumper stickers of both family cars.

And we conveniently forgot that the Hanoverians, who have ruled England since 1714 were, originally, German.

The local school, like many small-town schools, had only enough money for one language class. Unlike the others, which usually chose French or Spanish, New Dresden High, of course, chose German. I had been forced to take German for three years now but, in keeping with family tradition, I had managed to learn only *"Ich schreibe mit einem gelben bleistift."* ("I write with a yellow pencil.") I'd also picked up a few phrases accidentally from *Nick at Nite* reruns of *Hogan's Heroes* (*"Nein, nein puddin' head!"* and *"Schnell! Schnell!"* for instance).

What bothered me was that Mrs. Arnim—whoops, *Frau* Arnim—who taught the class, was a friend of the family. She was the first of the townsfolk to visit us when we moved in and she was always coming by when any of the kids were sick to drop off some vile smelling but doubtless effective folk remedy.

But, as I said before, we were English. So, family friend or not, I resolutely slaughtered every word she had me repeat and mangled the pronunciation of every phrase on the blackboard. But when she came to our house for parties and my parents were stuffing the guests with boiled potatoes and chicken curry, I would always sneak off and cook her some nice big German sausages by way of an apology. Maybe that's why she never flunked me.

In the last period on the first day of school that fall, I sat in Frau Arnim's classroom and wished I could allow myself to wrap my mind around the language she was speaking. I knew I was close. Even if you don't do any work on it, three years of listening to a language will get you remarkably close to comprehension. But when she began stringing sentences together that I was on the edge of understanding, I just hummed "Rule Britannia" under my breath and shut the guttural sounds out completely. When class ended I shot her an apologetic smile and ran out the door and home.

It was the longest I had been away from Victor since he had been born.

The house was quiet when I arrived. This was not unusual. The three middle monsters went to a K-6 school a longish bus ride away and I easily beat them home each day. And Victor had proved himself a quiet baby for the most part, only crying when very hungry, which Mom did not allow to happen very often.

I suspected both mother and child were sleeping and I snuck up the stairs so as not to wake anyone. The stairs creaked a little but I skipped the loudest one and peeked in the nursery. Mom was in the corner, sacked out in a gliding rocker, a paperback in one limp hand, her head back and eyes closed.

I tiptoed to the crib and peered over the side. Little Victor lay on his stomach, squinched face towards me, making soft snuffling noises as he slept. His skin seemed yellower. I would have to ask my Mom about jaundice. Two of my brothers and I had suffered from it when we were born but all I really knew about it was that it made your skin yellow. I didn't know if it was dangerous.

I did know that babies aren't supposed to sleep on their stomachs. We even had a special pillow designed to keep Victor on his side while he slept. He had pushed it aside when he rolled over. Strong boy. I extended both hands into the crib and prepared to roll him onto his side. As soon as I touched him his eyes shot open and I jumped back.

His eyes were jet black. And looking right at me. We stood frozen there for a moment, looking into each other's eyes. Week-old babies shouldn't be able to focus on anything, let alone stare directly at you. He looked at me, unblinking, for what felt like a full minute before I finally ripped myself away from his unnatural stare. Opening his mouth wide, he let out a horrible screeching wail. My mother sprung from her chair.

"What the . . ." she said, dropping her book to the floor.

"His eyes, Mom! They're black!"

She stood and took the two steps to the crib. She deftly scooped Victor up and he was already attached to a breast by the time she sat back down. She pulled his head back a little and examined his eyes, but quickly let him get back to feeding when he howled again.

"Why, so they are," she stated. "Three younger siblings before Victor and this is the first time you have noticed that babies' eyes change color, Vee?" she chided me.

"But so quickly? And so black?"

She shrugged. "They'll probably change three or four more times before we know what color they are going to be. I seem to remember *your* eyes doing that."

"Well, I can't argue with you," I said, "since I was a baby when my eyes changed."

She nodded. I was about to ask about babies staring a girl down but I realized how crazy it sounded. Deciding I had imagined it, I left the room. I forgot to ask about jaundice.

❖

Mom nursed Victor the rest of the day and into the night. He couldn't seem to get enough. They both fell asleep at midnight but Victor awoke a half-hour later and began caterwauling until he was fed again. This continued through the night and the next day as well. When the next night was spent sleepless as well, Dad decided enough was enough and packed my mother and youngest sibling off to the doctor, leaving me to get my three other brothers ready for school.

When I came home that afternoon I found my mother sick and exhausted and my father muttering about the doctor's diagnosis.

"A colicky baby," he said, maybe to me, maybe to himself. "That's helpful. 'And what do we do for a colicky baby, Doc?' 'Why you suffer, sir.'" He used a high persnickety voice for the doctor and lowered his natural voice a little to represent himself.

"Why does this happen?" asked the Dad voice.

"Do you believe in God?" asked the doctor voice.

"Why, yes I do," replied the Dad voice.

"Then it is because God is testing you," said the doctor voice.

I decided it was time to cut in. "Do you know anything about jaundice, Dad? Victor seemed a little yellow to me. Could that cause whatever's wrong with him?"

Dad blinked and looked at me, perhaps noticing I was there for the first time. "Jaundice? I don't know much about it. Three of you kids had it when you were born and it went away the next day. None of the doctors seemed overly concerned about it." He plucked his glasses from his nose and worked at them with his shirttail. "I'll ask when we go to another doctor. Tomorrow most likely."

❖

Over the next few weeks three more doctors gave my parents the same diagnosis. A colicky baby. Just wait it out.

The lack of sleep caused my mother to lose weight. She grew cranky and short-tempered. Her few moments of peace were spent barking at me or my brothers for any noises we made while she tried to grab a few minutes of slumber.

Meanwhile, despite the constant feedings, Victor seemed to grow skinnier and his skin became increasingly yellow and dry, stretching tight over long thin legs that should have remained short and chubby. The doctors could find nothing wrong with him physically: no jaundice, no wasting disease, no mysterious cancer. I began to wonder if they were looking at the same child I was. With his large head perched unnaturally on his skinny body and his wide black eyes staring unblinkingly—when he wasn't screaming his huge head off—he looked more freakish doll than human.

❖

Halloween night. I volunteered to stay home with Mom and Victor while Dad took the other boys trick-or-treating.

"I'm too old for that stuff anyway, Dad." Actually, I wasn't. We were reading Greek mythology in our Lit class and my friends, Allie and Jeanine, and I had planned to go out dressed as the three Fates. We would then claim trick-or-treating as extra credit as we ate ourselves into a sugar coma.

I called them and canceled at the last minute. They weren't surprised.

"It's okay, Vee," Allie said. "We know you gotta take care of your family."

My family. My family was taking up most of my time. My schoolwork was beginning to suffer and I looked as haggard as my mother did.

"Thanks, Vee," said my father, "You've been a real life saver." He didn't look so good either. He had lost weight and hair and had dark circles under his eyes. "I'm going to make it up to you when Vic is out of this stage." But he didn't sound convinced that this "stage" would ever end. I tried to give him an encouraging smile but it died before reaching my eyes.

"Bye, Vee," sounded my three middle brothers in unison. They were all dressed as their namesakes in royal purple robes—little Charles with the addition of gigantic rubber ears—and I gave them each a pat on their crowned heads as they left.

Victor began screeching. Dad winced and scampered out the door. I leaned on the windowsill, watching them tromp down the walkway: Dad, hunched and defeated, my three younger brothers—impervious to hardship as all young children are when faced with a night full of candy and costumes—scurrying around his legs, pushing each other in good-natured combat.

"Vee!" yelled Mom. She was practically bedridden now, only shuffling downstairs occasionally to feed herself when Victor was asleep. More often, I would fix her soup or sandwiches and bring them to where she lay, exhausted.

I sighed and pushed myself away from the window. Time to get to work. I went into the kitchen and snagged a pot. I started running water into it and went to the refrigerator. Sometimes I could keep Victor quiet for a few moments with a bottle and let Mom get a little more sleep. I grabbed a bottle out of the fridge and the pot of water from the sink before lighting the stove.

Mom yelled, "Vee!" again as Victor let loose with an especially loud howl.

"One sec, Mom!" I left the pot on the stove and jogged up the stairs. I was down the hall and into Vic's room in moments but it was nearly too late. Mom was out of her room and shuffling towards us in her bathrobe when I came out, Victor, still screaming, tucked in one arm.

"Lemme try a bottle, Mom. You keep sleeping." She may have thanked me but I couldn't hear her over the inhuman din. I went downstairs.

I rocked Victor by the stove until the water was hot and juggled him from one arm to the other when I tested the temperature of the milk. Lukewarm. Time to feed. We settled into the big easy chair in the living room and he finally quieted, taking great slurps from the bottle.

The doorbell rang and I nearly dropped Victor in surprise. *Trick-or-treaters!* I thought. I had forgotten what night it was. I couldn't handle Vic, the bottle, and the candy bowl all at once.

He's a little young for it but . . . I slithered out from underneath him and left him perched, hopefully not too precariously, on the chair. He grasped the bottle easily and settled back, apparently relieved to be left to his own devices. I shook my head and went to the front door.

"Trick or Treat!" yelled the pack of witches, wizards, and superheroes on the porch.

"And *guten Abend,* Miss Victoria," said a familiar voice, its heavy accent turning my name into Veektoria.

"Good evening, Frau Arnim. Bringing your grandchildren around this year?"

"*Ja.* My son, he is so busy, he works on Halloween! He says he will send them out alone but I say, 'It is not safe. I will take them.'" She stuck her head through the door as her countless grandchildren dug greedily into the candy bowl. "Now, where is this young *Liebchen* who is giving your mother such problems?"

Before I could answer she was inside. She got to the living room and stopped cold when she could see little Victor sitting in his chair. Even I, who was growing used to Victor's odd appearance, had to admit he cut a particularly bizarre figure right then. He had managed to get his feet up on one leg of the chair and crossed his skinny legs at the ankles. His hands, long and well-formed for one his age, held the bottle easily and he rocked it back and forth rhythmically as he drank.

Frau Arnim's behavior was even stranger. She clapped one hand over her mouth but was too late to stop the loud gasp that escaped from it. Victor heard the noise and swiveled his big head to face us. He stared at her with black unblinking eyes and her hands fell limp to her sides.

"Killcrop!" she shouted. Victor started at the sound, flung his bottle away, and started screaming again. Frau Arnim backed out of the room and started shooing her grandchildren to the door. "Out! Out, children, out! *Schnell!*"

"Frau Arnim!" I yelled, grabbing her arm before she could get out the door. I was angry. "How dare you come in here and upset him like that?"

She shook me off and made sure all her grandchildren were outside. Only then did she turn back to me.

"I am sorry, Victoria," she said. "But it would take more than just me screaming to upset that *massa carnis*. I will explain tomorrow."

And before I could ask her what she meant, she left, slamming the door behind her. I watched her through the glass, herding her grandchildren to the sidewalk and down the block like a mother goose. Or *the* Mother Goose.

Vic was still screaming and now Mom was yelling for me too. I gathered him up and, knowing he couldn't be settled down by anything but Mom now, I brought him upstairs to her.

❖

At school the next day, I was going to look for Frau Arnim right after homeroom, but she found me first, tapping me on the shoulder at my locker.

"Miss Victoria, come with me, please. I must show you something."

"But I have to get to homeroom!"

She showed me a pass and I followed her to her classroom. The room looked the same: an ordinary classroom in all aspects but on every identifiable item was a handmade sign identifying that object in German and English.

"Sit down, Miss Victoria," said Frau Arnim, perching on the edge of her desk. I sat at a desk in the front row and waited for her to continue. "I know what is wrong with your brother."

"What? Please, tell me!"

"*Ja,* I will. But you will not believe me." She ran her finger down the cover of one of the books. "I have brought some books to . . ."

"Frau Arnim!" I cried. "What is wrong with my brother?"

She pushed herself off her desk and laid an old leather-bound book on the desk where I sat. "Read the words of Martin Luther," she said.

"Martin Luther?"

"*Ja,* the founder of our church."

"Not my church. We're Church of England." Actually we weren't church of anything. But my father always said that as soon as they put a Church of England in town we would start going.

"Well then, the founder of all your friends' church."

She had me there. She opened the book to a page she had marked and pointed to a passage. It was in German.

"I can't read that," I said. She looked at me coldly.

"Well, why not, after three years of class?"

I had no answer for that except to ask why, after thirty years in this country, she still couldn't pronounce the letter *W* correctly. She stared at me open-mouthed—I was not normally that rude—and I apologized quickly.

"No, no, I am sorry," she said. "None of that is important now. Let me translate." She grabbed the book from me and perched a pair of reading glasses on her nose. " 'Eight years ago at Dessau, I, Dr. Martin Luther, saw and touched a changeling,' " she read, tracing the text with her finger. " 'It did nothing but eat; in fact, it ate enough for any four peasants or threshers.' " She skipped a few lines before going on. " 'I said to the Princes of Anhalt: "If I were the prince or the ruler here, I would throw this child into the water—into the Molda that flows by Dessau. I would dare commit *homicidium* on him!" Such a changeling child is only a piece of flesh, a *massa carnis,* because it has no soul.'" She slammed the book shut with a satisfactory thump and looked at me. "You see?" she asked.

"No, Frau Arnim, I don't see." I was confused and tired. It wasn't enough that my mother and brother were sick and I was going to fail school because I couldn't ever sleep or study; now I had to listen to a crazy German woman quote another crazy German at me. "You aren't making any sense."

"Ich bün so olt as Böhmer Gold," Frau Arnim intoned, her accent subtly different.

"What does that . . ."

"Listen, Victoria," she interrupted and grabbed me by my shoulders. "Victor is not your brother. He is a changeling, a killcrop."

"That's crazy!"

She shook her head. "No, it is not crazy. It is the truth. Victor has been taken by the underground people, the *Rotkaps,* and they have left a killcrop in his place."

I wriggled free from her grip. "Let's say I believe you—which I don't—how do I get him back?"

"In the old days a woman whose child had been stolen would brew beer in eggshells where the killcrop could see it. It would be so surprised it would exclaim, *'Ich bün so olt as Böhmer Gold, doch sonn Brug'n heww ik noch nie seihn.'* Its true nature revealed, the killcrop disappears, leaving the baby in its place."

I stood from my desk. "Well." I cleared my throat. "Frau Arnim, thank you for wasting my time with this insanity. Either you believe it and need serious help, or you think it's funny to tease me and my family when we are going through such hard times." I marched to the door and spoke over my shoulder. "Either way, I don't think you should come by the house anymore."

"Victoria!" I turned and looked at her. I hadn't realized it until then, but I had grown taller than her over the summer. "The *Rotkaps* have seen enough brewing beer in eggshells by now I would think. You will have to think of something new."

I ran from the classroom.

❖

I skipped German class for the next few days. Frau Arnim did not report me to the principal. I had trouble concentrating in the classes I actually went to.

Changelings. Killcrops. Rotkaps. It was all I could think about. Frau Arnim's story was crazy—but it did fit all the facts. I couldn't get it out of mind.

Friday, I skipped school entirely. It was Guy Fawkes day.

On November 5, 1605, a disgruntled Englishman by the name of Guy Fawkes was discovered in the basement of Parliament making ready to set off a great deal of explosives. He and his coconspirators were caught, tortured, and hanged by the neck until dead. Since then, every November 5 has been a holiday in England. And all over that country—and at a certain family's house in New Dresden, Wisconsin, as well—parties are thrown and bonfires are lit and Guy Fawkes is burned in effigy.

My father had wanted to cancel the party for this year but my mother, fearsome in her determination even while bedridden, convinced him to put it on anyway. My twin uncles drove in from Minnesota to help out with the preparations and I, having promised to help with the food, spent the day shopping.

When I got home from the grocery store, I scooped Victor up from next to my sleeping mother and plopped him into the stroller he almost never used. When I pushed it into the kitchen he woke but, for once, he kept quiet. His big dark eyes tracked me as I worked.

I began pulling food out of the paper bags I had carried inside: leeks, tomatoes, peppers, potatoes, and some roasted chicken breasts. The potatoes I washed and put in a bowl. Two pokes with a fork each and they went into the microwave. On the butcher block counter I chopped the other ingredients into bite-size pieces. I went to the pantry and rummaged through the shelves until I found a large can of chicken stock. I opened it in the kitchen and left it to sit next to the stove.

Beep.

The potatoes were done. I slipped an oven mitt on and grabbed the hot bowl out of the microwave. I shoved the vegetables and chicken to one side before dumping the hot tubers onto the counter next to them. These too, I chopped up.

I spared a glance for my youngest brother. Though unable to sit up completely, his head had stopped lolling to one side and his eyes were fastened on me, following my every movement. He really didn't look human.

Yes, I thought, *watch carefully.*

I sauntered over to the back door and grabbed one of my father's old leather work boots. It was a tan Timberland boot, size thirteen, with hardy laces, alternating tan and dark brown. It stank.

When I returned to the stove I plunked it down on top of the closest burner and peeked at my brother out of the corner of my eye. I swore he was sitting straight up now, rapt.

Changelings. Killcrops. Rotkaps.

The can of chicken stock went into the boot first. I didn't spill a drop but it began leaking out the bottom of the shoe almost immediately. I scooped up the vegetables and meat in the bowl I had microwaved the potatoes in and dumped them into the boot as well. I shook some garlic, salt, and black pepper in and topped it off with a pinch of basil. I began stirring it with a wooden spoon.

My brother said nothing.

In for a penny, in for a pound. I turned the dial for the front burner to *light*.

Click.

It failed to light on the first try. I dug the spoon into the boot with a vengeance and thought about how big an idiot I was.

Click.

Frau Arnim was obviously insane. And apparently, so was I, since I was about to burn a perfectly good boot to a crisp in front of a colicky baby.

Click.

"What are you doing?" The speaker's voice was deep and accented and it crackled, like old leaves.

I turned to see who had spoken thinking, *Maybe my father came home early,* but knowing it was still only me and my littlest brother. He was sitting forward in his stroller, leaning one elbow on the tray, index finger and thumb stroking his chin.

"Making soup," I said.

Whoosh!

The gas finally lit and blue flames shot forth. The plastic ends of the boot laces melted and sizzled in the first heat, dripping hot plastic onto the stove. I smelled toxic smoke and burning hair.

Burning hair! Shoots of orange flame had run up the laces in the initial burst and set fire to my arm hair. I leaped backwards in surprise.

But I forgot to let go of the spoon.

The spoon was still deep in the boot and I took the whole mess down on top of me. Plastic lava pocked my forearms and hands while cold chicken stock and hot potatoes splattered my face and hair.

"Ho, ho, ho. Ha, ha, ha," I heard from over me and I looked up into deep black eyes shining with an alien intelligence. He leaned out over his stroller to better see me and spoke once more. "I am as old as Bohemian gold and yet, in all my days, I have never seen anyone making soup in a boot." He leaned back, still chuckling. "Or failing so miserably in the attempt."

Uncooked soup dripped onto the floor and my brain howled at me to *Move! Run! Scream!* but I sat, slack-jawed, staring at what I had thought was my brother.

The back door flew open and my father charged in. The changeling fell back fully into the stroller and let his head loll to one side. A little drool leaked from the corner of his mouth and he was every bit the infant once more.

"Your uncles are itching to light the fire, Vee. Is all the food done?" He stopped when he saw me sitting on the floor covered in soup and boot. "What's going on here?"

I couldn't answer. What would I say? Frau Arnim was right: my brother had been stolen and this *thing* had been left in his place. She was wrong about one thing, though. Despite its true nature being revealed, the killcrop showed no signs of leaving any time soon.

I had to talk to Frau Arnim. I mumbled something about an accident to my father and told him I would clean it up in a second. Then I ran upstairs to my room and dialed Frau Arnim.

Out my window I could see the party preparations in the backyard. Lawn torches lit the area and chairs had been set up in a loose ring around the as-yet unlit bonfire. The bonfire was a man-high pyramid of wood and, once it was lit, no one could get within ten feet of it without being burned. Still, come ten o'clock, my insane uncles would risk singed eyebrows and deadly smoke inhalation to toss the straw effigy of Mr. Fawkes on to the flames.

Frau Arnim picked up on the fourth ring.

"It's a changeling," I blurted out before she could say hello. "I cooked it soup in a boot."

"Mein Gott!"

"What should I do?" I cried into the phone. "He said he was as old as Bohemian gold. I thought he was supposed to leave after that?"

"Listen, Victoria! If he has not left yet then you must beat him. Or threaten him in some way. Only if the killcrop is in danger will the *Rotkaps* bring your true brother back."

"You have to help me!" I was whining and hated the sound of my own voice. "Please, Frau Arnim."

"I am sorry, Victoria. I cannot." She sighed into the phone. "The *Rotkaps* will only deal with the family of the stolen baby. I could beat the killcrop to death and they would never come for him. And then you would lose your one hope of getting your real brother back."

There was nothing more to say. I took the phone from my ear and stood there, listening to the tinny voice of Frau Arnim repeating my name until she was replaced by the familiar recording: "Please hang up and dial again. If this is an emergency . . ."

I dropped the phone to the ground and, with a loud crash, its back flew open, sending batteries skittering across the floor.

"You okay, Vee?" called my dad from downstairs.

I didn't answer. His voice sounded small and distant. Like Frau Arnim's had when I held the phone away.

I trudged down the stairs and ignored my father's repeated, "Vee? Vee?"

The killcrop was where I had left him: drooling in his stroller, eyes shut tight. I pushed him towards the door.

"Could you get the door, Father?" I asked. He opened the door, looking at me with concern, and I pushed the stroller into the backyard. The cold hit me and I remembered we weren't wearing any coats. My father realized it at the same time.

"Coats, Vee!"

"We won't need them, Dad!" I called back, my breath frosting in the November air. I stopped next to a lawn torch. I guess the killcrop was trying not to draw more attention to himself because he hadn't started screaming yet. He wasn't strapped in and I grabbed a handful of his shirt front with my left hand and lifted him out. "We won't need coats, will we, Victor?" I spit the last word directly into his face. He opened one dark eye to look at me.

"Why not?" he whispered in his old, cold voice.

"Because we're going on the fire!" I replied. Both his eyes shot open as I wrenched the lawn torch out of the ground with my free hand.

He began screaming then. So did I, for that matter. I ran towards the bonfire, killcrop in one hand, torch in the other, screaming at the top of my lungs. When I got three feet away, I tossed the lawn torch onto the gasoline-drenched woodpile. It exploded into flames and the ensuing fireball knocked me to the ground.

I didn't let go of the killcrop.

I stood up, the heat trying to force me further back and yelled, "He goes on the flames! Hear me now you . . . you . . . *Rotkaps!* He goes on the flames!" I could barely hear myself over the killcrop's screeching. I grabbed him with both hands as he tried to squirm out of my grasp and made as if to toss him, arms extended over my head like I was throwing a soccer ball, into the raging fire.

"Into the flames!" I screamed, louder even then before. I could smell burning hair and knew my eyebrows would soon be gone if I stayed this close to the flames.

I saw movement. Out beyond the broken ring of lawn torches, and from a direction no neighbor would approach from, I saw movement. It resolved into the figure of a short old woman with wide hips, bustling towards the firelight on stubby legs. Her face was as wrinkled as a whole box of raisins and her nose was so big it looked like it was leading her around. She wore a coarse woolen dress and had stained rags wrapped about her shoulders. On her head was a black cap.

And she carried a fat, naked, *human* baby in one arm.

"Victor," I breathed. I froze with the killcrop high over my head and watched her approach. She waddled to the other side of the bonfire, waving her free hand at me in a frantic stop! stop! motion. I could see that what I had thought was a black cap was actually dark red.

Blood red.

She stopped before coming fully into the light.

"Come over here with my brother!" I yelled to her. But she was no longer waving her hand at me. She wasn't even looking at me anymore; she was looking at something over my shoulder.

Then her mouth opened in a malevolent grin, showing three yellowing teeth. The teeth came to sharp points and bobbed up and down as she looked behind me and began to laugh, cackling in a grating tenor voice.

I tried to turn to see what she was laughing about, but it was too late. Uncle Richard plucked the killcrop from my hands just as Uncle Robert hit me in the small of the back in a perfect football tackle, bringing me to the ground. I struggled to get up, or wriggle out, or grab the killcrop from my Uncle Richard. But I was held fast. I ranted and raved at them to throw the killcrop into the fire. I screamed for them to grab the old woman.

"What old woman?" Uncle Richard asked, now a safe distance away. He handed the screaming killcrop to my father who stared at me with wide sad eyes.

I strained against Uncle Robert's weight. I scratched at his face, I tried to bite his ear. I tried every dirty trick I had ever heard about or seen on TV but he held me down easily. With my cheek pressed hard into the frozen dirt, I watched in horror as the old woman walked off into the darkness, tickling Victor's pudgy feet with her long brown fingernails.

❖

The police eventually came and I was carted off. I was obviously insane and the prosecution refused to press criminal charges. Instead, I was moved to a juvenile facility where I got to spend the next seven months with other disturbed young people wandering the halls drooling, shaking, and mumbling to themselves.

It was enough to make you crazy—if you weren't already. But I wasn't crazy. No amount of drugs, counseling, or even ECT could change that.

My father visited yesterday. He hadn't come to see me in over a month. The last time he was here I had broken down. When I heard him talk about losing his job and Mom still being sick and the boys starting to get in trouble in school, I had begged him to destroy the killcrop—the source of all the family's bad luck. The orderlies had to drag me screaming out of the visiting room. The doctors thought that maybe my Dad's visit had triggered the relapse.

But this latest visit was a special occasion. The doctors had just told me I was to be moved to a halfway house next week. I think they arranged Dad's visit just to see if I would lose it again.

I didn't lose it.

I sat quietly and talked pleasantly and even patted my Dad on his bony knee and told him I was glad when he said that at least one person in the family was doing well: Victor. I kept my cool and when my father left the doctors were all smiles and I knew I was getting out. And if I could get to the halfway house and keep it together for a few months then they would have to send me home.

And this time, Victor goes on the fire for sure.

CATNYP

DELIA SHERMAN

❖

Stories that mix real places like the New York Public Library with faerie folk fall into a subgenre called "urban fantasy." Note how matter-of-factly Neef tells her story. She never lets you question, even for a moment, that fairies can exist side by side with humans in a kind of borderland of a modern city.

If you enjoy this story, try Holly Black's dark novel Tithe *in which a modern girl encounters faeries, or Will Shetterly's Borderland novels* Elsewhere *and* Nevernever, *or Emma Bull's award-winning novel* War for the Oaks, *about the seelie and unseelie courts living and warring in modern Minneapolis.*

The story I'm about to tell is a fairy story. It's got genuine fairies in it, and it's about how humans get catapulted into adventure through breaking a fairy law. The difference is that in fairy tales, the humans don't always know what law they're breaking or why.

I should have known better. I did know better. I grew up with the Folk. They stole me when I was just a few weeks old and left one of their own in my bassinet for my parents to raise. So I'm kind of bi-cultural, human and fairy. A changeling, in fact.

My story takes place in New York City. Not the one in the "I♥New York" posters, but the one that exists beside it, in the walls and crawl spaces and all the little pockets and passages of its infrastructure. Call it New York Between. That's what I call it. The Folk don't call it anything—they simply live there. Me, they call Neef, which was okay when I was a kid, but now I'm not a kid any more, I wish they'd picked something a little less lame.

So anyway, once upon a time, not all that long ago, I was sitting in the FolkXChange with Snowbell and Fleet. We were talking about men. Actually, Fleet, who'd just been dumped by the selkie she'd been dating, was talking about men, and Snowbell and I were listening. Snowbell is a swan maiden. Fleet's a changeling, like me. The FolkXChange is an open kind of place. Sometimes you even see vampires there.

Anyway, there we are, drinking nectar and eating fairy cakes and listening to Fleet carry on about her selkie. Her ex-selkie. "We'd been having this fight," Fleet was saying, "about how I didn't understand the stresses of being a shapechanger, and I just said if he wanted me to understand so bad, maybe he should lend me his sealskin, and he . . ."

Snowbell made a noise that was a lot more swan than maiden. Fleet shook her black braids forward over the cinnamon oval of her face. "It was all his fault," she muttered. "He started it. He was all, 'you're just human, you don't know what it's like, you haven't got any magic.' And I kind of lost it."

I snorted. "You can say that again. How could you be so dumb?"

Fleet sighed. "Love, I guess. It makes you do stupid things."

"Oh. Love. Like you know anything about love," I said.

"I know more about it than you do," Fleet countered. "I've had lots of boyfriends. When was *your* last date, huh?"

She had me there. Having a love life is hard for a changeling. There aren't that many Folk a girl can date. A lot of them are as ugly as a backed-up sewer, and would rather take you apart than out dancing. The beautiful ones know how to have fun, but they can be kind of temperamental. And changelings don't date changelings. We hang out together, we talk things over, we're friends, but we don't date. I mean, who'd go out with a human being when there are elves around?

Snowbell stretched out her long, white neck and gave her slender shoulders a swanny little ripple. "You will stop quarreling," she said.

"It is not interesting. Neither of you know anything of love. You are human. You are too frail to bear the intensity of true love. If you felt for one moment the heat of desire the least of the Folk feels, you would turn black and crumble, like toast."

"Dog doo," I said. Fleet stopped sniveling. "You know, I've heard that line before, and to be perfectly honest, I've never seen the slightest proof of it. It looks to me like we humans are the ones who do all the loving around here. All you guys do is eat it up with a spoon."

Snowbell isn't very big. She's all white skin and floaty hair and big, black eyes, wistful and delicate as a paper flower. But she's got a touchy temper and a mean bite. I thought for a minute she was going to go for me, but she laughed instead.

"I have an idea," she said. "You will try to prove that humans know more of love than the Folk."

"Why?" I asked.

"Because you will discover that I am right, and I look forward to watching you lose."

"And what happens if I do?"

"The usual, I think. Service for a year and a day. It's been ages since I had a human servant."

"And if I win?"

"You won't. But I'll give you a boon if you do. Whatever you like. We'll put it to the Genius of Central Park at the Solstice Dance." She got to her feet in a graceful surge and preened her tight black sweater. "Good luck."

Before I could tell her what she could do with her dumb bet, she was out the door. "You're in deep trouble, girlfriend," Fleet said.

"Not even. All I have to do is avoid her for a while and she'll forget all about it. I never said I accepted or anything."

Fleet just gave me a look. "Come *on*, girl. You make the rules around here? I don't think so. If you say you're not playing, she'll just collect anyway, and you know it."

Yeah. I knew it. "You gotta help me, Fleet," I said. "What am I going to do?"

Fleet looked thoughtful. "Well, I guess you could go ask the Genius of the New York Public Library. He knows everything, they say."

"Good idea. Thanks, Fleet. You're a peach."

And I walked out of the FolkXChange and took the Betweenways to the New York Public Library to ask the Genius about love.

The proper term is *genius loci*—the guardian of the place. There are a bunch of them, and they're the most New York of all New York Folk. A building or a park or even a street is around long enough, with people loving it and thinking it's important, and a genius appears—Poof! Like magic. The Genius of the New York Public Library isn't as old as the Genius of Broadway or as powerful as the Genius of Central Park. But he's pretty impressive anyway.

The Genius of the NYPL speaks every language he's got a book written in and he knows everything that's in the library, from agriculture to zoology. He can (and will) go on endlessly about any subject. He's kind of cute, in a lanky, long-haired, shortsighted way, and he rustles pleasantly when he moves.

"Love," he said thoughtfully. "A rich subject. A thorny subject. May I inquire why you are choosing to research it here?"

"I've got this bet with a swan maiden," I said. "I have to prove that humans know more about love than the Folk do."

He sighed. "And how do you propose to go about winning this, er, bet?"

"I don't really know," I confessed. "I thought I'd ask you to help me."

He took off his huge, square spectacles and polished them with a white handkerchief. *"Primus,"* he said dryly, "I am no expert on the subject of human love, being myself a supernatural being. *Secundus,* I am not a pedagogue. I am simply a repository of, admittedly human, knowledge and opinion. In short, I do not answer questions. My books do."

"Oh." This was going to be more complicated than I'd hoped. "Well then, I guess I'll read a few books about it."

The Genius replaced his glasses. "Reading is good," he said.

"'Histories make men wise; poets, witty; the mathematics, subtle; natural philosophy, deep; morals, grave; logic and rhetoric, able to contend.'" He fixed me with a bright, expectant look, like a pigeon waiting for a crumb. I nodded like I knew what he was talking about, but you can't fool a Genius. He sighed. "I was quoting Francis Bacon, child. From the essay 'On Studies.' I recommend it."

"'On Studies.' Bacon. Does that have anything to do with love?"

He turned back to his desk. "In a manner of speaking," he said. "Now. The New York Public Library is open to everyone. But you'll need a card, and you'll need to peruse this list of rules. The rules are very important." He opened one of the quadrillion drawers in his huge desk and pulled out a small cardboard rectangle and a sheet of paper, which he handed to me before dipping a long feather pen into an ornate inkwell. "Name?"

He didn't mean my real name, of course—there's a kind of don't-ask-don't tell policy on names in New York Between, where names are power. "Neef," I told him, and started to read.

Regulations for use of the New York Public Library Between
Department of Humanities and Social Sciences

DO NOT

1. Deface or write in a Book
2. Bring food or drink of any kind into the Library
3. Remove any Book from the Library
4. Create a Disturbance
5. Enter the Stacks

"Sir," I said, "I don't quite understand rule #5. If I can't go into the stacks, how am I supposed to get books?"

He turned his spectacles on me. "Consult CATNYP, of course, then ask one of the library pages to get it for you. Have you never been in a library before?"

"No."

He smiled, showing small, pointed teeth. "Stay out of the Stacks, child. They're dangerous."

I've lived in New York Between all my life; I know a fairy law when I hear one. I put the rules in my pocket and took my library card, which announced, in beautiful spidery lettering, that one Neef was allowed unlimited reading privileges at the NYPL. Then the Genius blew down a brass tube sticking out of the wall by his desk.

A page popped out of another brass tube and unrolled itself at my feet. I moved back so I wouldn't step on it and greeted it in Common Supernatural.

"Don't bother," the Genius said. "It's deaf."

Unrolled, the page came up to my waist. It looked like a giant paper doll with a smiley-face inked onto its circular head. "Don't tell me," it said. "You're a changeling, and you want to get in touch with your human heritage. What can I get you? A nice romance? Some pop psych? Or maybe something more challenging? Quantum physics? Sigmund Freud?"

The Genius glared at it. "The page will take you to the Reading Room and introduce you to CATNYP," the Genius said. "Good-bye." And he turned back to his desk.

The page was hard to see when it turned sideways, but I managed to follow it up and around and along the betweenways of the NYPL. We ended up in a room with a handful of changelings in it, sitting in comfy chairs with their noses in open books. It was a nice room, just perfect for reading in: plenty of soft, silver fairy light, little desks to write on if you needed to, and the happy hum of minds concentrating on stuff they were interested in.

"CATNYP's in here," said the page. "Come on."

I followed it into a side room, which was furnished, if you can call it that, with a couple of chairs and a lion on a marble pedestal. The lion's eyes were closed and its paws were stretched out in front of it. It was maybe the size of a big dog, and its fur was a grainy white.

The page tickled the lion between its furry ears. It opened its eyes, which were Easter-egg blue, and stared at us.

"This is CATNYP," the page told me. "It knows what books we have and where they're kept. It's a simple, user-friendly system, designed for you to be able to figure it out by yourself. Give it a little pat when you're done. That puts it to sleep." And it left me there, face to face with CATNYP, which yawned toothily.

Okay. I've dealt with enchanted animals before. You ask them questions, they answer. You just have to ask them the right questions. If I only knew what the right questions were.

Well, that was a place to start. "What should I ask you?" I said.

The lion blinked at me. "Title, Author, Subject, Keyword."

This was not very clear, but then, magic animals aren't supposed to be clear. I thought for a while. "Subject, I guess. Love."

The lion shut its eyes and seemed to go to sleep again. I tickled it between the ears, experimentally, which produced nothing more helpful than a slight, irritated growl. I was about to go out and tackle the page when the lion opened its china blue eyes again. "There are 28,073 entries under Love," it informed me.

"Ooo-kay," I said. "How about Romance?"

"Thirteen thousand two hundred ninety-eight entries," CATNYP said. "Would you like some search tips?"

Well, that was a little more user-friendly. I smiled into its eyes. "Yes. Please."

"Limit your search," CATNYP suggested.

"Say what?"

CATNYP sighed. "Love Poems. Divine Love. Love and Women. . . ."

"Oh. Thank you. It's hard to ask questions when you don't know what you're asking, you know?"

CATNYP had no answer to that, unless you counted a twitch of its tufted tail.

"Okay," I said, half to myself. "What I want to find out is . . ."

"You're never going to get anywhere like that," said a voice behind me. It was a nice voice, smooth and deep as double chocolate ice
cream. I turned around, and saw it belonged to a guy, maybe a little
older than me, brown eyes and brown hair, built like an athlete, and
almost too good-looking to be human. He was dressed in the
changeling uniform of jeans and T-shirt stolen from Salvation Army
bins, but it didn't matter. He looked like a prince in disguise as a
swineherd, or (because this was twenty-first-century New York and
not nineteenth-century Germany) like a rich boy pretending to be a
street person.

"What are you staring at?" he said. "Did I cut myself shaving?"

This wasn't a question I felt like answering, so I turned back to
the lion. It yawned and settled its chin on its paws.

"Don't go to sleep on me here," I said. "I haven't found a book
yet!"

"Here," the changeling said. "Let me help you."

In one way, it was easier, since he knew how to ask the right
questions. In another, it was just about the most embarrassing thing
in the world, to have to tell the cutest human guy I'd ever seen that I
was searching for books about love. Once I got it straightened out
that I wasn't looking for *The Joy of Sex,* though, it got better.

The way it worked was, you gave CATNYP your subject, properly limited, and CATNYP gave you mice. They hopped out of its
mouth and lined up on the pedestal and gave you their titles, authors,
and publication information, one after another, in tiny, clear voices.

The mice the handsome changeling had pulled up for me repre-
sented a couple of anthologies of love poetry, a couple of scientific-
sounding studies, and something called *Your Love Signs.*

"How many can I choose?" I asked.

"The pages will only bring you two volumes at a time."

I grabbed two mice at random. They snuggled cozily into my fingers. "What if I want the others later?"

"They'll come if you call them by title and author."

"Who designed this system anyway?"

The guy shrugged. "Nobody designed it—it just happened. Typical fairy magic."

"Yeah. Well, thanks for the help."

"You're not home free yet. You have to get a page. I'm Byron, by the way."

"And I'm Neef."

I was also in love. I was ready to can my mice and my bet with Snowbell and ask him if he'd like to cut out for a nice, long walk in Central Park. But he was already heading toward the back of the Reading Room, where there was a long wooden counter. It had a couple of books and a scattering of corn on it, and a small stack of pages.

Byron peeled a page from the stack and skimmed it across the counter. The page shook itself with an irritable rustle, chose a kernel of corn and gave it to me, took the mice, rolled itself tight around them, and dove into a brass tube.

Byron breathed into my ear. "That's your seat number. Okay now?"

I was anything but okay. His whisper had gone through me like an electrical charge. "What?" He tapped the kernel. I looked down, noticed that it had a number printed on it. "Oh. Sure. Thanks."

He flashed me a heart-stopping smile and went off to his own seat. Which wasn't, of course, anywhere near mine. I'm sure the page did it on purpose.

Glamour is usually a Folk thing, but Byron definitely had it. Not megawatt, like a fox spirit or a pooka. His was more subtle, like a couple of candles on a bedside table. It was enough, though, to make me want to go up behind him and run my fingers through his hair and across his shoulders, broad and square under the torn T-shirt.

But that would lead to breaking Rule # 4 (don't create a Disturbance) and possibly Rule # 1 (don't damage the Books) as well. So I didn't do anything. But thinking what I'd like to do passed the time until the page brought me my books.

"Here you go, girlie," it said. "Knock yourself out. And, girlie, you gotta quit thinking so loud. You're making us blush here."

I blushed myself. Then I picked up the top book and opened it and started reading.

Since this is a fairy tale, I'm not going to go on about what I learned at the NYPL. Fairy tales don't go into detail about what the characters do between adventures. I'll just say that those books—the poems especially—cast a spell of their own, a powerful enchantment that changed the way I felt about being human. I didn't always understand them, but I felt them curling up in my brain and making me feel stuff I'd never felt before.

The poems were enchanting enough to make me forget about Byron. Almost. I didn't sneak a peek at him more than every couple of pages or so. And when he closed his book and took it back to the book counter and put on a battered leather jacket to leave, I swear I got up and followed him just because I was hungry.

He waited for me by the door. I sauntered up to him—Miss Nonchalance of New York Between. "This part of town's not in my flight path," I whispered. "Where can I go to grab a sandwich?"

Instead of answering, he took my hand and pulled me with him out the door. I don't know how he felt when our hands clasped, but my mouth went dry and my face flamed hot as a sidewalk in August. I checked my symptoms against the poems. Love, for sure. Maybe this bet would be easier to win than I thought.

We ended up at a place I'd never been to before: the Wannabe, under Times Square. It was a changeling hangout—no Folk allowed—and it served human food, stolen from a deli Outside. It smelled kind of odd to me, but I was willing to try anything Byron liked. He ordered hamburgers and coffee for both of us, and I tried to think of a conversation-starter. After about forever, all I could come up with was, "What are you studying?" So I asked him that.

"Magic," he said.

"Oh," I said. "Why?"

He looked around and scooched his chair a little closer to me. "I want to get out of here, get back Outside, where I belong."

I nodded. Just my luck. I meet the answer to every changeling girl's prayer, and he turns out to be loony tunes. Everybody knows changelings can't get out of New York Between, not unless the Folk kick them out. Most changelings wouldn't go Outside if they could. I sure wouldn't. Go to a place without magic, where you need money to live, where the wind will chill you and the rain wet you, where you can't talk to cats or dance with the Vilis or match wits with a leprechaun? Not on your life. I was curious about Outside, sure. I read the newspapers and magazines that blew down the storm sewers and listened to the Folk's stories about their adventures with mortals. But no way did I want to live among mortals. They're way too unpredictable.

"I'm like a pet, a toy, and I'm sick of it," Byron said. "Nothing I do makes any difference here. I want to make a *difference*, Neef. I want to be somebody. I want to be a hero."

He might have been loony tunes, but he was definitely adorable. I made sympathetic noises and watched his brown curls flop endearingly over his forehead whenever he pushed them back.

"There's got to be a way. I mean, you know the precedents: Thomas the Rhymer, Tam Lin, Orpheus, Hercules. All I have to do is put it all together. I've got this theory, that it all has to do with chaos theory and alchemy. You see . . ."

While he talked, I admired how passion lit fires behind his soft brown eyes and wondered whether I could get him to look at me like that. Since I doubted he'd succeed in getting out of New York Between, I figured I'd have plenty of time to try.

I never got back to the Library that day. We stayed at the Wannabe for a while, and then we went dancing at the permanent floating Faerie Rave. I couldn't quite figure out why Byron was sticking with me when there were so many delicious Folk looking at him, but finally I didn't care. We had a good time. When we got tired of dancing, we swam with the mer-folk in New York harbor and stole clams from the Grand Central Oyster Bar and caught an act of *Song of Broadway,* the Folk's perpetual musical entertainment. We did stuff until we were too tired to do any more, and then we fell asleep. When I woke up, I was in a nest of were-bears underneath the Central Park Zoo, and Byron was nowhere. The were-bears didn't know where he had gone, but I did.

❖

When I walked into the Reading Room, there he was, curly brown head bent worshipfully over a huge book with black covers and red edges. I made sure to pass his chair on my way to the catalogue room and brushed his shoulder as I went by. He didn't even look up.

That was a disappointment. But then I reminded myself that he wanted to be a hero. Fine. I understand heroes. They go on impossible quests. Byron was just doing his thing. I decided to play with CATNYP for a while, and then I'd see if I could get him to come out to the Wannabe and tell me how it was going.

CATNYP was asleep when I came in, its mane a furry wave over its glistening shoulders. I scratched it gently between its teacup-sized ears. CATNYP's fur was soft and springy under my fingers, and it purred like an approaching subway.

"Hey there, CATNYP," I said. "What's up?"

It opened its ice-blue eyes, shook its mane, and yawned. "Author, Title, Subject, Keyword," it said sleepily.

"Okay," I said. "Today, I'm going to learn to talk to you."

It was fun, really. At one point, I had the room full of mice, nosing all over the floor while I tried to figure out how to organize my searches. Then I discovered how to get a list of titles without the mice, and the Subject Index, and all kinds of cool stuff. CATNYP was incredibly patient with me and, once I learned how to ask, showed me all sorts of useful shortcuts. Finally, I buried my fingers in CATNYP's stiff mane.

"Thanks," I said. "You're the best. Sleep tight, now." I tousled the coarse fur and watched the blue eyes drift shut.

That was when I heard the uproar in the Reading Room.

The first thing I thought was, "There's rule #4 down the tubes." And then I recognized Byron's voice, and got my butt out there on the double.

Byron was climbing over the counter. There wasn't a page in sight. The changelings were milling around like a flock of worried pigeons, cooing frantically:

"What's he *doing*?"

"He's breaking all the rules!"

"Come back, you idiot!"

"Somebody call the Genius!"

It took me about two breaths to take this all in, and then I was across the room and on top of the counter myself, by which time Byron was standing in front of a door I hadn't seen before, a wooden door with a frosted glass window in it, narrow, but human-sized. One hand was on the polished brass doorknob, and the other cradled a terrified mouse. He was flushed, determined, and totally, awesomely heroic-looking.

"Byron, stop!" I called. He glanced impatiently over his shoulder, dead set on breaking Rule #5, whatever the consequences. "Just a sec. I'm coming with you."

I was over the counter and through the door before I had time to think whether it was a good idea, then looked around for my dashing boyfriend, who had thoughtlessly dashed out of sight. I thought I heard his boots moving down a parallel aisle. I ran to intercept him, but when I reached the cross aisle, it was empty in both directions.

So here I was in the Stacks, alone. I could go back, but how lame would that be? The stacks stretched around me, dim and cramped. I could touch the ceiling without stretching and the aisles between the cast-iron shelves were not a lot wider than my shoulders. The air was cool and dry, not at all musty or dusty or book-smelling. It didn't seem dangerous, although I did notice that the books were all jailed behind iron grilles. I concentrated on listening for the sound of footsteps or breathing, anything to tell me which way Byron had gone.

That's when I began to hear voices.

It was real subtle at first, a vague, low murmuring that was so much a part of the atmosphere I might have been imagining it. But once I noticed it, it got louder. I started getting jittery. I mean, here I was in a forbidden place, a place I'd been warned against, and there were these mysterious voices getting louder by the second, like an invisible mob creeping up on me. I stood there, undecided, getting antsier and unhappier while the murmuring grew. I started picking up words: "Psyche"; "death"; "human condition." I put my hands over my ears.

A mouse ran across my foot, which made me jump about a mile and duck into the shelter of one of the side aisles. The mouse scrambled up the grill that covered the shelf, wiggled through the wire, and sat on a book spine. I shrank back to the end of the row and made like a bookcase just before a page appeared and opened the grill. The mouse disappeared to wherever magical constructs go when they're not needed and the page wrapped itself around the book and dived into a brass tube at the mouth of the aisle.

One mystery solved. Several million left to go. Beginning with: Where was Byron and how was I going to keep from going nuts? No wonder the pages were deaf. I wished, briefly, that I was too. And that's when I remembered that I'd already broken one rule that day: Rule #2, in fact. Do not bring food or drink of any kind into the Library. In my pocket was a corned beef and mustard on rye I'd picked up at the Wannabe. I fished it out of the pocket of my sweater and, tearing off two little pieces of fairly un-mustardy crust, squished them up and stuck them in my ears. Gross, but effective. The murmuring faded to a faint roar, like traffic through a closed window, easy to ignore for a city girl like me. Now I could think, and so I did.

It was a big library. Running around like an idiot was only going to tire me out, not to mention get me more lost by the second. What I needed was a mouse. To get a mouse, I needed CATNYP. Which was back in the Reading Room. Dead end.

So much for thinking. I crept out of my aisle and looked right and left. To the right, the corridor disappeared around a bend. To the left, I saw a narrow stair leading down to the next level. I turned left.

The Genius was right. The Stacks were dangerous. The only way I can explain it is to say that those books really, really wanted to get my attention. When I didn't respond to their whispering, they sent out fictional characters, metaphors, and dangerous ideas to reel me in. I was pelted with visions: the path between a snowy wood and a frozen lake; a man who was also a tree, with a woman twined ivy-like around him; a wild-haired woman with blood on her clothes, brandishing a knife and begging me with terrible eyes to listen to her story.

I'm calm about it now—I survived it, after all—but I wasn't very calm then. I was scared shitless. I knew it was all an illusion, that the woman's knife wouldn't cut me or the man and woman break my heart with their beauty, but it felt as if they could. Finally I shut my eyes and crawled, the floor reassuringly cold and stable under my hands and knees, until I got to the stairs. I crawled up a few steps and cautiously opened my eyes. All I saw was dim-lit aisles and the flat black ends of bookshelves. I'd reached neutral ground.

My face was sweating. I wiped it on my sleeve, and that's when I found the hair.

My sweater was black, and the hair, which was white, showed up like print against the dark wool. The were-bears were brown, and I don't have a cat of any color, so I must have picked it up in the catalogue room, just before the upheaval began.

Well. I may not know much about human love, but I do know what to do with a hair from a magic animal. Carefully, I tweezed it up between my fingernails and breathed on it.

CATNYP brave and CATNYP bold
Please boot me up before I'm old.

"Flattery," a deep voice remarked at my shoulder, "will get you everywhere. Although I must say I don't think much of the poem."

It was CATNYP, all right, bolt upright on the landing above me. "What happened to Title, Author, Subject, Keyword?" I said a little shakily.

CATNYP looked just as inscrutable as a cat can look. "I can do that, if you like."

"No. That's okay. This is fine. Listen. I need a mouse, big time."

"When you have me?" CATNYP sounded offended. "If you like, but I can move through the Stacks much faster than the mice. And there's really not a lot of time to spare, if it's that tiresome young hero you're looking for."

I couldn't let myself think about what might be happening to Byron. I didn't have time to panic. "You will? I mean, I never expected you'd help me yourself. I'd appreciate that, CATNYP. Really."

"How much would you appreciate it? How much does this young human mean to you?"

No one curses in New York Between unless they're prepared to deal with the consequences. But I came close. I hate unanswerable questions almost as much as I hate bargaining with a magical animal when I'm in a hurry. But what choice did I have? "Name your price," I said, "and we'll see if I can meet it."

"You," CATNYP said.

"Meaning?"

"I will not bargain with you. I'm offering you my help in return for your service. That's the trade. Time grows short, changeling girl."

Oh, boy. At this rate, I was going to be running errands for animal-Folk the rest of my life. "Okay," I said. "Yes. I agree. You help me get Byron out of here, and I'll scratch you behind your ears and bring you milk and whatever else you want."

"For as long as it pleases me."

It wasn't fair, but that's the Folk for you. I sighed. "For as long as it pleases you. But you'll have to wait your turn. There's a swan maiden with dibs."

"I don't think you'll have to worry about Snowbell," said CAT-NYP. "But it was honorable of you to mention it."

And then we were in another part of the library and I saw Byron. He was in deep trouble.

He was standing in the mouth of an aisle, with his hair blowing around his cheeks in a wind I couldn't feel. His back was straight, his head was high, his arms were stretched out before him. Beyond him was one of those purple and green gold-tusked demons with bug-eyes that look so comical in pictures. In the flesh, it wasn't comical at all. It was as beautiful and deadly as a gun. It was opening a door. Not an ordinary door, of course—a magical door, a dimensional door, a door that should not exist.

I turned to CATNYP. "I thought you said he was in trouble," I said. "It looks to me like he's just about to achieve his quest."

"Look again," said CATNYP.

Byron had moved a little closer to the door. He looked awfully rigid, standing there like a sleepwalker with his arms out. And I realized the demon was looking positively gleeful, which meant that it was doing something that made it happy, which was probably not good news for Byron.

"He conjured the demon to open a door Outside," CATNYP said. "He neglected to specify which Outside he wanted to go to."

"Oh, my." I took a step forward to pull him back, and fell over CATNYP, suddenly blocking my way.

"Touch him and you go with him," it growled.

"Okay," I said. "What do I do?"

"To rescue him?"

"Of course, to rescue him."

"The boy has broken a number of important prohibitions. He has entered the Stacks, he has Created a Disturbance and Defaced Books. He has sought to go Outside."

"Listen," I said. "I don't care what he's done. He doesn't deserve to go wherever that demon is taking him. I've already said I'll be your servant for as long as you want, which is way longer than the usual arrangement. Help me out here. Please, CATNYP?"

So I started out heroic and ended up pathetic. I'm only human, okay? And I was pretty upset. CATNYP wasn't. It sat down with its tail coiled around its front feet.

"You must break the bond between him and the demon," it said. "Once his concentration is broken, the demon will disappear and the door will close. Provided it is no more than half-way open."

By this time, Byron was about a third of the way down the row and the door looked to be about thirty-three degrees open. Swirls of darkness were leaping from the gap, and flashes of colors I didn't recognize. "Byron!" I screamed. "It's me, Neef. Come back!"

Nothing happened, except for the demon's grin creeping around under his ears. "He can't hear you," CATNYP remarked. "May I suggest a good book?"

It took every bit of self-control I had not to lose it. I know how these things work. This was a hint. I needed to keep my cool to figure it out. A good book could mean several things. I ran through the possibilities as fast as I could. With a magic book, I could turn Byron into something the demon wasn't interested in—a mouse, maybe. Or I could un-summon the demon. But finding the right book and the right spell would take longer than I had, even using CATNYP's Subject Index. I looked at the books nearest me. *The Art of Toulouse-Lautrec, The Architecture of Frank Lloyd Wright*, an illustrated folio edition of *The Canterbury Tales*. What they all had in common was their size. They were big books. Heavy books.

"The door is opening," CATNYP murmured.

There wasn't time to think. I yanked open the grill, grabbed the biggest and heaviest of the books in both hands, took three big steps down the aisle, and bopped Byron on the beezer.

Then several things happened at once. Byron collapsed in an untidy heap on the floor. The demon's grin disappeared into a roar that revealed more than I wanted to see of its crimson throat and knobbly blue tongue. The invisible door slipped from the demon's claws with a screech even louder than its roar and snapped shut with an ear-popping rush of pressure, taking the demon with it. All that remained were a few little eddies of darkness that rippled aimlessly around on the floor until CATNYP pounced on them and batted them still.

"Well," it said. "That was exciting. How's the book?"

I looked at the book—*The Canterbury Tales,* by Geoffrey Chaucer, the Kelmscott edition. It had held up very well—better than Byron, who groaned and lifted a hand to his head. I knelt down beside him, laid the book on the floor, and helped him sit up. He winced and felt the back of his head tenderly. He looked a whole lot less handsome than he had, and I loved him so much that my heart hurt.

"Byron," I said softly. "It's over, baby. You're safe now."

He pulled away from me. "What did you do that for?" he snapped. "I was nearly there!"

"The girl saved you," CATNYP said. "The only place you nearly were was a world even more inimical to you than this one."

"I knew what I was doing," Byron said.

"You did not," CATNYP said.

When the Catalogue of the New York Public Library tells you something, you can make book it's telling the truth. Byron squeezed his eyes shut very tight, took a deep breath, and let it go. "Okay." He opened his eyes. "Thanks, Neef. You saved my life. I appreciate it."

My heart, which had been standing still, thumped into action again. "No biggie. You'd have done it for me."

He smiled at me, dazzlingly. "Thanks anyway. And you, CAT-NYP. I owe you one."

"You do indeed."

It wasn't CATNYP's voice, and we weren't in the Stacks any more. We were in the Genius's office, sitting in library chairs facing his desk. CATNYP was on its haunches beside his wooden chair, staring at us with unblinking eyes.

"I am gravely disappointed in you," the Genius went on. "Gravely. Between the two of you, you have broken virtually every rule in the list. What do you have in your pocket, young lady?"

There are times when it's okay to lie to the Folk and times when it isn't. Besides, I was too tired. "A corned beef and mustard on rye, sir."

"And what were you intending to do with it?"

"Eat it. In the bathroom, where there aren't any books. I get hungry, and I hate having to go all the way to the Wannabe to get something to eat."

"Still," he said. "And you, young man. Why did you enter the Stacks?"

Byron was sitting up, very straight and proud. "I wanted a book," he said, looking the Genius firmly in the glasses.

"The pages would get it for you."

"There weren't any pages available," Byron said.

"That's right," I said. "There wasn't a page in the room."

CATNYP and the Genius exchanged an inscrutable look. "That's no excuse," the Genius said. "As you know very well. You've been told the Stacks are dangerous. You know what danger can mean here. You behaved foolishly." The glittering rectangles turned from Byron to me. "As did you. With better cause, perhaps, but still foolishly. I'm afraid I must ask you for your library cards."

I fished my card out of my jeans. I was astonished that our punishment wasn't any worse, but I was even more astonished at how sorry I was to be handing over my card. After the wonders I'd glimpsed, it was going to be hard to go back to soggy newspapers and torn magazine pages.

"I don't need it anyway," Byron said, pulling out his own card. "I know what I know. You can't take that away from me."

"Can I not?" the Genius said. His tone was mild, but the hair rose on the back of my neck. He held out his hand, and we gave him the cards.

Byron stood up and headed for the door. "Coming, Neef?"

I stood up, too. I felt tired and sad. "Yeah," I said. "Good-bye, CATNYP. I'll miss you."

"Not so fast," said the Genius. "I'm not done with you yet. Byron and Neef, you have broken the prohibitions and survived the ordeal.

If I recall my folklore correctly, a boon is customary in cases of this kind. One wish each, don't you think, CATNYP?"

The white lion nodded.

"Very well," the Genius said. "One wish it is. Byron?"

My jaw dropped. I could see why I'd get a boon—I mean, I rescued Byron and banished the demon. All he'd done was get bopped over the head just in time. In this scenario, he was the helpless one and I was the hero. So why was he getting a reward? I know the Folk aren't fair, but at least you can count on them to follow their own rules.

I was just about to ask this when Byron piped up. He'd recovered from his shock faster than I had, and was all bright-eyed and flushed with excitement and knowing exactly what he was going to say.

"I want to return Outside," he said.

"Very well," said the Genius. "When you go out that door, you will be in the Human Reading Room of the New York Public Library. A hero like you will have no difficulty in finding his way to the main entrance and onto Fifth Avenue. Good luck."

Byron turned toward the door. "Wait," I said. "First of all, how come he's a hero? He didn't do anything but almost get killed. And second of all, do you have any place to go out there, Byron? What are you going to do?"

Byron grinned. "Seek my fortune. Wanna come with?"

The Genius turned to me. "Is that your wish, Neef? To go with Byron and help him seek his fortune?"

You never know what you're going to be surprised by until it happens. Up until about a minute ago, I had thought that all I wanted in the world was to be with Byron and live happily ever after with him in the fairy-tale ending I'd earned for us. But then the hero question had come up and Byron had opted for New York Outside, and I suddenly wasn't so sure. What it boiled down to was that I knew I loved New York Between. I didn't know whether I loved Byron.

"Answer, child," said the Genius. "I'm getting bored."

I swear I had no idea what I was going to say. I opened my mouth and this is what came out: "My wish is to have my library card back."

"Let's get go . . . What did you say?" Byron's double take would have been funny, if I'd been in a laughing mood.

"I'm not going with you, Byron. I'm staying here."

I don't think the Genius would have allowed me to change my mind, but I might have tried if Byron had argued with me. Instead, he nodded sadly. "Good luck, Neef," he said. "I'll miss you." And then he gave me a hug and turned around and squared his shoulders and strode briskly through the door.

"Good riddance to bad rubbish," said CATNYP. "I never liked him."

"I did," I said, and started to cry. I hate crying. It makes my nose run and my eyes sting and it's so humiliatingly human. The Folk never cry.

I felt a weight on my knee and took my hands away from my face. CATNYP had its head in my lap, like a big dog, and was purring. My library card was in my lap too.

"Wish granted," the Genius said. "Now, one last piece of business, and we can all get back to work. I believe you have sworn service to CATNYP in return for its help in rescuing that singularly stupid young man from the consequences of his foolhardiness."

I sighed. What a bargain that was. "Yes. I did."

"CATNYP?"

The lion raised its chin from my leg. "I think," it said, "that I'll turn you into a Librarian. Come in and talk to me about it when you've had some rest. But now I'll take that corned beef sandwich. I've always been curious about human food."

I wanted to kiss it and cry into its mane and generally carry on like the crispy critter that I was, but the Genius cramped my style. So I took the sandwich out of my pocket and unwrapped it. It was kind of smooshed. CATNYP snapped it up, threw it back, and licked its chops with a long pink tongue.

"Interesting," it said. "You shall bring me another next time you come."

I turned to the Genius. "Can I ask you a question?"

"One wish," the Genius said. "You know what happens to mortals who are greedy with wishes."

"It's not a wish, Genius. It's information."

"Oh, very well. Byron is in the kind of tale in which the hero succeeds by attracting the right companions. If you had been his heroine, you would have chosen to go with him and used your superior common sense to help him to success in New York Outside. If the same rules obtain there."

"So what I get for saving Byron is to live happily ever after as a librarian?"

The Genius blinked, looking momentarily very like CATNYP. "What you get for saving Byron is the chance to be the hero in your own tale. Only time will tell what that will be."

❖

So that's it, really. In the tradition of the oldest fairy tales, Byron got his wish through someone else's help, and mostly I hope it turned out happily ever after for him. Sometimes, when I'm feeling sorry for myself, I hope he's a street person for real, seeing fairies wherever he looks without being able to talk to them. But mostly I'm happy enough, hanging out at the library, learning the ins and outs of the system, learning how to talk to the pages, feeding CATNYP corned beef sandwiches, and reading. I'm reading a lot: poetry, novels, plays, philosophy, history. And folklore. I was right. Mortals care a lot more about the Folk than the Folk care about them. At the Solstice Dance, I'll prove it, chapter and verse, so that even Snowbell will have to admit she's beat. In the meantime, I'm planning what boon I'll ask of Snowbell and figuring out what kind of a tale I want to be in. I don't know quite what it is yet. But I'm getting there.

They

RUDYARD KIPLING

❖

*Here's our Golden Oldie. First published a hundred years ago in
1904, this tremulous story is one of Kipling's finest tales. But
remember as you read it that this was written at a time when
certain prejudices were prevalent in British society. Even famous
authors like Kipling were not immune to them.*

If you like this story, try The Turn of the Screw *by Henry
James, or Phillipa Pearce's* Tom's Midnight Garden, *or Peter S.
Beagle's* A Fine and Private Place—*all wonderful ghost
stories.*

One view called me to another; one hill top to its fellow, half
across the county, and since I could answer at no more trouble than the snapping forward of a lever, I let the county
flow under my wheels. The orchid-studded flats of the East gave way
to the thyme, ilex, and grey grass of the Downs; these again to the rich
cornland and fig-trees of the lower coast, where you carry the beat of
the tide on your left hand for fifteen level miles; and when at last I
turned inland through a huddle of rounded hills and woods I had run
myself clean out of my known marks. Beyond that precise hamlet
which stands godmother to the capital of the United States, I found
hidden villages where bees, the only things awake, boomed in eighty-
foot lindens that overhung grey Norman churches; miraculous brooks
diving under stone bridges built for heavier traffic than would ever vex
them again; tithe-barns larger than their churches, and an old smithy
that cried out aloud how it had once been a hall of the Knights of the
Temple. Gipsies I found on a common where the gorse, bracken, and

heath fought it out together up a mile of Roman road; and a little further on I disturbed a red fox rolling dog-fashion in the naked sunlight.

As the wooded hills closed about me I stood up in the car to take the bearings of that great Down whose ringed head is a landmark for fifty miles across the low countries. I judged that the lie of the country would bring me across some westward running road that went to his feet, but I did not allow for the confusing veils of the woods. A quick turn plunged me first into a green cutting brimful of liquid sunshine, next into a gloomy tunnel where last year's dead leaves whispered and scuffled about my tyres. The strong hazel stuff meeting overhead had not been cut for a couple of generations at least, nor had any axe helped the moss-cankered oak and beech to spring above them. Here the road changed frankly into a carpeted ride on whose brown velvet spent primrose-clumps showed like jade, and a few sickly, white-stalked blue-bells nodded together. As the slope favoured I shut off the power and slid over the whirled leaves, expecting every moment to meet a keeper; but I only heard a jay, far off, arguing against the silence under the twilight of the trees.

Still the track descended. I was on the point of reversing and working my way back on the second speed ere I ended in some swamp, when I saw sunshine through the tangle ahead and lifted the brake.

It was down again at once. As the light beat across my face my fore-wheels took the turf of a great still lawn from which sprang horsemen ten feet high with levelled lances, monstrous peacocks, and sleek round-headed maids of honour—blue, black, and glistening—all of clipped yew. Across the lawn—the marshalled woods besieged it on three sides—stood an ancient house of lichened and weather-worn stone, with mullioned windows and roofs of rose-red tile. It was flanked by semi-circular walls, also rose-red, that closed the lawn on the fourth side, and at their feet a box hedge grew man-high. There were doves on the roof about the slim brick chimneys, and I caught a glimpse of an octagonal dove-house behind the screening wall.

Here, then, I stayed; a horseman's green spear laid at my breast; held by the exceeding beauty of that jewel in that setting.

"If I am not packed off for a trespasser, or if this knight does not ride a wallop at me," thought I, "Shakespeare and Queen Elizabeth at least must come out of that half-open garden door and ask me to tea."

A child appeared at an upper window, and I thought the little thing waved a friendly hand. But it was to call a companion, for presently another bright head showed. Then I heard a laugh among the yew-peacocks, and turning to make sure (till then I had been watching the house only) I saw the silver of a fountain behind a hedge thrown up against the sun. The doves on the roof cooed to the cooing water; but between the two notes I caught the utterly happy chuckle of a child absorbed in some light mischief.

The garden door—heavy oak sunk deep in the thickness of the wall—opened further: a woman in a big garden hat set her foot slowly on the time-hollowed stone step and as slowly walked across the turf. I was forming some apology when she lifted up her head and I saw that she was blind.

"I heard you," she said. "Isn't that a motor car?"

"I'm afraid I've made a mistake in my road. I should have turned off up above—I never dreamed—" I began.

"But I'm very glad. Fancy a motor car coming into the garden! It will be such a treat—" She turned and made as though looking about her. "You—you haven't seen any one, have you—perhaps?"

"No one to speak to, but the children seemed interested at a distance."

"Which?"

"I saw a couple up at the window just now, and I think I heard a little chap in the grounds."

"Oh, lucky you!" she cried, and her face brightened. "I hear them, of course, but that's all. You've seen them and heard them?"

"Yes," I answered. "And if I know anything of children one of them's having a beautiful time by the fountain yonder. Escaped, I should imagine."

"You're fond of children?"

I gave her one or two reasons why I did not altogether hate them. "Of course, of course," she said. "Then you understand. Then you won't think it foolish if I ask you to take your car through the gardens, once or twice—quite slowly. I'm sure they'd like to see it. They see so little, poor things. One tries to make their life pleasant, but—" she threw out her hands towards the woods. "We're so out of the world here."

"That will be splendid," I said. "But I can't cut up your grass."

She faced to the right. "Wait a minute," she said. "We're at the South gate, aren't we? Behind those peacocks there's a flagged path. We call it the Peacock's Walk. You can't see it from here, they tell me, but if you squeeze along by the edge of the wood you can turn at the first peacock and get on to the flags."

It was sacrilege to wake that dreaming house-front with the clatter of machinery, but I swung the car to clear the turf, brushed along the edge of the wood and turned in on the broad stone path where the fountain-basin lay like one star-sapphire.

"May I come too?" she cried. "No, please don't help me. They'll like it better if they see me."

She felt her way lightly to the front of the car, and with one foot on the step she called: "Children, oh, children! Look and see what's going to happen!"

The voice would have drawn lost souls from the Pit, for the yearning that underlay its sweetness, and I was not surprised to hear an answering shout behind the yews. It must have been the child by the fountain, but he fled at our approach, leaving a little toy boat in the water. I saw the glint of his blue blouse among the still horsemen.

Very disposedly we paraded the length of the walk and at her request backed again. This time the child had got the better of his panic, but stood far off and doubting.

"The little fellow's watching us," I said. "I wonder if he'd like a ride."

"They're very shy still. Very shy. But, oh, lucky you to be able to see them! Let's listen."

I stopped the machine at once, and the humid stillness, heavy with the scent of box, cloaked us deep. Shears I could hear where some gardener was clipping; a mumble of bees and broken voices that might have been the doves.

"Oh, unkind!" she said weariedly.

"Perhaps they're only shy of the motor. The little maid at the window looks tremendously interested."

"Yes?" She raised her head. "It was wrong of me to say that. They are really fond of me. It's the only thing that makes life worth living—when they're fond of you, isn't it? I daren't think what the place would be without them. By the way, is it beautiful?"

"I think it is the most beautiful place I have ever seen."

"So they all tell me. I can feel it, of course, but that isn't quite the same thing."

"Then have you never?" I began, but stopped abashed.

"Not since I can remember. It happened when I was only a few months old, they tell me. And yet I must remember something, else how could I dream about colours? I see light in my dreams, and colours, but I never see *them*. I only hear them just as I do when I'm awake."

"It's difficult to see faces in dreams. Some people can, but most of us haven't the gift," I went on, looking up at the window where the child stood all but hidden.

"I've heard that too," she said. "And they tell me that one never sees a dead person's face in a dream. Is that true?"

"I believe it is—now I come to think of it."

"But how is it with yourself—yourself?" The blind eyes turned towards me.

"I have never seen the faces of my dead in any dream," I answered.

"Then it must be as bad as being blind."

The sun had dipped behind the woods and the long shades were possessing the insolent horsemen one by one. I saw the light die from off the top of a glossy-leaved lance and all the brave hard green turn to soft black. The house, accepting another day at end, as it had accepted an hundred thousand gone, seemed to settle deeper into its rest among the shadows.

"Have you ever wanted to?" she said after the silence.

"Very much sometimes," I replied. The child had left the window as the shadows closed upon it.

"Ah! So've I, but I don't suppose it's allowed. . . . Where d'you live?"

"Quite the other side of the county—sixty miles and more, and I must be going back. I've come without my big lamp."

"But it's not dark yet. I can feel it."

"I'm afraid it will be by the time I get home. Could you lend me some one to set me on my road at first? I've utterly lost myself."

"I'll send Madden with you to the cross-roads. We are so out of the world, I don't wonder you were lost! I'll guide you round to the front of the house; but you will go slowly, won't you, till you're out of the grounds? It isn't foolish, do you think?"

"I promise you I'll go like this," I said, and let the car start herself down the flagged path.

We skirted the left wing of the house, whose elaborately cast lead guttering alone was worth a day's journey; passed under a great rose-grown gate in the red wall, and so round to the high front of the house which in beauty and stateliness as much excelled the back as that all others I had seen.

"Is it so very beautiful?" she said wistfully when she heard my raptures. "And you like the lead-figures too? There's the old azalea garden behind. They say that this place must have been made for children. Will you help me out, please? I should like to come with you as far as the crossroads, but I mustn't leave them. Is that you, Madden? I want you to show this gentleman the way to the cross-roads. He has lost his way but—he has seen them."

A butler appeared noiselessly at the miracle of old oak that must be called the front door, and slipped aside to put on his hat. She stood looking at me with open blue eyes in which no sight lay, and I saw for the first time that she was beautiful.

"Remember," she said quietly, "if you are fond of them you will come again," and disappeared within the house.

The butler in the car said nothing till we were nearly at the lodge gates, where, catching a glimpse of a blue blouse in a shrubbery, I swerved amply lest the devil that leads little boys to play should drag me into child-murder.

"Excuse me," he asked of a sudden, "but why did you do that, Sir?"

"The child yonder."

"Our young gentleman in blue?"

"Of course."

"He runs about a good deal. Did you see him by the fountain, Sir?"

"Oh, yes, several times. Do we turn here?"

"Yes, Sir. And did you 'appen to see them upstairs too?"

"At the upper window? Yes."

"Was that before the mistress come out to speak to you, Sir?"

"A little before that. Why d'you want to know?"

He paused a little. "Only to make sure that—that they had seen the car, Sir, because with children running about, though I'm sure you're driving particularly careful, there might be an accident. That was all, Sir. Here are the cross-roads. You can't miss your way from now on. Thank you, Sir, but that isn't *our* custom, not with—"

"I beg your pardon," I said, and thrust away the British silver.

"Oh, it's quite right with the rest of 'em as a rule. Good-bye, Sir."

He retired into the armour-plated conning tower of his caste and walked away. Evidently a butler solicitous for the honour of his house, and interested, probably through a maid, in the nursery.

Once beyond the signposts at the cross-roads I looked back, but the crumpled hills interlaced so jealously that I could not see where the house had lain. When I asked its name at a cottage along the road, the fat woman who sold sweetmeats there gave me to understand that people with motor cars had small right to live—much less to "go about talking like carriage folk." They were not a pleasant-mannered community.

When I retraced my route on the map that evening I was little wiser. Hawkin's Old Farm appeared to be the survey title of the place, and the old *County Gazetteer,* generally so ample, did not allude to it. The big house of those parts was Hodnington Hall, Georgian with early Victorian embellishments, as an atrocious steel engraving attested. I carried my difficulty to a neighbour—a deep-rooted tree of that soil—and he gave me a name of a family which conveyed no meaning.

A month or so later—I went again, or it may have been that my car took the road of her own volition. She over-ran the fruitless Downs, threaded every turn of the maze of lanes below the hills, drew through the high-walled woods, impenetrable in their full leaf, came out at the cross-roads where the butler had left me, and a little further on developed an internal trouble which forced me to turn her in on a grass way-waste that cut into a summer-silent hazel wood. So far as I could make sure by the sun and a six-inch Ordnance map, this should be the road flank of that wood which I had first explored from the heights above. I made a mighty serious business of my repairs and a glittering shop of my repair kit, spanners, pump, and the like, which I spread out orderly upon a rug. It was a trap to catch all childhood, for on such a day, I argued, the children would not be far off. When I paused in my work I listened, but the wood was so full of the noises of summer (though the birds had mated) that I could not at first distinguish these from the tread of small cautious feet stealing across the dead leaves. I rang my bell in an alluring manner, but the feet fled, and I repented, for to a child a sudden noise is very real terror. I must have been at work half an hour when I heard in the wood the voice of the blind woman crying: "Children, oh, children, where are you?" and the stillness made slow to close on the perfection of that cry. She came towards me, half feeling her way between the tree-boles, and though a child, it seemed, clung to her skirt, it swerved into the leafage like a rabbit as she drew nearer.

"Is that you?" she said, "from the other side of the county?"

"Yes, it's me from the other side of the county."

"Then why didn't you come through the upper woods? They were there just now."

"They were here a few minutes ago. I expect they knew my car had broken down, and came to see the fun."

"Nothing serious, I hope? How do cars break down?"

"In fifty different ways. Only mine has chosen the fifty-first."

She laughed merrily at the tiny joke, cooed with delicious laughter, and pushed her hat back.

"Let me hear," she said.

"Wait a moment," I cried, "and I'll get you a cushion."

She set her foot on the rug all covered with spare parts, and stooped above it eagerly. "What delightful things!" The hands through which she saw glanced in the chequered sunlight. "A box here—another box! Why you've arranged them like playing shop!"

"I confess now that I put it out to attract them. I don't need half those things really."

"How nice of you! I heard your bell in the upper wood. You say they were here before that?"

"I'm sure of it. Why are they so shy? That little fellow in blue who was with you just now ought to have got over his fright. He's been watching me like a Red Indian."

"It must have been your bell," she said. "I heard one of them go past me in trouble when I was coming down. They're shy—so shy even with me." She turned her face over her shoulder and cried again: "Children! Oh, children! Look and see!"

"They must have gone off together on their own affairs," I suggested, for there was a murmur behind us of lowered voices broken by the sudden squeaking giggles of childhood. I returned to my tinkerings and she leaned forward, her chin on her hand, listening interestedly.

"How many are they?" I said at last. The work was finished, but I saw no reason to go.

Her forehead puckered a little in thought. "I don't quite know," she said simply. "Sometimes more—sometimes less. They come and stay with me because I love them, you see."

"That must be very jolly," I said, replacing a drawer, and as I spoke I heard the inanity of my answer.

"You—you aren't laughing at me," she cried. "I—I haven't any of my own. I never married. People laugh at me sometimes about them because—because—"

"Because they're savages," I returned. "It's nothing to fret for. That sort laugh at everything that isn't in their own fat lives."

"I don't know. How should I? I only don't like being laughed at about *them*. It hurts; and when one can't see. . . . I don't want to seem silly," her chin quivered like a child's as she spoke, "but we blindies have only one skin, I think. Everything outside hits straight at our souls. It's different with you. You've such good defences in your eyes—looking out—before any one can really pain you in your soul. People forget that with us."

I was silent, reviewing that inexhaustible matter—the more than inherited (since it is also carefully taught) brutality of the Christian peoples, beside which the mere heathendom of the West Coast nigger is clean and restrained. It led me a long distance into myself.

"Don't do that!" she said of a sudden, putting her hands before her eyes.

"What?"

She made a gesture with her hand.

"That! It's—it's all purple and black. Don't! That colour hurts."

"But how in the world do you know about colours?" I exclaimed, for here was a revelation indeed.

"Colours as colours?" she asked.

"No. *Those* Colours which you saw just now."

"You know as well as I do," she laughed, "else you wouldn't have asked that question. They aren't in the world at all. They're in *you*—when you went so angry."

"D'you mean a dull purplish patch, like port-wine mixed with ink?" I said.

"I've never seen ink or port-wine, but the colours aren't mixed. They are separate—all separate."

"Do you mean black streaks and jags across the purple?"

She nodded. "Yes—if they are like this," and zigzagged her finger again, "but it's more red than purple—that bad colour."

"And what are the colours at the top of the—whatever you see?"

Slowly she leaned forward and traced on the rug the figure of the Egg itself.

"I see them so," she said, pointing with a grass stem, "white, green, yellow, red, purple, and when people are angry or bad, black across the red—as you were just now."

"Who told you anything about it—in the beginning?" I demanded.

"About the colours? No one. I used to ask what colours were when I was little—in table-covers and curtains and carpets, you see—because some colours hurt me and some made me happy. People told me; and when I got older that was how I saw people." Again she traced the outline of the Egg which it is given to very few of us to see.

"All by yourself?" I repeated.

"All by myself. There wasn't any one else. I only found out afterwards that other people did not see the Colours."

She leaned against the tree-bole plaiting and unplaiting chance-plucked grass stems. The children in the wood had drawn nearer. I could see them with the tail of my eye frolicking like squirrels.

"Now I am sure you will never laugh at me," she went on after a long silence. "Nor at *them*."

"Goodness! No!" I cried, jolted out of my train of thought. "A man who laughs at a child—unless the child is laughing too—is a heathen!"

"I didn't mean that of course. You'd never laugh *at* children, but I thought—I used to think—that perhaps you might laugh *about* them. So now I beg your pardon. . . . What are you going to laugh at?"

I had made no sound, but she knew.

"At the notion of your begging my pardon. If you had done your duty as a pillar of the state and a landed proprietress you ought to have summoned me for trespass when I barged through your woods the other day. It was disgraceful of me—inexcusable."

She looked at me, her head against the tree trunk—long and steadfastly—this woman who could see the naked soul.

"How curious," she half whispered. "How very curious."

"Why, what have I done?"

"You don't understand . . . and yet you understood about the Colours. Don't you understand?"

She spoke with a passion that nothing had justified, and I faced her bewilderedly as she rose. The children had gathered themselves in a roundel behind a bramble bush. One sleek head bent over something smaller, and the set of the little shoulders told me that fingers were on lips. They, too, had some child's tremendous secret. I alone was hopelessly astray there in the broad sunlight.

"No," I said, and shook my head as though the dead eyes could note. "Whatever it is, I don't understand yet. Perhaps I shall later—if you'll let me come again."

"You will come again," she answered. "You will surely come again and walk in the wood."

"Perhaps the children will know me well enough by that time to let me play with them—as a favour. You know what children are like."

"It isn't a matter of favour but of right," she replied, and while I wondered what she meant, a dishevelled woman plunged round the bend of the road, loose-haired, purple, almost lowing with agony as she ran. It was my rude, fat friend of the sweetmeat shop. The blind woman heard and stepped forward. "What is it, Mrs. Madehurst?" she asked.

The woman flung her apron over her head and literally grovelled in the dust, crying that her grandchild was sick to death, that the local doctor was away fishing, that Jenny the mother was at her wits' end, and so forth, with repetitions and bellowings.

"Where's the next nearest doctor?" I asked between paroxysms.

"Madden will tell you. Go round to the house and take him with you. I'll attend to this. Be quick!" She half-supported the fat woman into the shade. In two minutes I was blowing all the horns of Jericho under the front of the House Beautiful, and Madden, in the pantry, rose to the crisis like a butler and a man.

A quarter of an hour at illegal speeds caught us a doctor five miles away. Within the half-hour we had decanted him, much interested in motors, at the door of the sweetmeat shop, and drew up the road to await the verdict.

"Useful things cars," said Madden, all man and no butler. "If I'd had one when mine took sick she wouldn't have died."

"How was it?" I asked.

"Croup. Mrs. Madden was away. No one knew what to do. I drove eight miles in a tax cart for the Doctor. She was choked when we came back. This car 'd ha' saved her. She'd have been close on ten now."

"I'm sorry," I said. "I thought you were rather fond of children from what you told me going to the cross-roads the other day."

"Have you seen 'em again, Sir—this mornin'?"

"Yes, but they're well broke to cars. I couldn't get any of them within twenty yards of it."

He looked at me carefully as a scout considers a stranger—not as a menial should lift his eyes to his divinely appointed superior.

"I wonder why," he said just above the breath that he drew.

We waited on. A light wind from the sea wandered up and down the long lines of the woods, and the wayside grasses, whitened already with summer dust, rose and bowed in sallow waves.

A woman, wiping the suds off her arms, came out of the cottage next the sweetmeat shop.

"I've be'n listenin' in de back-yard," she said cheerily. "He says Arthur's unaccountable bad. Did ye hear him shruck just now? Unaccountable bad. I reckon t'will come Jenny's turn to walk in de wood nex' week along, Mr. Madden."

"Excuse me, Sir, but your lap-robe is slipping," said Madden deferentially. The woman started, dropped a curtsey, and hurried away.

"What does she mean by 'walking in the wood'?" I asked.

"It must be some saying they use hereabouts. I'm from Norfolk myself," said Madden. "They're an independent lot in this county. She took you for a chauffeur, Sir."

I saw the Doctor come out of the cottage followed by a draggletailed wench who clung to his arm as though he could make treaty for her with Death. "Dat sort," she wailed—"dey're just as much to us dat has 'em as if dey was lawful born. Just as much—just as much! An' God he'd be just as pleased if you saved 'un, Doctor. Don't take it from me. Miss Florence will tell ye de very same. Don't leave 'im, Doctor!"

"I know. I know," said the man, "but he'll be quiet for a while now. We'll get the nurse and the medicine as fast as we can." He signalled me to come forward with the car, and I strove not to be privy to what followed; but I saw the girl's face, blotched and frozen with grief, and I felt the hand without a ring clutching at my knees when we moved away.

The Doctor was a man of some humour, for I remember he claimed my car under the Oath of Aesculapius, and used it and me without mercy. First we convoyed Mrs. Madehurst and the blind woman to wait by the sick-bed till the nurse should come. Next we invaded a neat county town for prescriptions (the Doctor said the trouble was cerebro-spinal meningitis), and when the County Institute, banked and flanked with scared market cattle, reported itself out of nurses, for the moment we literally flung ourselves loose upon the county. We conferred with the owners of great houses—magnates at the ends of overarching avenues whose big-boned womenfolk strode away from their tea-tables to listen to the imperious Doctor. At last a white-haired lady sitting under a cedar of Lebanon and surrounded by a court of magnificent Borzois—all hostile to motors—gave the Doctor, who received them as from a princess, written orders which we bore many miles at top speed, through a park, to a French nunnery, where we took over in exchange a pallid-faced and trembling Sister. She knelt at the bottom of the tonneau telling her beads without pause till, by short cuts of the Doctor's invention, we had her to the sweetmeat shop once more. It was a long afternoon crowded with mad episodes that rose and dissolved like the dust of our wheels; cross-sections of remote and incomprehensible lives through which we raced at right angles; and I went home in the dusk, wearied out, to dream of the clashing horns of cattle; round-eyed nuns walking in a garden of graves; pleasant tea-parties beneath shaded trees; the carbolic-scented, grey-painted corridors of the County Institute; the steps of shy children in the wood, and the hands that clung to my knees as the motor began to move.

❖

I had intended to return in a day or two, but it pleased Fate to hold me from that side of the county, on many pretexts, till the elder and the wild rose had fruited. There came at last a brilliant day, swept clear from the south-west, that brought the hills within hand's reach—a day of unstable airs and high filmy clouds. Through no merit of my own I was free, and set the car for the third time on that known road. As I reached the crest of the Downs I felt the soft air change, saw it glaze under the sun; and, looking down at the sea, in that instant beheld the blue of the Channel turn through polished silver and dulled steel to dingy pewter. A laden collier hugging the coast steered outward for deeper water and, across copper-coloured haze, I saw sails rise one by one on the anchored fishing-fleet. In a deep dene behind me an eddy of sudden wind drummed through sheltered oaks, and spun aloft the first dry sample of autumn leaves. When I reached the beach road the sea-fog fumed over the brick-fields, and the tide was telling all the groins of the gale beyond Ushant. In less than an hour summer England vanished in chill grey. We were again the shut island of the North, all the ships of the world bellowing at our perilous gates; and between their outcries ran the piping of bewildered gulls. My cap dripped moisture, the folds of the rug held it in pools or sluiced it away in runnels, and the salt-rime stuck to my lips.

Inland the smell of autumn loaded the thickened fog among the trees, and the drip became a continuous shower. Yet the late flowers—mallow of the wayside, scabious of the field, and dahlia of the garden—showed gay in the mist, and beyond the sea's breath there was little sign of decay in the leaf. Yet in the villages the house doors were all open, and bare-legged, bare-headed children sat at ease on the damp doorsteps to shout "pip-pip" at the stranger.

I made bold to call at the sweetmeat shop, where Mrs. Made-hurst met me with a fat woman's hospitable tears. Jenny's child, she said, had died two days after the nun had come. It was, she felt, best out of the way, even though insurance offices, for reasons which she did not pretend to follow, would not willingly insure such stray lives. "Not but what Jenny didn't tend to Arthur as though he'd come all proper at de end of de first year—like Jenny herself." Thanks to Miss Florence, the child had been buried with a pomp which, in Mrs. Madehurst's opinion, more than covered the small irregularity of its birth. She described the coffin, within and without, the glass hearse, and the evergreen lining of the grave.

"But how's the mother?" I asked.

"Jenny? Oh, she'll get over it. I've felt dat way with one or two o' my own. She'll get over. She's walkin' in de wood now."

"In this weather?"

Mrs. Madehurst looked at me with narrowed eyes across the counter.

"I dunno but it opens de 'eart like. Yes, it opens de 'eart. Dat's where losin' and bearin' comes so alike in de long run, we do say."

Now the wisdom of the old wives is greater than that of all the Fathers, and this last oracle sent me thinking so extendedly as I went up the road that I nearly ran over a woman and a child at the wooded corner by the lodge gates of the House Beautiful.

"Awful weather!" I cried, as I slowed dead for the turn.

"Not so bad," she answered placidly out of the fog. "Mine's used to 'un. You'll find yours indoors, I reckon."

Indoors, Madden received me with professional courtesy, and kind inquiries for the health of the motor, which he would put under cover.

I waited in a still, nut-brown hall, pleasant with late flowers and warmed with a delicious wood fire—a place of good influence and great peace. (Men and women may sometimes, after great effort, achieve a creditable lie; but the house, which is their temple, cannot say anything save the truth of those who have lived in it.) A child's cart and a doll lay on the black-and-white floor, where a rug had been kicked back. I felt that the children had only just hurried away—to hide themselves, most like—in the many turns of the great adzed staircase that climbed stately out of the hall, or to crouch at gaze behind the lions and roses of the carven gallery above. Then I heard her voice above me, singing as the blind sing—from the soul:

> In the pleasant orchard-closes.

And all my early summer came back at the call.

> In the pleasant orchard-closes,
>   God bless all our gains say we—

> But may God bless all our losses,
>> Better suits with our degree.

She dropped the marring fifth line, and repeated—

> Better suits with our degree!

I saw her lean over the gallery, her linked hands white as pearl against the oak.

"Is that you—from the other side of the county?" she called.

"Yes, me from the other side of the county," I answered, laughing.

"What a long time before you had to come here again." She ran down the stairs, one hand lightly touching the broad rail. "It's two months and four days. Summer's gone!"

"I meant to come before, but Fate prevented."

"I knew it. Please do something to that fire. They won't let me play with it, but I can feel it's behaving badly. Hit it!"

I looked on either side of the deep fireplace, and found but a half-charred hedge-stake with which I punched a black log into flame.

"It never goes out, day or night," she said, as though explaining. "In case any one comes in with cold toes, you see."

"It's even lovelier inside than it was out," I murmured. The red light poured itself along the age-polished dusky panels till the Tudor roses and lions of the gallery took colour and motion. An old eagle-topped convex mirror gathered the picture into its mysterious heart, distorting afresh the distorted shadows, and curving the gallery lines into the curves of a ship. The day was shutting down in half a gale as the fog turned to stringy scud. Through the uncurtained mullions of the broad window I could see valiant horsemen of the lawn rear and recover against the wind that taunted them with legions of dead leaves.

"Yes, it must be beautiful," she said. "Would you like to go over it? There's still light enough upstairs."

I followed her up the unflinching, wagon-wide staircase to the gallery, whence opened the thin fluted Elizabethan doors.

"Feel how they put the latch low down for the sake of the children." She swung a light door inward.

"By the way, where are they?" I asked. "I haven't even heard them to-day."

She did not answer at once. Then, "I can only hear them," she replied softly. "This is one of their rooms—everything ready, you see."

She pointed into a heavily-timbered room. There were little low gate tables and children's chairs. A doll's house, its hooked front half open, faced a great dappled rocking horse, from whose padded saddle it was but a child's scramble to the broad window-seat overlooking the lawn. A toy gun lay in a corner beside a gilt wooden cannon.

"Surely they've only just gone," I whispered. In the failing light a door creaked cautiously. I heard the rustle of a frock and the patter of feet—quick feet through a room beyond.

"I heard that," she cried triumphantly. "Did you? Children, oh, children, where are you?"

The voice filled the walls that held it lovingly to the last perfect note, but there came no answering shout such as I had heard in the garden. We hurried on from room to oak-floored room; up a step here, down three steps there; among a maze of passages; always mocked by our quarry. One might as well have tried to work an un-stopped warren with a single ferret. There were bolt-holes innumerable—recesses in walls, embrasures of deep slitten windows now darkened, whence they could start up behind us; and abandoned fireplaces, six feet deep in the masonry, as well as the tangle of com-municating doors. Above all, they had the twilight for their helper in our game. I had caught one or two joyous chuckles of evasion, and once or twice had seen the silhouette of a child's frock against some darkening window at the end of a passage; but we returned empty-handed to the gallery, just as a middle-aged woman was setting a lamp in its niche.

"No, I haven't seen her either this evening, Miss Florence," I heard her say, "but that Turpin he says he wants to see you about his shed."

"Oh, Mr. Turpin must want to see me very badly. Tell him to come to the hall, Mrs. Madden."

I looked down into the hall whose only light was the dulled fire, and deep in the shadow I saw them at last. They must have slipped down while we were in the passages, and now thought themselves perfectly hidden behind an old gilt leather screen. By child's law, my fruitless chase was as good as an introduction, but since I had taken so much trouble I resolved to force them to come forward later by the simple trick, which children detest, of pretending not to notice them. They lay close, in a little huddle, no more than shadows except when a quick flame betrayed an outline.

"And now we'll have some tea," she said. "I believe I ought to have offered it you at first, but one doesn't arrive at manners, somehow, when one lives alone and is considered—h'm—peculiar." Then with very pretty scorn, "Would you like a lamp to see to eat by?"

"The firelight's much pleasanter, I think." We descended into that delicious gloom and Madden brought tea.

I took my chair in the direction of the screen, ready to surprise or be surprised as the game should go, and at her permission, since a hearth is always sacred, bent forward to play with the fire.

"Where do you get these beautiful short faggots from?" I asked idly. "Why, they are tallies!"

"Of course," she said. "As I can't read or write I'm driven back on the early English tally for my accounts. Give me one and I'll tell you what it meant."

I passed her an unburnt hazel-tally, about a foot long, and she ran her thumb down the nicks.

"This is the milk-record for the home farm for the month of

April last year, in gallons," said she. "I don't know what I should have done without tallies. An old forester of mine taught me the system. It's out of date now for every one else; but my tenants respect it. One of them's coming now to see me. Oh, it doesn't matter. He has no business here out of office hours. He's a greedy, ignorant man—very greedy or—he wouldn't come here after dark."

"Have you much land then?"

"Only a couple of hundred acres in hand, thank goodness. The other six hundred are nearly all let to folk who knew my folk before me, but this Turpin is quite a new man—and a highway robber."

"But are you sure I sha'n't be—?"

"Certainly not. You have the right. He hasn't any children."

"Ah, the children!" I said, and slid my low chair back till it nearly touched the screen that hid them. "I wonder whether they'll come out for me."

There was a murmur of voices—Madden's and a deeper note— at the low, dark side door, and a ginger-headed, canvas-gaitered giant of the unmistakable tenant-farmer type stumbled or was pushed in.

"Come to the fire, Mr. Turpin," she said.

"If—if you please, Miss, I'll—I'll be quite as well by the door." He clung to the latch as he spoke, like a frightened child. Of a sudden I realised that he was in the grip of some almost overpowering fear.

"Well?"

"About that new shed for the young stock—that was all. These first autumn storms settin' in . . . but I'll come again, Miss." His teeth did not chatter much more than the door latch.

"I think not," she answered levelly. "The new shed—m'm. What did my agent write you on the 15th?"

"I—fancied p'r'aps that if I came to see you—ma—man to man like, Miss—but—"

His eyes rolled into every corner of the room, wide with horror. He half-opened the door through which he had entered, but I noticed it shut again—from without and firmly.

"He wrote what I told him," she went on. "You are overstocked already. Dunnett's Farm never carried more than fifty bullocks—even in Mr. Wright's time. And *he* used cake. You've sixty-seven and you don't cake. You've broken the lease in that respect. You're dragging the heart out of the farm."

"I'm—I'm getting some minerals—superphosphates—next week. I've as good as ordered a truck-load already. I'll go down to the station to-morrow about 'em. Then I can come and see you man to man like, Miss, in the daylight. . . . That gentleman's not going away, is he?" He almost shrieked.

I had only slid the chair a little further back, reaching behind me to tap on the leather of the screen, but he jumped like a rat.

"No. Please attend to me, Mr. Turpin." She turned in her chair and faced him with his back to the door. It was an old and sordid little piece of scheming that she forced from him—his plea for the new cowshed at his landlady's expense, that he might with the covered manure pay his next year's rent out of the valuation after, as she made clear, he had bled the enriched pastures to the bone. I could not but admire the intensity of his greed, when I saw him out-facing for its sake whatever terror it was that ran wet on his forehead.

I ceased to tap the leather—was, indeed, calculating the cost of the shed—when I felt my relaxed hand taken and turned softly between the soft hands of a child. So at last I had triumphed. In a moment I would turn and acquaint myself with those quick-footed wanderers. . . .

The little brushing kiss fell in the centre of my palm—as a gift on which the fingers were, once, expected to close: as the all faithful half-reproachful signal of a waiting child not used to neglect even when grown-ups were busiest—a fragment of the mute code devised very long ago.

Then I knew. And it was as though I had known from the first day when I looked across the lawn at the high window.

I heard the door shut. The woman turned to me in silence, and I felt that she knew.

What time passed after this I cannot say. I was roused by the fall of a log, and mechanically rose to put it back. Then I returned to my place in the chair very close to the screen.

"Now you understand," she whispered, across the packed shadows.

"Yes, I understand—now. Thank you."

"I—I only hear them." She bowed her head in her hands. "I have no right, you know—no other right. I have neither borne nor lost—neither borne nor lost!"

"Be very glad then," said I, for my soul was torn open within me.

"Forgive me!"

She was still, and I went back to my sorrow and my joy.

"It was because I loved them so," she said at last, brokenly. "*That* was why it was, even from the first—even before I knew that they—they were all I should ever have. And I loved them so!"

She stretched out her arms to the shadows and the shadows within the shadow.

"They came because I loved them—because I needed them. I—I must have made them come. Was that wrong, think you?"

"No—no."

"I—I grant you that the toys and—and all that sort of thing were nonsense, but—but I used to so hate empty rooms myself when I was little." She pointed to the gallery. "And the passages all empty. . . . And how could I ever bear the garden door shut? Suppose—"

"Don't! For pity's sake, don't!" I cried. The twilight had brought a cold rain with gusty squalls that plucked at the leaded windows.

"And the same thing with keeping the fire in all night. *I* don't think it so foolish—do you?"

I looked at the broad brick hearth, saw, through tears I believe, that there was no unpassable iron on or near it, and bowed my head.

"I did all that and lots of other things—just to make believe. Then they came. I heard them, but I didn't know that they were not mine by right till Mrs. Madden told me—"

"The butler's wife? What?"

"One of them—I heard—she saw—and knew. Hers! *Not* for me. I didn't know at first. Perhaps I was jealous. Afterward, I began to understand that it was only because I loved them, not because— . . . Oh, you *must* bear or lose," she said piteously. "There is no other way—and yet they love me. They must! Don't they?"

There was no sound in the room except the lapping voices of the fire, but we two listened intently, and she at least took comfort from what she heard. She recovered herself and half rose. I sat still in my chair by the screen.

"Don't think me a wretch to whine about myself like this, but— but I'm all in the dark, you know, and *you* can see."

In truth I could see, and my vision confirmed me in my resolve, though that was like the very parting of spirit and flesh. Yet a little longer I would stay since it was the last time.

"You think it is wrong, then?" she cried sharply, though I had said nothing.

"Not for you. A thousand times no. For you it is right. . . . I am grateful to you beyond words. For me it would be wrong. For me only. . . ."

"Why?" she said, but passed her hand before her face as she had done at our second meeting in the wood. "Oh, I see," she went on simply as a child. "For you it would be wrong." Then with a little in-drawn laugh, "and, d'you remember, I called you lucky—once—at first. You who must never come here again!"

She left me to sit a little longer by the screen, and I heard the sound of her feet die out along the gallery above.

The Wings of Meister Wilhelm

THEODORA GOSS

❖

Historical fantasy can be set in any era, as the history itself is twisted around to serve the fantastic tale. Sometimes—as in this story—the reader is led slowly to the revelation of the imagined world's crucial difference. Other times it's clear from the beginning that the imagined world is bizarrely different from our own.

If you find this story fascinating, try some of R. Garcia y Robertson's short stories. Or try Judith Tarr's Lord of the Two Lands *or* His Majesty's Elephant, *in which she made Egypt and Byzantium vibrant with magic. Or Graham Joyce, whose* The Facts of Life *mixes magic with London during World War II.*

My mother wanted me to play the piano. She had grown up in Boston, among the brownstones and the cobbled streets, in the hush of rooms where dust settled slowly, in the sunlight filtering through lace curtains, over the leaves of spider-plants and aspidistras. She had learned to play the piano sitting on a mahogany stool with a rotating top, her back straight, hair braided into decorous loops, knees covered by layers of summer gauze. Her fingers had moved with elegant patience over the keys. A lady, she told me, always looked graceful on a piano stool.

I did try. But my knees, covered mostly by scars from wading in the river by the Beauforts' and then falling into the blackberry bushes, sprawled and banged—into the bench, into the piano, into Mr. Henry, the Episcopal Church organist, who drew in the corners of his mouth when he saw me, forming a pink oval of distaste. No matter how often my mother brushed my hair, I ran my fingers through it so that I looked like an animated mop, and to her dismay I never sat up straight, stooping over the keys until I resembled, she said, "that dreadful creature from Victor Hugo—the hunchback of Notre Dame."

I suppose she took my failure as a sign of her own. When she married my father, the son of a North Carolina tobacco farmer, she left Boston and the house by the Common that the Winslows had inhabited since the Revolution. She arrived as a bride in Ashton expecting to be welcomed into a red brick mansion fronted by white columns and shaded by magnolias, perhaps a bit singed from the war her grandfather the General had won for the Union. Instead, she found herself in a house with only a front parlor, its white paint flaking, flanked by a set of ragged tulip poplars. My father rode off every morning to the tobacco fields that lay around the foundations of the red brick mansion, its remaining bricks still blackened from the fires of the Union army and covered through the summer with twining purple vetch.

❖

A month after my first piano lesson with Mr. Henry, we were invited to a dinner party at the Beauforts'. At the bottom left corner of the invitation was written, "Violin Recital."

"Adeline Beaufort is so original," said my mother over her toast and eggs, the morning we received the invitation. "Imagine. Who in Balfour County plays the violin?" Her voice indicated the amused tolerance extended to Adeline Beaufort, who had once been Adeline Ashton, of the Ashtons who had given their name to the town.

Hannah began to disassemble the chafing dish. "I hear she's paying some foreign man to play for her. He arrived from Raleigh last week. He's staying at Slater's."

"Real-ly?" said my mother, lengthening the word as she said it to express the notion that Adeline Beaufort, who lived in the one red brick mansion in Ashton, fronted by white columns and shaded by magnolias, should know better than to allow some paid performer staying at Slater's, with its sagging porch and mixed-color clientele, to play at her dinner party.

My father pushed back his chair. "Well, it'll be a nice change from that damned organist." He was already in his work shirt and jodhpurs.

"Language, Cullen," said my mother.

"Rose doesn't mind my damns, does she?" He stopped as he passed and leaned down to kiss the top of my head.

I decided then that I would grow up just like my father. I would wear a blue shirt and leather boots up to my knees, and damn anything I pleased. I looked like him already, although the sandy hair so thick that no brush could tame it, the strong jaw and freckled nose that made him a handsome man made me a very plain girl indeed. I did not need to look in a mirror to realize my plainness. It was there, in my mother's perpetual look of disappointment, as though I were, to her, a symbol of the town with its unpaved streets where passing carriages kicked up dust in the summer, and the dull green of the tobacco fields stretching away to the mountains.

After breakfast I ran to the Beauforts' to find Emma. The two of us had been friends since our first year at Ashton Ladies' Academy. Together we had broken our dolls in intentional accidents, smuggled books like *Gulliver's Travels* out of the Ashton library, and devised secret codes that revealed exactly what we thought of the older girls at our school, who were already putting their hair up and chattering about beaux. I found her in the orchard below the house, stealing green apples. It was only the middle of June, and they were just beginning to be tinged with their eventual red.

"Aren't you bad," I said when I saw her. "You know those will only make you sick."

"I can't help it," she said, looking doleful. The expression did not suit her. Emma reminded me of the china doll Aunt Winslow had given me two summers ago, on my twelfth birthday. She had chestnut hair and blue eyes that always looked newly painted, above cheeks as smooth and white as porcelain, now round with the apple pieces she had stuffed into them. "Mama thinks I've grown too plump, so Caddy won't let me have more than toast and an egg for breakfast, and no sugar for my coffee. I get so hungry afterward!"

"Well, I'll steal you some bread and jam later if you'll tell me about the violin player from Slater's."

We walked to the cottage below the orchard, so close to the river at the bottom of the Beauforts' back garden that it flooded each spring. Emma felt above the low doorway, found the key we always kept there, and let us both in. The cottage had been used, as long as we could remember, for storing old furniture. It was filled with dressers gaping where their drawers had once been and chairs whose caned seats had long ago rotted through. We sat on a sofa whose springs sagged under its faded green upholstery, Emma munching her apple and me munching another although I knew it would give me a stomachache that afternoon.

"His name is Johann Wilhelm," she finally said through a mouthful of apple. "He's German, I think. He played the violin in Raleigh, and Aunt Otway heard him there, and said he was coming down here, and that we might want him to play for us. That's all I know."

"So why is he staying at Slater's?"

"I dunno. I guess he must be poor."

"My mother said your mother was original for having someone from Slater's play at her house."

"Yeah? Well, your mother's a snobby Yankee."

I kicked Emma, and she kicked back, and then we had a regular kicking battle. Finally, I had to thump her on the back when she choked on an apple from laughing too hard. I was laughing too hard as well. We were only fourteen, but we were old enough to understand certain truths about the universe, and we both knew that mothers were ridiculous.

❖

In the week that followed, I almost forgot about the scandalous violinist. I was too busy protesting against the dress Hannah was sewing for me to wear at the party, which was as uncomfortable as dresses were in those days of boning and horsehair.

"I'll tear it to bits before I wear it to the party," I said.

"Then you'll go in your nightgown, Miss Rose, because I'm not sewing you another party dress, that's for sure. And don't you sass your mother about it, either." Hannah put a pin in her mouth and muttered, "She's a good woman, who's done more for the colored folk in this town than some I could name. Now stand still or I'll stick you with this pin, see if I don't."

I shrugged to show my displeasure, and was stuck.

On the night of the party, after dinner off the Sêvres service that Judge Beaufort had ordered from Raleigh, we gathered in the back parlor, where chairs had been arranged in a circle around the piano. In front of the piano stood a man, not much taller than I was. Gray hair hung down to his collar, and his face seemed to be covered with wrinkles, which made him look like a dried-apple doll I had played with one autumn until its head was stolen by a squirrel. In his left hand he carried a violin.

"Come on, girl, sit by your Papa," said my father. We sat beside him although it placed Emma by Mr. Henry, who was complaining to Amelia Ashton, the town beauty, about the new custom of hiring paid performers.

The violinist waited while the dinner guests told each other to hush and be quiet. Then, when even the hushing had stopped, he said "Ladies and Gentlemen," bowed to the audience, and lifted his violin.

He began with a simple melody, like a bird singing on a tree branch in spring. Then came a series of notes, and then another, and I imagined the tree branch swaying in a rising wind, with the bird clinging to it. Then clouds rolled in, gray and filled with rain, and wind lashed the tree branch, so that the bird launched itself into the storm. It soared through turbulence, among the roiling clouds, sometimes enveloped in mist, sometimes with sunlight flashing on its wings, singing in fear of the storm, in defiance of it, in triumph. As this frenzy rose from the strings of the violin, which I thought must snap at any moment, the violinist began to sway, twisting with the force of the music as though he were the bird itself. Then, just as the music seemed almost unbearable, rain fell in a shower of notes, and the storm subsided. The bird returned to the branch and resumed its melody, then even it grew still. The violinist lifted his bow, and we sat in silence.

I sagged against my father, wondering if I had breathed since the music had started.

The violinist said "Thank you, ladies and gentlemen." The dinner guests clapped. He bowed again, drank from a glass of water Caddy had placed for him on the piano, and walked out of the room.

"Papa," I whispered, "can I learn to play the violin?"

"Sure, sweetheart," he whispered back. "As long as your mother says you can."

It took an absolute refusal to touch the piano, and a hunger strike lasting through breakfast and dinner, to secure my violin lessons.

"You really are the most obstinate girl, Rose," said my mother. "If I had been anything like you, my father would have made me stay in my room all day."

"I'll stay in my room all day, but I won't eat, not even if you bring me moldy bread that's been gnawed by rats," I said.

"As though we had rats! And there's no need for that. You'll have your lessons with Meister Wilhelm."

"With what?"

"Johann Wilhelm studied music at a European university. In Berlin, I think, or was it Paris? You'll call him Meister Wilhelm. That means Master, in German. And don't expect him to put up with your willfulness. I'm sure he's accustomed to European children, who are polite and always do as they're told."

"I'm not a child."

"Real-ly?" she said with an unpleasant smile, stretching the word out as long as she had when questioning Adeline Beaufort's social arrangements. "Then stop behaving like one."

"Well," I said, nervous under that smile, "should I go down to Slater's for my lessons?" The thought of entering the disreputable boarding house was as attractive as it was frightening.

"Certainly not. The Beauforts are going to rent him their cottage while he stays in Ashton. You'll have your lessons there."

❖

Meister Wilhelm looked even smaller than I remembered, when he opened the cottage door in answer to my knock. He wore a white smock covered with smudges where he had rubbed up against something dusty. From its hem hung a cobweb.

"Ah, come in, Fraulein," he said. "You must forgive me. This is no place to receive a young lady, with the dust and the dirt everywhere—and on myself also."

I looked around the cottage. It had changed little since the day Emma and I had eaten green apples on the sagging sofa, although a folded blanket now lay on the sofa, and I realized with surprise that the violinist must sleep there, on the broken springs. The furniture had been pushed farther toward the wall, leaving space in the center of the room for a large table cracked down the middle that had been banished from the Beauforts' dining room for at least a generation. On it were scattered pieces of bamboo, yards of unbleached canvas, tools I did not recognize, a roll of twine, a pot of glue with the handle of a brush sticking out of it, and a stack of papers written over in faded ink.

I did not know what to say, so I twisted the apron Hannah had made me wear between my fingers. My palms felt unpleasantly damp.

Meister Wilhelm peered at me from beneath gray eyebrows that seemed too thick for his face. "Your mother tells me you would like to play the violin?"

I nodded.

"And why the violin? It is not a graceful instrument. A young lady will not look attractive, playing Bach or Corelli. Would you not prefer the piano, or perhaps the harp?"

I shook my head, twisting the apron more tightly.

"No?" He frowned and leaned forward, as though to look at me more closely. "Then perhaps you are not one of those young ladies who cares only what the gentlemen think of her figure? Perhaps you truly wish to be a musician."

I scrunched damp fabric between my palms. I scarcely understood my motives for wanting to play the violin, but I wanted to be as honest with him as I could. "I don't think so. Mr. Henry says I have no musical talent at all. It's just that when I saw you playing the violin—at the Beauforts' dinner party, you know—it sounded, well, like you'd gone somewhere else while you were playing. Somewhere with a bird on a tree, and then a storm came. And I wanted to go there too." What a stupid thing to have said. He was going to think I was a complete idiot.

Meister Wilhelm leaned back against the table and rubbed the side of his nose with one finger. "It is perceptive of you to see a bird on a tree and a storm in my music. I call it *Der Sturmvogel*, the Stormbird. So you want to go somewhere else, Fraulein Rose. Where exactly is it you want to go?"

"I don't know." My words sounded angry. He did think I was an idiot, then. "Are you going to teach me to play the violin or not?"

He smiled, as though enjoying my discomfiture. "Of course I will teach you. Are not your kind parents paying me? Paying me well, so that I can buy food for myself, and pay for this bamboo, which has been brought from California, and glue, for the pot there, she is empty? But I am glad to hear, Fraulein, that you have a good reason for wanting to learn the violin. In this world, we all of us need somewhere else to go." From the top of one of the dressers, Meister Wilhelm lifted a violin. "Come," he said. "I will show you how to hold the instrument between your chin and shoulder."

"Is this your violin?" I asked.

"No, Fraulein. My violin, she was made by a man named Antonio Stradivari. Some day, if you are diligent, perhaps you shall play her."

I learned, that day, how to hold the violin and the bow, like holding a bird in your hands, with delicate firmness. The first time I put the bow to the strings I was startled by the sound, like a crow with a head cold, nothing like the tones Meister Wilhelm had drawn out of his instrument in the Beauforts' parlor.

"That will get better with time," he told me. "I think we have had enough for today, no?"

I nodded and put the violin down on the sofa. The fingers of my right hand were cramped, and the fingers of my left hand were crisscrossed with red lines where I had been holding the strings.

On a table by the sofa stood a photograph of a man with a beard and mustache, in a silver frame. "Who is this?" I asked.

"That is—was—a very good friend of mine, Herr Otto Lilienthal."

"Is he dead?" The question was rude, but my curiosity was stronger than any scruples I had with regard to politeness.

"Yes. He died last year." Meister Wilhelm lifted the violin from the sofa and put it back on top of the dresser.

"Was he ill?" This was ruder yet, and I dared to ask only because Meister Wilhelm now had his back to me, and I could not see his face.

"*Nein.* He fell from the sky, from a glider."

"A glider!" I sounded like a squawking violin myself. "That's what you're making with all that bamboo and twine and stuff. But this can't be all of it. Where do you keep the longer pieces? I know— in Slater's barn. From there you can take it to Slocumb's Bluff, where you can jump off the big rock." Then I frowned. "You know that's awfully dangerous."

Meister Wilhelm turned to face me. His smile was at once amused and sad.

"You are an excellent detective, *kleine* Rose. Someday you will learn that everything worth doing is dangerous."

❖

Near the end of July, Emma left for Raleigh, escorted by her father, to spend a month with her Aunt Otway. Since I had no one to play with, I spent more time at the cottage with Meister Wilhelm, scraping away at the violin with ineffective ardor and bothering him while he built intricate structures of bamboo and twine.

One morning, as I was preparing to leave the house, still at least an hour before my scheduled lesson with the violinist, I heard two voices in the parlor. I crept down the hall to the doorway and listened.

"You're so fortunate to have a child like Emma," said my mother. "I really don't know what to do with Elizabeth Rose."

"Well, Eleanor, she's an obstinate girl, I won't deny that," said a voice I recognized as belonging to Adeline Beaufort. "It's a pity Cullen's so lax with her. You ought to send her to Boston for a year or two. Your sister Winslow would know how to improve a young girl's manners."

"I suppose you're right, Adeline. If she were pretty, that might be some excuse, but as it is . . . Well, you're lucky with your Emma, that's all."

I had heard enough. I ran out of the house, and ran stumbling down the street to the cottage by the river. I pounded on the door. No answer. Meister Wilhelm must still be at Slater's barn. I tried the doorknob, but the cottage was locked. I reached to the top of the door frame, pulled down the key, and let myself in. I banged the door shut behind me, threw myself onto the sagging sofa, and pressed my face into its faded upholstery.

Emma and I had discussed the possibility that our mothers did not love us. We had never expected it to be true.

The broken springs of the sofa creaked beneath me as I sobbed. I was the bird clinging to the tree branch, the tree bending and shaking in the storm Meister Wilhelm had played on his violin, and the storm itself, wanting to break things apart, to tear up roots and crack branches. At last my sobs subsided, and I lay with my cheek on the damp upholstery, staring at the maimed furniture standing against the cottage walls.

Slowly I realized that my left hip was lying on a hard edge. I pushed myself up and, looking under me, saw a book with a green leather cover. I opened it. The frontispiece was a photograph of a tired-looking man labeled "Lord Rutherford, Mountaineer." On the title page was written, "*The Island of Orillion: Its History and Inhabitants,* by Lord Rutherford." I turned the page. Beneath the words "A Brief History of Orillion" I read, "The Island of Orillion achieved levitation on the twenty-third day of June, the year of our Lord one thousand seven hundred and thirty-six."

I do not know how long I read. I did not hear when Meister Wilhelm entered the cottage.

"I see you have come early today," he said.

I looked up from a corner of the sofa, into which I had curled myself. Since I felt ashamed of having entered the cottage while he was away, ashamed of having read his book without asking, what I said sounded accusatory. "So that's why you're building a glider. You want to go to Orillion."

He sat down on the other end of the sofa. "And how much have you learned of Orillion, *liebling?*"

He was not angry with me then. This time, my voice sounded penitent. "Well, I know about the painters and musicians and poets who were kicked out of Spain by that Inquisition person, Torquesomething, when Columbus left to discover America. How did they find the island in that storm, after everyone thought they had drowned? And when the pirate came—Blackbeard or Bluebeard or whatever—how did they make it fly? Was it magic?"

"Magic, or a science we do not yet understand, which to us resembles magic," said Meister Wilhelm.

"Is that why they built all those towers on the tops of the houses, and put bells in them—to warn everyone if another pirate was coming?"

Meister Wilhelm smiled. "I see you've read the first chapter."

"I was just starting the second when you came in. About how Lord Rutherford fell and broke his leg on a mountain in the Alps, and he thought he was going to die when he heard the bells, all ringing together. I thought they were warning bells?"

"Orillion has not been attacked in so long that the bells are only rung once a day, when the sun rises."

"All of them together? That must make an awful racket."

"Ah, no, *liebling*. Remember that the citizens of Orillion are artists, the children and grandchildren of artists. Those bells are tuned by the greatest musicians of Orillion, so that when they are rung, no matter in what order, the sound produced is a great harmony. From possible disorder, the bells of Orillion create musical order. But I think one chapter is enough for you today."

At that moment I realized something. "That's how Otto Lilienwhatever died, didn't he? He was trying to get to Orillion."

Meister Wilhelm looked down at the dusty floor of the cottage. "You are right, in a sense, Rose. Otto was trying to test a new theory of flight that he thought would someday allow him to reach Orillion. He knew there was risk—it was the highest flight he had yet attempted. Before he went into the sky for the last time, he sent me that book, and all of his papers. 'If I do not reach Orillion, Johann,' he wrote to me, 'I depend upon you to reach it.' It had been our dream since he discovered Lord Rutherford's book at university. That is why I have come to America. During the three years he lived on Orillion, Lord Rutherford charted the island's movements. In July, it would have been to the north, over your city of Raleigh. I tried to finish my glider there, but was not able to complete it in time. So I came here, following the island—or rather, Lord Rutherford's charts."

"Will you complete it in time now?"

"I do not know. The island moves slowly, but it will remain over this area only during the first two weeks of August." He stood and walked to the table, then touched the yards of canvas scattered over it. "I have completed the frame of the glider, but the cloth for the wings—there is much sewing still to be done."

"I'll help you."

"You, *liebling*?" He looked at me with amusement. "You are very generous. But for this cloth, the stitches must be very small, like so." He brought over a piece of canvas and showed me his handiwork.

I smiled a superior smile. "Oh, I can make them even smaller than that, don't worry." When Aunt Winslow had visited two summers ago, she had insisted on teaching me to sew. "A lady always looks elegant holding a needle," she had said. I had spent hours sitting in the parlor making a set of clothes for the china doll she had given me, which I had broken as soon as she left. In consequence, I could make stitches a spider would be proud of.

"Very well," said Meister Wilhelm, handing me two pieces of canvas that had been half-joined with an intricate, overlapping seam. "Show me how you would finish this, and I will tell you if it is good enough."

I crossed my legs and settled back into the sofa with the pieces of canvas, waxed thread and a needle, and a pair of scissors. He took *The Island of Orillion* from where I had left it on the sofa and placed it back on the shelf where he kept the few books he owned, between *The Empire of the Air* and *Maimonides: Seine Philosophie*. Then he sat on a chair with a broken back, one of his knees crossed over the other. Draping another piece of canvas over the raised knee, he leaned down so he could see the seam he was sewing in the dim light that came through the dirty windows. I stared at him sewing like that, as though he were now the hunchback of Notre Dame.

"You know," I said, "if you're nearsighted you ought to buy a pair of spectacles."

"Ah, I had a very good pair from Germany," he answered without looking up from his work. "They were broken just before I left Raleigh. Since then, I have not been able to afford another."

I sewed in silence for a moment. Then I said, "Why do you want to go to Orillion, anyway? Do you think—things will be better there?"

His fingers continued to swoop down to the canvas, up from the canvas, like birds. "The citizens of Orillion are artists. I would like to play my *Sturmvogel* for them. I think they would understand it, as you do." Then he looked up and stared at the windows of the cottage, as though seeing beyond them to the hills around Ashton, to the mountains rising blue behind the hills. "I do not know if human beings are better anywhere. But I like to think, *liebling,* that in this sad world of ours, those who create do not destroy so often."

❖

After the day on which I had discovered *The Island of Orillion,* when my lessons had been forgotten, Meister Wilhelm insisted that I continue practicing the violin, in spite of my protest that it took time away from constructing the glider. "If no learning, then no sewing—and no reading," he would say. After an hour of valiant effort on the instrument, I was allowed to sit with him, stitching triangles of canvas into bat-shaped wings. And then, if any time remained before dinner, I was allowed to read one, and never more than one, chapter of Lord Rutherford's book.

In spite of our sewing, the glider was not ready to be launched until the first week of August was nearly over. Once the pieces of canvas were sewn together, they had to be stretched over and attached to the bamboo frame, and then covered with three layers of wax, each of which required a day and a night to dry.

But finally, one morning before dawn, I crept down our creaking stairs and then out through the kitchen door, which was never locked. I ran through the silent streets of Ashton to Slater's barn and helped Meister Wilhelm carry the glider up the slope of the back pasture to Slocumb's Bluff, whose rock face rose above the waving grass. I had assumed we would carry the glider to the top of the bluff, where the winds from the rock face were strongest. But Meister Wilhelm called for me to halt halfway up, at a plateau formed by large, flat slabs of granite. There we set down the glider. In the gray light, it looked like a great black moth against the stones.

"Why aren't we going to the top?" I asked.

He looked over the edge of the plateau. Beyond the slope of the pasture lay the streets and houses of Ashton, as small as a dolls' town. Beyond them, a strip of yellow had appeared on the hilltops to the east. "That rock, he is high. I will die if the glider falls from such a height. Here we are not so high."

I stared at him in astonishment. "Do you think you could fall?" Such a possibility had never occurred to me.

"Others have," he answered, adjusting the strap that held a wooden case to his chest. He was taking his violin with him.

"Oh," I said, remembering the picture of Otto Lilienthal. Of course what had happened to Lilienthal could happen to him. I had simply never associated the idea of death with anyone I knew. I clenched and unclenched my hands.

"Help me to put on the glider," said Meister Wilhelm.

I held the glider at an angle as he crouched under it, fastened its strap over his chest, above the strap that held the violin case, and fitted his arms into the armrests.

"Rose," he said suddenly, "listen."

I listened, and heard nothing but the wind as it blew against the face of the bluff.

"You mean the wind?" I said.

"No, no," he answered, his voice high with excitement. "Not the wind. Don't you hear them? The bells, first one, then ten, and now a hundred, playing together."

I turned my head from side to side, trying to hear what he was hearing. I looked up at the sky, where the growing yellow was pushing away the gray. Nothing.

"Rose." He looked at me, his face both kind and solemn. In the horizontal light, his wrinkles seemed carved into his face, so that he looked like a part of the bluff. "I would like you to have my books, and my picture of Otto, and the violin on which you learned to play. I have nothing else to leave anyone in the world. And I leave you my gratitude, *liebling*. You have been to me a good friend."

He smiled at me, but turned away as he smiled. He walked back from the edge of the plateau and stood, poised with one foot behind the other, like a runner on a track. Then he sprang forward and began to sprint, more swiftly than I thought he could have, the great wings of the glider flapping awkwardly with each step.

He took one final leap, over the edge of the plateau, into the air. The great wings caught the sunlight, and the contraption of waxed canvas fastened on a bamboo frame became a moth covered with gold dust. It soared, wings outstretched, on the winds that blew up from the face of the bluff, and then out over the pasture, higher and farther into the golden regions of the sky.

My heart lifted within me, as when I had first heard Meister Wilhelm play the violin. What if I had heard no bells? Surely Orillion was there, and he would fly up above its houses of white stucco with their belltowers. The citizens of Orillion would watch this miracle, a man like a bird, soaring over them, and welcome him with glad shouts.

The right wing of the glider dipped. Suddenly it was spiraling down, at first slowly and then faster, like a maple seed falling, falling, to the pasture.

I heard a thin shriek, and realized it had come from my own throat. I ran as quickly as I could down the side of the bluff.

When I reached the glider, it was lying in an area of broken grass, the tip of its right wing twisted like an injured bird. Meister Wilhelm's legs stuck out from beneath it.

I lifted one side of the glider, afraid of what I might see underneath. How had Otto Lilienthal looked when he was found, crushed by his fall from the sky?

But I saw no blood, no intestines splattered over the grass—just Meister Wilhelm, with his right arm tangled in a broken armrest and twisted under him at an uncomfortable angle.

"Rose," he said in a weak voice. "Rose, is my violin safe?"

I lifted the glider off him, reaching under him to undo the strap across his chest. He rolled over on his back, the broken armrest still dangling from his arm. The violin case was intact.

"Are you going to die?" I asked, kneeling beside him, grass tickling my legs through my stockings. I could feel tears running down my nose, down to my neck, and wetting the collar of my dress.

"No, Rose," he said with a sigh, his fingers caressing the case as though making absolutely sure it was unbroken. "I think my arm is sprained, that is all. The glider acted like a helicopter and brought me down slowly. It saved my life." He pushed himself up with his left arm. "Is it much damaged?"

I rubbed the back of my hands over my face to wipe away tears. "No. Just one corner of the wing."

"Good," he said. "Then it can be fixed quickly."

"You mean you're going to try this again?" I stared at him as though he had told me he was about to hang himself from the beam of Slater's barn.

With his left hand, he brushed back his hair, which had blown over his cheeks and forehead. "I have only one more week, Rose. And then the island will be gone."

Together we managed to carry the glider back to Slater's barn, and I snuck back into the house for breakfast.

Later that day, I sat on the broken chair in the cottage while Meister Wilhelm lay on the sofa with a bandage around his right wrist.

"So, what's wrong with your arm?" I asked.

"I think the wrist, it is broken. And there is much pain. But no more breaks."

His face looked pale and old against the green upholstery. I crossed my arms and looked at him accusingly. "I didn't hear any bells."

He tried to smile, but grimaced instead, as though the effort were painful. "I have been a musician for many years. It is natural for me to hear things that you are not yet capable of hearing."

"Well, I didn't see anything either."

"No, Rose. You would see nothing. Through the science—or the magic—of its inhabitants, the bottom of the island always appears the same color as the sky."

Was that true? Or was he just a crazy old man, trying to kill himself in an especially crazy way? I kicked the chair leg, wishing that he had never come to Ashton, wishing that I had never heard of Orillion, if it was going to be a lie. I stood up and walked over to the photograph of Otto Lilienthal.

"You know," I said, my voice sounding angry, "it would be safer to go up in a balloon instead of a glider. At a fair in Brickleford last year, I saw an acrobat go up under a balloon and perform all kinds of tricks hanging from a wooden bar."

"Yes, you are right, it would be safer. I spent many years in my own country studying with Count Von Zeppelin, the great balloonist. But your acrobat, he cannot tell the balloon where to go, can he?"

"No." I turned to face him again. "But at least he doesn't fall out of the sky and almost kill himself."

He turned away from me and stared up at the ceiling. "But your idea is a good one, Rose. I must consider what it is I did wrong. Will you bring me those papers upon the table?"

I walked over to the table, lifted the stack of papers, and brought it over to the sofa. "What is this, anyway?" I asked.

Meister Wilhelm took the stack from me with his left hand. "These are the papers my friend Otto left me." He looked at the paper on top of the stack. "And this is the letter he wrote to me before he died." Awkwardly, he placed the stack beside him on the sofa and lifted the letter to his nearsighted eyes.

"Let me read it to you," I said. "You'll make yourself blind doing that."

"You are generous, Rose," he said, "but I do not think you read German, eh?"

I shook my head.

"Then I will read it to you, or rather translate. Perhaps you will see in it another idea, like she of the balloon, that might help us. Or perhaps I will see in it something that I have not seen before."

He read the letter slowly, translating as he went, sometimes stumbling over words for which he did not know the English equivalent. It was nothing like the letters Emma and I were writing to each other while she stayed in Raleigh. There was no discussion of daily events, of the doings of family.

Instead, Otto Lilienthal had written about the papers he was leaving for his friend, which discussed his theories. He wrote admiringly of Besnier, the first to create a functional glider. He discussed the mistakes of Mouillard and Le Bris, and the difficulties of controlling a glider's flight. He praised Cayley, whose glider had achieved lift, and lamented Pénaud, who became so dispirited by his failures that he locked his papers into a coffin and committed suicide. Finally he wrote of his own ideas, their merits and drawbacks, and of how he had attempted to solve the two challenges of the glider, lift and lateral stability. He had solved the problem of lift early in his career. Now he would try to solve the other.

The letter ended, "My dear Johann, remember how we dreamed of gliding through the air, like the storks in our native Pomerania. I expect to succeed. But if I fail, do you continue my efforts. Surely one with your gifts will succeed, where I cannot. Always remember that you are a violinist." When he had finished the letter, Meister Wilhelm passed his hand, still holding a sheet of paper, over his eyes.

I looked away, out of the dirty window of the cottage. Then I asked, because curiosity had once again triumphed over politeness, "Why did he tell you to remember that you're a violinist?"

Meister Wilhelm answered in a tired voice, "He wanted to encourage me. To tell me, remember that you are worthy to mingle with the citizens of Orillion, to make music for them before the Monument of the Muse at the center of the city. He wanted—"

Suddenly he sat up, inadvertently putting his weight on his right hand. His face creased in pain, and he crumpled back against the seat of the sofa. But he said, in a voice filled with wonder, "No. I have been stupid. Always remember, Rose, that we cannot find the right answers until we ask the right questions. Tell me, what did the glider do just before it fell?"

I stared at him, puzzled. "It dipped to the right."

He waved his left forefinger in the air, as though to punctuate his point. "Because it lacked lateral stability!"

I continued to look puzzled.

He waved his finger again, at me this time. "That is the problem Otto was trying to solve."

I sat back down. "Yes, well he didn't solve it, did he?"

The finger waved once again, more frantically this time. "He solved it in principle. He knew that lateral stability is created with the legs, just as lift is controlled with the position of the body in the armrests. His final flight must have been intended to test which position would provide the greatest amount of control." Meister Wilhelm sat, pulling himself up this time with his left hand. "After his death, I lamented that Otto could never tell me his theory. But he has told me, and I was too stupid to see it!" He rose and began pacing, back and forth as he spoke, over the floor of the cottage. "I have been keeping my legs still, trying not to upset the glider's balance. Otto was telling me that I must use my body like a violinist, that I must not stay still, but respond to the rhythm of the wind, as I respond to the rhythm of music. He thought I would understand."

He turned to me. "Rose, we must begin to repair the glider tomorrow. And then, I will fly it again. But this time I will fly from the top of Slocumb's Bluff, where the winds are strongest. And I will become one with the winds, with the great music that they will play through me."

"Like the Stormbird," I said.

His face, so recently filled with pain, was now filled with hope. "Yes, Rose. Like *Der Sturmvogel*."

❖

Several days later, when I returned for dinner after a morning spent with Meister Wilhelm, Hannah handed me a letter from Emma.

"Did the post come early?" I asked.

"No, child. Judge Beaufort came back from Raleigh and brought it himself. He was smoking in the parlor with your Papa, and I'm gonna have to shake out them parlor curtains. So you get along, and don't bother me, hear?"

I walked up the stairs to my room and lay on top of the counterpane to read Emma's letter. "Dear Rose," it began. "Aunt Otway, who's been showing me an embroidery stitch, asks what I'm going to write." That meant her letter would be read. "Father is returning suddenly to Ashton, but I will remain here until school begins in September." She had told me she was returning at the end of August. And Emma never called Judge Beaufort "Father." Was she trying to show off for Aunt Otway? Under the F in "Father" was a spot of ink, and I noticed that Emma's handwriting was unusually spotty. Under the b and second e in "embroidery," for instance. "Be" what? The letters over the remaining spots spelled "careful." What did Emma mean? The rest of her letter described a visit to the Museum of Art.

Just then, my mother entered the room. "Rose," she said. Her voice was gentler than I had ever heard it. She sat down on the edge of my bed. "I'm afraid you can't continue your lessons with Meister Wilhelm."

I started at her in disbelief. "You don't want me to have anything I care about, do you? Because you hate me. You've hated me since I was born. I'll tell Papa, and he'll let me have my violin lessons, you'll see!"

She rose, and her voice was no longer gentle. "Very well, Elizabeth. Tell your father, exactly as you wish. Until he comes home from the Beauforts', however, you are to remain in this room." She walked out, closing the door with an implacable click behind her.

Was this what Emma had been trying to warn me about? Had she known that my mother would forbid me from continuing my lessons? But how could she have known, in Raleigh?

As the hours crept by, I stared at the ceiling and thought about what I had read in Lord Rutherford's book. I imagined the slave ship that had been wrecked in a storm, and the cries of the drowning slaves. How they must have wondered, to see Orillion descending from the sky, to walk through its city of stucco houses surrounded by rose gardens. How the captain must have cursed when he was imprisoned by the citizens of Orillion, and later imprisoned by the English as a madman. He had raved until the end of his life about an island in the clouds.

Hannah brought my dinner, saying to me as she set it down, "Ham sandwiches, Miss Rose. You always liked them, didn't you?" I didn't answer. I imagined myself walking between the belltowers of the city, to the Academy of Art. I would sit on the steps, beneath a frieze of the great poets from Sappho to Shakespeare, and listen to Meister Wilhelm playing his violin by the Monument of the Muse, the strains of his *Sturmvogel* drifting over the surface of the lake.

After it had grown dark, I heard the bang of the front door and the sound of voices. They came up the stairs, and as they passed my door I heard one word—"violin." Then the voices receded down the hall.

I opened my door, cautiously looking down the hall and then toward the staircase. I saw a light under the door of my father's study and no signs of my mother or Hannah.

Closing my bedroom door carefully behind me, I crept down the hall, stepping close to the wall where the floorboards were less likely to creak. I stopped by the door of the study and listened. The voices inside were raised, and I could hear them easily.

"To think that I let a damned Jew put his dirty fingers on my daughter." That was my father's voice. My knees suddenly felt strange, and I had to steady them with my hands. The hallway seemed to sway around me.

"We took care of him pretty good in Raleigh." That was a voice I did not recognize. "After Reverend Yancey made sure he was sacked from the orchestra, Mr. Empie and I visited him to get the money for all that bamboo he'd ordered on credit. He told us he hadn't got the money. So we reminded him of what was due to decent Christian folk, didn't we, Mr. Empie?"

"All right, Mr. Biggs," said another voice I had not heard before. "There was no need to break the man's spectacles."

"So I shook him a little," said Mr. Biggs. "Serves him right, I say."

"What's done is done," said a voice I knew to be Judge Beaufort's. "The issue before us is, what are we to do now? He has been living on my property, in close proximity to my family, for more than a month. He has been educating Mr. Caldwell's daughter, filling her head with who knows what dangerous ideas. Clearly he must be taken care of. Gentlemen, I'm open for suggestions."

"Burn his house down," said Mr. Biggs. "That's what we do when niggers get uppity in Raleigh."

"You forget, Mr. Biggs," said Judge Beaufort, "that his house is my house. And as the elected judge of this town, I will allow no violence that is not condoned by law."

"Then act like a damned judge, Edward," said my father, with anger in his voice. "He's defaulted on a debt. Let him practice his mumbo jumbo in the courthouse jail for a few days. Then you can send him on to Raleigh with Mr. Biggs and Mr. Empie. Just get him away from my daughter!"

There was silence, then the sound of footsteps, as though someone were pacing back and forth over the floor, and then a clink and gurgle, as though a decanter had been opened and liquid were tumbling into a glass.

"All right, gentlemen," said Judge Beaufort. I leaned closer to the door even though I could hear his voice perfectly well. "First thing tomorrow morning, we get this Wilhelm and take him to the courthouse. Mr. Empie, Mr. Biggs, I depend on you to assist us."

"Oh, I'll be there all right," said Mr. Biggs. "Me and Bessie." I heard a metallic click.

My father spoke again. "Put that away, sir. I'll have no loaded firearms in my home."

"He'll put it away," said Mr. Empie. "Come on, Biggs, be sensible, man. Judge Beaufort, if I could have a touch more of that whiskey?"

I crept back down the hall with a sick feeling in my stomach, as though I had eaten a dozen green apples. So this was what Emma had warned me about. I wanted to lie down on my bed and sob, with the counterpane pulled over my head to muffle the sounds. I wanted to punch the pillows until feathers floated around the room. But as I reached my door, I realized there was something else I must do. I must warn Meister Wilhelm.

I crept down the stairs. As I entered the kitchen, lit only by the embers in the stove, I saw a figure sitting at the kitchen table. It was my mother, writing a note, with a leather wallet on the table beside her.

She looked up as I entered, and I could see, even in the dim light from the stove, that her face was puffed with crying. We stared at each other for a moment. Then she rose. "What are you doing down here?" she asked.

I was so startled that all I could say was, "I heard them in the study."

My mother stuffed the note she had been writing into the wallet, and held it toward me.

"I was waiting until they were drunk, and would not miss me," she said. "But they think you're already asleep, Rose. Run and give this to Meister Wilhelm."

I took the wallet from her. She reached out, hesitantly, to smooth down my mop of hair, but I turned and opened the kitchen door. I walked through the back garden, picking my way through the tomato plants, and ran down the streets of Ashton, trying not to twist my ankles on invisible stones.

When I reached the cottage, I knocked quietly but persistently on the door. After a few minutes I heard a muffled grumbling, and then a bang and a word that sounded like an oath. The door opened, and there stood Meister Wilhelm, in a white nightshirt and nightcap, like a ghost floating in the darkness. I slipped past him into the cabin, tossed the wallet on the table, where it landed with a clink of coins, and said, "You have to get out of here, as soon as you can. And there's a note from my mother."

He lit a candle, and by its light I saw his face, half-asleep and half-incredulous, as though he believed I were part of some strange dream. But he read the note. Then he turned to me and said, "Rose, I hesitate to ask of you, but will you help me one final time?"

I nodded eagerly. "You go south to Brickleford, and I'll tell them you've gone north to Raleigh."

He smiled at me. "Very heroic of you, but I cannot leave my glider, can I? Mr. Empie would find it and take it apart for its fine bamboo, and then I would be left with what? An oddly shaped parachute. No, Rose, I am asking you to help me carry the glider to Slocumb's Bluff."

"What do you mean?" I asked. "Are you going to fly it again?"

"My final flight, in which I either succeed, or—But have no fear, *liebling*. This time I will succeed."

"But what about the wing?" I asked.

"I finished the repairs this afternoon, and would have told you about it tomorrow, or rather today, since my pocket watch on the table here, she tells me it is after midnight. Well, Rose, will you help me?"

I nodded. "We'd better go now though, in case that Mr. Biggs decides to burn down the cottage after all."

"Burn down—? There are human beings in this world, Rose, who do not deserve the name. Come, then. Let us go."

The wind tugged at the glider as we carried it up past the plateau where it had begun its last flight, toward the top of Slocumb's Bluff. In the darkness it seemed an animated thing, as though it wanted to fly over the edge of the bluff, away into the night. A little below the top of the bluff, we set it down beneath a grove of pine trees, where no wind came. We sat down on a carpet of needles to wait for dawn.

Through the long, dark hours, Meister Wilhelm told me about his childhood in Pomerania and his days at the university. Although it was August, the top of the bluff was chilly, and I often wished for a coat to pull over my dress. At last, however, the edges of the sky looked brighter, and we stood, shaking out our cold, cramped legs.

"This morning I am an old man, *liebling*," said Meister Wilhelm, buckling the strap of the violin case around his chest. "I do not remember feeling this stiff, even after a night in the Black Forest. Perhaps I am too old, now, to fly as Otto would have me."

I looked at the town. In the brightening stillness, four small shapes were moving toward Judge Beaufort's house. "Well then, you'd better go down to the courthouse and give yourself up, because they're about to find out that you're not at the cottage."

Meister Wilhelm put his hand on my shoulder. "It is good that you have clear eyes, Rose. Help me to put on the glider."

I helped him lift the glider to his back and strap it around his chest, as I had done the week before. The four shapes below us were now moving from Judge Beaufort's house toward Slater's barn.

Meister Wilhelm looked at me sadly. "We have already said our goodbye, have we not? Perhaps we do not need to say it again." He smiled. "Or perhaps we will meet, someday, in Orillion."

I said, suddenly feeling lonelier than I had ever felt before, "I don't have a glider."

But he had already turned away, as though he were no longer thinking of me. He walked out from under the shelter of the trees and to the top of the bluff, where the wind lifted his gray hair into a nimbus around his head.

"Well, what are you waiting for?" I asked, raising my voice so he could hear it over the wind. Four shapes were making their way toward us, up the slope above Slater's barn.

"The sun, Rose," he answered. "She is not yet risen." He paused, as though listening, then added, "Do you know what day this is? It is the ninth of August, the day that my friend Otto died, exactly one year ago."

And then the edge of the sun rose over the horizon. As I had seen him do once before, Meister Wilhelm crouched into the stance of a runner. Then he sprang forward and sprinted toward the edge of the bluff. With a leap over the edge, he was riding on the wind, up, up, the wings of the glider outspread like the wings of a moth. But this time those wings did not rise stiffly. They turned and soared, as though the wind were their natural element. Beneath them, Meister Wilhelm was twisting in intricate contortions, as though playing an invisible violin. Then the first rays of the sun were upon him, and he seemed a man of gold, flying on golden wings.

And then, I heard them. First one, then ten, then a hundred— the bells of Orillion, sounding in wild cacophony, in celestial harmony. I stood at the top of Slocumb's Bluff, the wind blowing cold through my dress, my chin lifted to the sky, where the bells of Orillion were ringing and ringing, and a golden man flying on golden wings was a speck rapidly disappearing into the blue.

"Rose! What in heaven's name are you doing here?" I turned to see my father climbing over the top of the bluff, with Judge Beaufort and two men, no doubt Mr. Biggs and Mr. Empie, puffing behind. I looked into his handsome face, which in its contours so closely resembled mine, so that looking at him was like looking into a mirror. And I answered, "Watching the dawn."

❖

I managed to remove *The Island of Orillion* and the wallet containing my mother's note from the cottage before Mr. Empie returned to claim Meister Wilhelm's possessions in payment for his bamboo. They lie beside me now on my desk, as I write.

After my father died from what the Episcopal minister called "the demon Drink," I was sent to school in Boston because, as Aunt Winslow told my mother, "Rose may never marry, so she might as well do something useful." When I returned for Emma's wedding to James Balfour, who had joined his uncle's law practice in Raleigh, I read in the Herald that the Wrights had flown an airplane among the dunes near Kitty Hawk, on the winds rising from the Atlantic. As I arranged her veil, which had been handed down through generations of Ashton women and made her look even more like a china doll, except for the caramel in her right cheek, I wondered if they had been searching for Orillion.

And then, I did not leave Ashton again for a long time. One day, as I set the beef tea and toast that were all my mother could eat, with the cancer eating her from the inside like a serpent, on her bedside table, she opened her eyes and said, "I've left you all the money." I took her hand, which had grown so thin that blue veins seemed to cover it like a net, and said, "I'm going to buy an airplane. There's a man in Brickleford who can teach me how to fly." She looked at me as though I had just come home from the river by the Beauforts', my mouth stained with blackberries and my stockings covered with mud. She said, "You always were a troublesome child." Then she closed her eyes for the last time.

I have stored the airplane in Slocumb's barn, which still stands behind the remains of the boarding house. Sometimes I think, perhaps Orillion has changed its course since Lord Rutherford heard its bells echoing from the mountains. Perhaps now that airplanes are becoming common, it has found a way of disguising itself completely and can no longer be found. I do not know. I read Emma's letters from Washington, in which she complains about the tedium of being a congressman's wife and warns about a war in Europe. Even without a code, they transmit the words "be careful" to the world. Then I pick up the wallet, still filled a crumbling note and a handful of coins. And I consult Lord Rutherford's charts.

Displaced Persons

LEAH BOBET

❖

Taking a well-known story and telling it from a different point of view is known as "redaction." In this story, Leah Bobet has shown us what happens to the henchmen (or hench monkeys) of a famous villainess. It lets us see the tale we thought we knew so well in a different way.

If you enjoyed this, try "Spillage," by Nancy Kress, about Cinderella's rat coachman. Or Jane Yolen's "The Bridge," about the friendship between the bridge and the doomed troll who meet up with three billy goats. Or try the novel I Was a Rat *by Philip Pullman.*

Regime change is a bitch, and we never saw it coming. Although I suppose nobody ever does. One day you're in public service, the next you're out of a job. One day you're on top of the world, the next, in the gutters of the Emerald City and being driven out of there, too.

One day you have wings, and the next you crawl.

❖

Louis-Chance is the leader now, for our generals are all dead. He was a porter once; they did not think he was dangerous enough to kill, and it's easy to see why. He's bent from age, exhaustion, defeat, as well as the sudden lightness on his back. He wants us to bide our time, up on the mountain where nobody goes. *If primates were meant to fly,* he says, *the Great Monkey would have given us wings himself. We have transgressed horribly, my fellows. It is no more than we deserve.* She offered us wings;

she gave us somewhere to live, all the fruit we could eat and throw, travel opportunities, learning and leisure. It was a good life: I can't see how we could have offended by taking that which was given.

There was no way we could have known.

And then one day we came home and she was naught but a puddle on the floor. We collected as much of her as we could for a decent burial: some had already leaked through the cracks in the flagstones, run into the drains and then the river and the sea, and was lost for good. We poured what was left around the roots of a mighty oak, meaning to tend it until the end of our days. But there was no place for us in the New World Order, no place for monkeys and trees amidst scarecrows and men of tin and other artificialities.

We were tried, and we were found guilty. To this day I'm not sure what exactly the charge was.

❖

I still have nightmares, some nights, of those last days: the smell of burning flesh, the pain in my back, the shouts that followed us for days and nights of nonstop running, running some of us had never done in our lives. The blood that marked our path until it stopped, and the tears that kept on going.

She gave us wings; the mob lined us up, one by one, and took them away again.

It hurt more than I expected from the sounds of chopping coming down the line. It sounded more solid: like an axe moving through nerveless, stubborn wood, something that could offer at least token resistance to the blade. The wings made no sound as they were piled high in the centre of the green-paved square, feathers ruffling in the afternoon breeze.

"Death to the Witch!" they cried as the torches came down and the stink rose into the air. "Death to her kingdom!"

I'm told I fainted.

❖

Nobody goes up into the mountains, so we went up into the mountains.

There is little to eat; those we have not lost to pain or injury we are losing to despair. Those who are still brave, still strong, are building a life. Our gardens are not like her gardens. Our caves are not like her castle, and when we pluck fruit from the trees we have nursed so carefully in crevices, away from the wind, we have to climb their rough and horrid trunks.

These days, we do a lot of waiting.

We wait for their anger to heal, for their memories to fade, for our next generation to be born and weaned. For this I believe: the wings of our children will be their own. Not grafted: inseparable from their small brown bodies by axe or trial or fire. They will hunt through the skies, play in the clouds, alight on the tops of trees instead of reaching from below. They will bring us news of the world, delicacies from afar, sights to be tasted and savoured on cold nights. They will not walk, or crawl, or beg.

They will fly.

Sergeant Chip

BRADLEY DENTON

❖

The augmentation of animals to make them smarter, or handier for human wars, is a well-known science fictional device. Bradley Denton uses this idea to write a poignant novella that leaves the reader questioning the idea of war itself. It is a tale of betrayed loyalty, so don't miss the sinister stuff going on in the background.

If you like this story, try Pierre Boulle's novel, Monkey Planet, *which was later made into the movie* Planet of the Apes. *Or Harlan Ellison's hard-hitting novella,* A Boy and His Dog, *also made into a movie. Or Robert Silverberg's prize-winning story of an augmented dolphin, "Ishmael in Love."*

To the Supreme Commander of the soldier who bears this message—

Sir or Madam:

Today before it was light I had to roll in the stream to wash blood from my fur. I decided then to send You these words.

So I think of the word shapes, and the girl writes them for me. I know how the words are shaped because I could see them whenever Captain Dial spoke. And I always knew what he was saying.

The girl writes on a roll of paper she found in the stone hut when we began using it as our quarters three months ago. She already had pencils. She has written her own words on the paper many times since then, but she has torn those words from the roll and placed them in her duffel. Her own words have different shapes than the ones she writes for me now. She doesn't even know what my word shapes mean, because the shapes are all that I show her. So the responsibility for their meanings is mine alone.

Just as the responsibility for my actions is mine alone.

Last night I killed eighteen of Your soldiers.

I didn't want to do that. They reminded me of some of the soldiers I knew before, the ones who followed Captain Dial with me. But I had to kill them because they came to attack us. And if I let them do that, I would be disobeying orders.

I heard them approach while the girl, the two boys, and the old man slept. So I went out and climbed the ridge behind the hut so I could see a long way. I have good night vision, and I had no trouble spotting the soldiers as they split into two squads and spread out. Their intent was to attack our hut from different angles to make its defense more difficult. I knew this because it was one of the things Captain Dial taught me.

So I did another thing Captain Dial taught me. As the two squads scuttled to their positions to await the order to attack, I crept down toward them through the grass and brambles. I crept with my belly to the earth so they couldn't see me coming. Not even with their infrared goggles.

Captain Dial once said I was black as night and silent as air. He was proud when he said it. I remembered that when I crept to Your soldiers.

They didn't hear me as I went from one to another. They were spread out too far. Their leader wasn't as smart as Captain Dial. I bit each one's throat so it tore open and the soldier couldn't shout. There were some sounds, but they weren't loud.

The first soldier had a lieutenant's bar on his helmet. I had seen it from a long way away. It was the only officer's insignia I saw in either squad. So I went to him first. That way he couldn't give the order to attack before I was finished.

But the others would have attacked sooner or later, even without an order from their lieutenant. So I had to kill them all.

The last soldier was the only female among the eighteen. As I approached her, I smelled the same kind of soap that Captain Dial's wife Melanie used. That made me pause as I remembered how things were a long time ago when I slept at the foot of their bed. But then the soldier knew I was there and turned her weapon toward me. So I bit her throat before she could fire.

I dragged the soldiers to the ravine near the southern end of the ridge. You'll find them there side by side if You arrive before the wild animals do. I did my best to treat them with honor.

Then I went to the stream. The stream is near the hut, so I tried to be quiet. I didn't want to wake my people before sunrise.

After washing, I went into the grass and shook off as much water as I could. But there was no one to rub me with a towel. There was no one to touch my head and tell me I was good.

I remembered then that no one had ever told Captain Dial he was good, either.

This is what it means to be the leader.

I wanted to howl. But I didn't. My people were still asleep.

I take care of them. I don't let anyone hurt them. These were Captain Dial's orders, and I will not disobey.

Captain Dial was my commanding officer. I was his first sergeant. If You examine the D Company roster, You will see that my pay grade is K-9.

My name is Chip.

❖

Whenever Captain Dial gave me an order, I obeyed as fast as I could. And then he always touched my head and told me I was good. Sometimes when I was extra fast, he gave me a treat. I liked the treats, but I liked the touch even more.

There was never a time when Captain Dial wasn't my leader. But he wasn't always a captain, and I wasn't always his first sergeant. In the beginning he was a lieutenant, and I was his corporal.

We were promoted because of the day we demonstrated our training to the people in the bleachers.

That morning, in our quarters, Lieutenant Dial said that what we would participate in that afternoon was political bullshit. Money for the war was about to be cut, so public-relations events like this were an attempt to bolster civilian support. But Lieutenant Dial said that only two things had ever motivated the public to support the military—heroism and vengeance.

He also said that we had to do well regardless. He said I would have to do a good job and make him proud. So I stood at attention, and I thought about running fast to find mines and attack enemies. I thought about making Lieutenant Dial proud.

Then he touched my head. He knew my thoughts. He always knew my thoughts. He told me I was good and gave me permission to be at ease.

So I wiggled and pushed my head against his knees, and my tail wagged hard as he buckled my duty harness. Even though he had said it was bullshit, I could smell that he was excited about the job ahead. That made me excited too. And as we left our quarters, Lieutenant Dial's wife Melanie came with us. That made me even more excited, because she was almost never with us except in our quarters.

Melanie spoke to me every morning, and although I couldn't understand her thoughts too well, I knew she was telling me to take care of Lieutenant Dial throughout our day of training. And every night when Lieutenant Dial and I returned, Melanie touched my head and said I was good. Then, after we all ate supper, she and Lieutenant Dial would climb into their bed, I would lie down on my cushion at its foot, and we would sleep. Sometimes in the night their scents grew stronger and blended together, and they made happy sounds. But I stayed quiet because I wanted them to stay happy. Other times I smelled or heard strangers outside our quarters, and I would go on alert even though Lieutenant Dial was still asleep and had not given me an order. But the strangers always went away, and then I slept again too.

Those were the only times Melanie was with us, and that one or-der every morning was the only order she ever gave me. All of my other orders, all of my treats, and all of my food came from Lieu-tenant Dial.

But Lieutenant Dial loved Melanie. I could see the word "love" whenever he thought of her. And that made me glad because it made him glad. So we were all happy on the day she came with us. She smelled like a hundred different flowers all mixed together, and she was wearing new clothes that seemed to float around her.

She also wore a gift that Lieutenant Dial had given her the night before. It was a shiny rock on a silver chain that she wore around her neck. Lieutenant Dial told me that Melanie liked the color of the rock. It just looked like a rock on a chain to me. But when Lieutenant Dial put it around Melanie's neck, it made me think of the chain and tags that Lieutenant Dial wore around his own neck whenever he was on duty. And it also made me think of the collar he put on me when I wasn't wearing my duty harness. So then I understood why Melanie was so happy to receive the rock and chain. Now we all had things to wear around our necks.

We didn't go to our usual training area at the fort that day. In-stead we went to a park by the ocean. There were flags and people everywhere. It was busy and noisy, and I wanted to run around and smell everything. But Lieutenant Dial ordered me to stay beside him, and that was fun too. I still got to smell everything. We walked from one tree to another, with me on one side of Lieutenant Dial and Melanie on the other. And at every tree, people gathered around while Lieutenant Dial told them who he was and who I was. Then he would give me a few orders—easy things like attention, on guard, and secure-the-perimeter—and we would move on. A lot of people asked if they could touch me, but Lieutenant Dial said they couldn't. He explained that I was on duty. I wasn't a pet. I was a corporal.

He was proud when he said it, and that made me proud too.

As we walked from place to place, sometimes Lieutenant Dial held Melanie's hand in his. And once, Melanie reached across and touched my head. This violated the rule Lieutenant Dial had been telling everyone. But even though I was on duty, it seemed all right. I was glad she did it.

After a while we walked away from the trees to a broad stretch of lawn beside the ocean. I saw a long pier floating on the water. And across the lawn from the pier were bleachers with people in them. There were more people in the bleachers than I had ever seen in one place before, and some of them were high-ranking officers in dress uniforms. So I knew that even if what was going to happen here was bullshit, it was important bullshit.

Out on the lawn were little flags, mud puddles, wooden walls, sandbag fortifications, and some mock-enemies. I knew they were mock-enemies because they wore dark, padded suits. All of these things were familiar to me from training. But there were more things on the lawn than I had ever seen in one training session, and that excited me.

Melanie went to the bleachers while Lieutenant Dial took me onto the lawn, where we were joined by other soldiers. Some of the other soldiers were also K-9s. I knew most of them. Lieutenant Dial and I had trained with them many times.

Out on the pier, men and women dressed in white stood at attention. And when Lieutenant Dial and I reached a spot in the middle of the lawn, he told me to stand at attention as well. So I did, and all of the other soldiers did too.

A colonel stood in front of the bleachers and addressed the crowd. He said a lot of words through a loudspeaker, but I couldn't understand them. Since they didn't come from Lieutenant Dial, they were meaningless.

When the colonel stopped talking, the people in the bleachers clapped their hands. Then a soldier ran onto the lawn and handed Lieutenant Dial a microphone. Lieutenant Dial signaled that I should remain at attention, so I didn't move as he took a step forward and addressed the people.

He told them a lot of things about K-9 soldiers. One thing he said was that while war dogs required a lot of training, we didn't have to be trained to understand loyalty or rank. A dog who was raised and trained by one soldier would always see that soldier as his or her pack leader. So if Lieutenant Dial was put in charge of a platoon, that platoon would become my pack. And I would see my duty to that pack as absolute and unquestionable.

It surprised me that Lieutenant Dial had to explain that to people. It was as obvious to me as knowing that food is for eating. But then I remembered that people didn't always think the same way that Lieutenant Dial and I thought. Melanie, for example. Melanie was always kind to me, but sometimes I could smell that she also feared me a little. And I always wondered how that could be. Lieutenant Dial loved Melanie, so I would never hurt her. And as long as I was near her, I would never let anything else hurt her, either. So I hoped that what Lieutenant Dial was saying to the people in the bleachers would help Melanie understand that she never had to be afraid.

Then Lieutenant Dial said something that made him sad as he said it. I don't think the people knew how sad it made him, but I knew. The other K-9s knew, too.

He said that during a war in the past, some high-ranking officers had decided that K-9s weren't really soldiers. Instead, they were classified as equipment. That meant that when their units left the field, K-9s were abandoned or destroyed. They were treated like utility vehicles or tents. They weren't allowed to return to their home quarters with their handlers.

Lieutenant Dial always spoke the truth, but this truth was difficult for me to comprehend. I knew I wasn't equipment. I knew the difference between a vehicle and a dog. And the K-9s in that past war must have known the difference too. So I was glad the regulations had changed. But I wondered then, and wonder now, whether there might still be some high-ranking officers who don't think of me as a soldier.

I urge You not to make that mistake.

Lieutenant Dial's sadness went away as he continued talking. He described some of the duties K-9 soldiers perform, and as he described those duties, different handlers ordered their K-9s to perform them. And as the dogs obeyed, their images appeared on a big screen that had been set up beside the pier.

One dog, a pointy-eared shepherd, attacked and subdued first one mock-enemy, then three, and then five. He was good at it. Even though the mock-enemies were padded so he couldn't really hurt them, I could smell that they were afraid of him.

Another dog, a lean pinscher, ran fast fast fast, dodging and leaping over obstacles that popped up before him, and he delivered a medical kit to another soldier at the end of the lawn. Then he dragged that soldier to a designated safety point while avoiding some booby traps. The booby traps went off bang bang bang after the pinscher and his soldier were past them.

A big-chested Malinois destroyed a machine-gun nest.

Another shepherd crept on her belly to flank an enemy platoon.

A hound pointed out hidden land mines and howled as he found each one.

Lieutenant Dial announced each K-9's name and rank, each handler's name and rank, and the task to be performed. The K-9s were all good, and the people in the bleachers clapped. So I was glad because everyone was happy. But I was getting more and more excited because I wanted it to be my turn. In fact, as the second shepherd completed her flanking maneuver and took down a mock-enemy from behind, I almost broke attention. I wanted to help. I wanted to be a good soldier, too.

I whimpered, and Lieutenant Dial gave me a corrective glance. So I tried extra hard to remain still and silent. I didn't want to disappoint Lieutenant Dial. Disappointing Lieutenant Dial would be the worst thing in the world.

When all of the other dogs had performed their tasks, Lieutenant Dial told the people that the modern K-9 soldier went beyond those of the past. He told them that K-9s and their handlers were now matched according to their skills, temperaments, and rapport—because there were some dogs and humans who had a gift for understanding each other, and some who didn't. And he told them that such matchings had been so successful that dogs often knew what their handlers wanted them to do even before any verbal or visual orders had been issued. In addition, a subcutaneous device implanted in each dog made it possible for handlers to send pulsed signals that their K-9s had been trained to recognize as orders. And the implants, in turn, sent biometric signals to the handlers to indicate their K-9s' levels of anxiety and confidence as orders were carried out. So even when a dog and handler weren't in close proximity, they could still communicate and complete their mission.

I didn't remember receiving my implant, but I knew it was under the skin between my shoulders. I almost never thought about it because Lieutenant Dial almost never used his transmitter anymore. He had used it often in our early days of training. But as our training had progressed, our thoughts had become clearer and clearer to each other, and one day we had both known the electronic signals weren't needed anymore. So Lieutenant Dial had unstrapped the transmitter from his wrist and put it in a pouch on his belt. After that day, he would sometimes send a signal just to be sure my implant was working, but I always started carrying out his orders before I felt the pulses anyway. That was because I paid attention to him, and I could see his thoughts even when he was far away.

When Lieutenant Dial finished telling the people about the communication implants, he told them about me. He told them I had been rescued from a municipal shelter as a puppy, and that a military veterinarian had determined that the dominant breeds in my genetic background were black Labrador and standard poodle. That made me a Labradoodle. Some of the people in the crowd laughed when they heard that name, but Lieutenant Dial didn't laugh when he said it.

He said I had the intelligence of a poodle and the temperament of a Labrador. He said I was three years old and in peak physical condition. He said I weighed eighty pounds, which was big enough to be strong, but small enough to be fast and to squeeze into places too tight for people. He said my black, wavy coat was good camouflage at night. He said I was at the top of my training class. He said I was a corporal and my name was Chip.

Then Lieutenant Dial looked across the lawn at a sandbagged machine-gun nest and gave me the hand signal to attack. I knew he was going to give me the signal as soon as he looked across at the sandbags, but I also knew I should wait for it. The people in the bleachers wouldn't like it if I didn't.

But I jumped away fast when he gave it. I ran for the sandbags, and the machine gun opened fire. It was firing blank cartridges, but I knew from training that I had to act as if the ammunition could hurt me. So I zigzagged and made quick stops behind cardboard rocks, stacks of tires, and other things that were on the lawn between Lieutenant Dial and the machine-gun nest. The machine-gun barrel swiveled to follow me, but I was too fast and tricky for it, because when I ran behind a cardboard rock, I would come out in a different direction. The machine-gun barrel couldn't keep up, and soon I was right under it so it couldn't point at me. Then I jumped up over the sandbags and pushed the gunner onto his back. Two mock-enemies on either side of him pointed rifles at me, so I bit one in the crotch and twisted so that he fell against the other one. Then all three mock-enemies were on their backs, and I bit the pads at their throats. A bell sounded over the loudspeaker as I broke the skin of each pad and the mock-blood came out. After the third bell, the people in the bleachers clapped.

Then I felt a quick series of pulses between my shoulders, but I was already jumping away from the machine-gun nest because I knew what Lieutenant Dial wanted me to do next. I ran as fast as I could to the farthest end of the lawn, dodging mock-enemies as they popped up and tried to shoot me, until I reached the wooden wall with the knotted rope at the top. The wall was high, but I liked that. I'm good at jumping.

I ran hard and jumped high, and I grabbed the bottom knot on the rope with my teeth. Then I pushed against the wall with all my feet so I could grab the next knot, and the next, and the next. Just before the next-to-last knot, a piece of the wall broke away as my feet pushed it, and I almost missed the knot. I caught it with just my front teeth. But that made me angry at the wall and the knot, because they were trying to make me disappoint Lieutenant Dial. So I bit as hard as I could with my front teeth, and I kicked and scratched the wall until another piece broke away and gave me a good place for my hind feet. Then I pulled with my teeth and pushed with my legs, and I went all the way over the wall without having to grab the last knot.

On the other side of the wall, two soldiers lay on the ground. They had mock-wounds on their legs and chests, but they weren't pretending to be unconscious. So I went to the nearest one and let him grab the handle on my duty harness. Then I dragged him through a mock-minefield to a medical station. The mines weren't marked with flags the way they often were in training, but I didn't need the flags. I know the smells of many different explosives, so I could smell the mines even though they were just smoke-bangs. It was easy to drag the soldier around them. Some of them went off when we were past, but it didn't matter. None of the smoke touched us, and I got the soldier to the medical station in the same shape I found him in.

I ran back for the other soldier, but when I reached him he was pretending to be unconscious. I whined and licked his face, but I knew it wouldn't make him stop pretending. So then I grabbed one of his flak-jacket straps and began to drag him toward the medical station. But when we were halfway through the minefield, an open utility vehicle carrying four mock-enemies came driving across it, straight for us. The mines didn't go off as the vehicle drove over them, and the mock-enemy manning the mounted gun began firing at me and my soldier.

They were trying to prevent me from obeying Lieutenant Dial's orders. I wouldn't let them do that.

I dropped my soldier and started running so the mock-enemies would chase me. When they did, and when we were far enough from the wounded soldier that I knew he would be safe, I made a quick stop, turned around, and jumped. I cleared the vehicle's windshield and had just enough time to bite the pad on the gunner's throat. The bell rang. Then I hit the ground behind the vehicle and tumbled, but got up and turned back around in time to see the gunner slump over and the driver turn the steering wheel hard. The other two mock-enemies were raising their pistols.

As the vehicle made its turn, exposing the driver, I ran and jumped again. But when I bit the pad on the driver's throat, the skin didn't break right away. So I hung on and bit harder. The driver gave a yell that I don't think was a word. Then the pad broke, the mock-blood came out, and I heard the bell. So I jumped away, spinning as my paws hit the ground so I could be ready to attack the remaining two mock-enemies.

But I didn't have to. The vehicle rolled over so its wheels went up, and three of the four enemies fell out. Then it was still. The driver was still strapped in his seat, but his neck was bent against the ground, and he didn't move. The three mock-enemies on the ground didn't move either. So I ran to the two I hadn't bitten yet, broke the skins on their throat pads, then returned to my soldier in the minefield.

The soldier was sitting up with his eyes and mouth open. But I grabbed his flak-jacket strap anyway and resumed dragging him to the medical station. Then he tried to pull away from me. But I was still under orders. So I growled, and then my soldier was still again. I delivered him to the medical station, ran back to Lieutenant Dial, and stood at attention.

The people in the bleachers began to smell unhappy. They made growling noises, and none of them clapped their hands. So for a moment I was afraid I had done something wrong. But then I knew it wasn't so, because Lieutenant Dial touched my head and said I was good.

That was all that mattered.

From Lieutenant Dial's next thoughts, I knew that the driver in the utility vehicle had made a mistake. He'd been supposed to drive farther away from me after the gunner was bitten. But he had turned back toward me too soon, and I had been faster than he had thought I would be. Then, when his throat pad hadn't broken right away, he had panicked and turned the steering wheel too sharply. So the vehicle had rolled over. But by then I had broken the throat pad and jumped away.

All four of the mock-enemies in the utility vehicle had to be taken away for real medical care, and I could hear that some of the people in the bleachers felt bad about that. But Lieutenant Dial didn't. Instead, he became angry. He wasn't angry with me, but I didn't want him to be angry with anything. Being angry made him unhappy. And that made me unhappy too. Anger was like smoke with a bad smell in his head.

The K-9 demonstration was over then, and Melanie came down from the bleachers to meet us. I was glad to see her. But Lieutenant Dial was still angry. He told Melanie that the driver of the utility vehicle had done the exercise incorrectly, and that what had happened wasn't my fault. I had done what I was supposed to do, but the mock-enemies had screwed it up.

Melanie told him she already knew that, and that everyone else knew it too. She said he shouldn't worry about what people would think of him, or of me, or of any of the K-9s, because we had all been wonderful.

I didn't always know what Melanie was saying, but that time I understood every word. And as she spoke, Lieutenant Dial's anger drifted away. Just like smoke. And then he was happy and proud again. And so was I.

I rubbed my nose against Melanie's knee, and she touched my head. I wished I could tell her she was good.

Then Lieutenant Dial, Melanie, and I walked to the edge of the water with some of the people from the bleachers, and we stood on a boardwalk while the people on the pier performed demonstrations with water animals. We had a good view even though we were about thirty meters from them. Lieutenant Dial said the animals that stayed in the water all the time were called dolphins, and the ones that hopped from the pier to the water and back again were called sea lions. One of the sea lions barked, but I couldn't understand it.

The water animals delivered equipment to people underwater, and they also searched for mines and mock-enemies. Pictures of them doing those things appeared on the big screen. Sometimes a sea lion carried a clamp in its mouth, and when it found a mock-enemy, it swam up behind him and put the clamp on his leg. Then the mock-enemy was pulled up to the pier by a rope attached to the clamp, while the sea lion jumped from the water and got a treat from its handler. It looked like fun, and I wished I could go underwater and sneak up on the mock-enemies down there too.

Then the sea lions had a contest. They were supposed to find some small dummy mines and push buttons on the mines with their noses, then attach handles and bring the mines up to the pier. It was a race to see which sea lion could bring up the most mines in two minutes. So the sea lions were swimming fast and splashing a lot, dropping the mines on the pier and grabbing new handles before plunging into the ocean again.

The dummy water mines looked like black soccer balls, and they had lights that came on if the button had been pushed. Once one of the sea lions brought up a mine that didn't have its light on, and his handler threw the mine back into the water. Then the sea lion had to go get it again, and he had to be sure to push the button before putting it on the pier. If I had been that sea lion, I would have felt bad for not doing it right the first time. But I couldn't tell whether he felt bad or not, because he kept on swimming for more mines. So then I was glad because he was still being a good soldier.

He didn't win the contest, though. He came in second. At the end of two minutes, he had eleven mines, and the winner had twelve. All the people who had watched the race clapped and cheered, and the four sea lions who had raced got up on their hindquarters and barked. The people cheered even more then, and Lieutenant Dial and Melanie did too. But Lieutenant Dial didn't clap because he had one hand on the handle of my duty harness.

Both Lieutenant Dial and Melanie were happy. So I should have been happy too.

But I wasn't. Something was wrong.

I didn't know what it was at first, so I lifted my head high and sniffed the air. There were many smells. There was sweat, soda, and popcorn. There were buckets of little fish. The sea lions smelled salty. Melanie still smelled like flowers. The other K-9s smelled thirsty. The practice mines smelled like wet Frisbees.

Except there was another smell with the Frisbee smell. It wasn't big. But it was there. It was a bad smell. It was a bad smell like the real mines that had been in the practice minefield during the hardest part of training. It was a bad smell like the real mine that had killed another K-9 who wasn't careful enough.

And as soon as I had identified that bad smell, I knew where it was coming from. The final mine that the winning sea lion had brought up wasn't like the others. It looked like them, but it didn't smell like them. It was different. It was bad.

It wanted to explode and kill someone.

But none of the sea lions were doing anything about it. They were still on their hindquarters, swaying back and forth, while the people clapped. One of the dolphins was splashing and chattering out in the water, so I think she might have known. But none of the handlers paid any attention to her. They were smiling at the clapping people.

I was under no specific orders. But Lieutenant Dial had given me one General Order many training sessions ago: If I ever knew something was wrong, I had to act.

So I bolted for the pier, and Lieutenant Dial released my harness handle. I knew his thoughts, and he knew mine. He knew I was being good.

I ran fast between people's legs. Some of them yelled. And then I was on the pier. It moved up and down a little, but I kept on running fast even though it tried to make me fall. Two of the people in white stepped into my path, but I zigzagged around them. The pier was wet there, and my feet slipped. But I scrabbled hard like I did at the wall and kept going.

One of the sea lions came down from his haunches as I approached, and he opened his mouth as if to bite me. It was a big mouth with big teeth. The whole sea lion was as big as five of me, and he lunged at me when I came close. So I jumped over his head and kicked the back of his neck with my hind feet. That pushed me the last three meters to the end of the pier.

My front feet hit the pier right beside the bad mine, so I grabbed its handle with my teeth, whipped it forward, and let go so it flew into the water. Two of the dolphins swam away fast as the mine splashed and sank.

Then I couldn't smell the bad mine anymore, so I was glad. But when I turned around and saw the white-clothed people and their sea lions, none of them seemed glad. The people were shouting and the sea lions were barking. The sea lions' barks still didn't make sense.

I saw Lieutenant Dial running down the pier toward me, so I started running toward him too. And just as I began to zigzag around the sea lions, I heard a rumble and a splash, and the pier rose up under me. I fell, and the pier hit my jaw and made me bite my tongue. Then the pier bounced up and down, and I couldn't stand up because my feet kept slipping. One of the people in white had fallen down beside me, and he kept slipping too. That made me worry about Lieutenant Dial, so I looked up to see if he was all right. But a sea lion was in the way.

Then I yelped. Later, a news reporter would say that I yelped because my tongue was hurt. But that wasn't the reason. It was because I couldn't see or hear Lieutenant Dial, and I couldn't find his thoughts. There were too many people thinking and yelling all at once. I couldn't even smell him because I was too close to the sea lions.

That was a bad moment. But the pier moved a little less each time it bounced, and finally I could stand up. And then I could see Lieutenant Dial. He was in the middle of the pier helping another person stand up, so I ran to him and stood at attention. When he had finished helping the other person, he looked down at me and saluted.

And he told me I was good. He told me I was more good than I had ever been before.

And the bad moment was gone.

Later, investigators said that a real enemy had replaced one of the sea lions' dummy mines with a live one, intending to hurt or kill as many people and animals as possible. But because I threw it back into the water, only one dolphin was hurt. And no one was killed.

A few weeks later, Lieutenant Dial was promoted to Captain, and I was promoted to Sergeant. Captain Dial received silver bars for his uniform, and then he leaned over and showed me a new metal tag before clipping it to the ring in my collar. It was shaped like the insignia for Sergeant First Class. I knew I couldn't wear it on combat duty, because it would get in the way and make noise. But it was still a fine thing, because that was how it looked in Captain Dial's thoughts.

Other soldiers were promoted during that ceremony as well, but I was the only K-9. Also, Captain Dial and I were commended for finding the live mine. We were called heroes.

Melanie was there for the ceremony, and both she and Captain Dial were proud and happy. So I was proud and happy too.

But I still wasn't as happy as I had been on the pier. That was where I had been more good than I had ever been before. Captain Dial had said so.

That was how I knew it was true.

❖

Soon after our promotions, Captain Dial and I left the fort with many other soldiers, and we all went to the war. Melanie came to the fort to say good-bye to us. She and Captain Dial hugged each other for a long time while I stood at ease. Most of the other soldiers were hugging people too. There were wives and children, and even a few dogs who weren't soldiers.

Then Melanie knelt down and put her head against mine. It surprised me. She had never done anything like that before. I think she was trying to help me understand her thoughts the way I understood

Captain Dial's. It helped a little. But even if she hadn't done it, I would have known she was telling me the same thing she had told me every morning before training. She was telling me to take care of Captain Dial.

So I kissed her face. I wanted her to be glad that Captain Dial and I were going to the war together. Her face tasted like ocean water.

Then Melanie took her head away from mine and put her arms around Captain Dial again. After a while, Captain Dial pulled away from her and gave me the signal to proceed. We left Melanie and went to the D Company bus.

When all the soldiers of D Company had boarded the bus, it took us to the air transport. Captain Dial was quiet during the bus ride. He just looked out the window. And for the first time, his thoughts weren't clear to me. It was as if they were far away in a fog, and a fuzzy sound ran through them. I glimpsed Melanie, but that was all. Captain Dial kept his hand on my neck, though, and every now and then his fingers rubbed behind my ears. So I didn't worry. Captain Dial always had some thoughts that I couldn't understand anyway. The only ones I really needed to know were the ones that were orders.

The air transport took a long time, and it was loud. I didn't like it. By the time it stopped at an island to refuel, all my muscles were sore. But I felt better after marking some trees near the airstrip, and better still after some food. We got back on the transport then, and Captain Dial gave me a pill to help me sleep through the rest of the flight. It helped a lot. But I was still glad when we were on the ground again. When we finally left the transport we were in a place that was dry and sunny, and all of the smells were sharp.

The soldiers of D Company spent one night in a tin-roofed barracks at the combat zone airfield, and Captain Dial and I slept there with them. There was no kennel or cushion for me, so I slept on a blanket beside Captain Dial's cot. I was the only K-9 in the company, and some of the other soldiers were nervous around me. But Captain Dial made sure that I met each one and learned that soldier's smell.

Captain Dial wanted to keep them all safe. So I wanted to keep them safe too.

I could see some soldiers' thoughts, although none of them were as clear to me as Captain Dial's. But that was all right, because the soldiers' voices and smells told me all I needed to know about them. Most of them were friendly, although several stayed nervous even after they met me. And a few smelled frightened or angry.

One of the angry ones was an officer, Lieutenant Morris, who was in charge of First Platoon. I couldn't see his thoughts at all, but I still knew he didn't like me. I knew he didn't like Captain Dial, either. When he stood before us, his sweat smelled bitter, and his voice was low. And even when he saluted, his muscles were tense as if he were about to run or fight.

Captain Dial was aware of all this, because he knew my thoughts. But unlike me, he was able to think of a reason for Lieutenant Morris's attitude. He thought Lieutenant Morris believed he should have been promoted to Captain and given command of D Company.

This troubled Captain Dial, because he had never wanted to lead a company of regular soldiers anyway. But I was the only one who knew it. What he really wanted to do was serve in a K-9 unit. But when we were promoted, he was ordered to command D Company because its original captain had died in training. So he requested that I be allowed to join the company with him, and we were both happy when his request was granted. We joined D Company on the same day we went to the war. And I knew that all of the soldiers in D Company were lucky to have Captain Dial as their leader.

The morning after our arrival in the combat zone, D Company was assigned to guard four checkpoints on highways that led to the airfield. So Captain Dial put a platoon at each checkpoint, splitting the soldiers among three separate road barriers per checkpoint. He told the lieutenants and sergeants to stop and inspect each vehicle at each barrier, and to detain the occupants of any vehicle found to contain contraband. He also told them to have their soldiers fire warning shots over any vehicles that passed the first barrier without stopping for inspection. They were to aim at the tires and engines of any vehicles that also passed the second barrier without stopping. And any vehicles that passed the third barrier without stopping were to be destroyed. But any vehicles that stopped at all three barriers and were found to contain no contraband were to be allowed to proceed unless the soldiers had reason to believe that a more thorough inspection was needed. In that case, the suspicious vehicle was to be reported to Captain Dial so he could bring me to it and I could smell whether anything was wrong.

I thought these orders were easy and clear.

Captain Dial and I spent our first five days in the combat zone riding from checkpoint to checkpoint in a utility vehicle, inspecting cars and trucks and seeing to the needs of D Company. I liked doing the inspections. In those first days, I found three pistols, four rifles, a rocket-propelled grenade launcher, and a brick of hashish. Captain Dial arrested the people with the guns and sent them to Headquarters. But he laughed at the man with the hashish and let him drive away. Hashish wasn't contraband here, he told me, so long as no one gave any to our soldiers. This was a new rule to me, but I'm good at learning new rules.

The first five days were fun. All of our platoons did their jobs, and so did Captain Dial and I.

Then, on the morning of the sixth day, Lieutenant Morris ordered First Platoon to open fire on a van that had gone past the first barrier without stopping. It didn't reach the second barrier. By the time Lieutenant Morris ordered his soldiers to cease fire, all seven people inside the van had been killed.

Captain Dial and I weren't there when it happened. We were two checkpoints away. By the time we arrived, the incident had been over for fifteen minutes. Lieutenant Morris and a few other soldiers had dragged three of the bodies from the shot-up van and laid them by the side of the road. They were heading back toward the van when Captain Dial stopped our utility vehicle in front of them and ordered them to stay away from the van and the bodies.

Then he ordered me to search the van, and I obeyed. It was a bad place. It smelled of spent machine-gun rounds, explosive residue, and human blood.

The driver was still in her seat. She had been a woman about the size of Melanie. The three other bodies still in the van had been small children. There were two boys and a girl. I had seen children of their sizes on the day by the ocean. But the ones in the van had been shot through and through. Their blood was all over the floor and seats, and I had to step in it to conduct my search.

There was no contraband. There were no guns, and the only bullets were spent rounds. And I couldn't smell any explosives except the residue of a grenade that had been fired into the van by someone in First Platoon.

After I had searched the van, Captain Dial ordered me to search the three bodies on the ground. So I did. They were all girls. Two were even smaller than the children in the van. The third was larger, about the size of the girl who writes these words. But she wasn't fully grown. All of them had been shot many times. One of the younger girls had most of her face gone. The older girl had a narrow cut on her neck. None of them possessed any contraband.

Captain Dial was angrier than he had ever been before. The smoke in his head was thick and turbulent. And there were sounds. I could hear Melanie crying. I could hear a hundred Melanies crying.

Then Captain Dial began shouting at Lieutenant Morris. I had never heard him shout like that before, and it made me cringe even though he wasn't shouting at me. All the soldiers of First Platoon cringed, too, especially when Captain Dial said he would bring Lieutenant Morris up on charges for disobeying orders.

But Lieutenant Morris's bitter smell was acrid and strong now, and he stood with his head thrust forward and his arms straight down at his sides. He didn't salute. It was as if he was challenging Captain Dial. It was as if he thought he had done a good thing, and that Captain Dial's orders had been wrong.

That made me angry, because Captain Dial always gave good orders. So I took a step toward Lieutenant Morris and growled.

Lieutenant Morris reached for his sidearm, but Captain Dial slapped his hand away from it. Then Lieutenant Morris made a fist and started to swing it at Captain Dial's face. I was on him before his fist was halfway there, and I put him on his back on the highway.

I stood with my front paws on Lieutenant Morris's chest and my teeth touching his throat, and Captain Dial ordered him to remain still. This time, Lieutenant Morris obeyed. I could feel the pulse in his neck and the shallow motion of his chest as he breathed, but those were the only movements he made until Captain Dial ordered me to stand down. Then I took my paws from Lieutenant Morris's chest and backed away.

But now I smelled something wrong in a pocket of Lieutenant Morris's fatigues. It smelled like the girl with the cut on her neck. It smelled like her blood.

I pointed at Lieutenant Morris's pocket and barked. So Captain Dial knelt down, opened the pocket, and brought out a slender chain with a shiny rock on it. It wasn't just like the one he had given Melanie, but it didn't look much different. Except that this one had blood on its chain.

The clasp on the chain was closed, but the chain had been broken in another place. The rock slid down against the clasp when Captain Dial pulled the chain from Lieutenant Morris's pocket, and it dangled there as he held it up. It caught the sun so that it seemed to have a light inside it.

Captain Dial remained on one knee, looking at the necklace, for a long time. Lieutenant Morris started to speak, but I growled and he shut up. I was doing him a favor, because one of Captain Dial's thoughts was clear. He was thinking of using his sidearm to shoot Lieutenant Morris in the head. He was thinking that if Lieutenant Morris said even one word, that was what he would do.

What happened instead was that Captain Dial stood up and told a First Platoon sergeant to call for military police. Then he returned to our utility vehicle, leaving Lieutenant Morris on his back on the highway. I went with Captain Dial, and we waited in our vehicle until the military police came. When they did, Captain Dial gave the rock and chain to one of them.

I didn't understand everything that happened after that. But Lieutenant Morris was back with D Company just two days after he ordered First Platoon to attack the van. And Captain Dial was unhappy because he didn't think there would ever be a court-martial. For one thing, none of the soldiers of First Platoon were sure about what had happened. Some of them even thought that the van had been loaded with explosives, and they continued to think so even after Captain Dial told them I hadn't smelled any. Also, Lieutenant Morris said that he had found the girl's necklace on the ground. And there were no soldiers who would say that he hadn't. Except me. I hadn't smelled any dirt or asphalt on it. All I had smelled was skin and blood from the girl's neck plus sweat from Lieutenant Morris's hand. But the only officer who could hear my testimony was Captain Dial. And unless there was a court-martial, he had already done all he could do.

Besides, the military police said they lost the necklace.

Captain Dial was sad from then on. I don't think anyone else in the company knew that. But I did.

I wanted to make Captain Dial happy again, so I tried even harder to be good. And he told me I was. He told me I was the best sergeant he had ever seen.

But he was still sad. So I was sad too.

❖

Two weeks later, D Company was assigned to a combat mission. A few hours before dawn on a Friday morning, thirty enemy guerrillas had attacked our supply depot using mortars and small arms—and although they had been repelled, four of our soldiers had been killed. So the guerrillas had to be followed and destroyed, and D Company was chosen to do it. Captain Dial thought it was strange that an entire company was being sent after only thirty enemies, but he followed the order without hesitation.

D Company was in pursuit of the guerrillas within an hour of the attack. The guerrillas had a big head start, but they were on foot, and D Company had armored personnel carriers, utility vehicles, and me. So we were able to move fast over both roads and fields, and every few minutes Captain Dial had me run ahead and correct the direction of our pursuit. The guerrillas were staying in one group, so their trail was easy to smell.

We had almost caught up to them as they reached the hills fifteen kilometers west of our airfield. We were so close that Captain Dial could see them through his night-vision field glasses. They were making their way up a narrow, ascending valley, and they were still in one group.

This troubled Captain Dial. It seemed to him that once the guerrillas had reached the hills, they should have scattered to make our pursuit more difficult. But they were staying together. So Captain Dial used his radio to consult with Headquarters, and Headquarters said a refugee camp of about three hundred souls lay a short distance up the valley, a few hundred meters beyond a natural curve. The guerrillas probably intended to stay together long enough to reach that camp—and then they would disperse and blend in with the civilians. This would force Captain Dial to either let them escape, or arrest the entire camp.

So we had to stop the guerrillas before they reached the refugee camp. Captain Dial increased our speed, then dropped off two squads from Fourth Platoon with ten mortars as soon as we were in range. His plan was for those squads to fire the mortars just beyond the guerrillas, forcing them to turn away from the refugee camp . . . and perhaps also to run back into our pursuit.

As the rest of D Company started up the valley, the mortar squads put a dozen rounds where Captain Dial had ordered. But instead of reversing direction, the guerrillas began to ascend a hill on the south side of the valley. They remained in one group, though, and we gained on them. When we were close enough that we might be hit by stray mortar rounds, Captain Dial radioed the squads and told them to hold fire. But they were to stay put to intercept any enemies that might be flushed back toward them.

We rushed toward the base of the hill the guerrillas were climbing. They were moving much more slowly now, and in the light of dawn it was clear that we would overtake them before they reached the crest of the hill. I became excited as I thought of knocking them down and holding them, one by one, until my fellow soldiers could take them prisoner. And as the utility vehicle that carried me, Captain Dial, and Staff Sergeant Owens began to climb the hill, I readied myself to leap out and attack.

Our vehicle was in the lead, so most of the company was still on the valley floor as we started up the hill. It was at that moment that rocket-propelled grenades and mortar shells began raining down around us from the opposite hillside to the north. And then the guerrillas we were chasing took up positions and began to fire down on us with small arms.

Captain Dial radioed orders to our platoon leaders to take cover and return fire. Then he had Staff Sergeant Owens turn our utility vehicle broadside to the enemy fire, and the three of us exited on the downhill side. We crawled downhill as fast as we could until we reached one of D Company's APCs, and we took cover behind it with soldiers from First and Second Platoons. The soldiers were jumping up and leaning out to fire quick bursts from their rifles, and Captain Dial shouted for them to keep it up as he got on the radio again to call Headquarters for air support. Our helicopters and drones were always out on missions, but two or three could be diverted if soldiers were in trouble. And we were in trouble.

But now Captain Dial couldn't raise Headquarters on the radio. He tried every possible frequency, and there was nothing but silence.

Lieutenant Morris crawled to us and told Captain Dial that we were all going to be killed, and that it was Captain Dial's fault. I wanted to bite Lieutenant Morris's throat then. But Captain Dial ignored him, so I tried to ignore him too. He wasn't a good soldier. He didn't belong in D Company.

There was a loud explosion up the hill, and a soldier told Captain Dial that our abandoned utility vehicle had been hit by a rocket from the other side of the valley. They were zeroing in on us. So Captain Dial said we couldn't stay behind the armored personnel carrier, because it would be targeted next. He ordered First and Second Platoons to retreat to the valley floor, and then he got on the radio and told the mortar squads from Fourth Platoon to fire on the northern hillside. Finally he called to Third Platoon and the remaining two squads of Fourth Platoon, who were all still at the base of the hill, and told them to abandon their APCs and move up the valley on foot, doubletime. All platoons were to return fire as best they could. No one was to retreat back toward the plain.

As Captain Dial and I moved downhill with First and Second Platoons, Lieutenant Morris shouted that Captain Dial's orders were insane. The soldiers in APCs should stay in them, he said. Without armor, he said, they would be picked off in the valley like cattle in a chute.

But Captain Dial knew that the armor was what the enemy would try to destroy first, unless it was moving fast. And it couldn't move fast in the terrain we were in. So getting the soldiers away from it was the only thing to do. And sure enough, before we reached the bottom of the hill, the APC we had been using for cover was hit by a rocket and destroyed.

Our mortars began hitting the northern hill as Captain Dial and I reached the base of the southern hill, and Captain Dial stood his ground there while urging the soldiers of First and Second Platoons to run past our abandoned APCs and continue up the valley. And even now, Lieutenant Morris kept telling him he was wrong, and that D Company ought to be heading back to the plain in full retreat.

But I knew Captain Dial's thoughts, and I knew he was right. Headquarters had been tricked into having D Company follow the guerrillas into an ambush—but Captain Dial wouldn't let the guerrillas trick him any further. He knew that once the ambush began, the enemy would expect D Company to retreat toward the plain. So there would be another trap waiting at the mouth of the valley. The enemy would close us in, then fire down upon us until we were annihilated.

So Captain Dial would confound their expectations. D Company would continue up the valley, on foot, until we could reach an elevated position. With our mortar squads out on the plain providing harassing fire, we could be well up the valley before the guerrillas could leave their hillsides. And then we would transform the enemy's ambush into an attack of our own.

But we would have to take up our battle position before reaching the refugee camp. So we would doubletime around the curve to get out of sight of the enemy, then run up the hill on the backside of the curve. The guerrillas would have no clear shot from their current positions—and if they followed us, we would be able to pour fire down on them as they rounded the curve. So even without air support, we could prevail.

Captain Dial's plan was good, and as D Company rushed up the valley, it began to work. Two more of our abandoned vehicles were hit and began to burn, but despite the constant fire from the enemy, we had not yet lost a single soldier. Our mortar squads were hitting the hillsides as ordered, and the guerrillas' weapons fire became erratic. Captain Dial paused every few meters to shout orders and encouragement to his running soldiers, and once he sent me back to nip at the heels of a few stragglers. But the stragglers weren't stragglers for long, and I was able to rejoin Captain Dial in less than a minute. Then, bringing up the rear, he and I rounded the curve and began running up the slope to take our positions with the rest of our soldiers. They were already following Captain Dial's orders, taking cover behind rocks and in gullies. And they were readying their weapons.

Some of the guerrillas had chased after us, and a few of them came around the curve before Captain Dial and I were far enough up the slope to take our positions. But we hit the dirt so our soldiers could fire on them, and only two of these enemies survived long enough to come within twenty meters of me and Captain Dial. So I turned, charged, and bit their throats. Then I returned to Captain Dial, and we joined several of our soldiers behind a jumble of rocks and dirt.

More guerrillas came around the curve, and D Company shot them. Then some came up the slope in a truck, and one of our soldiers destroyed it with a rocket-propelled grenade. We were winning the battle despite being ambushed.

Then strange things happened.

They didn't seem strange at first. At first, I heard the buzz of airborne drones. Captain Dial couldn't hear them yet, but he knew that I could, and he was glad. It seemed that Headquarters had heard his request after all.

But almost as soon as I heard the drones, I also heard distant explosions, and our mortar squads stopped firing. So Captain Dial radioed them for a status report. But there was no reply. Then he tried again to contact Headquarters, but there was still no reply there either.

The buzz became loud, and two drones appeared around the curve of the valley, flying low. They were narrow-winged and sleek, and almost invisible against the sky. They didn't have any insignia on their wings.

Then they fired rockets at us. They fired rockets at D Company. And at least twenty soldiers died as the rockets exploded. Dirt and rocks pelted me and Captain Dial where we crouched. My ears hurt.

The drones rose up over the opposite hill, then turned back toward us. Captain Dial shouted into his radio, trying one frequency after another, doing his best to raise Headquarters, to raise the remote drone pilots, to raise anyone who should have been listening. He shouted to his lieutenants to try their own radios too. And they did. But no one received a reply.

The drones came swooping toward us, and it became clear that their first attack hadn't been a mistake. Captain Dial's thoughts were tangled as he realized this. The enemy had no such weapons. So he couldn't understand why the drones were attacking us. Their cameras should have seen who we were, and their pilots should have known that D Company wasn't the enemy.

But even in his confusion, Captain Dial was a good leader. He ordered Sergeant Owens to fire a flare to identify us, but he didn't wait to see whether the cameras had seen it and understood its meaning. Instead, he shouted for D Company's surviving lieutenants and sergeants to get their soldiers up and moving again. If the drones were returning to attack our position again, he was going to put us somewhere else.

The soldiers of D Company were already running down the slope when the drones launched their second wave of rockets, so most of them made it to the valley floor. But eight more were killed. Captain Dial and I were bringing up the rear again, and the rocket that killed the eight exploded in front of us just as another exploded behind us. Captain Dial dove to the ground, putting his arms around me and pushing me down. Then he covered me with his body as more rockets exploded on the slope above us.

I didn't like it. Captain Dial wasn't supposed to shield me from harm. I was supposed to do that for him. So I tried to reverse our positions, but Captain Dial ordered me to stay put. Of course I had to obey. But I didn't understand. Captain Dial was more important to D Company than I was.

The rockets stopped exploding, and the drones passed over us again. They were so close that the dirt under my jaw hummed. Then Captain Dial was on his feet again, shouting orders as the drones flew behind the hilltop. The surviving soldiers of D Company were to run like hell up the valley and to take whatever cover they could find— rocks, trees, ditches, anything—if the drones made another pass. But the soldiers were to avoid entering the refugee camp, wherever it was, at all costs. If they came upon it while still on the run, they were to find a way around it.

❖

Captain Dial was smart. But even Captain Dial could only make his choices based on what he knew. And he didn't know that the refugees weren't gathered in a single camp, as Headquarters had said. He didn't know that they were scattered in small clusters throughout the rest of the valley.

And he didn't know that the drones would return so soon, or that they would swoop up and down the valley firing their Gatling guns at anything that moved. The valley was full of sunlight now, so the pilots should have been able to see our soldiers' uniforms. There was nothing to block the view of the cameras. But the drones kept firing on us.

I wished I could jump high enough to tear them out of the sky.

As D Company's lieutenants and sergeants began shouting and radioing Captain Dial, telling him that they were losing more soldiers and that every scrap of cover was occupied by noncombatants, Captain Dial made a decision he didn't want to make. He tried one more time to contact Headquarters—and when that failed, he ordered D Company to return fire. Then he took a rifle from a fallen corporal and fired the first shots at the lead drone as it swooped toward us again.

I couldn't fire a weapon, so I did the only thing I could do to help. I ran in a zigzag pattern toward the drones in an attempt to draw their fire and give the rest of D Company a better chance to make their shots count. And I could hear Captain Dial shouting that I was good.

That made me glad.

The lead drone turned toward me, and in that instant the soldiers of D Company were able to hit it broadside with small-arms fire and at least one RPG. The drone began spewing smoke, and then it turned and almost collided with the second drone. The second drone pulled up and vanished behind a hill just as the first one began to spiral downward.

I returned to Captain Dial, who ordered me and the soldiers who were closest to follow him. We ran up a hillside and dove into a gully that cut across it. There were six of us: Captain Dial, Lieutenant Morris, Sergeant Owens, two specialists, and me. And in the gully we found five civilians: An old man, a woman, an adolescent girl, and two young boys. They scrambled away from us as we tumbled into the gully, and they seemed about to climb out until Captain Dial spoke to them in their language. I think he told them they would be safer if they stayed put.

He had no sooner gotten the words out than the ground shook with the biggest explosion yet. I smelled burning fuel, and I knew the drone had crashed. Captain Dial shouted for everyone to hit the dirt, but I was the only one in the gully who heard him. There was a roaring noise and more explosions. The drone's remaining weapons were detonating.

One of the boys tried to climb out of the gully. The woman jumped up to stop him, and something from the exploding drone hit her in the face. She fell back into the gully. So Captain Dial tried to get to the panicked boy to pull him down. But Lieutenant Morris clutched Captain Dial's leg and stopped him.

Captain Dial made a gesture, and I followed the order. I leaped over him and Lieutenant Morris, and I grabbed the boy's ankle and pulled him down. My teeth broke his skin, but it couldn't be helped. When the boy fell to the dirt beside the woman, I pressed my chest against his to hold him there.

The girl started to move as if to protect the boy from me, but then she looked at my eyes. And for that moment, she knew my thoughts. So she crawled to the woman instead and wiped blood from her face.

The woman wasn't breathing, and I knew she was dead. The girl knew it too, but she tried to make the woman breathe again anyway.

There were a few more explosions from the fallen drone, and then the only noise from it was a muted roar as it burned. So I listened for the other drone, and I heard it flying farther and farther away.

Captain Dial told me I could let the boy up, so I did. He tried to run away again, but this time the girl stopped him. He was crying, and so was the girl. So was the other boy. The girl looked at me again, and I knew then that the dead woman was their mother and the old man was their grandfather. The old man was sitting against the wall of the gully with his knees pulled up to his face and his eyes closed tight.

I looked at Captain Dial then and saw that he was hurt. His left sleeve was turning dark at the shoulder, just below the edge of his flak jacket. But I could hardly smell his blood among all the other bloody smells. I went to him and whined, and he touched my head and told me he was all right. I wanted to go find a medic for him, but he ordered me to stay.

Then he used his radio to ask the rest of D Company for a status report, but he couldn't hear the replies because Lieutenant Morris began shouting. I couldn't understand all of the words, but I understood that Lieutenant Morris blamed Captain Dial for what had happened. He accused Captain Dial of treason for shooting down one of our own aircraft. And he said that the civilians weren't refugees at all, but guerrillas like those we had been pursuing. He said that was why the drones had attacked. And he said it was Captain Dial's fault that D Company had been in the line of fire when that happened.

Nothing Lieutenant Morris was shouting made any sense. But nothing that had happened to us had made any sense either. I knew that much from Captain Dial's thoughts. He didn't understand why things had happened the way they had happened. He slumped with his back against the wall of the gully, and he wondered whether Melanie would still love him after this.

Lieutenant Morris turned to Sergeant Owens and the two specialists, and he announced that Captain Dial was incapacitated. So he was now ranking officer, he said, and he ordered them to turn their weapons toward the old man, the girl, and the boys. If any of them moved, he said, the soldiers were to shoot them all.

Sergeant Owens and the specialists did as they were told. Then Lieutenant Morris reached for the radio in Captain Dial's right hand, but I jumped in his way and snarled at him. So Lieutenant Morris unholstered his sidearm and pointed it at me.

But before he could fire, Captain Dial spoke. He ordered Lieutenant Morris to lower his weapon, and after some hesitation, Lieutenant Morris obeyed. Then Captain Dial ordered Sergeant Owens and the specialists to lower their weapons as well, and they obeyed too.

Captain Dial was strong again. His shoulder was bleeding, but his thoughts were clear. He stood up, pushing himself off the gully wall with his right forearm, and peered over the rim at the burning drone. He spoke into his radio and told his soldiers to stay put if they were in a safe place, and to keep trying to find one if they weren't. He would assess the situation and issue new orders within the next few minutes.

But we didn't have a few minutes. I could hear the second drone returning.

I barked to let Captain Dial know it was coming. So then he shouted into his radio and ordered all of his soldiers to remain still and refrain from returning fire unless directly fired upon. Then he ordered those of us in the gully to hit the dirt. The girl and the two boys didn't understand at first, but the old man put his hands on their shoulders and made them lie down close to their dead mother.

Then Captain Dial lowered himself to a sitting position with his back against the gully wall. He couldn't lie down flat with his wounded shoulder. I lay down next to him and put my chin on his knee, and we waited while the drone flew back and forth. Its Gatling gun chattered three or four times, and I hoped it was shooting enemy guerrillas and not D Company soldiers or civilians.

One of the little boys began to cry, but the girl and the old man whispered to him, and then he was quiet again. I was glad they could calm him like that. They were being good leaders. Like Captain Dial.

But a good leader needs good soldiers.

On the drone's fourth pass, Lieutenant Morris stood and fired his weapon into the air. I was on him fast, my front paws hitting his back and pushing him down, but it was too late. Even as I pinned Lieutenant Morris to the bottom of the gully, I could hear the drone turning and the barrels of its Gatling guns beginning to spin.

Lieutenant Morris shouted into the dirt that we had to show ourselves to the drone so it would know who we were and so it could help us kill the rest of the enemy. He worked a hand free from under his chest and pointed at the family with the dead mother.

I wanted to bite Lieutenant Morris and bite him hard. And I smelled something in one of his pockets that made me feel that way even more. It smelled like the dead girl at the highway checkpoint.

But I didn't bite him, because I knew Captain Dial wouldn't like it. Captain Dial was busy with his radio, telling the rest of D Company that they were not to give away their positions by firing on the drone if it attacked those of us in the gully—not unless there was a clear shot for an RPG. Otherwise, we were on our own. But D Company would survive.

I heard the drone dip low. It was flying on a path directly in line with our gully. It would be able to pour bullets and rockets on us with ease.

Captain Dial was on his feet. It was as if he had been yanked up on a rope from the sky. His left sleeve was so wet that it dripped.

He shouted two orders. First, Sergeant Owens and the two specialists were to get out of the gully at the south rim and run through the smoke of the downed aircraft until they could find other cover in the valley. Second, I was to take the civilians over the north rim and head up into the hills until I could find another gully, a cave, or some other sheltered position. I was to keep them safe.

Sergeant Owens and the specialists clambered over the south rim, rolled, and ran into the smoke. I jumped off Lieutenant Morris and started toward the civilians. But after a few steps, I stopped. The drone's Gatling guns had begun to fire.

I looked back and saw Captain Dial pull Lieutenant Morris to his feet. Captain Dial could only use his right arm, so he had dropped his radio. Lieutenant Morris seemed dazed, and Captain Dial had to hold him up and drag him.

Captain Dial shouted for me to obey my order. I was not to wait for him and Lieutenant Morris. They would catch up, he said.

But I knew Captain Dial's thoughts. I knew he didn't think that he and Lieutenant Morris would make it.

So for the first time ever, I decided to disobey a direct order. I would obey my General Order instead. That was what I had done on the day beside the ocean, and Captain Dial had told me I was good. He had told me I was more good than I had ever been before. So I would do that again.

I ran back to Captain Dial, and he yelled at me. He said I had to obey his order immediately.

But instead I grabbed one of Lieutenant Morris's flak-jacket straps, and I pulled him away from Captain Dial and began dragging him up the gully wall. He was heavy, but I'm strong.

Captain Dial knew then that he should take charge of the civilians. Dragging soldiers to safety was one of my jobs, and keeping civilians safe was one of his. But first, he jumped to me and hooked Lieutenant Morris's arm through my harness loop. Then he pulled the strap to tighten the loop. Now I could let go of the flak-jacket strap and drag Lieutenant Morris a lot faster.

Captain Dial touched my head and told me to go.

I went up the gully wall and over the top with Lieutenant Morris while Captain Dial ran to the civilians and told them that they must go with him. One of the boys cried because he wanted to stay with his mother, but the old man and the girl listened to Captain Dial and wouldn't let the boy stay. They all climbed up from the gully.

Captain Dial's foot slipped on the way up and he almost fell, but the girl grabbed his arm to steady him. It was his wounded arm, but she couldn't reach the other one. I saw a flash like a grenade exploding in Captain Dial's thoughts. But Captain Dial didn't cry out even though it hurt a lot. He was a good soldier. The girl was, too. She didn't hesitate to help Captain Dial. She didn't flinch from his blood.

When we were all out of the gully, we ran north through the smoke. Captain Dial and the civilians were a few meters west of me and Lieutenant Morris, and they were moving up the slope a little faster. Every few steps, Captain Dial would look back and call encouragement to me. And I would pull harder and could feel Lieutenant Morris's boots bouncing on the ground behind us.

I didn't look back, but I heard the buzz of the drone as it flew low over the gully we had just left. I could smell its exhaust. Its Gatling guns chattered, and the slugs made dull thumps in the dirt.

And then, as we ran higher and came up out of the smoke, I heard the drone swoop out over the valley, turn, and head right for us. It was attacking us from behind, and there was no place for us to take cover when its guns started firing again. I looked ahead and saw a shadow on the ground that looked like another gully, but it was too far away. Lieutenant Morris and I wouldn't reach it before the drone strafed us.

I looked over at Captain Dial. Although he was wounded, he was now carrying one of the boys. The girl was carrying the other one. The old man was breathing hard and stumbling. So they were losing speed, and Lieutenant Morris and I had almost caught up to them. They wouldn't reach the next gully either. The drone would be able to hit all of us with the same burst of gunfire, or with just one rocket.

Captain Dial looked over at me as I looked at him, and we each knew the other's thoughts. There was only one thing to do. And when his thoughts said *Now,* I followed his order.

He and the civilians cut left, where there was still a little smoke, and I cut right, where the air was clear. We ran away from each other as fast as we could. I could hear Captain Dial's breath getting farther and farther away behind me. I could hear it even over the noise from Lieutenant Morris's boots.

I would have dropped Lieutenant Morris if I could, because he would have been safer lying still. But I couldn't. The loop on my harness was pulled tight around his arm, and there was no time for me to turn my head to yank it loose.

The drone came after me and Lieutenant Morris. I was sorry for what that meant for Lieutenant Morris, but glad because it gave Captain Dial a better chance to get himself and the civilians to cover. And I was glad because it gave me a chance to be good.

I ran hard, and I zigzagged as much as I could while dragging Lieutenant Morris. The engine buzz became a roar, and the Gatling gun chattered loud and long. And it almost missed us. But the last slugs in the burst came ripping through the dirt right behind us, and Lieutenant Morris jerked as they reached him. I was slapped down at my hindquarters, and I fell. Lieutenant Morris and I rolled a little way down the hill, and the drone flew over us so low that I could see the rivets in its belly. It rose up over the ridge, hung there for a moment, and then started toward us again.

But this time it bloomed fire from its tail, and it twisted sideways and dove into the hillside above us. There was a loud noise and more fire when it hit, and smoke like there had been from the first one.

I tried to get up, but Lieutenant Morris was lying on my hind legs. And my back hurt, close to my tail. But I couldn't see or hear Captain Dial, and I had to find him. So I twisted my head around far enough to tug on my harness loop until Lieutenant Morris's arm slipped out. I couldn't hear Lieutenant Morris's breath or heartbeat, and I could smell that he had blood coming out of his legs, back, chest, and neck. He was dead, and there was no place I could drag him where he would be all right again.

When his arm came free, I was able to scramble with my front legs and pull myself out from under him. And then I was able to stand up all the way even though my back hurt. I looked for Captain Dial and the civilians, but I couldn't see them. There was a lot more smoke now, and it made my eyes itch. It also made it hard to smell anything else. But I heard the girl say something, faint and soft, so I left Lieutenant Morris and followed her voice.

I found her with the other civilians and Captain Dial. Captain Dial was lying on the ground, and the girl was kneeling beside him with her hand on his head. The old man was standing nearby holding the little boys' hands. The boys were scared. They were looking at the body of a D Company soldier lying nearby. It was torn in two.

Captain Dial smiled when I came up to him and licked his face. I had to step over an RPG launcher to reach him, and when I touched him I knew what he had done. He had found the RPG launcher with the dead soldier, and he had used it to bring down the second drone. But it had recoiled against his wounded shoulder, and now the wound was bleeding even more.

He saw my thoughts and knew what had happened to Lieutenant Morris. But he said I had done everything right. He said he was proud of me. He said I was good.

And just as he said that, I heard a buzzing noise far off in the south. It was heading toward us fast. More drones were coming.

Captain Dial couldn't hear them. But he knew I did. And he said that they might not be coming to attack us, because their pilots might have realized that the first two had been firing on allies and civilians. But we couldn't count on it. So I was to take the four civilians away and find shelter for them. I was to do so immediately.

I didn't understand at first, because the picture I saw in Captain Dial's thoughts was a picture only of me and the civilians. He wasn't in it. He wasn't walking with us, and I wasn't dragging him with my harness.

And then he made me understand. He was too dizzy to walk, and I couldn't drag him without making his wound worse.

I wanted to follow his orders, but first I wanted to go back down the hill and find a D Company medic to take care of him. But Captain Dial said there was no time for that. Not if I was going to take the civilians to safety before the new drones arrived. And I knew he was right, because the girl could hear the drones now too. She still had her hand on Captain Dial's head, but she was looking at the sky.

I whined. I didn't want to go off with the civilians and leave Captain Dial all alone, even for a little while.

Captain Dial reached up with his right hand to touch my head. He told me it was all right to leave him for now, because I could come back as soon as I had taken the civilians to a safe place. It could be a cave or a deep ravine. It just had to be somewhere they couldn't be hurt. Once I had made sure of that, I could return. And if a medic hadn't come to help Captain Dial yet, I could go find one for him then.

But for now, I had to go. I had to keep the civilians safe.

Captain Dial took his hand from my head and spoke to the girl, and he took his pulse transmitter from the pouch on his belt and gave it to her. I knew he was telling her to go with me, and that the transmitter would help us communicate. She shook her head at first, but I could understand her thoughts well enough to know that it wasn't because she was afraid of me. It was because she didn't want to leave Captain Dial alone any more than I did.

I knew then that I liked her. But we were under orders now, and we had to follow them. So I took the girl's hand in my mouth, and I gave a tug to pull her away from Captain Dial. She didn't want to go, but she didn't fight me. She knew what we had to do. She strapped the transmitter to her wrist and stood up. She was good, too.

We left Captain Dial and went to the old man and the boys. I released the girl's hand as she told them they were all going with me. She put the old man's hand on the handle of my harness, and then he held the hand of one of the boys. The girl held the hand of the other one. We all started up the hill again, pushing through the smoke. My hind legs hurt, but I was still strong. I helped the old man go fast. The girl kept pace beside me as I sniffed and listened to find the best path for us.

I could still see Captain Dial's thoughts for a long way up the hill. At first he was thinking of me and what I was doing, and he was proud. That made me glad.

Then he thought the two words he had thought about on the day we performed our demonstration by the ocean. He thought the words "heroism" and "vengeance."

And then he worried about the other soldiers in D Company. So that made me worry, too. But I couldn't go back to check on them yet. I had orders to follow.

Finally, as the civilians and I came out of the smoke onto a sloping field of rocks, I saw one last strong thought from Captain Dial. It was of Melanie. It was of Melanie with him in their bed, sleeping. And I was on my cushion at their feet.

It was a happy thought, and it made me happy too.

Then Captain Dial's thoughts became fuzzy as the civilians and I went higher, and soon they were gone. I paused near the crest of the hill and looked back down the slope, but I couldn't see the place where Captain Dial lay because of the rocks and smoke. And I thought for a moment that maybe the civilians were safe now, and that I could leave them and go back to where I could know Captain Dial's thoughts again.

But the sound of the approaching drones was loud now, and as I watched, one of them came flying up out of the smoke below us. So I led the civilians behind a big rock. We all crouched down, and I heard the drone turn away and fly back down the hillside again.

Then I heard Gatling guns firing, and I remembered my orders. So I got up from my crouch, and the girl and I took the old man and the boys over the top of the hill and down the other side.

I didn't like not being able to see Captain Dial's thoughts. But now I could see the girl's thoughts almost as well as I had seen his, and she had some good ideas about where we might find a safe place to hide. So we started off in the direction she thought was best.

We had to alter our path many times because of things I smelled or heard. And once we had to make a long detour because the girl remembered there were land mines ahead. I couldn't smell them yet, but she warned me by sending pulses to my implant. And then I saw her thoughts, and I knew they were true. So we found another way.

I became tired and thirsty, and my hind legs hurt. The girl and her family became tired and thirsty too. But we could hear gunfire and explosions behind us, so the girl and I wouldn't let the others stop. Not until we found someplace safe.

Not until we had done what Captain Dial had ordered us to do.

❖

We went up and down through the hills all that day. At dusk we found a guerrilla camp that had been bombed many weeks before. But there were still some matches, a knife, and three plastic jugs of water. So we were able to get a drink. The water tasted like plastic, but we drank a lot of it. There was only one jug left when we were finished. The girl tied it to my harness, and we set out again. The girl carried the matches and the knife.

After nightfall, the girl couldn't see where we were or where we were going. Clouds covered the sky, so she couldn't find any stars to help her. That meant our path was up to me. So I followed my nose and my ears, and I took us farther and farther away from cities, camps, and roads. I took us away from anything that smelled or sounded like people with weapons. We had to go a long way.

At last, when the eastern sky had begun to brighten, we found a shelf of rock in the side of a hill. Under the shelf was a cave that was narrow but deep. It was well hidden by brush. I went in first and found some bone fragments and a ring of stones for a fire, but I could smell that they were old. No one had used the cave in a long time.

So I brought the people inside, and they slept on the bare rock. I didn't sleep right away because I had to lick the cuts on my hind legs. Then I dozed. But I kept my ears and nose alert. The only sounds were of the wind blowing through the rocks and brush. The only smells were of rabbits, birds, and other small animals nearby. There were no guerrillas, soldiers, or other people anywhere near us.

When I had rested for a few hours, I went out into the morning sunlight and killed three rabbits. I had to chase them, and that made my legs hurt again. But I still caught them with no trouble. I tore one apart and ate most of him, and then I took the other two back to the cave. The girl was awake, and she knew what to do. She woke up the boys and had them gather brush and sticks while she used the knife from the guerrilla camp to skin the rabbits. The old man made a spit from the sticks, and they cooked the rabbits over a fire the girl started inside the old ring of stones. It filled the cave with smoke, but the people didn't care. They were hungry.

While they ate, I scouted the area around the cave in widening circles. I sniffed, smelled, and listened. I marked a broad perimeter to warn off animal intruders. Then I did it all over again. And then I was sure my people were safe.

I had followed and completed Captain Dial's order. So I went to the girl and pushed my nose into her hand to be sure she knew my thoughts. I made sure she knew that she and her family should stay close to the cave. They could kill more rabbits to eat, and they still had the jug of water from the guerrilla camp. When that ran out, they could catch rain and dew.

The girl understood.

So I started back to the battlefield where I had left Captain Dial. I was able to go faster now because I didn't have people with me, and because my legs felt better. I could also choose a path that took me closer to dangerous smells. And I found a pond where I could get a drink. But that was the only time I stopped. I wanted to get back to Captain Dial as soon as I could.

There was still some light in the sky when I came over the hilltop and looked down the rocky slope at the battlefield. The two fallen drones had stopped burning, and there was no more smoke. A number of people were walking around down near the gully where Captain Dial and I had found the civilians, and the wind brought me their smells along with the smells of many dead D Company soldiers and refugees. The walking people didn't smell like soldiers or refugees. But they didn't smell like the enemy, either. They didn't make much noise, but occasionally one of them would fire a single shot. It sounded as if they were firing into the ground.

I didn't care who they were, or why they were shooting at the ground. Because now I smelled something else, too.

When I reached Captain Dial, I lay down beside him with my chin on his chest. There was nothing else I could do. I didn't nudge him with my nose or lick his face. I didn't try to wake him up. I'm not stupid. That was one of the things Captain Dial liked best about me. He liked that I was smart.

I closed my eyes. I didn't have an order for what to do next, so I would do nothing. I was tired, and there were no D Company soldiers left for me to help. I would stay there with my chin on Captain Dial.

I closed my eyes and fell asleep. And I dreamed. I dreamed about the day I found the live mine on the pier and about how proud Captain Dial was. I dreamed about running fast in training so I could complete my orders and get back to Captain Dial before the buzzer sounded. I dreamed about lying curled up on my cushion on the floor while Captain Dial and Melanie made soft noises above me.

Then I woke up and opened my eyes. Three of the people below were coming up the slope. They were solid shadows in the dusk. And their smell was sharper now. They smelled like men who used shampoo and soap and who wore clean clothes. They smelled like the men in the crowd the day I found the mine. They smelled like civilians from home.

And as they came toward me and Captain Dial, I heard something behind me. Something higher up the slope, moving down through the rocks. It wasn't loud, so I knew the men coming up the slope couldn't hear it. I couldn't identify it by scent because the wind was blowing the wrong way, but I could hear that it was small and alone. So I didn't think it would hurt anyone. Besides, none of the men coming up the slope was my commanding officer. I wasn't required to alert them.

The three men approached within a few meters of me and Captain Dial, and now I saw that they were dressed in dark clothes that weren't uniforms. But they carried pistols in holsters. One of them pointed a camera at me and Captain Dial. I couldn't see the men's thoughts, but they spoke in the same language as D Company, so I understood some of what they said. One of them said something was great, and the others agreed.

I didn't know what they thought was great, but I knew there was nothing there that was.

One of them stepped closer and leaned down as if about to touch Captain Dial. So I raised my head and snarled at him, and he moved back. Then I put my head down again, but I stayed ready. I didn't know who they were, but they weren't part of D Company. They weren't even soldiers. I wouldn't let them touch Captain Dial.

The one with the camera kept aiming it at me and Captain Dial. But the other two put their hands on their pistols and conferred. And I understood enough to know they were talking about shooting me. So I did what Captain Dial had taught me to do. I planned how to attack them so they couldn't get off a shot. If either of their pistols began to rise from its holster, I would execute the plan. And I would decide what to do about the one with the camera based on how he reacted.

But another thing that Captain Dial had taught me was that a battlefield situation can change quickly.

The thing coming down the slope sent some pebbles skittering through the brush. And the three men heard it. They backed away from me and Captain Dial, and the one with the camera let it drop to dangle on a cord around his neck. They all three began taking their pistols from their holsters. But now they were looking past me toward whatever had made the pebbles skitter.

I kept my eyes on the three men. But I sniffed the air, and even though the wind was still going the wrong way, I caught a faint scent that told me who was on the slope behind me. It was the girl I had taken to safety on Captain Dial's order. She was still and quiet now, probably crouched behind a rock. But even so, she wasn't safe anymore.

All three men were raising their pistols. They were farther away from me than when I had made my plan of attack. But they weren't looking at me now. The light of day was almost gone. And I am black as night. I am silent as air.

The third one got off a shot as I hit his chest, but the bullet went into the sky. The other two were already on the ground, their throats torn out, their weapons in the dirt. The third one tried to fight me off once he was down, but that didn't last long.

When he was still, I looked back up the slope, beyond Captain Dial, and saw the girl standing beside a clump of brush. She was almost invisible because the sun was gone now. But I saw her shape against the brush. And the wind had shifted so I could smell her better. She smelled scared.

I was angry that she had returned to the battlefield. I had done my duty and made her safe, and she had spoiled it. I didn't understand why she had done that.

Then she came down the hill past Captain Dial, past me, and past the three men on the ground. She didn't walk fast, but she walked steady and strong even though she was scared. She said something soft to me as she went by, and I saw a flash of her thoughts. Then I understood. She was going down to the gully, to her mother. She wanted to wrap the body and take it somewhere to bury it. She had returned by herself to do this, leaving her brothers in the care of the old man.

I looked past her and knew I couldn't let her do as she planned. There were more people down there. They were like the three men I had just killed. The girl wouldn't be safe among them. Already, I could see and hear several of them starting toward her. She couldn't see them yet. But she would encounter them before she could reach the gully.

So I ran down to the girl and got in front of her. But she just walked around me. Then I took her hand in my mouth, but she just pulled it away and kept going. She wouldn't stay in contact with me long enough to see my thoughts. She was determined to reach her mother.

I couldn't knock her down or bite her to make her come with me. But I couldn't let her keep going. I had to make her pay attention to me long enough so she would understand what we had to do. So I turned and ran fast across the hillside, away from both the girl and Captain Dial. I ran to the body of Lieutenant Morris, and I tore open one of his pockets. Some ammo clips fell out, but that wasn't what I wanted. I wanted what I had smelled when I'd pushed Lieutenant Morris down in the gully.

And I found it curled up in the corner of the pocket. It was the necklace from the dead girl at the checkpoint. There was still enough blood on it that I had been able to smell it. The necklace had been taken from Lieutenant Morris for the investigation, but he had stolen it back. Now I took it from him again.

I ran back to the girl with it, got in front of her, and pushed my nose against her hand so she would feel the necklace hanging from my mouth.

She stopped walking. Her palm was against my nose. Her fingers brushed the silver chain. The transmitter on her wrist hummed. And then, as someone shouted below us, I thought hard and showed her what had happened to the girl who had worn the necklace. So she saw that girl lying on the side of the road with her sisters. She saw me find the necklace in Lieutenant Morris's pocket. She saw how angry Captain Dial had been at what Lieutenant Morris had done.

The shouting below us grew louder. I could hear six voices now, and weapons being readied. More of the armed-men-who-weren't-soldiers were coming toward us.

But I didn't turn away from the girl. I kept my nose in her palm because I had to be sure she understood. I had to be sure she understood that Captain Dial was my commanding officer, and that I hated to leave him there on the hillside again. But I would. And she would have to leave her mother there, too. We both had to follow Captain Dial's last order. And if the men coming up the hillside reached us, we would fail. I wouldn't be good. And she would be like the other girl. The one who had worn the necklace.

The girl was smart. I saw in her thoughts that her mother wouldn't want her to die like that other girl. But when she understood what I was telling her, she began to cry. She hadn't cried before this. But she cried now, taking the necklace from my mouth and clutching it in her fist. She wanted to fight the men coming up the hill. She thought they were responsible for her mother's death. She thought they had made the drones attack.

I didn't know why she thought that. But I understood why she would want to fight whoever had made the drones fire on D Company. I wanted to fight those people too. But even if those people were the men who were coming up the hill, we couldn't fight them now. I had already killed three of them, but I had caught those three by surprise. There were more than three coming now, and they had their weapons ready to fire.

So we had to go back up over the hill. And while the girl stood there with the necklace clenched in her fist, I took her other hand in my mouth. And then I started up the hill, pulling her with me.

At first, she came with me without knowing what she was doing. She was still crying and thinking of what she wanted to do to the people who had sent the drones. So the men coming up the hill gained on us, and a shot was fired. I heard the bang and then heard the slug hiss through the air. It hit the dirt several meters ahead of us.

Then the girl's thoughts came back to where we were and what we needed to do. So she began to run, and I was able to release her hand. We ran together back up the hill, through the rocks and brush, up toward the night sky.

We paused for a few seconds when we reached Captain Dial again. He lay still in the twilight. He made no sound. He had no thoughts. He didn't even smell like Captain Dial anymore. So it was all right for the girl to take his sidearm and empty his pockets. And this time, it was easier to leave. This time, I knew I wouldn't need to return.

In training, Captain Dial had told me that when a soldier was gone, he was gone forever. But he had also told Melanie that they would be together forever. So *forever* was always a hard word for me to understand. But whenever I didn't understand something, it was because it was something only someone as smart as Captain Dial could understand. And in those cases, I would just have to believe whatever Captain Dial said. Because Captain Dial always spoke the truth.

So that was what I did as I left his body there on the hillside for the last time. I remembered what Captain Dial had said, and I was

glad that even though he was gone, he and Melanie would still be together.

I wished I could be with them, too. But I didn't know how to get
to wherever they were.

The girl and I went up over the top of the hill, and soon I
couldn't smell or hear the men behind us anymore. Then the twilight
was gone, and the girl held my harness so I could lead her through
the darkness. She knew my thoughts most of the time now, so I
promised her I would do a good job. And she promised me the same
thing.

We had our orders. So we would follow them.

Forever.

❖

I took the girl back to the cave where the old man and the boys were
waiting, and we stayed there several weeks until I smelled men with
weapons approaching. Then we left, and I led the way deeper into the
hills, taking us as far from danger as I could. The weather grew
colder, but my fur grew thicker, and we found winter clothing in an
abandoned village. The old man also found sewing tools, and he
made blankets from the skins of the rabbits I caught. The girl
stretched some skins between two long pieces of wood, and that was
where we kept our growing collection of supplies. The people and I
took turns dragging it as we traveled.

We traveled this way for many days, until we came upon the
stone hut near the stream.

It's been a good place. We found more things that my people
could use here. But the people who had stayed in the hut before us
had been gone for a long time when we arrived. I couldn't even smell
them on the things they had left. So I believed my company would be
safe here for the winter.

Food was easy to obtain. All I had to do was go up and down the
stream until I found rabbits. Once I killed a small deer, and the girl
said its skin should be my bed. So now I sleep on it even though I

like the bare ground just as well. I have thick fur. But it makes my people happy to see me lie down on the deer's skin, and that makes me glad.

In recent weeks the bushes and trees have grown leaves, and the grass that was dry and thin is now thick and juicy. The girl and the old man have been making plans to plant seeds they found in the abandoned village. We've all been looking forward to warmer days.

Then, last night, eighteen of Your soldiers came to kill us. You must have told them we were the enemy. So they didn't know I was trained by Captain Dial. They didn't know that even when I sleep, my ears and nose are awake.

I took the girl to their bodies this morning, and it made her sad. But she understood that I had to follow orders. She understands a lot. She and I often help each other figure out things that are puzzling.

I didn't understand how Your soldiers could have found us, or why You would want them to, because we've traveled far from anything that should matter to You. Besides, we're not Your enemies. And even if we were, we wouldn't be important enough for You to bother with. Or so I thought.

Then the girl remembered the implant under the skin between my shoulders, and the transmitter that Captain Dial had given her. We had used these things to help us understand each other in our first weeks together, but then—just as Captain Dial and I had found— they had become unnecessary. So the girl had placed the transmitter in her duffel, and we hadn't thought of it or of my implant since. But now the girl said that machines in the sky could probably hear signals from them at any time, and that the machines could then tell You where I was. So that was how Your soldiers found us.

The girl also says she knows why You want to attack us.

She found a radio receiver in the abandoned village, and now she listens to its voices for a few minutes each evening. I can't understand the voices, but the girl has told me some of the things they've said. They've said that all Your soldiers were about to be sent home because the money for the war was almost gone. But then D Company was ambushed and destroyed by enemy guerrillas, and the bad publicity from what Lieutenant Morris had done at the checkpoint was obliterated by the heroism of his company's sacrifice. So Your public support surged, and more money was provided so Your soldiers could avenge the ambush by destroying the enemy.

This is what the radio voices say. They don't say anything about the drones. But if the drones hadn't come, D Company would not only have beaten the guerrillas, but would have suffered almost no casualties. Captain Dial would have seen to it.

But the drones did come. They came from our own airfield. They came from You.

Then the men-who-weren't-soldiers came too, and the girl thinks she knows why they fired shots at the ground. She thinks they killed any soldier or refugee who was still alive. And we believe those men were sent by You as well.

The girl says that our knowledge of this is why You want to attack us. We're the only survivors of that battle. So as long as we still live, You fear that we may reveal the truth of what happened to D Company and the refugees. And the girl says that then all of Your public support and money will go away again.

I have tried to think of what Captain Dial might do if these things had been revealed to him. But he was much smarter than me. And I can't see his thoughts anymore.

But I still know the final order he gave me: To keep my people safe.

So I've thought of things I can do to obey.

The first thing I thought of was to have the girl write this message. Again, she doesn't know what she writes. Only that I require her to write it. And what I'm asking her to write now is a promise that You have nothing to fear from me if You leave us alone. If You allow me to keep my people safe, we will never tell the radio voices what Your drones and men-who-weren't-soldiers did to D Company.

The second thing made the girl cry again. Before beginning this message, I told her to use her knife to cut between my shoulders and find the communication implant. She cried because she didn't want to hurt me, and then she cried more because the device was smaller than we had imagined, and it was hard to find. She had to make the cut longer and deeper. But she finally found the tiny glass bean and gave it to the boys, who took turns hitting it and the transmitter with a hammer until both were dust. Then the old man cleaned my wound and sewed it shut. I growled once because the needle hurt, and he stepped back. But then I licked his hand, and he finished the job. Afterward, I was proud of all of them for following orders so well.

The third thing makes us unhappy. But it's necessary. We must leave the stone hut. We must leave this good place with its water and rabbits. Your soldiers found us here, so You know where we are.

But since I no longer have the communication implant, You won't know where we'll go next.

Finally, there is a fourth thing I'll do.

If the above measures fail, and if You send more soldiers or men-who-aren't-soldiers to find us, I will kill them all. I'll always know they're coming, so they'll never be able to attack us before I attack them first.

You may even send some of my fellow K-9s, because they could find us more quickly than people could. But Captain Dial said that the K-9s in my training class were the best war dogs there had ever been, and I was ranked first in that class. So there are no K-9s that I can't find and defeat before they can find and defeat me.

And if You attack us with drones instead of people or dogs, we're now equipped to fight them. Some of the soldiers I killed last night were carrying RPGs, and others carried guns with armor-piercing rounds. We have taken these weapons.

But if You bomb us from high in the sky so we can't fight, there may be nothing I can do to stop You. Then You will have made me fail to carry out my orders.

In that event, I'll do whatever I must to survive. And then I will find You. I don't know Your name or Your rank, but I will find You anyway. I will hunt and kill every officer in every company and every battalion until I reach You. I will read their thoughts as they die and use that knowledge to hunt You. I will climb walls and dig tunnels. I will swim and run. I will stow away in trucks, ships, and aircraft that will bring me closer to You. I will find something You have touched so I know Your scent. And then I will find You in Your bed or at Your table or wherever You may be.

And I will bite Your throat so it tears out.

So I hope You heed this message. It will be left with one of Your dead soldiers, so I know it will reach their unit's commanding officer. And then it will reach that officer's commanding officer, and then that officer's commanding officer, and so on until it reaches the officer who gave the orders that resulted in the current situation. Until it reaches You.

My company has its equipment and is ready to move out. The two boys are my specialists. The old man is my medic and quartermaster.

As for the girl—

She now wears the metal tag I received when I was promoted to sergeant. She found it in Captain Dial's pocket as we left the battlefield, and today she put it on the chain of her necklace beside the shiny rock. Sergeant is the toughest enlisted job. But she can do it.

I myself am no longer a sergeant. I didn't realize that until this morning. But after I showed the girl what I had done in the night, she touched my head. And I heard her thoughts. I heard what she called me.

She called me Captain.

Then she took the silver bars that she found with the sergeant's tag, and she pinned them to my duty harness.

I am the ranking survivor of D Company, and my final order from Captain Dial was a commission. I know this because what he told me to do was what a good officer does.

A good officer takes care of his soldiers.

But if You attack us again, You will not be a good officer. You will not be taking care of Your soldiers. And if You make me fail in my duty to take care of mine, You will not be an officer of any kind for much longer.

Captain Dial told me what I am, and he always spoke the truth. So now I tell You:

I am black as night. I am silent as air.

My sergeant touches my head, and I tell her she's good.

This message is complete.

Respectfully,
Chip, K-9
Captain and Commanding Officer
D Company

HONOR ROLL 2004

The Year's Best Science Fiction and Fantasy for Teens

Peter S. Beagle, "Quarry," *The Magazine of Fantasy and Science Fiction,* May 2004.

Emma Bull, "De la Tierra," *The Faery Reel,* edited by Ellen Datlow and Terri Windling (New York: Viking, 2004).

Russell Davis, "The Last Day of the Rest of Her Life," *Little Red Riding Hood in the Big Bad City,* edited by Martin H. Greenberg and John Helfers (New York: DAW Books, 2004).

Charles de Lint, "Riding Shotgun," *Flights: Extreme Visions of Fantasy,* edited by Al Sarrantonio (New York: Roc, 2004).

Rudi Doremann, "Embers," *Realms of Fantasy,* October 2004.

Esther Friesner, "Johnny Beansprout," *The Magazine of Fantasy and Science Fiction,* July 2004.

Lisa Goldstein, "Finding Beauty," *The Magazine of Fantasy and Science Fiction,* October/November 2004.

Nina Kiriki Hoffman, "Heart's Desire," *Realms of Fantasy,* February 2004.

Nina Kiriki Hoffman, "The Laily Worm," *Realms of Fantasy,* August 2004.

Tracina Jackson-Adams, "Making a Sparrow," *Abyss & Apex,* March/April 2004.

James Patrick Kelly, "Serpent," *The Magazine of Fantasy and Science Fiction,* May 2004.

Jay Lake, "Tiny Flowers and Rotten Lace," *Realms of Fantasy,* February 2004.

Margo Lanagan, "Rite of Spring," *Black Juice* by Margo Lanagan (Crows Nest, NSW, Australia: Allen & Unwin, 2004).

Margo Lanagan, "Singing My Sister Down," *Black Juice* by Margo Lanagan (Crows Nest, NSW, Australia: Allen & Unwin, 2004).

Mike Lewis, "The Smell of Magic," *Realms of Fantasy,* August 2004.

Bruce McAllister, "The Seventh Daughter," *The Magazine of Fantasy and Science Fiction,* April 2004.

Gordon McAlpine, "Rowboat with Moon and Star," *Cicada,* March/April 2004.

Lyn McConchie, "The Boy Who Stuffed Chooks," *Rogue Worlds,* July 2004.

Paul Melko, "Fallow Earth," *Asimov's SF,* June 2004.

Elizabeth Moon, "Gifts," *Masters of Fantasy,* edited by Bill Fawcett and Brian Thomsen (Riverdale, N.Y.: Baen Books, 2004).

Catherine Morrison, "Elvis in the Attic," *Sci.Fiction,* April 2004.

Tim Pratt, "In the Glass Casket," *Realms of Fantasy,* October 2004.

Jenn Reese, "Memree," *Polyphony 4,* edited by Deborah Layne and Jay Lake (Wilsonville, Ore.: Wheatland Press, 2004).

Bruce Holland Rogers, "Egypt," www.shortshortshort.com, August 2004.

Bruce Holland Rogers, "The One Who Conquers," *Realms of Fantasy,* February 2004.

Benjamin Rosenbaum, "Start the Clock," *The Magazine of Fantasy and Science Fiction,* August 2004.

Kristine Kathryn Rusch, "Collateral Damage," *Asimov's SF,* August 2004.

Kristine Kathryn Rusch, "Forest for the Trees," *Asimov's SF,* July 2004.

Ellen Steiber, "Screaming for Fairies," *The Faery Reel,* edited by Ellen Datlow and Terri Windling (New York: Viking, 2004).

Beverly Suarez-Beard, "Lady of the Birds," *Paradox,* Summer 2004.

Vivian Vande Velde, "Morgan Roehmer's Boys," *Gothic: Ten Original Dark Tales,* edited by Deborah Noyes (Cambridge, Mass.: Candle-wick Press, 2004).

Michelle West, "The Colors of Augustine," *Summoned to Destiny,* ed. Julie E. Czerneda (Markham, Ontario: Fitzhenry & Whiteside, 2004).

Gene Wolfe, "Calamity Warps," *Realms of Fantasy,* April 2004.

George Zebrowski, "My First World," *Microcosms,* ed. Gregory Benford (New York: DAW Books, 2004).

NOTES ON CONTRIBUTORS

Born in Australia, LYNETTE ASPEY has lived in England, Wales, Scotland, Canada, Sweden, and on a houseboat in Trinidad. Her work has appeared in *Aurealis* and *Asimov's SF.*

Canadian LEAH BOBET's stories have appeared in *Realms of Fantasy, Strange Horizons, Arabella Romances,* and many other venues.

BRADLEY DENTON's works include the science fiction novels *Wrack and Roll* and *Buddy Holly Is Alive and Well on Ganymede,* the psychological thriller *Blackburn,* and the contemporary fantasy *Lunatics.* His paired story collections *A Conflagration Artist* and *The Calvin Coolidge Home for Dead Comedians* jointly won the World Fantasy Award.

DAVID GERROLD's distinguished career in science fiction includes novels such as *When HARLIE Was One, The Martian Child,* the *War Against the Chthorr* series, and the enduringly popular *Star Trek* episode "The Trouble with Tribbles." His SF novels for young readers include *Jumping Off the Planet* and *Bouncing Off the Moon.* He won the Hugo and Nebula awards for the novella version of "The Martian Child."

Hungarian-born THEODORA GOSS's stories have appeared in *Polyphony, Realms of Fantasy,* and *Strange Horizons,* among other places. In 2004, her collection *The Rose in Twelve Petals & Other Stories* was published by Small Beer Press.

RUDYARD KIPLING (1865–1936) was born in Bombay, India, of English parents, and spent much of his life on the Indian subcontinent. His literary works include the fanciful *The Jungle Book* and the espionage novel *Kim*. A significant number of his stories include fantasy and science fiction elements. He won the Nobel Prize for Literature in 1907.

KELLY LINK's acclaimed short stories include the Nebula Award–winning "Louise's Ghost," the World Fantasy Award–winning "The Specialist's Hat," and the James Tiptree, Jr. Memorial Award–winning "Travels with the Snow Queen." A selection of her best work can be found in her collection *Stranger Things Happen*. With Gavin Grant, she runs Small Beer Press, a distinguished small publisher of SF and fantasy; and with Gavin Grant and Ellen Datlow, she coedits the annual *Year's Best Fantasy and Horror* series published by St. Martin's Press.

Australian GARTH NIX's critically acclaimed and internationally popular fantasy novels for young readers and adults include *The Ragwitch, Shade's Children,* the "Seventh Tower" series, and the Old Kingdom trilogy, comprising *Sabriel, Lirael,* and *Abhorsen.* He is currently working on a seven-book series, *The Keys to the Kingdom*.

DELIA SHERMAN's historical fantasy *The Porcelain Dove* won the Mythpoeic Fantasy Award. With Ellen Kushner, she cowrote *The Fall of the Kings.* Her short fiction has appeared in *The Magazine of Fantasy and Science Fiction, Xanadu,* and *Sandman: Book of Dreams,* among other places.

ADAM STEMPLE is a working musician, lead guitarist for Boiled in Lead, the Tim Malloys, and (years ago) the legendary Cats Laughing, a band that also included fantasy writers Emma Bull and Steven Brust. With his mother, Jane Yolen, he has cowritten several songbooks for children, and a fantasy novel for young readers, *Pay the Piper,* forthcoming in 2005. Also forthcoming in 2005 is his debut solo novel, *Singer of Souls.* His story in *The Year's Best Science Fiction and Fantasy for Teens* was selected by the non-Yolen side of this anthology's editorial staff.

S. M. STIRLING's many science fiction and fantasy novels include his own "Draka" novels (*Marching Through Georgia* and its sequels), *Snowbrother, The Peshawar Lancers,* and collaborations with a wide range of other SF and fantasy writers, including Jerry Pournelle, Greg Bear, Anne McCaffrey, and David Drake. His "Nantucket" series of alternate-history adventures, of which "Blood Wolf" is a part, includes the novels *Island in the Sea of Time, Against the Tide of Years,* and *On the Oceans of Eternity.*